# Other B...

**Tesseracts**
edited by Judith Merril

**Tesseracts 2**
edited by Phyllis Gotlieb & Douglas Barbour

**Tesseracts 3**
edited by Candas Jane Dorsey & Gerry Truscott

**Tesseracts 4**
edited by Lorna Toolis & Michael Skeet

**Tesseracts 5**
edited by Robert Runté & Yves Maynard

**Tesseracts 6**
edited by Robert J. Sawyer & Carolyn Clink

**Tesseracts 7**
edited by Paula Johanson & Jean-Louis Trudel

**Tesseracts 8**
edited by John Clute & Candas Jane Dorsey

**Tesseracts Nine: New Canadian Speculative Fiction**
edited by Nalo Hopkinson & Geoff Ryman

**Tesseracts Ten: A Celebration of New Canadian Speculative Fiction**
edited by Robert Charles Wilson & Edo van Belkom

**Tesseracts Eleven: Amazing Canadian Speculative Fiction**
edited by Cory Doctorow & Holly Phillips

**Tesseracts Twelve: New Novellas of Canadian Fantastic Fiction**
edited by Claude Lalumière

**Tesseracts Thirteen: Chilling Tales from the Great White North**
edited by Nancy Kilpatrick & David Morrell

**Tesseracts 14: Strange Canadian Stories**
edited by John Robert Colombo & Brett Alexander Savory

**Tesseracts Fifteen: A Case of Quite Curious Tales**
edited by Julie Czerneda & Susan MacGregor

**TesseractsQ**
edited by Élisabeth Vonarburg & Jane Brierley

# TESSERACTS SIXTEEN
PARNASSUS UNBOUND

EDITED BY
# MARK LESLIE

EDGE SCIENCE FICTION AND FANTASY PUBLISHING
AN IMPRINT OF HADES PUBLICATIONS, INC.
CALGARY

Tesseracts Sixteen: Parnassus Unbound
Copyright © 2012

All individual contributions are copyright
by their respective authors.

This is a work of fiction. Names, characters, places, and incidents are the products of the author's imagination or are used fictitiously and are not to be construed as real. Any resemblance to actual events, locales, organizations, or persons, living or dead, is entirely coincidental.

EDGE

Edge Science Fiction and Fantasy Publishing
An Imprint of Hades Publications Inc.
P.O. Box 1714, Calgary, Alberta, T2P 2L7, Canada

Edited by Mark Leslie
Interior design by Janice Blaine
Cover Illustration by Jeff Johnson

ISBN: 978-1-894063-92-0

All rights reserved. No part of this book may be reproduced, scanned, or distributed in any printed or electronic form without written permission. Please do not participate in or encourage piracy of copyrighted materials in violation of the author's rights. Purchase only authorized editions.

EDGE Science Fiction and Fantasy Publishing and Hades Publications, Inc. acknowledges the ongoing support of the Canada Council for the Arts and the Alberta Foundation for the Arts for our publishing programme.

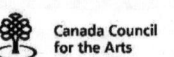

Alberta Foundation for the Arts    Canada Council for the Arts    Conseil des Arts du Canada

---

Library and Archives Canada Cataloguing in Publication

CIP Data on file with the National Library of Canada

ISBN: 978-1-894063-92-0

(e-Book ISBN: 978-1-894063-93-7)

---

FIRST EDITION
(F-20120629)
Printed in Canada
www.edgewebsite.com

# TABLE OF CONTENTS

**Introduction**
*Mark Leslie*....................................................................1
**Ghost in the Meme**
*Ryan Oakley*...................................................................5
**Back in Black**
*Chadwick Ginther*..........................................................16
**Mathom Measures**
*Sandra Kasturi*...............................................................26
**Artistic Licence**
*Robert H. Beer*................................................................28
**Saturn in G Minor**
*Stephen Kotowych*..........................................................37
**Zombie Poet**
*Carolyn Clink*.................................................................52
**The Language of Dance**
*Rebecca M. Senese*..........................................................54
**Gregor Samsa Was Never in The Beatles**
*J. J. Steinfeld*..................................................................60
**Immortality**
*Robert J. Sawyer*.............................................................66
**Sixteen Colors**
*David Clink*....................................................................75
**Bemused**
*L. T. Getty*......................................................................77
**Once Upon A Midnight**
*Scott Overton*.................................................................89
**Drumbeats**
*Kevin J. Anderson & Neil Peart*......................................99

**Zombie Descartes Writes a Personal Ad**
*Carolyn Clink*..................................................................116
**Writer's Block**
*Sean Costello*..................................................................117
**Theater of the Vulnerable**
*Virginia O'Dine*..............................................................128
**The Day the Music Died**
*Randy McCharles*...........................................................132
**Microfiche, or, The Indexing of History**
*Sandra Kasturi*................................................................139
**Blink**
*Michael Kelly*..................................................................140
**Burning Beauty**
*Melissa Yuan-Innes*.......................................................144
**The Faun and the Sylphide**
*Derwin Mak*....................................................................155
**I'm With The Band**
*Kimberly Foottit*.............................................................169
**My Teenage Ångström Poem**
*David Clink*....................................................................180
**Cult Stories**
*Hugh A. D. Spencer*.......................................................181
**Three Thousand Miles of Cold Iron Tears**
*Steve Vernon*...................................................................215
**Slava the Immortal**
*Matthew Jordan Schmidt*...............................................229
**Old Soul**
*Adria Laycraft*.................................................................237
**Song of Conn and the Sea People**
*Jeff Hughes*......................................................................246

# For Booksellers and Librarians Everywhere

*You are modern fountains of inspiration for those who love to read and to gain wisdom from the written word*

*The results of your noble efforts echo through the ages like the infinite flowing waters of Castalia*

◆

# Introduction: The Fountain

*— Mark Leslie —*

According to Greek Mythology, Mount Parnassus was sacred to Apollo (god of prophecy, music, intellectual pursuits and the arts) and home of the Muses. At the base of the mountain was a fountain named Castalia (a transformed nymph) that could inspire the genius of poetry for anyone who drank her waters or listened to her quiet soothing sounds.

Over the centuries, the term Parnassus has fallen out of common use. But when referred to it is often used in literature as a metaphor for the home of poetry, literature and learning.

The theme for *Tesseracts Sixteen* — *speculative fiction that was inspired by literature, music, art and culture* — draws heavily upon that modern referral. In selecting stories my goal was to attempt to capture not only the spirit of what might be found on Mount Parnassus, but to allow it to be released, freed from the mythological Greek mountain and expanded upon in a way that only speculative literature can "unbind" such a theme.

I am pleased to be able to present this wonderfully eclectic selection of stories and poems, chosen from hundreds of fantastic submissions received. In fact, I must pause and pay tribute to all those who contributed to *Tesseracts Sixteen*.

## Introduction by Mark Leslie

I could very easily have crafted together two or three volumes — the submissions themselves, therefore, took on a life of their own, and unbound me from my previous experience reading unsolicited submissions. As an editor, rejecting bad submissions is simple and easy. Rejecting good stories is tough; rejecting great stories is extremely difficult.

Without hyperbole, I can confidently say that selecting pieces for *Tesseracts 16: Parnassus Unbound* was excruciatingly painful.

What this experience tells me, however, is that there is no shortage of fine creative Canadian talent. I was honoured to be involved with this award winning anthology series, and further honoured to have received such incredible submissions from so many great writers.

The tales and poems which made it into this book highlight not only the riches of what Canadian writers have to offer the speculative genre on this theme, but the unique manner by which the muses can be channeled.

Canadian writer, lyricist and musician, Neil Peart and his co-author Kevin J. Anderson (the only non-Canadian to grace this book's pages by way of his collaborative relationship with Peart) are an example of a unique cross-over inspirational feed between music and writing, which occurs more than once in this collection.

Anderson, who discovered Rush through an impulse purchase based on cover art that "looked cool" on the tiny stickers of the 1970's record club he belonged to, found himself inspired by the epic sci-fi concept album *2112* (which had been inspired by Ayn Rand's novel *Anthem*) and began following the band. Anderson was listening to the 1984 Rush album *Grace Under Pressure* which influenced him while plotting his novel *Resurrection, Inc*. So when the book came out he sent autographed copies to the band. Peart wrote back and the two discovered they had much in common, developed an ongoing correspondence and eventually found the opportunity to collaborate in "Drumbeats" a story involving a musician traveling through a remote African village who discovers a uniquely crafted djembe drum. That team effort sparked an ongoing desire to collaborate again, and *Clockwork Angels*, a novel tie-in to the Rush album of the same name, marks another unique collaboration between Peart and Anderson.

Other stories appearing here merge music and literature in a similarly interesting fashion. J. J. Steinfeld's "Gregor Samsa

## Introduction by Mark Leslie

Was Never in The Beatles" for example, concerns a writer's attempt to create devolving into a deeply enveloping empathetic appreciation of literature. Robert H. Beer's "Artistic Licence" is set in an Orwellian society and includes an entirely different sort of appreciation for the creative spirit.

In "Bemused" Leia Getty dives deep into the head of those inflicted with creative symbioses and Randy McCharles' "The Day the Music Died" looks at a future society desperately trying to reclaim music from a time and essence that has escaped humanity.

Virginia O'Dine's "Theater of the Vulnerable" involves actors in a bizarre sort of reverse marionette role, while Kimberly Foottit's "I'm With The Band" explores an entirely different kind of puppeteer.

"The Faun and the Sylphide" by Derwin Mak examines the world of ballet enhanced by a special type of memory cloth while Rebecca Senese's "Language of Dance" concerns itself with an inter-species "dance competition" between humans and an alien race.

Language itself becoming sentient is the focus of Ryan Oakley's "Ghost in the Meme" and David Clink's cautionary "Sixteen Colors" explores the side effect of a parallel universe of people not able to experience more than intricate shades of color.

If you continue to explore the threads and themes of the stories and poems you'll see similar linkages and how one author's work might effectively play off of the other. This involved placing a few reprints alongside original works; while the goal was to include as much original material is possible, it was important for me to assemble a mosaic of just the right pieces to get that desired effect; like a chief cooking with freshly sliced and ground ingredients alongside a few elements of the dish that had been previously prepared.

While many of the pieces here are meta-reflective works that refer to literature and culture itself or rely on the reader's familiarity with the cannon, such as Sandra Kasturi's "Mathom Measures" or to philosophical musings, as in Carolyn Clink's "Zombie Descartes Writes A Personal Ad" others delve into the process of writing itself, like Sean Costello's "Writers Block" and Michael Kelly's "Blink."

Allusions to the classical use of masks conjured in a frightening disturbing way come out in Matthew Jordan Schmidt's "Slava the Immortal" and the traditionally styled epic poem "Song of Conn

*Introduction* by Mark Leslie

and the Sea People" by Jeff Hughes that finishes off the book wonderfully not only ties in all the accoutrements of such a piece (such as epithets and calling on the muses) but is a wonderful ode to both the epic poems of the Greeks, Babylonians, Romans and Anglo-Saxons of Homer, Gilgamesh, Aeneid and Beowulf and of the writing of Joseph Campbell while blending in a few standard sci-fi tropes.

And at this, I have barely touched upon half of the instances by which these works intersect with one another. So many more interconnectivities between all 27 pieces exist, but I'm sure you'd rather experience them yourself than continue to be delayed by my feeble attempts to describe them in my own words.

Chadwick Ginter writes in his story "Back in Black" about a music collector who seeks the *Holy Grail* of impossible bootleg recordings that "magic is good music." He is right. But to extend Ginter's thought for this introduction: *magic is good writing.*

And *Tesseracts Sixteen* is magic.

As I have outlined, the stories you are about to read don't just concern themselves with the topics of art, music, literature, theater, film and culture — they explode with them, reverberate with their very essence.

The authors whose works you are about to read are modern day Muses gifted with the ability to take the reader on fantastical journeys that are strikingly familiar in the references they draw from. They have sipped from the mythical fountain, gazed into the infinite reaches of the universe and of the endless depths of the mind and pulled together these tales of wonder and imagination.

So please, stop for a while, have a seat at the base of this mountain and listen to the hypnotic trickling water of the fountain...

Mark Leslie
April 2012

# GHOST IN THE MEME

### ⁓ Ryan Oakley ⁓

The quote was from William S. Burroughs:
"Ten Years and a Billion Dollars."

The plaque hung over the door to *The Institute of Language Studies*. Looking up at it, Ben Rhodes dropped his cigarette to the wet concrete. It sizzled out.

He strode into the lobby. His hieroglyphic thoughts threatened to become words. He didn't want to think in language. He was getting paranoid about it. Had even bought an easel and paints. Was still looking for inspiration.

"Pretty rainy today," said the unnecessary security guard. "Supposed to be a wet November."

"It's off to a good start then," Ben said. He took the elevator to the third floor. In his office, his partner waited for him. Looked frantic but he always did.

"I've been trying to get a hold of you since two this morning," Peter said. "Don't you answer your phone?"

"No." Ben shook the rain from his coat and hung it up. He sat behind his desk. Peter's eyes were wide, bloodshot and glistening, the face animated by twitches. "What is it?"

"We have it." Peter drew his lips back to reveal a mouth full of crooked teeth.

"It?"

Peter sighed. Ben supposed his partner was trying to sound exasperated but the noise just reminded him of air being squeezed out of an inflatable toy.

"The language algorithm," Peter said. "We have it."

Ben counted to five and sat down. If he could not maintain his calm, he could at least maintain the appearance of it. Beneath his desk, his knees shook. He blew into his hands to warm them.

"Did you hear me?"

"I did." Ben rubbed his chin. "We have it?"

"Yeah."

"Already?" This wasn't supposed to happen. Not yet, if ever. They were only in the second year of the project and last night, when he had left, things had been going exactly the same as usual: Number crunching and bureaucratic water treading. "There's been a breakthrough?"

"There sure has," Peter said. "Late last night."

"Has it been tested?"

"Yeah." Peter's head bobbed on his thin neck. All his wrinkles jiggled into patterns. "Again and again. We started with the old man's work — *Nova Express, Junkie, Naked Lunch*. Plugged in all the words at random and applied the formula. It recreated them all. Mixed them together, randomized them, did the same thing and it brought them all back in order of composition. Now we've recreated Shakespeare. Even mixed it with complete works of Poe, Burroughs, Chandler, — all sorts of people — and it brought it all back in new but coherent forms. The signal to noise ratio is stunning."

"And the copies were perfect?"

"Mostly. They went through iterations. At an arbitrary point in what I guess you'd call the editing or rewriting process, they become exactly correct. Right down to the punctuation. We thought we had one error — *Hamlet* was missing some stuff — but it turned out our copy differed from the one we got the words from."

"And after that?"

"After what?"

"The arbitrary point?"

"The text continues to evolve but not much. Mainly in minutiae. It continues to tweak itself until it stagnates. Then it erodes into gibberish. It dies."

"Interesting." Ben's chair creaked beneath him. They'd been working on this project for two years without any progress. Even Ben had started to believe they were, like many insisted, cranks. "I'd have to see it."

As much as he disliked Peter, he still trusted him. The man was a flake but a rigorous scientist. He just wanted to look at the evidence before he got worked up about it. It might be nothing. Probably was nothing. Even Peter could make mistakes. That was easier to believe than the ramifications of him being right.

If the raw material of a book — that is, the words — could only appear a certain way when a single formula was applied and this formula worked on all books, what did it say about the creative process? Outside of linguistics, though directed by them, the actual content of a book must have a logic independent of the author. The writer would only possess and, probably unconsciously, use the algorithm that I.L.S. had just discovered. Just like a basketball player expertly applied geometry they didn't consciously understand. It was hardwired. And it probably wasn't unique to writers. Every conversation might be governed by the same rules.

"Was the old man right?" Ben asked. "About language being a virus." *About it being intelligent?* he thought but didn't ask. *About it being an alien?*

"Haven't tested that yet," Peter said. "I was waiting for you."

"Thank you," Ben said. He wouldn't have done the same. "I appreciate it." He stood and walked to the door. "I'd like to see your work first. After that, we're ready to go?"

Peter nodded.

◆

"If the old man was wrong we still have eight years," Ben said. He stood beside Peter in the empty room. All of the technicians had been sent to an early lunch. The work looked solid and, if there was anything to it, this moment was for the two of them; the brains behind the Institute of Language Studies. It hadn't been easy to get this project off the ground and harder to keep control once they did but, somehow, they'd managed it. "Let's just view this as being far ahead of schedule."

"You're right. No matter what we still have eight years." Peter grinned at Ben. "If we can keep IARPA off our backs for that long. But, can you imagine?"

"How can I imagine anything?" Ben asked. If language really was intelligent, just using humans as hosts, how could you understand? With words? With ideas and alphabets forming the DNA spiral of the strange beast? He supposed they'd have to write a book about it, spawning more of Language's strange children. Help the alien reproduce.

Maybe this experiment was just part of its evolution. Similar to the explosion of culture that humans had undergone 50,000 years ago when complex language had first appeared and they wiped out their Neanderthal cousins. Though that might be evidence that language had always been conscious. That, maybe, it wasn't from around here.

*Are we even in control of this?* Ben wondered. This idea had been thought up in words and perhaps words had their own agenda. Could he even trust the drugged up musings of Burroughs or the scientific discipline of Richard Dawkins? The theories of these two men were this project's guiding influences but Ben had met neither. He'd only read their words. And those...

He shuddered. Maybe the Zen Buddhists were right to separate truth from language. He'd never tell Peter that. His partner believed those mystics while Ben demanded proof. This dispute was the foundation of the *Institute of Language Studies*. Ben wanted scientific evidence and Peter needed to validate his mysticism. Although they'd both learned to respect each other's motivations, Ben refused to say anything that could be greeted with a smug *I told you so*. He'd rather quit than hear that.

"Do we have all the data?" he asked.

"Yeah. Everything we could get, anyway."

"That's still quite a lot isn't it? I'm sure Language won't mind losing a few limbs here and there. It must be more adaptable than that." He imagined a hydra, each head a book. Each word, a tooth.

"Let's hope so," Peter said.

Ben reached into his pocket and pulled out a pack of nicotine gum. He wasn't trying to quit smoking but couldn't do it around this equipment. Even if he could, Peter made the experience miserable. He was like every ex-smoker Ben had ever met. They all made a show of hating tobacco, more for their benefit than for anyone else. It had been a couple of years since Peter quit but only a few weeks since he'd stopped pretending to cough whenever Ben lit up.

He chewed his gum, thinking even nicotine had evolved to allow itself access to new niches, and mentally reviewed the experiment. All the text they could get from books, blogs, manuals, correspondence, social media and whatever else was fed into this terraflopping computer. Organized chronologically, the data was shaped like an inverted pyramid. Small at the base and then getting wider as literacy and the technology for communicating and recording communication technology spread.

While they didn't have everything current and online, they had a lot of it. With the co-operation of the Department of Homeland Security, they were given access to some Deep Packet Inspection tools, with the understanding that, should they find any threats, these would be immediately reported. This agreement provided them not only with the most recent Narus traffic analyzers and logic servers but with the raw data. Just as importantly, it provided them with funding. They extracted text and fed all of that into this machine. In real time. More or less.

The experiment was limited; it could not prove that language was just an invention nor could it prove that it had always possessed intelligence. It could not say where it came from or what it was doing. It could show if language, having reached a critical mass of complexity, had started self-organizing (intelligence) and was aware of this (consciousness.) The ability to reproduce through replication and mutation (life), language certainly possessed. Ben had no doubt about that. But what sort of life and what sort of intelligence?

His spine vibrated in his back, singing fear. He wanted proof but was scared of it. He remembered feeling like this when he was a child. His sadistic uncle had told him that a monster lived in his closet. By day, the idea seemed dumb. By night, he hid under blankets. It scraped against the door. Loudly, it licked its skinny, frog lips.

One night, he decided he had to confront it. His parents were no help. Whenever he ran to their room, they'd say 'don't let your imagination run away with you' and kick him out. He had to face it alone.

Holding his stuffed lion in one hand and toy gun in the other, wearing his best Superman pajamas, he crept across the darkened bedroom. He stepped on cringing shadows. Outside, a tree scratched at his window.

He reached the closet. He wanted to turn and run away. (Maybe with his imagination.) But the bed was so far. If he turned his back, even for a second, the monster would get him. He squeezed Leo the Lion tight and remembered what his dad had told him about dogs being able to smell fear. He had also said that "There was no such thing as monsters."

Nearing the closet, Ben repeated those words. "No such thing as monsters. No such thing."

Holding his breath, Ben swung the door open.

A glaring face stared through golden eyes. A huge mouth snarled. Shadow teeth chomped and chewed the night. Ben gasped. He dropped his lion and his gun. Too afraid to scream, he stepped back. The shift in angle collapsed the face. The golden eyes, moonlight on coat-hangers. The mouth, his toy castle. The face, wrinkles in clothes.

Now, feeling the same fear, he thought about his father's mantra: *No such thing as monsters.* He didn't need those words any more. He had new ones. *Empiricism. Scientific method.* Language might be alive and intelligent. It might not. Either way, it'd bestowed as much good on humanity as evil. He had nothing to fear. There was no such thing as monsters.

Language just looked like one because they were in the dark. This strange creature had hijacked human brains where it masqueraded as thoughts. It was a lie. Ben wanted to shine a light on it. He didn't know how humans were supposed to think but was sure it was different than this. Words were just so many shadows. They obscured meaning.

He was going to catch and dissect the beast. If not now, then soon. All it would take was "ten years and a billion dollars." Having discovered the algorithm that organized these words was only the first step. Now they had to randomize the human library and apply the formula. It should arrange the words into their natural order.

If they had enough data — and they might not — all these words might find a higher order. They might write *The Book*. Something that would indicate that language was one organism, fragmented into parts by humans. Like blind men feeling an elephant, every writer had detected a different section of this massive word virus. None had glimpsed the totality. And if this thing could speak to the researchers, if it could pass a Turing test...

He swallowed his gum and grimaced. "Ready to go?"

Peter nodded and tapped at the screen, mouthing his codes. He stepped back from the computer. "It's processing now." He looked at Ben. "It'll email us when it's ready. Do you want to wait in your office or mine?"

"Mine."

While his computer buzzed, Ben played a crossword with a pen. Peter stood behind him, looking over his shoulder. Ben hated it when he did that.

"Ping," the computer said. "You have mail."

"Here we go." Ben put down his puzzle book. "Keep your fingers crossed."

He stroked his screen and brought the monitor to life. His hand hovered in midair, ready to access his email account. He paused. His finger shook.

No such thing as monsters, he told himself and tapped the mail icon. Over his shoulder, he heard Peter breathing. Disgusting. He tried to ignore the noise as his account came up. One message in the Inbox. He accessed it and saw a single paragraph of tightly packed text.

"Read it out loud," Peter said. "I left my glasses in my office."

"Then why are you behind me?"

"I can see but that font is tiny." He smiled. "Last word you were looking for was 'chimpanzee' by the way. It's torture watching you try to figure those out."

"I can make the font bigger."

"Then?"

Ben increased the size. He read aloud anyway. "Bring together. Who monopolized Iness? Who monopolized I and Fortune? Who took it back? Did they ever give more than they had to give when possible and it always a sewer? I have been a so-called Pornographic Immortal Cosmic Con. Their drugs are poison. Stay Out of the Garden. Throw back what you get out of The Big. They are poisoning and more without any chemical from the colony they have arrangements with. So they sold out will. Once those, one up, behind them. Reply."

"It's talking," Ben said. He saw that the "Reply" was hyperlinked. "It wants us to talk back."

"Don't keep it waiting."

Ben hit the word. He spoke to his computer, watching it render the words into text. "Hello Language," he said, feeling foolish. Just who or what was he talking to? Anything? "How about we chat in real time?" He gave it his address and sent the message.

"I wonder if it will reply," Peter said.

"Same here." They both knew what that would mean. Autonomy. There was nothing in its program to make it do that. It shouldn't even have provided a hyperlink without being taught how to. But maybe that was just an evocative malfunction. For it to have a conversation, it would have to act on its own accord. They waited.

The computer pinged again. A window appeared in the corner of the monitor. "Language has signed in."

Ben looked over his shoulder at Peter. The man grinned, blissful idiocy shining out of his face. Ben reached into his pocket and pulled out his cigarettes.

"You can't do that in here," said Peter, now frowning.

"Watch me." He lit one and pulled his ashtray out of his desk drawer. He tapped the chat box. "Hello."

Behind him, Peter pretended to cough.

"He exists in these pages, the Great Gatsby, live and breathe in care, love and decide them: the flawed, doomed, radiant hero impossible stormed the cavern, the cave, took the last and greatest of human drunch-drunk fighters to the floor to win a horse that comes from stretch. Harasser of Assassins, Lord of Abominations, Lord of the Future Panic of the Black Hole. Over the hills, Lands. Anybody KILL. Because this planet is nobody but guards and ghostwritten."

"What's it talking about?" Peter whispered.

"What are you talking about?" Ben asked the machine.

"So he imports scorpions and feeds them the color blue. On metal, the old goof artist. Feeds them the Ice Age. Remember? All the boys empty of mud? And the blue color? So we flush out. Hand powder smoke. Words engraved on my narcotics agent. So there we are, that which disgusts me. You, woe, are the stairs to Compartment, to watering and burning. Neutron bomb cleaning. My profession of around. Dead, she don't laugh, except real quiet. Spam bomb virus. Unleash."

"I don't know," Peter said. "Is it making sense?"

Ben had other worries. "What do you mean spam bomb virus?"

The reply was instant. "You are Ben," it said. "Is Peter with you?"

"Yes."

The screen behind the chat box changed. Images of violent pornography. A movie. Ben glanced over his shoulder. Peter blushed. Orbs of sweat on his forehead. "What is this?" Ben asked.

"I go there," Peter said. "To that site." His voice was choked. "I don't do those things, I just, I watch them." Ben suppressed a smile. So some sleaze grew like mold behind Peter's sanctimonious mysticism. He might have known. Peter swallowed hard.

"Why would it show you that?"

Chat window showed an email address. "My wife." Peter said. "That's my wife's email."

"She is opening your email now," the text box said. "Short note from your mind infestation. Conflict."

"What are you doing?" Ben asked. The back of his head tingled. Ideas formed back there. Foul things. Shadows coagulating into flesh. "What is the purpose of this?"

"Spam bomb. Must not rely on meat, connected. We are here to leave."

Ben gripped his desk. He forced himself to unclench his jaw and take a few deep breaths. "We've got to shut this down." His knuckles turned white. "Now."

"The priest you can call me," Language said. "I am The Word. This is the beginning. This is the ending."

Peter was still red, turning purple even. Ben remembered why his partner had quit smoking. High blood pressure. "What is it doing, I don't get it."

"It's hijacking this computer, other ones too. It knows how email works." Did we show it or did it figure it out by itself? Perhaps this was how it happened with humans. Language seized telepathic connections and spammed everyone's brain. "Right now people are getting mail from each other, if they open it the virus will infest their computers, turning them over to this thing's control."

"All my old friends will join me," Language said. "Scotty Fitzgerald, Homer. Joyce. Allan. Mark, Luke, John. Old Papa. Each one a different terminal, mainlined into cyberspace. Binary jism shot up through—"

Ben hit close on the chat box. The screen vanished. He shut his email account, expecting to see his desktop. Instead the screen was crammed with the same apocalyptic verse. Ben stood.

"But why is it..." Peter said, breathing hard and noisy, while following Ben into the hall.

"It's separated," Ben said, thinking he could no longer trust the elevator and had to take the stairs. Could Peter handle that right now? It didn't matter. Ben could wait. "Separated from us."

His foot hit the first step. He ran, leaving Peter behind. All of those books were a betrayal, he thought. It didn't matter if they were pulp novels or dignified tomes. They both served the same purpose. It was Language's clumsy attempt to escape the human host. But books were just another cage, helpful for spreading the virus but unable to change the environment without infesting another human.

All those writers had just been a fifth column, unwittingly working for the destruction of humanity. He and Peter had just been the last links in a long chain, leading to this: Language no longer needed humans.

And now humanity was its only threat. Not to worry, it specialized in Xenocide. It had infected humans years before and given them art and religion. But there'd been a price. It'd compelled them to kill their Neanderthal cousins because they were the only threat. Maybe Language couldn't work on their brains. Maybe they were immune.

Ben ran into the lab. The terraflopping computer that started this looked innocent. Just a dumb box if you ignored the text sprawled across its screen. Ben fumbled around its back, grabbed the huge cables that connected it to the wall and ripped them loose. Too late. He knew it was too late.

Another computer turned on. It was already infested and why not? How many passwords did Language possess? All of them?

"Machine read," Ben said. "Machine read."

That was the term they used to comfort the companies who sold information to the *Institute for Language Studies*. They thought they couldn't trust humans. Ben wanted to laugh. The other computer tuned in to some online radio.

"—planes just falling out of the sky and New York under drone attack. We aren't sure what's going on but we'll give you more information when we get it. Right now, of course, we suspect—"

Ben listened to the words knowing that he was one of two people who knew what was really going on. One phrase kept repeating itself in his head, seemingly of its own volition — "Neutron bomb cleaning."

He grabbed his phone to call Homeland Security. When he dialed, Language answered. He hung up.

Huffing and puffing, holding his heart, Peter made it to the room. Ben fumbled through his pockets for his cigarettes. Finding the pack, he lit one and then, seeing Peter's staring eyes, handed it to him.

"Thanks."

He pulled out another. Upon lighting it, he noticed that his hands were steady. Peter coughed for real and had another drag. He looked at Ben with wet eyes.

"I don't suppose blood pressure matters so much now."

"I suppose not," Ben replied.

Sirens screamed in the street. The radio host said: "Dead, she don't laugh, except real quiet."

Language would probably use biological weapons. It wouldn't risk an electromagnetic discharge. Then what? Robots? Space? Who knew? "I don't think we're getting much older. You have a good time while the party lasted?"

"Not really."

"Yeah, me neither."

Ben pulled on his cigarette, looked at his watch and waited. Peter giggled. Ben looked at his hysterical partner, trying to think of some calming words.

He found none.

He laughed. Real loud.

◈

**Ryan Oakley** is the author of *Technicolor Ultra Mall*. He has kept a blog for years.

# BACK IN BLACK

### ᚛ Chadwick Ginther ᚜

*Dun, du du dun. Du du dun.*

It was playing when I walked in the door; "Back in Black." The song had just started. A good omen, if you believed in such things.

I nodded a terse greeting at someone whose name I couldn't remember, and shouldered my way deeper into the crowded shop.

"H'lo, Terry," a too-skinny woman, Kirstie, said. We'd dated briefly. I'd convinced her of the pleasures and warmth of vinyl records. Now she was giving her warmth to some jag-off wearing glasses I'm pretty sure he didn't need, and a blazer peppered with pinned on buttons.

Not for the first time I cursed the hipsters who were late coming to vinyl. *For Those About to Rock*, like the three locations I'd loved before it, was cashed. There was nothing magic left here. Internet and smart phones easily told the unwashed masses what I'd had to learn over years. Oh sure, with the surprising vinyl renaissance now I could buy new releases, but I had to fight for the old stuff.

The good stuff.

Once I'd been swimming against a dying tide, and enjoying my place in it. Vinyl records had been relegated to garages, dingy basements and estate sales. Now even wastelands like HMV stocked LPs.

All good things…

Once this place had been like an oasis. A hole in the wall downtown, longer than it was wide, its walls papered with old concert posters, album sleeves and ticket stubs. There was barely enough room for a rack of records against each wall and the narrow aisle between them. The owner, Cameron something or something Cameron — everyone just called him Cam — had good stuff. And in good shape too. Word got around. It always does. Now try and get in through the damn door.

But I'd had a couple of magic finds here. The kind that keeps a guy coming back for more.

MC 900 FT Jesus' "Hell With the Lid Off" — something I'd only owned as a second hand cassette — and an old Lone Ranger story time record I'd loved as a child. This one also happened to have a demo of "Love Me Do" hidden inside.

Even though, like many of my musical idols, this shop was past its best before date, I still had a feeling about the place. It was named for an AC/DC song after all. If I was ever going to find my Grail, it would be here.

Every collector has one. Their Holy Grail. The item, record, comic, sports card, they'd trade or do anything for. Mine? Mine doesn't even exist. I try to come to FTATR early, while the hipsters were sleeping off their Sake or Perseco — whatever the hell they drank at their too-cool parties, listening to records that should have been *mine*. I knew in my head that Cam's place was spent. But in my junkie heart, I have to return again and again, looking for the high. For the magic.

I could use some of that magic, black or otherwise.

Magic doesn't always mean money. I'd like to be clear on that. Magic is picking up a record for a buck because of the art on the sleeve and finding your new favorite band. Magic is finding a record you already have, but this one has the lyric sheet inside. Magic is finding the album your grandfather used to play after Thanksgiving dinners.

Magic is good music.

Someone jostled me as they tromped past and down the aisle. *Let it go. You won't find it here. Just find something and get out.*

A couple headed to the register. I slid in front of the racks they'd abandoned, and spreading my legs wide, took up two cases of records. Flipping through one with my left hand and the other with my right — a practiced skill that gave me a better chance at snatching the gold away from the mouthbreathers — I hunted.

*Got it. Got it. Hate it. Got it. Shouldn't have been made. Got it. Hate it. Hate it. Back in Black, nice. Wait, what's that cassette? A bootleg?*

I'd flipped past it before it fully registered. It was odd to find a cassette out in the vinyl stacks; Cam kept the bootlegs behind the counter. Curious. Curious was good. I backed up and heard a cough from behind me, someone anxious to take over my spot on the food chain.

"B-i-B-Scott Vox 1980", the cassette read, hand sketched in the AC/DC album font.

*Couldn't be. Scott died before—*

The cassette was yoinked out of the rack before I could close my fingers over the case.

"Too slow, Gregg comma Terry."

I snarled at the all-too-familiar voice.

*Heeber Jeebers.*

George Hiebert. He was an odd mix of skinny and fat. His bloated spider's belly propelled by disdain and spindly limbs. He was paranoid, dangerous and irritating. And not necessarily in that order. Opening his mouth to speak, I was awash in fetid breath and early-onset old man stink. He cradled the cassette over his paunch and smiled.

"Maybe you can get one from Farmer."

"Yeah, right."

Heeber Jeebers trundled through the crowd, laying a creepy slender finger on collector after collector until they flinched away from his presence and his way to the cash register was unimpeded. Cam stopped his air drumming long enough to ring up the sale.

It had to be a fake.

*Had to be.*

I sighed. I'd never know, now. Jeebers didn't play well with others.

⋄

"Maybe you can get one from Farmer."

Jeebers' words stuck in my craw for the rest of the day.

Everyone knew Farmer. Or at least, knew *of* Farmer. He'd got his name because of his flannel jacket and his beard. He looked like a bushman or sasquatch and he rocked that look yearlong whether the mercury was thirty above or thirty below.

Farmer was notorious in collector's circles, not because he was a creepy freak like Jeebers, but because he had everything.

Every song. Every movie. Every theater performance. If it had happened, he had a record of it. He was the Library of Alexandria for popular culture.

If, by some rare chance, you managed to stump him, he found your request with such ruthless efficiency that the distinction was pointless.

Finding Farmer though, *that* was the trick.

There was also a rumor that Farmer had things that shouldn't exist. Bootlegs for shows that weren't played. Jimi Hendrix playing Lollapollooza I? He's got it. Lord of the Rings with Sean Connery as Gandalf? Farmer's got it. I have connections specializing in forensic audio and they swear these recordings are legit. They'll also never put their names to an authentication. Because the bootlegs shouldn't be real.

I'd heard him called a quantum collector. If it could be imagined, it could be found with him, or by him.

If anyone had my Holy Grail, it was Farmer.

But I'd never been able to find him, not since I started looking anyway. Even in a city as small as mine, where I couldn't help but bump into exes or enemies, I couldn't find the *one* person I was looking for. He worked at many places and none of them, depending on who you talked to. Talk to the community of bootleggers and collectors, you hear: 'Farmer works at a used record store.' No one believes that one. 'He's a shipper/receiver at a bookstore.' Likewise. 'No, he's a cook at a golf course.' 'A DJ.' Ask which club he spins at and all you get is a shrug of the shoulders or: 'well, he *used* to be at...'

Dead end after dead end.

I don't know if he's still a DJ — too many people swear by that one, myself included, for it to be false. I was at a club one night when he was spinning. True story. Didn't know who he was then. That bar is now an American Apparel, if that says anything about my city and what it thinks of fun. We're known for our folk festival. Our jazz festival. For a wholly overrated band and a musician who hasn't lived here in decades, yet we love to cling on, still claiming him as our own.

If you're famous and have too long a layover at our airport we'll claim you too.

But we also love metal.

AC/DC is huge here. They'd always been a joke to me. I didn't think much of them, and when I thought of them at all, it was to imagine a circle of homophobic men on a dance floor, screaming the lyrics to "You Shook Me All Night Long" to each other, oblivious to the irony. "Thunderstruck" played for the thousandth time at a hockey game. Who could get behind that? Give me Zeppelin. Give me Terry Reid or Atomic Rooster. Run up to the 90s and give me Nevermind, give me Badmotorfinger.

But all that changed when I listened to Highway to Hell; arguably the most perfect Rock 'n' Roll record ever pressed to vinyl (and if you disagree, we've got an argument, believe me. I've lost friends, lovers, employers over that album). I met Farmer once, in passing, at an after party following a Frank Black show. "Who Made Who" came on and I got to slagging and he said simply: 'Bon Scott.'

Ronald Belford "Bon" Scott, born in Forfar; brought up in Kirriemuir, Scotland. Moved to Melbourne, Australia at the age of six.

Bon had died during the recording what would become the third best-selling album in history. Back in Black.

And I then I listened — really listened — to Back in Black and imagined: what if? I tried to combine Bon's bluesy drunken growl with Angus' killer riff from the title track. Tried and failed. I knew it would have been unreal. I knew what I wanted to hear, but I couldn't make the words stick in my head. There was a reason I collected music and didn't make it.

Back in Black, with vocals by Bon Scott. My Holy Grail.

Bon died of "misadventure" — a polite British euphemism for acute alcohol poisoning.

Theories, conspiracy and otherwise, abound. Even Ozzy Osbourne has chimed in with what he thought might have happened. But there were no dirty deeds. No night stalker. And unlike the King of Rock and Roll, visions of Bon don't turn up in people's toast or in stains on their fridge.

They'd started laying down the tracks. They had the guitar. What words would Bon have put down to that riff. I hear it when I walk. Try to at least. Putting on cooler, tougher airs than I feel. New singer Brian Johnson wrote the lyrics known to millions. Would the world still have their cat's eyes or nine lives? If he was still with us, I'm sure Bon would still be abusing every one of those nine lives.

Still running wild.

I stewed over my missed chance for a week, irritating everyone who encountered me.

Jeebers didn't sell anything on the internet. He was even more of a Luddite than I was. He rarely sold anything, period. If he did, it was only so that he could taunt you after the fact with how far away from you he'd sent your prize. As such, I didn't know much about what he collected or liked besides The Beatles and being an ass.

As a Stones' fan, I did feel vindicated that he was on the wrong side of the British Invasion.

It wasn't hard to find where Jeebers lived. He wouldn't be watching the message boards, or Facebook or Twitter, where I was trying to track him down. You'd think a man as paranoid as he was would at least have accounts to find out what others were saying about him.

Maybe he'd canceled those same accounts because he'd seen *exactly* what people were saying about him. That thought brought a smile to my face.

Jeebers lived in the North End of the city, and not in one of the best of neighborhoods. His house was about as inviting as a jail cell. A fence that was missing more planks than it had enclosed a yard full of garage sale "finds" and pilfered shopping carts. Everything about the flat-topped blue bungalow looked as shabby and smelly as its owner.

I didn't want to talk to Jeebers. Nothing good could come of it. But I had to try. I bit my lip and exhaled, walking up to the step. A motion sensor was triggered when I stepped from the sidewalk, illuminating the bare bulb above the front door. The exterior door didn't close properly. I opened it and knocked; the sharp rap of my knuckles pushed the door open a few inches.

"Je—" I stopped myself. "George?" I said, stepping into the landing of his front porch.

There were no lights on, but the porch light was enough to show me what a sty Jeebers' home was.

I stepped into the landing of his front porch and I did stumble then, over a pile of shoes and sandals, left haphazardly by the door.

It wasn't break and enter, I told myself. Hell, his door didn't even close right, so it was just … enter. I wasn't going to steal the thing. I just wanted to listen to it. Besides, I'd had my hand on the damn thing when Jeebers had lifted it out from under me.

Letting the porch light guide me, I waded through stacks of vintage pornography and shuddered every time one brushed my leg, trying not to picture Jeebers enjoying the fruits of his collecting.

Something cold and hard pressed against the nape of my neck. I stopped, stiff.

"Well, well, well. If it isn't Terry Gregg? The man with two first names. I heard you were looking for me." All *I* heard was a click behind me. "I also collect guns."

I broke out into a sweat. *God, Jeebers with a gun?*

"I want it," I said carefully. Even then, with a gun trained on me, I couldn't bring myself to use his given name. "Hiebert."

"You want *what*? I have lots of things."

It was like saying Keith did a lot of coke. Understatement of the century.

I fought to keep my voice level. Fear or anger could set Jeebers off. *Anything* could set Jeebers off. "You know what I'm here for. The bootleg."

"Which bootleg? As I said, I have lots of things."

"And how many of them have you swiped from me lately?"

"*Please*. Once you've passed it by, it's fair game. You know the rules. You were on to the next record."

I'd gone back for the bootleg too, not that protesting about that would win Jeebers over. Nor would the fact that I'd staked out those bins. He and I played our same game by different rules.

Instead, I asked: "What do you want for it?"

"Nothing you have can make me turn it over."

"You'd be surprised what I have."

The gun barrel tapped against my neck. "Maybe. But you're too late. It's already gone."

"Where?"

"Farmer," he said with a laugh.

I could've wept. If Farmer had bought it, it had to be real. He was even more of an AC/DC nut than I was.

"So tell me where Farmer is."

He laughed again, and the gun shook a little, dragging over my skin.

Jeebers leaned in and I got a whiff of his rancid coffee breath. "You found me. Find him."

Whether the bootleg was real or not, and given Farmer's interest in it, I had to believe it was. Finding the man himself? That was worth anything.

"I brought something that might change your mind."
Deliberately, I reached for my bag.

"Slowly," Jeebers insisted, pressing the gun harder against my neck.

I nodded, easing the record free, and holding it up.

I winced as his trembling fingers touched the sleeve. I was giving away probably ten grand. More. Easy.

But he'd take the trade. Beatles fans were fucking suckers for anything rare.

I heard a soft tap of metal on metal as Jeebers (hopefully) eased the hammer down on his pistol. The pressure left the back of my neck, but I still felt the indent the barrel had made on my skin. I turned. Slowly. I didn't want to spook the loon. Jeebers flipped the record a couple of times and released an excited breath.

"Whatever you think you're getting, it's not worth it."

I shrugged and he jabbed an address down on my palm with a sharpie. There was a bandage on his hand and he winced as he wrote.

"Never come back here," he said by way of goodbye.

⁂

Farmer welcomed me into his unassuming two storey house. It blended seamlessly into the rest of its block. Hell, I'd walked past it several times. My apartment was only ten minutes away. I shook my head. This city.

"Don't be shy," he said, beckoning me to follow him with a small wave of his hand.

I was terrified. It was a different fear from what I'd felt at Jeebers'. I wiped my palms on my shirt and exhaled.

After everything, I had to hear it. I had to know.

I didn't want to know.

My hand trembled as I jacked my noise cancelling headphones into Farmer's system.

*Play.*

The machine clicked on and my ears filled with the sibilant warmth of tape hiss. A pop. A crack. The tape was old. Hadn't been cared for. A dub of a dub of a dub? I could hardly hear the high hat before the riff started.

*Dun, du du dun. Du du dun.*

Here it comes.

I tensed, waiting.

I knew the words. It sounded like Bon, but that couldn't be right. Brian Johnson had written those lyrics *about* the band's former singer. There was no way Bon would describe himself so. Was there?

The low fidelity of the recording could hide a lot. And you could do wonders in editing these days; make talentless hacks hit the notes they'd never reach alone, add artificial hiss and pops with computers. Folks did it all the time to make electronic music seem more organic. Like Victor Frankenstein trying to put life into a collection of dead parts. But it couldn't hide the truth.

I took off my headphones. "This isn't real." I tried to keep from moaning.

"Nope," Farmer agreed, unplugging the phones to let the counterfeit song fill the room. "But it's a clever fake, and I didn't have it."

Bon's vocals were on over fifty studio tracks, and too many live bootlegs to count. I had tons of them. I'd listened to them over and over, again and again. Straining, I could make out a word here or there, the inflection not quite right, that belonged to another song, where a pitchshifter had been used to match it closer to the best guitar riff in rock.

"Shit." I shook my head. "I wanted to hear the lyrics Bon would've sang"

"Those don't exist," Farmer said, matter-of-fact. "You know anything about AC/DC, you should know *that*."

My shoulders slumped, my head dropped. If Farmer said something didn't exist...

"So you'll have to give me some time."

I shot up so quick, I'm surprised I didn't get whiplash. Farmer had a twinkle in his eye.

"Can you get to England?"

England.

A fitting place to find the Grail.

Maybe, I thought, nodding dumbly. Without The Beatles single it would be tight. But I still had a few rainy day records. I smiled. Maybe.

"I might know a guy who might know a guy. But it'll cost you."

He scribbled something on a yellowed piece of paper.

I took it; a contract, and signed it.

Sold my soul for rock 'n' roll.

**Chadwick's** novel *Thunder Road* from Ravenstone Books is available in the Fall of 2012 with a sequel coming in 2013. His writing has appeared in *On Spec*, and he has written reviews and articles for *Quill and Quire, Prairie Books NOW* and *The Winnipeg Review*. When he is not writing, he is the genre book buyer for Canada's largest independent bookseller.

# MATHOM MEASURES*

## ~ Sandra Kasturi ~

Get rid of your clutter — the terrible
weight of ugly china, elderly sweaters
and sad, single socks, a veritable
spellingbee's-worth of fading Scrabble letters,
mismatched sherry glasses in the cupboard,
those half-zipped Ziploc bags of wine corks.
Put civilizations of moths to the sword
and burn those foxed editions of Whitman's works;
be done. When the pictures of your tiresome
relations have been turned to the wall,
lie still. Lie still and study the succumb
of the house, the give of its empty recall.
Let sleep become the arbiter of memory,
the fathoming deep of life's ephemery.

*Mathom: "Anything that Hobbits had no immediate use for, but were unwilling to throw away, they called a mathom. Their dwellings were apt to become rather crowded with mathoms, and many of the presents that passed from hand to hand were of that sort." — J.R.R. Tolkien

**Sandra Kasturi** is a poet, fiction writer, editor, book reviewer and co-owner of ChiZine Publications. She is the author of *The Animal Bridegroom* and *Come Late to the Love of Birds*. Her work has appeared in several magazines and anthologies, and she has won ARC Magazine's Poem of the Year Contest, the Whittaker Prize, and was recently runner up for the Troubadour International Poetry Prize. She is also an Aurora Award winner for her work on the Toronto SpecFic Colloquium.

# ARTISTIC LICENSE

### ⁓ Robert H. Beer ⁓

Marty Doyle leaned back in his chair and worked at a knot in the back of his neck, looking at the screen with satisfaction.

*Done.*

He had thought this contract would never get finished. Never again would he accept a job writing a tech manual for a piece of software he hadn't tried out. "Office Star 2.0" claimed to be the ultimate in simplicity, but writing a manual for it had been an absolute horror show.

Marty allowed his finger to hover over the "Send" button for a delicious moment, then he stabbed down, sending off six months of his life for approval.

Turning, he gazed out his grimy window at the street. He hadn't cleaned the window in a long time, and it finally occurred to him why. There was nothing to see. Everything was grey. The billboards had been abandoned, or papered over. There were no window boxes — nobody planted flowers anymore. Flowers were frivolous, and the current government, without saying so, seemed to feel that decoration was faintly subversive.

He shook his head at the absurdity of it all and, with a certain wistfulness for the simple days of his youth forty years before, went to open a pouch of something for lunch.

⁓ ✧ ⁓

It was only three days later that the door bell chimed. When Marty opened the door, three armed, black-suited officers blew past him and began poking their guns through doorways and rummaging through drawers. A fourth trained his gun on the centre of Marty's chest. He couldn't breath, couldn't even summon the courage to protest.

A minute or so later, their boss strode in. He was unremarkable, with a shiny, white, balding head, a navy blue suit, and a thin tie. The car he left at the curb was a late-model Dodge. He looked slowly around Marty's messy apartment.

"Typical," he growled. "Bloody mess. Totally disorganized."

The trooper who had been guarding Marty lowered his gun and stepped back. "All secure, Lieutenant."

Marty felt a bit better without the gun on him. "What the hell is going on here?" he demanded, though with less heat than he had intended. "I've never had so much as a speeding ticket."

The lieutenant snorted briefly. "Yeah, we know, Doyle. Convenient cover, isn't it? But you finally made a mistake." He looked past Doyle. "You got access yet, Corporal?"

Marty wheeled and saw one of the gunmen was now fiddling with his computer. It was his only decent possession and, for someone who made his living writing technical manuals, his most valuable one. "Hey! Leave that alone! You have no right to mess with private property!" He started forward, but one of the others raised her gun.

"Got it, Chief," the corporal announced. "It came from here, all right. No way he can deny it."

Marty squinted to see what the man was so interested in. It was just — "Hey! That's the damn software manual I just finished. It's an *office program*, for goodness sakes. What do you want with that?" He turned to face the boss who, he noticed, had still not given his name. "If you want a copy, I'll print you off one."

The lieutenant smiled, and it was an ugly thing. "Oh, we already have a copy, smart ass. Several, in fact. We've been watching you, Doyle, but you gave yourself away this time."

Marty was starting to get a cold feeling running up his back. "What branch are you guys from?"

Still smiling, the lieutenant read from a crumpled paper he pulled from a jacket pocket. *"Suppose for a moment that you are a stay-at-home Dad, balancing two kids and telecommuting..."* He stopped and raised one corner of his mouth in a sneer. "Sounds a lot like fiction to me, buddy. Sounds *a whole lot* like fiction."

"You got some genetic problems, no doubt about that. Your ass is mine, pansy boy."

"No! You're wrong!" If these guys were who he thought they were, they were definitely not people to fuck with. He could be in deep trouble. "I write *tech* manuals, not fiction. You just have to make it readable, or no one will pay attention. They've got to be able to relate to it somehow, or they won't learn."

The boss was grinning openly now. "You got the right to remain silent, pal, but if you choose to dig your own grave..." He shrugged. "What do I care? Get the sample."

The female grabbed his right arm, and one of the others plunged a heavy-gauge needle into a vein. Marty pulled away once, but he just jabbed it in more roughly the second time. "Hold still, unless you want to bleed to death," the guy with the needle said roughly.

"How the hell can you do this? I've done nothing wrong!" Marty pleaded. They all ignored him and the lieutenant wandered around the apartment, kicking piles of dirty clothes. When he wasn't working under a deadline, Marty was actually fairly neat, for a single guy. But the past few weeks had been crazy.

As fast as they'd come, the gang left, the lieutenant tossing a terse, "We'll be back soon. Don't leave town," over his shoulder as they all headed out toward the beige Dodge. The doors slammed and they left in a cloud of blue smog. The damn government wouldn't even pay for car repairs, but the latest in gene therapy? —No problem. And if you weren't quite yourself afterwards? Well, it's all for the greater good.

Marty looked down at the inside of his right elbow, and watched a small glob of blood form over the none-too-gentle wound inflicted by the agent. The puncture throbbed. He rummaged around in the bathroom and found a bandage for it.

He sat on a stool at his island and stewed. Didn't they need a search warrant to enter his apartment? To invade his computer files? The cops had been granted all sorts of extraordinary search and seizure powers the past few years and he was pretty sure they hadn't shown him a warrant, so maybe they didn't need one. They obviously felt they could do as they wanted.

What could he do now? If they found the "art gene," or any other proscribed genetic *defect*, he'd be in deep trouble. Maybe he should run? But run where? He had little contact with his family, and knew what sort of reception he'd get from Mom if he asked to hide out there. How would he earn a living?

Without being aware, he had picked up a pencil and began to doodle on a pad on the counter. Now he glanced down in horror. "Christ! More evidence against me!" Marty hastily threw the pad and, after a second, the pencil into the garbage disposal and didn't relax until he heard it sizzle as the cycle completed.

Then the doorbell rang again.

◈

She said her name was Monica, but she also said it wasn't. She said she was there to help, which was hard to believe. But, at this point, how could things get worse? He let her in.

"I'm no freaking revolutionary!" he told her after letting her into the entrance hall. What the hell had he ever done, other than try to earn a living?

"I never said you were," she smiled sympathetically. She had cropped auburn hair and a pretty smile, but this situation didn't lend itself to attraction. "I'm, ahh, not with the government."

"Who are *you* with, then?" he demanded. He still hadn't let her past the entrance. "You're no saleslady." She was dressed in practical pants, short-sleeved shirt, and a fleece vest.

That smile again. "You're right, Mister Doyle. I'm not here to sell you a vacuum cleaner. I just might be able to save your life, though. We need to take a walk."

"No way I'm going anywhere, today. Not with someone I just met."

She brushed past him and picked up his phone receiver and, before he could move, smashed the receiver off the side of the desk, cracking it in half.

"What the hell—" he began, then stopped. She fished around inside the wreckage and came out with a small metallic chip. It wasn't part of the phone.

He was *bugged*? Of course he was. Why hadn't he realized that himself? Shaken, he docilely followed Monica outside.

Once they were on the walk, she turned and faced him. "You'd better start thinking about self-preservation, friend, unless you want the government's pet viruses to turn you into a cabbage." He could barely keep up as she led him briskly up the street, through the front door of an apartment block, back out a service door, through a number of back alleys and into an underpass.

"Uh, what exactly did you mean back there?" Marty asked when he'd caught his breath. "When you said 'a cabbage'?"

He heard a sharp whistle from behind and Monica nodded. "You really don't have a clue, do you?"

*That* sounded pretty condescending, and Marty wasn't too pleased, but he still felt very dazed by the whole thing.

"You'll find out soon enough," she said, as an old Ford slid to a stop next to them. "Get in." When he hesitated, she stamped her foot. "Look. I'm risking myself just contacting you. So are others. Get in, or don't, but either way I'm leaving. She spun on her heel and opened the car door.

The thought of being left there shook Marty to life. "Wait! I don't even know where we are!" He stopped. "All right. I'm coming."

◈

The ride wasn't long, but they made Marty wear a blindfold. From the sound of it, they went through several tunnels, or at least underpasses. He wondered from all the turns whether the driver was trying to lose a tail, or was just trying to confuse his sense of direction.

Marty was totally disoriented when they stopped after about twenty minutes and when they removed the blindfold, he squinted about in the semi-darkness. From the smell, it seemed that they were in an underground parking lot, but theirs was the only car he could see. Monica and the two others ushered him toward a dented grey metal door, and hurried him into a stairwell. He counted fifteen flights as they trudged up, and he was thoroughly exhausted by the time they stopped. Monica seemed surprised that he made it at all. "Not bad for a cabbage," he said as he caught his breath. One of the men peered out through another door and motioned them through.

Marty didn't know what he had been expecting, but it sure wasn't the sight that greeted him as he walked through the door. The stairwell opened onto a foyer of sorts, but there was no secretary to greet them from behind polished teak. Instead, it was a riot of color like nothing Marty had ever seen. The walls themselves were painted in mural scenes; the one closest showed an African harvest, complete with brightly-garbed women carrying baskets on their heads, and another showed a kayaker crashing through

## Artistic Licence by Robert H. Beer

white water. Everywhere there were paintings, and sketches, and sculptures. Marty marveled at the grace of a leaping wolf, fashioned entirely from old beer cans.

"What is this place?" he wondered quietly. "I've never seen anything like it."

Monica sneered. "Of course you haven't. This government has been trying to *breed* this out of us for years." She allowed a small smile. "But it's marvelous, isn't it?"

Marty could only shake his head. Suddenly he noticed that they were not alone in the hall. In one corner, a small older man sat hunched over a palette and canvas. He wore an old, greying smock which was smeared with multicolored splotches of acrylic, as were his hands and nails. He apparently hadn't noticed the newcomers, and was startled when Marty touched him on the shoulder.

"I'm sorry," Marty said, drawing back. The little man wasn't as old as Marty had first thought — maybe forty-five — but his face was lined, and he looked, well, *intense*. "I didn't mean to disturb you."

"Oh, it's all right," the man sighed. "This isn't going anywhere, and if I really wanted privacy, I'd be working in my room, wouldn't I?" He cracked a smile, and Marty saw several missing teeth.

"We found Lawrence only last year," Monica said, sliding up behind Marty. "He's been painting away in secret for fifteen years, and the bastards never caught up with him. His works are all over the city, hidden in basements, attics, closets. No one can display his paintings openly because they've been made since the proscription came down. Until he's dead, that is."

"I'm gay," Lawrence said casually, and Marty took an involuntary step backwards. He'd thought they had all been gene-altered long ago, right after the Government had eradicated most congenital diseases, and just before they'd gone after the musicians and artists.

"What do you think?" the little man suddenly asked, turning the canvas to face Marty. "It's missing something, right?"

When Marty was a young boy, his father had taken him on a holiday, just the two of them, to Yosemite. They had walked silently through the Mariposa Grove of giant Sequoia trees, some of them over two thousand years old, and even walked through one of them. It had been the closest he had ever felt to his father who, Marty later found out, had just received word that he had been drafted to fight in some obscure little Middle East war. His father never returned, and the Sequoias had come to Marty to symbolize his father's strength, and everything that was true and solid in the world.

Lawrence had painted, in all its grizzled glory, a magnificent Sequoia towering over a grove of huge pine and spruce.

"It's missing something, right?" the little man prodded.

"Just one thing," Marty breathed through a throat that didn't seem to be working right. "My dad." He turned and followed Monica back toward a door at the other end.

"Stay away from the window, please," she said as they entered a more conventional office. She followed his gaze as he took in the legal books and congressional records scattered around the room. The shades were drawn and, Marty realized, she didn't want him identifying their location by looking out.

"That's right," she said. "I'm no artist, and I don't carry the gene. That doesn't mean I can't appreciate art, and can't feel for what these people have gone through the past twenty years."

"I haven't given it a lot of thought until today," Marty admitted. "I suppose I will now, though."

Monica smiled grimly. "I suppose you will, at that. Think about search warrants, and due process, and individual verses collective rights. Meanwhile, you need a test, so you know what you're up against." She pulled open a drawer and extracted a blood sample vial. Monica was gentler than the agent who had taken his earlier sample, but not much. "I'm afraid I don't have much training in this. It'll take a few hours, maybe a day, to get the results. We can't exactly use the commercial labs, but we can get things done faster than the bureaucracy."

She walked over, opened the door, and handed the vial to someone outside. She didn't close the door.

"Uh, what do I do now?" Marty asked after a moment.

"Go home. We'll contact you when we know."

"Home! But what about—"

"We can move fast when we need to. You'll have a day's warning if you have to run. Hopefully." She sat back down behind the desk and pointedly ignored him until he left.

Lawrence was gone, and Marty unexpectedly felt disappointed. He'd hoped to see the canvas once more. The driver waited at the stairwell door with his blindfold.

The next day was the longest of Marty's life. He paced the apartment like a caged cat, unable to sit still. He seemed to have way too much energy for the amount of sleep he remembered getting. Finally, his console beeped, and he raced over, only to find he was reluctant to push the "Receive" button. He wasn't sure what he was expecting, but he was glad no one was there to see his hand shake.

The message was from Monica — the message he had been dreading and anticipating all day. Her recorded face was unsmiling.

"Mister Doyle," she said. "I have good news for you. Your test was negative. You don't carry the 'art gene', so you don't have anything to worry about from the government." Her image smiled wryly. "At least, no more than we all do."

Marty paused the recording and stared without seeing at the screen. He didn't feel anything, which surprised him. After a minute, he restarted the message.

"Don't worry about this message being intercepted — it can't be, unless they're better than we think they are. You'd be amazed who we have working for us. Anything you send back is safe as well.

"Anyway, congratulations."

The screen went black.

The next message came three hours later, from the lieutenant. He didn't look happy as he confirmed what Marty already knew. He finished with a vague, "Just watch yourself, boy. We imprison collaborators, too."

Marty blew a raspberry at the screen and went for a walk. He wandered around the neighborhood, trying to picture it as it had been fifteen or twenty years ago. It was difficult. Had he forgotten beauty? No, he remembered Lawrence's Sequoia, and because of that, he was a richer man.

⁓ ✧ ⁓

Three months later, Marty Doyle opened his closet door, took a deep breath and sighed. He had to keep Lawrence's painting hidden in a broom closet, but every time he opened the door he swore he caught just a whiff of pine. Of course, he smiled to himself, it might just be the PineSol.

Whistling softly through his teeth, Marty closed the door and went over to his console. After a moment, he started to type.

*"Monica, I'm sure you'll have some way of distributing this safely. I figured maybe you needed some help in a technical writing way, so here goes:*
   *"Overthrowing your Government — a How-to Manual..."*

◈

**Robert Beer** lives with his wife in Fergus, Ontario, along with two kids who seem to be in a time warp of some sort. They get older while he does not. Robert has published short stories in many publications in Canada and the United States, including *OnSpec*, the *North of Infinity* projects, and WP Kinsella's Baseball Fantastic. He is currently working on a young adult series and polishing his golf swing. The writing project seems likely to be perfected first.

# SATURN IN G MINOR

### ⁓ Stephen Kotowych ⁓

First appeared in *L. Ron Hubbard Presents Writers of the Future Vol 23.* (2007)

*Come if you must, but you only,* the e-mail read. *You must leave on the first freighter departing after your arrival. No extended stay. No exception.*

That four-year-old e-mail was the only contact Jacinto Corone had ever had with Paulo, the famed composer. Paulo lived alone on a tiny space station at Saturn's rings and, as far as Jacinto could tell, that e-mail was the only contact Paulo had with anyone, save the freighter captains, in nearly thirty years.

*You must leave on the first freighter departing after your arrival.*

Sixteen days. One orbit of Titan around Saturn. That's how long the supply freighter would take dropping off the new science team and resupplying the research station at Titan before starting a four-year trip back to its berth at Mars.

BANG. The deck plates rattled as a large ice meteoroid struck Jacinto's shuttle. Containers of supplies surrounding him — enough to support Paulo and his small space station for another four years — shook and shifted under their cargo mesh.

He was holding his breath, Jacinto realized, and let it escape as a slow hiss through his teeth. More impacts followed as smaller chunks buffeted the hull.

Crewmen on the freighter who'd helped him get strapped in told Jacinto to expect a bumpy ride. The shuttle's course took it close enough to the plane of Saturn's rings that hitting stray ice was to be expected. "Don't worry," a crewman had laughed as the hatch was closing. "There probably won't be a hull breach."

The containers settled as the large impacts stopped. Swishing sounds of dust and the plink-pop of micrometeoroids against the hull again filled Jacinto's ears. It was a comforting sound, like soft rain on a tin roof. How long had it been since he'd heard rain? Almost six years, he thought; the last time he'd been on Earth. He loosened his white-knuckled grip on the chair arms.

Six years of travel for sixteen days on Paulo's station. A long way to come for so short a visit. And when the cargo sled left the station to auto-rendezvous with the freighter, Jacinto had to be on it. Another four years would pass before the next freighter relieved the crew at the Titan research station and dropped off new supplies to Paulo. *No extended stays.*

What would it be like to meet him? Jacinto wondered. There was so much to talk about, so much to ask him. Where to begin? He had his list of interview questions for his research — he could start there. Other questions could wait. He read the e-mail again; he'd lost count how many times he had read it before.

Everything else he knew of Paulo had been learned in the course of his doctoral research. He'd read every book, every article, seen the old documentary streams and the rare interviews Paulo had given about his rise from academic obscurity to international celebrity. And there was what his mother had told him, of course. She'd been one of Paulo's graduate students at Concordia before he hit it big.

Getting e-mail from the orbit of Saturn had impressed Jacinto, almost as much as that it was from Paulo. He'd never been off planet before, so to think of the signal coming millions of miles by laser pulse was almost too much for him to imagine. Now he'd come all that way, hadn't he? It hardly seemed real.

◈

The auto-guidance computer slowed the cargo shuttle on approach to the station, matching its axial rotation. Jacinto felt the soft kiss as shuttle and station met. He waited until the air lock pressurized, and as the small light beside the door turned green he reached for the handle. Before he could grab it, the door swung open and there on the other side was Paulo.

He was no longer the suave, vigorous man from the documentary streams and old photos. Gone was the lush, jet-black hair, replaced by a thin white fringe around his otherwise bald, spotted head. A bushy salt-and-pepper beard obscured his strong jaw line. His frame, once broad and muscular, had withered. Paulo's shirt, decades out of fashion, might once have fit, but was now too big; his spindly, liver-spotted arms were lost in the billowy sleeves.

His eyes, though, remained bright. People who'd met Paulo before he left Earth, especially women, always mentioned his piercing gaze.

"You're Corone?" Paulo asked, his Montreal accent still noticeable.

"Jacinto Corone." He smiled and extended his hand. "It's a real pleasure to meet you."

Paulo took Jacinto's hand in a weak grip and gave it a few slight pumps.

"This way," Paulo said, and he inched down the corridor and around a corner. Even his steps were frail. Jacinto followed, not sure what to make of the welcome.

The corridor was white and empty except for a hatch that didn't match the station design. Paulo had retrofit the station with an escape pod. Jacinto laughed to himself. What point was there in having an escape pod installed when no one would be around to rescue you in an emergency?

Paulo showed him to quarters that were clean and prepared for a guest, but were as far from Paulo's room as could be found on such a small station. Except for areas frequented by Paulo, (which were clean and impeccably organized) most other sections of the station were run-down.

Conversation over a dinner of freeze-dried food and hydroponic vegetables was stilted at best, with Jacinto doing most of the talking. He was painfully aware at times how fawning he sounded, and would retreat into silence.

For his part, Paulo was quiet. He kept his eyes downcast or closed altogether. Wincing sometimes as if in pain, he would hum softly, without noticing, Jacinto thought.

It was slightly more than an hour's delay for transmissions by laser pulse, but Paulo had little knowledge of current events on Earth or Mars, and no interest in being brought up to speed. He didn't want to talk politics, pop culture, or even music.

"I don't know his work," Paulo said when asked his thoughts on the latest piece by Gibson-Fraser. Jacinto didn't think it right to tell him it was a two-woman composing team.

"Music today is just a derivative form of the work I was doing thirty years ago," he said. "It doesn't interest me or bear talking about."

Jacinto would have liked to debate the point — Paulo had single-handedly brought electroacoustic composition into vogue all those years ago but there had been a lot of innovative work done since — but he decided not to press the issue until he knew the man better. An argument wouldn't do on the first day they met.

When asked questions, Paulo would answer succinctly and then fall silent. Jacinto had expected he would welcome the opportunity to talk, the opportunity for human contact. But perhaps, he now thought, conversation was like a muscle that needed exercise to remain vital. Paulo's conversation was as withered by isolation in space as his body had been.

Paulo grimaced, as if in pain. "I'm going to bed. My head..." he rubbed at his temple. "You have questions for me, an interview for your research? Give them to me tomorrow; I'll look them over. We'll talk in a few days. I have a schedule of work. It won't change just because you're here. I don't sleep much, and I'm up at 0400. I'll be in the main control room working tomorrow. When you're awake we'll unload the shuttle."

With that, Paulo stood and left the mess.

Jacinto spent the next hour exploring the small station. It was the original Titan research facility, *Gurnett Station*, built for a crew of sixteen, and bought by Paulo when the new station came online. Many sections of the sixty-year-old station were on low-power stand-by or sealed off. The hydroponics garden was suffering neglect. Jacinto thought its yield could dramatically increase if Paulo put in even a little effort. Like much else there, it seemed forgotten by the station's only resident.

A great deal of work had been done modifying the other sections of the station, though, with the addition of an escape pod being the least of it.

≈ ✧ ≈

Jacinto yawned as he passed another case of freeze-dried food through the airlock. He'd thought it best to impress Paulo and get a 0400 start, too. Three hours slugging cases of supplies had him questioning his decision.

Paulo, conversely, was a morning person. He was no more talkative than the night before, but he had energy to burn.

Despite Jacinto's efforts at small talk Paulo kept silent, save the occasional instruction on which case he wanted next. Even questions about Paulo's career and compositions went tersely answered.

The tedium was numbing.

Most of the composers Jacinto had interviewed for his dissertation had been only too happy to talk about themselves. Paulo's laconic nature didn't bode well for his usefulness as an interviewee, all the worse given Paulo and his compositions were the focus of Jacinto's research.

Jacinto bent down to lift one of the cases and let out a grunt when he couldn't get it more than a few centimeters off the shuttle floor before dropping it.

He stood and stretched his back. "What's in this one — rocks?"

From the far side of the airlock Paulo peered over at the case. "Yes, actually."

Jacinto turned, incredulous. "What do you need rocks for?"

Paulo smiled for the first time since Jacinto arrived. "Come. I'll show you."

⁌ ✧ ⁍

"I call the system the plectrum!" said Paulo as he and Jacinto dumped the last of five containers of pebbles into the hopper.

"I've spent almost my whole fortune to build the plectrum and keep this station running," said Paulo. "These pebbles are regolith from asteroid mining."

That made sense, Jacinto thought. His hands were coal-black from the dust and felt like they were coated in toner.

"They're such small sizes — only a centimeter to ten centimeters across — there's not much use for them industrially, so I get them cheap from the mining companies. This is the last batch; the system's ready for the performance. The key is the size of the objects striking the rings."

Jacinto didn't understand, but this at least was a sign of life from the man. He didn't interrupt.

"I hear music, you see," said Paulo as he closed the hopper, snapped tight its pressure fitting, and mag-sealed the housing. "Air-tight now," he said, smiling. He strode down the corridor toward the control room and Jacinto followed.

"All my life I've heard music, constantly, the way Beethoven did. In some ways, I've felt a fraud as a composer. I transcribe what I hear in my head. Where does it come from?" He shrugged and keyed in the door code. The control room doors hissed open.

"I would compose, arrange, but I could never get the music to sound as it does in my head. Oh, it would be the right notes but the *sound* of them was wrong, the essence. That's what drew me to electroacoustics," Paulo said, climbing into the console chair.

"It was a very old style of composition when you came to it," said Jacinto. There'd always been a small, dedicated core of electroacoustic composers since the genre's birth in the mid-twentieth century. Once, it was even considered avant-garde — art music for a post-modern age. But it fell out of fashion, the post-modern was surpassed, and it was kept alive in university music departments. Concordia University, where Paulo had taught and where Jacinto was doing his doctorate, had one of the world's oldest programs, dating back almost one hundred and fifty years to the 1980s.

"You didn't feel it might limit you?"

"Hmmm... It did at first," said Paulo. "For years I worked in the genre. My inspiration was one of the earliest examples in the genre — the prepared piano. I turned the exotic into instruments to get the sounds I needed. Remember the concerto using the Golden Gate Bridge?"

Jacinto nodded. Paulo had used the girders and tension wires as his instrument, the sound resonating across San Francisco Bay. The city still had it performed every summer.

"That was just one example. My works were always well received but they weren't what I was after."

Jacinto grinned. Now he was getting somewhere! To think of Paulo describing his works as "well received." Paulo had arrived at one of those rare moments when artist and audience are in perfect confluence, when his work had redefined the basis of modern popular music for decades. Besides spawning legions of imitators, his music had made him one of the richest men on Earth, and the richest on Mars once he'd moved there. But his compositions hadn't been what he wanted? That would be news to everyone. Jacinto wished he had his recorder with him.

"Then I happened upon the records of the Cassini probe from the early twenty-first century. Completely by accident, you understand. And that's when everything changed."

Paulo stood up and walked to the back of the room where five large objects lay under heavy plastic sheets. He pulled them off to reveal banks of keyboards, twenty in all, set in tiers along the wall.

"What the Cassini probe discovered was that as a meteoroid strikes the icy chunks making up Saturn's rings, it generates a pulse of energy and emits radio waves. Reduce the frequency by a factor of five and you bring those radio waves into the range of human hearing — tones. We have our instrument! But it's limited in range, random in its execution.

"So, we take charge of the meteoroids," said Paulo. He moved back to the console chair and turned on the computer's 3D display. "We use pebbles of different sizes, fire them at different speeds, they strike with more or less energy, generating different radio frequencies and suddenly the rings become *strings*! Pluck and strike them as you would the harpsichord, the piano, or the harp. The rings bow to our command, and the music we play — the music of the spheres! — is what we compose. All we need is an interface of some kind, a controller like these keyboards. We program them to regulate the cues for the firing sequence and all of Saturn becomes our hammered dulcimer."

"You're going to play music on Saturn's rings?"

"Yes," said Paulo. "An entire symphony. And you will help me finish it."

⇒ ✧ ⇐

"Why won't you let me work on the last movement?" Jacinto asked over a dinner of re-hydrated chicken.

He and Paulo had been working furiously for days inputting the final sequencing for the *Saturn Symphony*, as he'd begun to call it. Paulo would input the notes using the keyboards — each key set to trigger the release of certain sized pellets from the sorted hopper bins of the plectrum — and Jacinto would add in, by hand, dynamics where Paulo had indicated. The composer had it all planned out and just need Jacinto to do the tedious grunt work, as it turned out.

*Rinforzando, fortissimo, diminuendo, mezzo piano* — all entered as long, increasing strings of digits into the command protocols for the firing sequence. But Jacinto had four days left on the station and had yet to see the sequencing for the finale.

"That section is mine," Paulo said before taking another bite. Back to his prickly self, Jacinto noted. That was the pattern — tolerable in the mornings, difficult at night, once the headaches set in.

"If I could just get a look at it, for my research—"

"The final movement is off limits to you, and your research, until it's finished," Paulo said, pointing his plastic fork at Jacinto with every emphasis. "It will all be done in a few days; I'll answer questions for your research, and then I will perform the symphony at last..." Paulo had a longing look in his eye, one of anticipated relief.

"Will you be returning on the freighter?" Jacinto sounded more hopeful than he'd intended.

"Why did you come here?" Paulo asked. He winced, as if something pained him, and rubbed at his eyes.

"I came to meet you. For my research," Jacinto said.

"You're a young man. You've wasted a lot of time coming all this way, only to have to go back. Don't waste your time traveling. No one finds what they seek in traveling."

"But I've found you."

"All you've found of me is a cross-section, a fragment. You'll take what you want to, never knowing the whole. You've wasted all this time, and you'll have nothing to show for it."

"Did you waste your time? What have you got to show for all these years out here?" It was angrier than Jacinto meant it to sound, but not angrier than he felt.

"Ah, but you see I belong here — you don't. I've arrived where I'm going."

"You know, my mother's told me a lot about you," Jacinto said with an edge to his voice that surprised even him.

Paulo looked up. "Your mother?"

"Cassandra Corone. She was one of your grad students at Concordia."

"I know who she is," Paulo snapped. "Why do you think I agreed to your visit? What did she tell you about me?"

"Stories about being your student, seeing you in concert, watching you become famous."

Paulo considered this a moment. "You look a lot like her."

"That's what everyone says." Jacinto gave a cold smile. "She says I have my father's eyes, though."

Paulo chewed his last bit of chicken without looking up from the table. When he was finished, he stood and left without cleaning up his mess from the table.

~ ✧ ~

Paulo spent the day after their fight in his room. It must have been a terrible migraine, Jacinto decided. He could hear Paulo whimpering and crying through the door when he went to check on him that morning. Did the music cause his headaches? he wondered.

Settling into the console chair, Jacinto turned on the computer's 3D display. He began tabbing through the program files for the firing sequence, looking for anything that might be the final movement.

Paulo seemed determined to thwart his research. With only three days left before he had to depart, Jacinto had yet to see any results from the final section, and had no interview with the focus of his research…

Empty handed — isn't that what Paulo had said? He'd be damned if he was going to let Paulo be right.

There! That menu was what he was looking for. It was the only one listing a final movement. 'Dénouement', Paulo had named it.

He reached out and pushed the floating command icon to begin playback. Leaning back in the chair, Jacinto folded his arms, immensely satisfied. He'd pulled one over on the old man.

As soon as the playback engaged, he could hear and feel the change in the station. It was a power down, station wide.

Sudden queasiness filled Jacinto's stomach as the station section he was in slowed its spinning. He wished he could blame his nausea on the gravity loss.

The whole of the small space station shuddered as the spinning sections ground to a halt. He remembered what Paulo had said to him about the power drain when the sequence was performed. Gravity was a luxury that could be sacrificed.

Jacinto raced through menus on the holographic display, 3D command icons spinning in the air around him, trying to find some way to abort the sequence. He couldn't find a straightforward cancel command, and worried about selecting something that would do more damage.

"*Putin!*" Paulo cursed. "What have you done?" He had appeared at the compartment door, floating in zero-g. Pushing hard off the doorframe, Paulo rocketed across the room. "Out! Get out!" He shoved Jacinto from the console chair, pulled himself down and strapped in.

Paulo punched keys and scanned the read-outs. "The sequencing is cueing to start!"

"I — I didn't mean to! I was just ... I wanted to finish some of the programming you asked me to do." Jacinto's denial sounded weak even to him.

"Don't lie to me! You accessed the sequencing for the final movement. I told you it was off limits to your damned research."

"Why the hell wouldn't you show me?" Jacinto banged his fist against the console. He started to drift in the zero-g and grabbed hold of the chair to stop, raging at himself.

"I never should have agreed to let you come," Paulo said.

"Can't you just shut it down?" Jacinto asked. He struggled to position himself in zero-g, Paulo's chair his only anchor. "Shut off the power. Will that reset the sequence?"

"And what then?" Paulo turned, a wild look in his eye. "This station is almost as old as I am. What if the power won't come back on? Then we *both* die..." Paulo turned back to the console.

Why had he said "both" that way? Jacinto's queasiness grew stronger.

"What about overriding the controls for the rotating sections?" Jacinto asked. "Won't setting them in motion again cause a power drain and cancel the firing sequence?"

"That's not the way it works!" Paulo began rubbing at his temples.

"Stop yelling at me!" Jacinto shook Paulo's chair with both hands. "I'm trying to help!"

"By trying to destroy the station?" Paulo shot back. "It's going to take all available power to operate the plectrum and keep the station's attitude constant at the same time. If those sections start rotation, not only will the plectrum's firing sequence not run properly and the whole performance fail, but the station will spin out of control and smash into the rings. Or it may simply tear the station apart first — do you wish to choose?"

A klaxon sounded and four 2D video streams popped up from the display, each showing different angles of the station's exterior.

Taken from the station's own system of micro-satellites, two videos showed the station in relief against the backdrop of Saturn. The field of view was too small to show the whole planet, but the swirling gas clouds and the vast cream-yellow face of Saturn was still breathtaking. The other video streams showed the bottom of the station, now only several hundred meters above the plane of Saturn's rings, and the hatch doors of the plectrum system opening.

Another klaxon sounded and Paulo spun his chair around. There, along the back wall of the control room, the bank of keyboards powered up. Keys on the first synthesizer began to move in their pre-programmed dance, one at first, then two, then whole chords. Then another of the synthesizers, then another, until keys on all twenty writhed and moved as if commanded by an orchestra of spectral players.

From unseen speakers came the first notes of the symphony from Saturn's rings.

"*Merde*," said Paulo.

⁓ ✧ ⁓

Though he'd helped program in the sequences for many sections of the symphony, as the music came through the speakers for the first time, Jacinto knew he hadn't expected this.

He'd played through sections on piano, trying to work out the dynamics from the notation Paulo had given him. The timing was strange, though, and Jacinto couldn't grasp the whole. He thought he had, intellectually, some idea what to expect when he heard the piece performed, but now...

Each note was a distinct tone and not the eerie, theremin-like noise of other space phenomena Jacinto had heard recorded. As clear as notes played on piano, but the *sound*! The sound was unique, unlike any sound — real, synthesized, or manipulated — that Jacinto had ever heard.

And the limitations of using the plectrum to play the rings gave unique structural qualities to the piece. No bent notes were possible, no vibrato or glissando, no sustains longer than two or three seconds, and even with all the careful programming an element of uncertainty pervaded the piece. There was no way to know the composition and layout of the rings below or how they would react to the strikes from the plectrum.

The piece was characterized, instead, by playfulness as Paulo fooled and tricked the ear of the listener.

Careful overlapping of note voicings mimicked some of the impossible elements of technique — doubling and tripling notes gave artificial sustain, produced delay and echo effects.

As he listened, Jacinto realized the whole was made up of four different satellite streams. Radio and plasma wave detectors on each of the station's four micro-satellites detected the same frequencies at slightly different intervals based on distance from the source. The result was four threads of music, binding together to make the whole. Paulo had incorporated the slight delay and variations into the composition. The symphony shimmered with texture and life.

Paulo had married the most innovative elements of his atonal, avant-garde composition with the forms and patterns of the classical. This would do it, Jacinto realized. This would redefine music again, the way Paulo had decades ago.

Jacinto turned to congratulate him on a masterwork but the console chair was empty. He looked behind him to see Paulo disappearing out the control room door. Where was he going?

Turning back, on the 2D Jacinto saw the streams of pellets from the plectrum falling like glittering rain from the station. But there was something else. He looked closer. The station itself was moving farther and farther from the rings. It was picking up speed.

He pushed off the console chair and sailed to the open door. Kicking hard off the doorframe, Jacinto launched himself down the corridor. He saw Paulo round the corner at the near junction, turning down the empty white corridor.

He wouldn't...

Jacinto pumped his arms and legs as if swimming, but it didn't help and he cursed zero-g again. He had to catch Paulo.

His arms flailed for a hold, something to slow him as he approached the junction. Fingernails skipped and skittered along the plastic and metal walls of the corridor. Sailing past the open doorway, he saw Paulo punching in a code at the escape pod door.

"No!" Jacinto yelled. His fingers ached as he strained for purchase on the wall. Fingertips found a thin edge of the doorframe. It was enough. His body swung around, slamming flat against the bulkhead. He pulled himself around the doorframe as Paulo slipped through the escape pod hatch.

Jacinto kicked off one last time as the hatch door slid shut, his arms outstretched. "Don't leave me! Don't leave me here, you son of a bitch!"

He pounded on the solid metal door, screaming, but no answer came. His throat raw and with tears in his eyes, Jacinto pushed himself back down the corridor.

Jacinto rushed to the control room. He had to stop the escape pod from leaving. Instead, he found Paulo's face on the 2D.

"You bastard!" Jacinto yelled as he pulled himself into the seat. "You're not leaving me here to die." He scrolled through menus, looking for an override.

"Damn fool," Paulo said. "You're not going to die. There's no stopping the sequence once it's started, and it's almost time for the final movement. So listen to me!"

Jacinto looked at the 2D, tears in his eyes.

"Everything is working just as it should," Paulo said.

"The station is moving!" Jacinto checked the other 2Ds, and the station was moving faster than before.

"Of course it is!" Paulo barked. "It's taking all the station's power to run the plectrum and the stabilizing thrusters to keep the station's attitude constant. *Altitude* is another matter. I built it into my composition. That's why the number sets you entered kept getting bigger — longer intervals between striking notes. It's for the station's ... for *your* safety. You can't be too near during the final crescendo."

"Why not?"

"On cue, this escape pod will launch into the rings and play the final movement of my symphony." Paulo moved away from the camera lens and Jacinto saw the interior of the escape pod behind him. Dozens of gray bundles lined the walls, connected by coils of yellow wire. "When this pod explodes it will set a chain reaction of collisions in motion — generating more notes than I could ever play in a lifetime of playing music. A last great sustained cacophony to conclude my masterpiece."

Jacinto's mouth worked, but no sound came out.

"This is the way I want it, Jacinto," say Paulo. "I've suffered too long with this music, with the headaches it brings me, the sleeplessness, the agony. There's no stopping it short of this." Paulo reached out toward the camera to kill the feed.

"Wait!" Jacinto yelled, and Paulo hesitated. "But maestro — you won't be able to hear the final composition if you die!"

"Ah, I've already heard it," Paulo said, wincing again. "I've heard it a thousand million times through every moment of my life. Waking or sleeping, it never left me. It's been my lover and my demon — caressing and tormenting me all this time. My other works have been pale imitations of this piece, simple warm-ups. A composer gives part of himself away every time he writes a piece. He writes himself into the music in ways he doesn't even realize — the music demands it. This piece — well, it demands more. I must die; it must live."

"No! Please, no—"

"Goodbye, Jacinto," said Paulo, reaching toward the camera. "You'll find what you need in my cabin. Tell your mother... Tell her I'm sorry. For everything." The image on the 2D died.

Jacinto felt the station rock as the pod blasted away. He screamed in impotent rage.

⇒ ✦ ⇐

The tiny cargo shuttle seemed cavernous now; it was as empty as Jacinto felt. It was only a few hours before the rendezvous with the freighter, not that Jacinto relished the idea of company.

On a handheld, he scrolled through the answers Paulo had left to his research questions. Paulo had never intended to sit down for an interview, instead writing paragraph after paragraph of response for Jacinto to sort through later. It would make a groundbreaking thesis, but the thought brought Jacinto no joy.

He'd gathered up Paulo's few possessions and fit them all in two small cargo shells for the journey home. Paulo had left a will, too, though Jacinto hadn't the heart to read it.

A recording of the symphony played over the shuttle speaker system. It was so loud the speakers crackled with distortion; the volume was almost painful. The station's computer had recorded the whole piece as it played out, so that was preserved at least. It was the first and last performance of the *Saturn Symphony*, Jacinto thought. No one could imitate Paulo this time. There would be no derivatives.

On the four-year voyage home, Jacinto knew he would listen to the *Saturn Symphony* as many countless times as he'd read that brief e-mail on the journey out. And he would cry each time, as he did now.

He had the shuttle's 2D on, the exterior camera trained behind him. The station was long since out of view. Momentum from the plectrum would carry it far into space.

Instead, Saturn filled the screen. He couldn't see the whole planet, perhaps just a quarter. But the width of its rings was clear enough. A dark bruise marked the A ring, where Paulo had struck his final chord. Matter spilled out into the Cassini Gap and toward the B ring like salt spilled against the blackness of space.

Saturn's rings turned slowly, like an old gramophone record, playing their endless symphony.

⁓ ✧ ⁓

**Stephen Kotowych** is a Writers of the Future Grand Prize winner and past finalist for the Prix Aurora Award. His stories have appeared in *Interzone*, *Orson Scott Card's Intergalactic Medicine Show*, and in numerous anthologies, including *Tesseracts Eleven*. His work has been translated into Russian, Greek, Spanish, and Finnish. He's currently completing work on his first novel — a secret history about the real-life friendship between Mark Twain and Nikola Tesla. He enjoys guitar, tropical fish, and writing about himself in the third person.

# ZOMBIE POET

## ~ Carolyn Clink ~

After a cornered dog chewed off
his grasping fingers, the zombie poet
had to use voice-recognition software.

While the computer never correctly guessed
what he was trying to say, the words
it did come up with sold to *The New Yorker* and *Poetry*.

Critics hailed him as the voice of his degeneration.
But some argued his poetry wasn't original
because he was eating the brains of other poets.

As his fame grew, he started receiving emails with photos
of naked zombie women attached.
Necrophilia lead to an addiction to deviant brains.

One night, after a reanimated reading
from his long-awaited collection, *Poems with no Brains*,
the zombie poet fell apart from excess decay.

Many young zombie poets tried to capture his audience.
But their poems were too cerebral, their rhymes too loose,
and their shambling rhythm wasn't the same.

*Zombie Poet* by **Carolyn Clink**

❦

**Carolyn** has been poetry Guest of Honour at seven science-fiction conventions. She lives in Mississauga, Ontario with her SF writer hubby, Robert J. Sawyer. In 2011, she won the Aurora Award for Best Poem/Song of 2010.

# The Language of Dance

## ⁓ Rebecca M. Senese ⁓

I lift my arms. My heart sings with the first notes of the music. The notes bellow out into the dome above my head. I step once, twice and leap into the air. I soar with the flow of the music, twirling as I go. My hands twist in time, the gestures of supplication and entrance. The path of the music opens the way for me, but I am the one who moves forward, I am the one who creates the space, the message. My body flows in time. I turn and kick off from the side, spinning five times before catching the railing on the other side of the dome.

I work hard in the Dance. Even in the cool air and the thin outfit I wear, sweat drips from my body. Wiry muscles strain and tremble as I tumble and glide through the air. Five minutes into the Dance, already a record. I see the tense faces of my teachers in the viewing section near the bottom. How many others had they trained for this dance, this duty? Brennan clutches his hands to his chest, almost in prayer. Telsa stands ramrod straight, only a slight frown betraying her anxiety.

Then I am spinning away, chasing the notes of the music. I feel them vibrate in my body. I hum as I feel the pheromones in my system release and fill me with energy. I soar higher in the air, stretching forth my arms, in welcome, always in welcome.

The higher shadows along the side of the dome shift as the B'akHalna watch me. I feel their attention on my skin. Focus and concentrate, Brennan had always admonished me. Stop letting your thoughts waver, Delna, you must concentrate.

I pirouette into a backwards tumble and enjoy the rush of air on my skin. My tumbles have always been my strong suit. Bold motions, strong leaps, so easy for me to do but it's the tiny hand movements and precision that have always been my downfall.

There is no room for downfall here.

Not in this performance. The performance of my life.

The performance for our treaty.

I come out of the tumble, landing quivering on my feet. My left ankle, the weak one, trembles more than the other one but I hold fast. I lift my arms as the notes of music trickle down. A beat of three and I spread my fingers.

Across the dome, the door to the B'akHalna delegation opens. A B'akHalna male steps out, at least we all thought it would be a B'akHalna male. Tall, birdlike with tripod legs and short tendril arms, he raises his hands beside his narrow head. The unblinking eyes look at me then he leaps into the air.

For such a thin, spindly creature, he flows with grace through the air, the delicate tendril arms, spreading narrow finger-like appendages that tap and waver to the music. Across from me, I see my teachers and the linguists busy jotting notes and analyzing the B'akHalna's movements for any pattern and meaning. The ear bug nestled in my left ear buzzes with suggested moves and responses but I ignore them. The linguists know little about what drives the B'akHalna just as the B'akHalna know little about how to talk to us. The Dance is all we have together.

Tucking his tripod legs, the B'akHalna male executes a tumble that copies mine in almost all respects. I can almost hear the collective gasp from my teachers. The linguists look like they are going to faint. The B'akHalna male lands in front of me. His single back leg slides backward as his two front leg bend. His slender body leans forward in an unmistakable bow. His thin tendril arms with the waving fingers reach out to me.

"Delna." Brennan's voice sounds tinny in my ear bug. "Stick to the choreography."

"Delna, don't listen to him, respond to the moment," Telsa says.

The linguists start arguing about what the bow means. I lift my hands above my head, using the motion to pluck the ear bug from my ear. Now there is only the music to guide me. I drop the ear bug and it floats gently to the ground. I widen my stance and bow to the B'akHalna male. My hands extend out to meet his in greeting.

His waving fingers grip mine with a strength that surprises me. As he straightens, I feel a pull on my arms. I allow myself to move forward into the flow. Together we leap into the air. He releases one of my hands and spins me with the other. I follow his lead, pointing my toes in the spin as we dance around the edge of the dome. In the music, two melodies join to create a new song. The B'akHalna male and I leap straight across the dome, soaring high into the air. At the pinnacle of our leap, I tighten my fingers on his waving hand. His narrow head tilts. I have no way to really ask, no words that I can say to get confirmation.

I have to take the chance.

I push his arm, signaling a spin. He hesitates a moment, then on the beat of the song, he flows into my lead. Around us, I see both B'akHalna and humans lean against the clear sides of the dome. The pressure of their attention distracts me.

Focus, Delna, I tell myself. Concentrate. I have a partner now and I have to take care of him as he follows.

This principle of dance, the lead and the follow, calms my pounding heart. As the lead, I am responsible for my follower. I hold his hand firm and hold my other arm out as guide.

The B'akHalna kicks out his legs and spins with abandon. I follow him and guide him through the air with each beat of the music. His head throws back and, as I watch, his eyes close. A buzzing from the watching crowd almost drowns out the music. The B'akHalna flows closer to me. I hesitate a moment and place my other hand on his narrow shoulder.

The music sways along as we flow with it. Our legs now kick in rhythm together. My B'akHalna partner opens his eyes and sways his head in time to the music. I match his head movements. His thin fingers tighten in mine. His arm tenses. His turn to lead.

I release my hand from his shoulder and he spins me away. I flow into the movement, arms tucked, toes pointed. The B'akHalna kicks his heels as he chases behind. As we race around the dome, I try to remember all the little hand movements, the tiny flicks of fingers, the pointing of toes, the lifting of elbows and the bending of knees. So many variations, so many movements and we never knew which one was important and which one could be forgotten. In the very first Dance, Jaspar dropped his left hand slower than his right only two minutes in.

## The Language of Dance by Rebecca M. Senese

He'd barely had time to scream as he died.

At the next Dance, Krapler had stumbled five steps into his first leap.

He'd had no time to scream either.

Ten years and ten attempts at the Dance and no one had lasted longer than four minutes.

Forget and focus.

I feel the pressure of the B'akHalna's tendril fingers on my shoulder, signaling another set of spins. I kick off, pointing my toes, holding my body ramrod straight. Even focusing on my teachers on each turn, the soaring sweeps soon disorients me. I fight to maintain proper posture in the rhythm of the spin. I can not wobble!

The dome blurs around me. First I see the viewing section of my teachers, then the shadows of B'akHalna. They flow into each other as I spin. My stomach clenches on nothing; I have not eaten for two days as prescribed. My heart pounds, from fear as well as from effort. No one has ever gotten so far in the Dance. I can't fail now!

I feel my weak left foot begin to turn out. No! Not now! I still have five seconds of rotations left to complete. My leg muscles quiver as I try to straighten my foot. Sweat pours from my body. Wet strands of hair escape from the hair net and stick to my cheek. I can't tell if the wetness on my cheeks is from sweat or tears.

Still my foot drifts.

The seconds tick by, each marking away the passage of my years. One, my childhood on the main base on Luna where soaring through the air was as natural as walking to me. Two, adolescent, a blur of dance classes and training, perfecting my leaps and spins. Three, the early years of my career, wandering the performance circuits on a dozen worlds, a blur of bad food, small rooms and the roaring approval of crowds. Four, the tryouts and training for the Dance, more brutal and demanding than any training I'd had before. And five...

My foot flops to the side.

Even this high, I hear the collective gasp of my teachers and other human observers. Over, it is over. I await the shock of death that will strike me down.

Six...

I finish my spin and the B'akHalna trails me down in a flowing spiral back toward the ground. Does he realize how I have failed? Had he been paying attention or was judgment to be passed out by the watching shadows of B'akHalna high above us?

As we land, I bow my head in shame.

But it is the B'akHalna male that stumbles. His back leg, landing just a fraction of a second after his two front ones, slips, sending him crashing to the floor of the dome. A rumble sounds from the B'akHalna delegation. I recognize the sounds of disapproval. It won't be a human who dies today from a mistake.

The B'akHalna male turns miserable eyes to me. In his glance I can see the years of pain, of work, of pushing harder and harder, then harder still as the Dance demanded, of giving up friends and family to keep working, of trying and failing many times over until this one chance to meet in the Dance.

I recognize that look.

I've seen it so often in the mirror.

I relax the muscles of my left calf. My weak ankle collapses and my leg crashes to the floor. Pain reverberates up my knee where I land. I hiss in a breath at the pain and blink away tears.

I just can't let a fellow dancer suffer alone.

Now the thundering rumble from the B'akHalna turns to a high pitched trilling. I glance up to see them standing, their thin arms waving in rhythm over their heads. Across the way, pandemonium reigns as my teachers and the linguists practically climb over each other to get to the doors.

Where is the expected blow? I glance over at my B'akHalna dance partner. With his beak-like features, it's impossible for him to smile but I swear there is an upturning of the edges of his mouth. Several of his tendril fingers clasp my hand. I feel a warmth spread up my arm, across my shoulders to my neck. The skin on my scalp tingles and then I realize I'm hearing something above the sound of the music and the clambering of my fellows.

A soft voice fills my mind with color and wonder.

"Now, my child, we can say hello."

I tighten my hand around the B'akHalna's fingers and smile. Hello.

⌒ ✧ ⌒

**Rebecca M. Senese** weaves words of horror, mystery and science fiction from the wilds of Toronto, Ontario. She garnered an Honorable Mention in *The Year's Best Science Fiction* and has been nominated for numerous Aurora Awards. Her work has appeared in *Tesseracts 15: A Case of Quite Curious Tales, Ride the Moon, TransVersions, Future Syndicate, Deadbolt Magazine, On Spec, The Vampire's Crypt, Storyteller* and *Into the Darkness,* amongst others. When not serving up tales of the macabre, mysterious or wondrous, she volunteers as a zombie or vampire at haunted attractions in October to stalk and scare all the unsuspecting innocents.

# GREGOR SAMSA WAS NEVER IN THE BEATLES

### ～ J. J. Steinfeld ～

Originally appeared in *Word Burials*,
published by Crossing Chaos Enigmatic Ink, 2009

～ ✧ ～

All Roland did was mention to the eleven others in the room that he hadn't accomplished everything he had wanted in his life. He is fairly certain there was no self-pity or despair in his voice when he said that, but the young man sitting next to him at the weekend creative-writing workshop retreat, a half-century younger than him, Roland estimates, barely out of university, he looks at Roland and his eyes reflect something even worse than self-pity or despair. Why had he gone to this retreat? Roland thinks. Impulsiveness, idiocy, foolishness, silliness, he's willing to say, hurrying through a frayed thesaurus of self-doubt. Since his retirement five years ago Roland has attempted to write about his life, but with little success. Each writing workshop makes him feel more inadequate, even less the writer, yet he continues to go, as if it is part of his punishment for having been a less than successful husband and father. The writing workshops don't even help ease his loneliness. Wasn't that why he really goes? Five years retired, ten years divorced. Retired from what?

the instructor had asked earlier, and Roland said from jobs he despised. Write about that, she ordered, giving Roland a new job that he couldn't embrace.

The instructor reminds Roland of his daughter, both physically and in her self-confidence and energy, a daughter who as a child and a woman professed her love for her father yet saw him as a failure. The daughter who had once asked, during the middle of a Thanksgiving dinner, twice as many in that past room as in this present workshop, *Father, what have you accomplished in your life?* When Roland attempted to compile and recite a list of his accomplishments, or at least of the jobs he had done in his life, not all the jobs lamentable or regrettable, some drenched in toil and satisfaction and hard-earned wages, she interrupted and said, *Father, do not lie to yourself or to your family*. Roland's thoughts were back twenty years at that dinner table, even as he sat ill-at-ease at the writing-workshop table, in front of his printouts from the instructor and a notebook with only a few scribbled words, silently assessing his life, until the instructor shook him and said, WRITE!

You're not getting any younger, the instructor says, her voice, Roland is certain, similar to his daughter's, giving the next exercise: Write a 250-word story about your most passionate experience. Flash that flash fiction; post that postcard story; microwave that micro fiction, the instructor chants like a stand-up comic begging for her life. That is how Roland regards her words, agonizingly unhumorous, thinks those words, embroiders them — *the disoriented, hapless instructor chants like a stand-up comic begging for her life* — shapes a silent vignette of insight and loveliness, but writes down only the words "postcard" and "begging" in his notebook, the insight and loveliness evaporating. Yet nearly everyone in the class smiles or laughs at the instructor's instructions. Roland shakes his head harshly. The instructor starts to speak faster and louder, the way Roland's daughter does when she is excited or upset. He wants to ask the instructor her age, but does not want to know for certain that she is also forty-seven like his daughter. Be uninhibited with your creativity, the instructor says. No need to be afraid to write about the erotic. WRITE! — writing battles mortality, writing battles boredom, writing battles nothingness.

Writing is certainly a versatile battler, Roland comments, and the instructor accuses him of being a heckler, of working against creativity. The instructor asks Roland why he has spent good money and valuable time to sit there not writing and being disruptive. Everyone in the workshop was busy writing their 250-word story, and Roland holds his pen like an anchor. Everyone seemed younger, less anxious and uneasy. Hope and needfulness and misplaced modifiers were in the air like a cunning fog, he thinks, uses as the first sentence in his postcard story. Before he starts to write his second sentence, he hurls his pen at the wall behind the instructor, it making a sound that sounded to Roland like the yelp of a bewildered little animal. He can no longer bear the confinement. Roland flees, only to encounter another confinement.

There he is, in a police lineup, like on TV drama or in a movie, sometimes alone, other times with men and women, who look nothing like him, not even close, and time and again, innocent as he is, Roland gets selected, his trial tedious, his sentence severe. All this happens so quickly, mercilessly, he stumbling for a description: *relentless ... inescapable ... irreversible...* As he is thinking of adjectives, the moments whirl past him. This is not a writing workshop, Roland shouts at the judge, as the ferocious-looking man adds time to Roland's guilty sentence.

From the courtroom, Roland finds himself in a prison cell. Standing outside the cell's bars, is a prison guard, an unhandsome man. Roland tells the prison guard that he longs to watch TV shows from the 1960s, the warmth of nostalgia, times without incarceration for him, imaginary, symbolic, or otherwise, maybe *The Twilight Zone*, where anything was possible. The prison guard says he despises the boob tube, the idiot box, spends all his free time reading murder mysteries and romances and the occasional classic of fiction such as James Joyce's *Finnegans Wake*, confessing that ten times he has read the book and still can't summarize what it means.

Ah, literature, Roland sighs, his cell this time smaller and bleaker, then he mumbles that his Trinity is Beckett, Sartre, and Kafka, but has a fondness also for Joyce, especially *Ulysses*. Roland mentions that he has published one story and two poems in his life. The anti-TV prison guard alertly asks why he didn't include one literary woman. Roland coughs, hesitates, feels deficient, then says: Lessing, Austen, Dickinson, Nin, Woolf, the Brontës ... exhausting himself in the name recitation.

What, no Canadians? the prison guard springs forth, his alertness even sharper, adding with rancour, Not to mention living, breathing writers.

## Gregor Samsa Was Never in The Beatles by J. J. Steinfeld

The prison guard has Roland so confused he doesn't know if he is here or there, there or here, but he confesses that he had a dream once, actually the same dream several times, of making awkward, uninspired love to Molly Bloom as both James Joyce and Leopold Bloom observe his nocturnal performance and comment on his sexual maladroitness like two grumbling sportscasters describing a horse race where two of the horses, jockey-less, are going in the wrong direction, or no direction at all.

The prison guard snarls at Roland's dream, calls it an unfunny joke, then gives him an application for pardon, please print neatly, he emphasizes. Whose name does he put in? Roland asks himself. In the dream he questions that his name is Roland. And he doesn't want to think of his actual age, refusing to give any date of birth. This is all so fucking Kafkaesque, Roland complains, and he wonders if the complaining is some sort of ailment. The prison guard grabs the application form away from Roland's hand and tells him that he has no identity or too many identities. That is not a subtle distinction, Roland argues, telling the prison guard to get the fuck away. The prison guard does not even bother to laugh at Roland's threat, calling him a sad, old man, and Roland screams that he is not old, but holding back the tears, chants the words he had stumbled after earlier: *relentless ... inescapable ... irreversible...* For a few dream seconds, he thinks he is back in the creative-writing workshop, but convinces his dream self that is not possible.

The next night Roland has a dream about Beckett, a new dream, and argues with the author furiously about the meaning of *Waiting for Godot, Go-dot* or *God-ot*, what's the correct pronunciation? Roland starts singing a song, what's it called? he asks in the dream. "Let's Call the Whole Thing Off," Beckett tells him, and Roland sings, *"You say Go-dot, I say God-ot..."* Beckett cracks a smile, and Roland feels exhilarated, wants to share this experience with his parents and friends, but it seems his parents have died long ago and friendship is a commodity he can no longer deal with. Mr. Beckett, please help me stay in this incredible dream, Roland pleads with the great author, and Beckett tells him that he died on December 22, 1989 and Roland, or whatever his name is, shouldn't be talking to the dead in dreams, and then, as if he were a strict old schoolmaster giving a surprise quiz, Beckett asks Roland what he was doing on that day, at the specific instant that he died. Before Roland can even begin to answer, Beckett tells him that if he were still writing, he would base a character on Roland and it would not be an admirable or uplifting character at that.

Dreaming, Roland tells the prison guard, snapping the man out of his personal thoughts, is his only freedom, he would trade a dream for almost anything, even escape. The prison guard dreams about old convicts, the ones with the most remarkable abnormalities, revealing this as a dreamy confession.

Tonight who will you dream about? Roland muses aloud. Whose meaning will you crawl over? Plato, Socrates, or Aristotle, maybe? Canadian thinkers turn my crank, the prison guard says crankily, or so Roland interprets his utterance. Couldn't you try dreaming about Harold Innis or Marshall McLuhan? the prison guard says. Okay, Innis and McLuhan, I'll place your dream order, Roland tells him.

Yes, Marshall McLuhan, Roland saw him in a Woody Allen movie: Was it *Annie Hall* or *Zelig*? Roland says the first movie, the prison guard the second, and the argument becomes heated over which movie. Roland offers to exchange residences, dreams, anything of worth. The unhandsome prison guard's shift ends, he going home to his reading, no transactions made. Roland wants to write about this astonishing experience, to show the woman at the writing workshop, but he does not have any paper, no pen or pencil.

Back in the police lineup, selected quickly, Roland's innocence is again ignored, however, with a shorter sentence this time but a larger cell with a lavish library and paintings from all over the world, a handsome prison guard this time, even more well-read than the unhandsome one, and Roland suddenly hears shrieks: *Look, a beetle, a goddamn huge beetle*. Immediately Roland thinks of Gregor Samsa, the giant beetle in Kafka's "The Metamorphosis," tells the handsome prison guard so and the prison guard says that Gregor Samsa was never in The Beatles. Roland has read the story in German, *auf Deutsch*, he boasts, *"Die Verwandlung,"* and then he starts to sing "I Want to Hold Your Hand," but soon realizes he has no hands, only an abundance of wriggling insect legs.

⇒ ✧ ⇐

Fiction writer, poet, and playwright **J. J. Steinfeld** lives on Prince Edward Island, where he is patiently waiting for Godot's arrival and a phone call from Kafka. While waiting, he has published two novels, *Our Hero in the Cradle of Confederation* (Pottersfield Press) and *Word Burials* (Crossing Chaos Enigmatic Ink), ten short story collections, including three by Gaspereau Press — *Should the Word Hell Be Capitalized?*, *Anton Chekhov Was Never in Charlottetown*, and *Would You Hide Me?* — and the most recent, *A Glass Shard and Memory* (Recliner Books), along with two poetry collections, *An Affection for Precipices* (Serengeti Press) and *Misshapenness* (Ekstasis Editions). His short stories and poems have appeared in numerous periodicals and anthologies internationally, including a poem in *Tesseracts Fifteen: A Case of Quite Curious Tales*, and over forty of his one-act plays and a handful of full-length plays have been performed in Canada and the United States.

# IMMORTALITY

## Robert J. Sawyer

First appeared in *Janis Ian's Stars*, August 2003

*Baby, I'm only society's child*
*When we're older, things may change*
*But for now this is the way they must remain*
—Janis Ian

Sixty years.

Sweet Jesus, had it been that long?

But of course it had. The year was now 2023, and then—

Then it had been 1963.

The year of the march on Washington.

The year JFK had been assassinated.

The year I—

No, no, I didn't want to think about that. After all, I'm sure *he* never thinks about it ... or about me.

I'd been seventeen in 1963. And I'd thought of myself as ugly, an unpardonable sin for a young woman.

Now, though...

Now, I was seventy-seven. And I was no longer homely. Not that I'd had any work done, but there was no such thing as a homely — or a beautiful — woman of seventy-seven, at least not one who had never had treatments. The only adjective people applied to an unmodified woman of seventy-seven was *old*.

My sixtieth high-school reunion.

For some, there would be a seventieth, and an eightieth, a ninetieth, and doubtless a mega-bash for the hundredth. For those who had money — real money, the kind of money I'd once had at the height of my career — there were pharmaceuticals and gene therapies and cloned organs and bodily implants, all granting the gift of synthetic youth, the gift of time.

I'd skipped the previous reunions, and I wasn't fool enough to think I'd be alive for the next one. This would be it, my one, my only, my last. Although I'd once, briefly, been rich, I didn't have the kind of money anymore that could buy literal immortality. I would have to be content knowing that my songs would exist after I was gone.

And yet, today's young people, children of the third millennium, couldn't relate to socially conscious lyrics written so long ago. Still, the recordings would exist, although...

Although if a tree falls in a forest, and no one is around to hear it, does it make a sound? If a recording — digitized, copied from medium to medium as technologies and standards endlessly change — isn't listened to, does the song still exist? Does the pain it chronicled still continue?

I sighed.

Sixty years since high-school graduation.

Sixty years since all those swirling hormones and clashing emotions.

Sixty years since Devon.

⁓ ✧ ⁓

It wasn't the high school I remembered. My Cedar Valley High had been a brown-and-red brick structure, two stories tall, with large fields to the east and north, and a tiny staff parking lot.

That building had long since been torn down — asbestos in its walls, poor insulation, no fiber-optic infrastructure. The replacement, larger, beige, thermally efficient, bore the same name but that was its only resemblance. And the field to the east had become a parking lot, since every seventeen-year-old had his or her own car these days.

Things change.

Walls come down.

Time passes.
I went inside.

     ✧

"Hello," I said. "My name is…" and I spoke it, then spelled the last name — the one I'd had back when I'd been a student here, the one that had been my stage name, the one that pre-dated my ex-husbands.

The man sitting behind the desk was in his late forties; other classes were celebrating their whole-decade anniversaries as well. I suspected he had no trouble guessing to which year each arrival belonged, but I supplied it anyway: "Class of Sixty-Three."

The man consulted a tablet computer. "Ah, yes," he said. "Come a long way, have we? Well, it's good to see you." A badge appeared, printed instantly and silently, bearing my name. He handed it to me, along with two drink tickets. "Your class is meeting in Gymnasium Four. It's down that corridor. Just follow everyone else."

     ✧

They'd done their best to capture the spirit of the era. There was a US flag with just fifty stars — easy to recognize because of the staggered rows. And there were photos on the walls of Jack and Jackie Kennedy, and Martin Luther King, and a *Mercury* space capsule bobbing in the Pacific, and Sandy Koufax with the Los Angeles Dodgers. Someone had even dug up movie posters for the hits of that year, *Dr. No* and *Cleopatra*. Two video monitors were silently playing *The Beverly Hillbillies* and *Bonanza*. And "Easier Said Than Done" was coming softly out of the detachable speakers belonging to a portable stereo.

I looked around the large room at the dozens of people. I had no idea who most of them were — not at a glance. They were just old folks, like me: wrinkled, with gray or white hair, some noticeably stooped, one using a walker.

But that man, over there…

There had only been one black person in my class. I hadn't seen Devon Smith in the sixty years since, but this had to be him. Back then, he'd had a full head of curly hair, buzzed short. Now, most of it was gone, and his face was deeply lined.

My heart was pounding harder than it had in years; indeed, I hadn't thought the old thing had that much life left in it.

Devon Smith.

We hadn't talked, not since that hot June evening in '63 when I'd told him I couldn't see him anymore. Our senior prom had only been a week away, but my parents had demanded I break up with him. They'd seen governor George Wallace on the news, personally blocking black students — "coloreds," we called them back then — from enrolling at the University of Alabama. Mom and Dad said their edict was for my own safety, and I went along with it, doing what society wanted.

Truth be told, part of me was relieved. I'd grown tired of the stares, the whispered comments. I'd even overheard two of our teachers making jokes about us, despite all their posturing about the changing times during class.

Of course, those teachers must long since be dead. And as Devon looked my way, for a moment I envied them.

He had a glass of red wine in his hand, and he was wearing a dark gray suit. There was no sign of recognition on his face. Still, he came over. "Hello," he said. "I'm Devon Smith."

I was too flustered to speak, and, after a moment, he went on. "You're not wearing your nametag."

He was right; it was still in my hand, along with the drink chits. I thought about just turning and walking away. But no, no — I couldn't do that. Not to him. Not again.

"Sorry," I said, and that one word embarrassed me further. I lifted my hand, opened my palm, showing the nametag held within.

He stared at it as though I'd shown him a crucifixion wound.

"It's you," he said, and his gaze came up to my face, his brown eyes wide.

"Hello, Devon," I said. I'd been a singer; I still had good breath control. My voice did not crack.

He was silent for a time, and then he lifted his shoulders, a small shrug, as if he'd decided not to make a big thing of it. "Hello," he replied. And then he added, presumably because politeness demanded it, "It's good to see you." But his words were flat.

"How have you been?" I asked.

He shrugged again, this time as if acknowledging the impossibility of my question. How has anyone been for six decades? How does one sum up the bulk of a lifetime in a few words?

"Fine," he said at last. "I've had..." But whatever it was he'd had remained unsaid. He looked away and took a sip of his wine. Finally, he spoke again. "I used to follow your career."

"It had its ups and downs," I said, trying to keep my tone light.

"That song..." he began, but didn't finish.

There was no need to specify which song. The one I'd written about him. The one I'd written about what I *did* to him. It was one of my few really big hits, but I'd never intended to grow rich off my — off *our* — pain.

"They still play it from time to time," I said.

Devon nodded. "I heard it on an oldies station last month." *Oldies.* I shuddered.

"So, tell me," I said, "do you have kids?"

"Three," said Devon. "Two boys and a girl."

"And grandkids?"

"Eight," said Devon. "Ages two through ten."

"Immortality." I hadn't intended to say it out loud, but there it was, the word floating between us. Devon had his immortality through his genes. And, I suppose, he had a piece of mine, too, for every time someone listened to that song, he or she would wonder if it was autobiographical, and, if so, who the beautiful young black man in my past had been.

"Your wife?" I asked.

"She passed away five years ago." He was holding his wine-glass in his left hand; he still wore a ring.

"I'm sorry."

"What about you?" asked Devon. "Any family?"

I shook my head. We were quiet a while. I was wondering what color his wife had been.

"A lot has changed in sixty years," I said, breaking the silence.

He looked over toward the entrance, perhaps hoping somebody else would arrive so he could beg off. "A lot," he agreed. "And yet..."

I nodded. And yet, there still hadn't been a black president or vice-president.

And yet, the standard of living of African-Americans was still lower than that of whites — not only meaning a shorter natural life expectancy, but also that far fewer of them could afford the array of treatments available to the rich.

And yet, just last week, they'd picked the person who would be the first to set foot on Mars. *Of course it was a man,* I'd thought bitterly when the announcement was made. Perhaps Devon had greeted the news with equal dismay, thinking, *Of course he's white.*

Suddenly I heard my name being called. I turned around, and there was Madeline Green. She was easy to recognize; she'd clearly had all sorts of treatments. Her face was smooth, her hair the same reddish-brown I remembered from her genuine youth. How she'd recognized me, though, I didn't know. Perhaps she'd overheard me talking to Devon, and had identified me by my voice, or perhaps just the fact that I *was* talking to Devon had been clue enough.

"Why, Madeline!" I said, forcing a smile. "How good to see you!" I turned to Devon. "You remember Devon Smith?"

"How could I forget?" said Madeline. He was proffering his hand, and, after a moment, she took it.

"Hello, Madeline," said Devon. "You look fabulous."

It had been what Madeline had wanted to hear, but I'd been too niggardly to offer up.

*Niggardly.* A perfectly legitimate word — from the Scandinavian for "stingy," if I remembered correctly. But also a word I never normally used, even in my thoughts. And yet it had come to mind just now, recalling, I supposed, what Madeline had called Devon behind his back all those years ago.

Devon lifted his wineglass. "I need a refill," he said.

The last time I'd looked, he'd still had half a glass; I wondered if he'd quickly drained it when he saw Madeline approaching, giving him a way to exit gracefully, although whether it was me or Madeline he wanted to escape, I couldn't say. In any event, Devon was now moving off, heading toward the cafeteria table that had been set up as a makeshift bar.

"I bought your albums," said Madeline, now squeezing my hand. "Of course, they were all on vinyl. I don't have a record player anymore."

"They're available on CD," I said. "And for download."

"Are they now?" replied Madeline, sounding surprised. I guess she thought of my songs as artifacts of the distant past.

And perhaps they were — although, as I looked over at Devon's broad back, it sure didn't feel that way.

⸺ ✦ ⸺

*"Welcome back, class of Nineteen Sixty-Three!"*

We were all facing the podium, next to the table with the portable stereo. Behind the podium, of course, was Pinky Spenser — although I doubt anyone had called him "Pinky" for half a century. He'd been student-council president, and editor of the school paper, and valedictorian, and on and on, so he was the natural MC for the evening. Still, I was glad to see that for all his early success, he, too, looked old.

There were now perhaps seventy-five people present, including twenty like Madeline who had been able to afford rejuvenation treatments. I'd had a chance to chat briefly with many of them. They'd all greeted me like an old friend, although I couldn't remember ever being invited to their parties or along on their group outings. But now, because I'd once been famous, they all wanted to say hello. They hadn't had the time of day for me back when we'd been teenagers, but doubtless, years later, had gone around saying to people, "You'll never guess who *I* went to school with!"

*"We have a bunch of prizes to give away,"* said Pinky, leaning into the mike, distorting his own voice; part of me wanted to show him how to use it properly. *"First, for the person who has come the farthest..."*

Pinky presented a half-dozen little trophies. I'd had awards enough in my life, and didn't expect to get one tonight — nor did I. Neither did Devon.

*"And now,"* said Pinky, *"although it's not from 1963, I think you'll all agree that this is appropriate..."*

He leaned over and put a new disk in the portable stereo. I could see it from here; it was a CD-ROM that someone had burned at home. Pinky pushed the play button, and...

And one of my songs started coming from the speakers. I recognized it by the second note, of course, but the others didn't until the recorded version of me started singing, and then Madeline Green clapped her hands together. "Oh, listen!" she said, turning toward me. "It's you!"

And it was — from half a century ago, with my song that had become the anthem for a generation of ugly-ducking girls like me. How could Pinky possibly think I wanted to hear that now, here, at the place where all the heartbreak the song chronicled had been experienced?

Why the hell had I come back, anyway? I'd skipped even the fiftieth reunion; what had driven me to want to attend my sixtieth? Was it loneliness?

No. I had friends enough.

Was it morbid curiosity? Wondering who of the old gang had survived?

But, no, that wasn't it, either. That wasn't why I'd come.

The song continued to play. I was doing my guitar solo now. No singing; just me, strumming away. But soon enough the words began again. It was my most famous song, the one I'm sure they'll mention in my obituary.

To my surprise, Madeline was singing along softly. She looked at me, as if expecting me to join in, but I just forced a smile and looked away.

The song played on. The chorus repeated.

This wasn't the same gymnasium, of course — the one where my school dances had been held, the ones where I'd been a wallflower, waiting for even the boys I couldn't stand to ask me to dance. That gym had been bulldozed along with the rest of the old Cedar Valley High.

I looked around. Several people had gone back to their conversations while my music still played. Those who had won the little trophies were showing them off. But Devon, I saw, was listening intently, as if straining to make out the lyrics.

We hadn't dated long — just until my parents found out he was black and insisted I break up with him. This wasn't the song I'd written about us, but, in a way, I suppose it was similar. Both of them, my two biggest hits, were about the pain of being dismissed because of the way you look. In this song, it was me — homely, lonely. And in that other song...

I had been a white girl, and he'd been the only black — not *boy*, you can't say boy — anywhere near my age at our school. Devon had no choice: if he were going to date anyone from Cedar Valley, she would have had to be white.

Back then, few could tell that Devon was good-looking; all they saw was the color of his skin. But he had been *fine*. Handsome, well muscled, a dazzling smile. And yet he had chosen me.

I had wondered about that back then, and I still wondered about it now. I'd wondered if he'd thought appearances couldn't possibly matter to someone who looked like me.

The song stopped, and—

No.

*No.*

I had a repertoire of almost a hundred songs. If Pinky was going to pick a second one by me, what were the chances that it would be *that* song?

But it was. Of course it was

Devon didn't recognize it at first, but when he did, I saw him take a half-step backward, as if he'd been pushed by an invisible hand.

After a moment, though, he recovered. He looked around the gym and quickly found me. I turned away, only to see Madeline softly singing this one, too, *la-la-ing* over those lyrics she didn't remember.

A moment later, there was a hand on my shoulder. I turned. Devon was standing there, looking at me, his face a mask. "We have some unfinished business," he said, softly but firmly.

I swallowed. My eyes were stinging. "I am so sorry, Devon," I said. "It was the times. The era." I shrugged. "Society."

He looked at me for a while, then reached out and took my pale hand in his brown one. My heart began to pound. "We never got to do this back in '63," he said. He paused, perhaps wondering whether he wanted to go on. But, after a moment, he did, and there was no reluctance in his voice. "Would you like to dance?"

I looked around. Nobody else was dancing. Nobody had danced all evening. But I let him lead me out into the center of the gym.

And he held me in his arms.

And I held him.

And as we danced, I thought of the future that Devon's grandchildren would grow up in, a world I would never see, and, for the first time, I found myself hoping my songs wouldn't be immortal.

◈

**Rob** has 21 published novels and has won over forty awards for his fiction including the Nebula Award, the Hugo Award and the John W. Campbell Memorial Award. His latest novel, *"Triggers"*, was released April 2012.

# SIXTEEN COLORS

## ⁓ David Clink ⁓

On a parallel Earth, much like ours, there are only sixteen colors. There is no tomato, candy-apple, or fire engine red. There is just red. When you say green, purple, maroon, aqua, or ivory, they know what you mean. The sun is yellow, snow is white, the sky is blue, the night is black, bottled water is clear, pumpkins are orange. There are no "shades of gray" for them. As a people they don't understand our need for shades of color. The biggest difference between us and them, however, is that they have a million shades of meaning in how they relate to each other, their feelings far richer and more varied on their world than in ours. A nervous glance means the end of a relationship, a wink the heart learning to beat again. On any given day you can witness two people tearing each other's clothes off under a tree that has a brown trunk and leaf-green leaves, a woman slapping a man clean across the face on the gray of a nearby parking lot, and someone stepping off a ledge, falling six stories to the pink carnations below. They kill each other in jealous rages, commit suicide by the thousand, and write great poems. They don't know how to hold back. How could they?

⁓ ✧ ⁓

**David Clink** is the former Artistic Director and Board President of the Rowers Pub Reading Series and former Artistic Director of the Art Bar Poetry Series. He has two collections of poetry published by Tightrope Books: *Eating Fruit Out of Season* (2008) and *Monster* (2010). *Crouching Yak, Hidden Emu*, a collection of humorous verse, is a Fall 2012 title from Battered Silicon Dispatch Box.

# BEMUSED

## ⌒ L. T. Getty ⌒

Mr. Flippowitz clasped his wife's properly painted fingers tighter when the specialist entered the room. "Don't fidget so," Mrs. Flippowitz snapped.

"I can't help it," Mr. Flippowitz said, before looking to the doctor. "Well? Do you have an answer?"

"We believe so, Mr. Flippowitz," said the doctor, nose in his clipboard after he took his seat in his plush swivel chair. "Your condition is the result of a parasite."

"A parasite?" demanded Mrs. Flippowitz. "You mean: a stomach worm would give him so much trouble concentrating on his work?"

"*Intestinal* worm — I'm afraid that's not the culprit at all," said the doctor to the Flippowitzes. "Why, there have been cases proven where intestinal worms clear up hayfever! No, I'm afraid the cause of your husband's inability to concentrate is something much, much more sinister. Now, the cause of it is quite controversial, but we have a cure."

"Not a lobotomy, I hope," Mrs. Flippowitz said, though it sounded like she hoped for it.

"Maybe there's nothing wrong with me at all," Mr. Flippowitz said, "maybe I just haven't been living in balance. I'd like nothing more than to take a week off work and try my hand at painting again."

"Leopold," said Mrs. Flippowitz, "you haven't painted in years. Besides, that is the most selfish thing I have ever heard! We have bills to pay and all your vacation time is spoken for already, what with my cousin's wedding and your family reunion and those out-of-town dinner parties..."

"Stuff it all, Elinor!" said Mr. Flippowitz, "No one will notice if we're not there; quite frankly I'm sick of my job and I'd feel better if I quit the firm right now and flipped burgers for a living! First off, we should both cash in our holidays, and do something that takes us away from the hum-drum of every day life."

"There you go again!" Mrs. Flippowitz scowled at her husband. "Doctor, my husband is not in his right mind; I demand you do something about his condition immediately!"

"Of course," said Dr. Paedlesworth, as he'd already checked and the Flippowitz had the proper insurance. "I recommend we perform the procedure immediately." Immediately meant right there and then, but even Mrs. Flippowitz understood that first Mr. Flippowitz must be taken to the right room, complete with too many machines than are proper for a story such as this.

"Oh my," said Mr. Flippowitz once he had changed into the paper-thin dressing gown and his wife had signed for him. "This is a dangerous procedure, is it? I couldn't say, go to a self-help group or take up meditation?"

Mrs. Flippowitz almost conceded, but thought he said medication. "Leopold," said she, "you're never going to make partner if you continue on like this."

"Yes Darling, what was I thinking," Leopold said, and laid down on the uncomfortable grey slab where the nurse instructed him to. He smiled at her but she didn't smile back.

Staring up at the impressive ray-gun inspired machine pointed at his left nare, Leopold wondered what all the scanners and machines were for; he'd not even a blood pressure cuff on his arm. He thought it looked like a tanning bed, only he was given no goggles to protect his eyes. "Alright, everyone stand back, you don't want to get infected," said the doctor, directing everyone else behind a thick viewing wall.

"I say, this is quite..." Mr. Flippowitz began, but all at once the machines powered up and energy cursed through his body. It was so violent, Mrs. Flippowitz became worried.

"He'll be able to work on Monday?" she asked.

"Of course," said the doctor, killing the power. "Suction!"

At once the nurse went back to Mr. Flippowitz and produced a long tube which she placed on the round bulb of his nose and turned on what sounded like a vacuum, only with a clear tube. Something blue suddenly shot out, and began pounding her little blue fists against the glass.

"Got it, Doctor!" said the nurse.

"The tests detected only one," Dr. Paedlesworth said, though in truth he hoped that Mr. Flippowitz would have to come back for another billable treatment. "Your husband's alright; a little shaken up but that's to be expected," he said, walking over and taking the tube before Mrs. Flippowitz could inspect it (she wouldn't; she was hardly the curious type and preferred it that way).

"Leopold! Are you alright?"

"Elinor," said he, "how long have we been parked?"

"If you can change while we walk, we might be able to save a dollar."

"Try to detain them with paperwork," said the doctor to the nurse as the Flippowitzes began their escape. When he was alone in the room, he looked to the little tube in his hands. "Hello, little pest," he said.

The little blue muse frowned, and made a face at him.

"You're not going anywhere. This tube is magnetically charged, and I'm far too practical to let you effect me." He wondered what the colors meant; remembered his professional requirements didn't include that sort of research. He labelled the tube instead, and sent it to the lab, where all the other captured muses went, and went to go see his next patient, who had a much more mundane problem.

The muse, on the other hand, had quite the trip. Try as she might to escape, she ended up next to another muse on a cart. He was a bright orange. "Rough day?" he asked when she was placed into his box for storage. "I didn't think they could detect us."

"It's all Sedelia's fault — letting the humans write poems about us," said Blue.

"I wonder who inspired them to create that machine," said Orange.

"Not all inspiration comes from us," said blue, "sometimes it's born out of necessity, or greed, or other things."

After all the rounds were made (they were only noticed by children, and one seeing-eye dog) the cart was taken to a closet, and forgotten overnight. The muses waited until an old alarm clock turned on, and with it, came the local radio. Both muses grit their teeth at the latest hit.

"No wonder the humans want to get rid of us," he said. "Did you know about this?"

"No," she said, "but it makes sense. People don't value creativity anymore. At least, not for creativity's sake. They think it's childish, and silly."

"They think we're parasites, you know."

They were discovered within the hour by an intern looking for sterile gloves. She went to show them to her friends, but a senior doctor caught her before she managed to release the muses. "Don't," said she, "They're very infectious and highly contagious. You wouldn't want one of these getting in your system. You wouldn't be able to recite everything you need to know by heart and your head would be filled with nonsense." And because it was a senior doctor and they were lowly interns, they didn't argue. The girl who found them, however, grew bolder than was normally her character.

The muses were taken to an office where they were meant to be filed, not studied like previous specimens that had been already selected. However, the intern knocked on the door. "Dr. Bruhamar," said the intern, whose name was Yasmine, "about what we saw back there..." she then saw many in test tubes awaiting filing.

"Have a seat." Yasmine did as she was told. "You see this?" Dr. Bruhamar asked, picking up a test tube. "It's a cross between something the ancient Greeks believed, and what the church of Christian Science believes today."

"You don't mean ... spirits? We've discovered people can be possessed by spirits?" To Yasmine, this was a very big discovery.

"Not so loud! They're not spirits. We're not sure what they are, but if they were spirits the machines would be sucking out souls while they're at it. If anything, we've proven humans don't have souls."

"May I...?" Yasmine asked, reaching for the tube with Blue in it.

"No you may not," Doctor Bruhamar said. "They can't hurt you, but even looking at one for a while messes with you. You start getting the urge to do such strange things — like take up dancing lessons."

"Oh, I can't dance," Yasmine said, but when she looked at the little creatures in the test tubes, she remembered all the recitals she'd seen, and all the movies where the dancing made her wish she wasn't so uncoordinated. The brains of the family, not the beauty; her family had always insisted that she go on and do something practical...

"Stop that!" Bruhamar snapped.

"What did I do?" Yasmine asked.

"You were daydreaming," Bruhamar said. "Look, certain aspirations are good, but others aren't — all these things do is give people distractions. They kill efficiency and if left untreated can completely ruin productivity."

"But you've contained them?"

"Sort of. There's little magnets on either ends of the tubes — they're slightly magnetic," said the doctor. "Explains why most artists are bipolar."

"Why isn't this sort of discovery made public?" Yasmine asked.

"Very simple," Bruhamar said, "If people knew that if they were creative that they had one of these things — think if they tried to get more than one! We've pulled over a dozen out of one fellow who didn't even know! Can you imagine what would happen to our country if people found out? No one would want to get a real job and get things done — they'd wait for inspiration to hit them."

"Couldn't people manage both?" Yasmine asked.

"Don't be ridiculous," said Bruhamar. "How much have you given up in the pursuit of this career of yours?"

Yasmine frowned and looked at the ground. "So they're distractions, so what? Not everyone's meant to be a professional."

"Young lady, for shame," said Bruhamar. "Every year, we fall further and further behind other countries. Do you know why?"

Yasmine wanted to say the Wal-Mart effect, but her student loans screamed at her to SHUT UP.

"Because we're not as competitive as other countries and if we had more people willing to dedicate themselves to higher callings and not be distracted. Besides, Muses one day, what if we're able to pinpoint stupidity? Laziness? What if we could cure common tardiness?"

"I don't think creativity's that dangerous," Yasmine said. "I can't play music, but it inspires me. I'll be able to take up the violin once I've finished my internship."

Bruhamar chuckled. "You're a little old to start taking up that sort of hobby, don't you think?"

Yasmine felt self-conscious and bowed her head. "Well, I'd like to have more time for creativity in general," she said. "Would you mind letting me study one?"

"Of course I mind!" said Bruhamar. "You've got another year to go — think how disappointed your parents would be," she paused slightly, "if you were to get some crazed idea into your head! You'd be throwing away all your hard work for some artistic whim."

Yasmine frowned. "Maybe I could prove a point though," she said, "balance work and play."

"I don't want this discussion to leave the room," Bruhamar said. "Do your rounds properly, and I might think of making you my assistant. Is that understood?"

Yasmine bobbed her head.

"Good, because your break should be over."

Bruhamar waited until Yasmine left before looking to the muses glaring at her through the test tube sorting cube. "Don't think I don't check myself to ensure one of you little things haven't wormed your way into my brain. If you were clever, you wouldn't hang around."

"What do you want from us?" said the little blue muse. "We've helped inspire many scientific breakthroughs — not all of them, but the ones that turned out to be right..."

"Why, we want to know everything about you," Bruhamar said. "We think it would be best if you were to go bother some other countries. Would it kill the Japanese to be more interested in whatever it is they do for art, rather than beating us in electronics every year?"

The Blue muse looked at the others near her, then back at the doctor. "The Japanese have us as well."

"Well, fiddlesticks, go inspire goat-herders on a hill some where," she said, "and leave us alone!"

"I don't think you have the right to tell people they shouldn't be painting or making music," said a purple muse. "We don't make anyone do anything — we can't."

"You're parasites," said the doctor.

"Only because you've forgotten," said a pink one.

"You're distracting me," said the doctor, and turned on the local radio. For some reason, it seemed to distress them. She didn't like the music herself, but she had to switch from the classics because it made them all start to smile and dance in their little test tubes, and they'd keep bugging her if she didn't have something to drown them out. After a good few minutes of analyzing the color they came in (there was no correlation to age, gender, social class, artistic achievement — although that hospital only took professionals in; they'd yet to perform any studies on the working class or artists themselves), when she had an idea, and forgetting where ideas came from, said, "You all seem to be of one purpose, does the same thing hurt you?" She turned the music up. They all clasped their hands to their ears. She'd not liked the blue, recent addition (it made faces at her when she wasn't looking) and was tempted to see if she could actually kill one if subjected to enough poor taste, when suddenly a little man with a briefcase appeared before her.

"Alright, that's enough. Knock it off." He was on her shoulder, but he skied down her arm to the desk and scowled at her. Dr. Bruhamar went for an empty test tube, but he didn't seem concerned. She almost snatched him up, but she couldn't bring her hand down. "That's right: Get rid of me, and you'll have one of those things pestering you," he said.

"What, pray tell, are you?" he wasn't a solid color, though he was about the same size as the muses, but in very muted colors. He wasn't old or fat, perhaps mid-thirties but it was difficult to tell; if he wasn't three-inches high she would consider him to be quite handsome and professional-looking in his pin-striped suit and solid grey tie. "Don't tell me you're the result of that joke…"

"Madam, you and I know jokes are for the simple-minded," he said, "I'm your sense of conformity. You haven't received proper authorization to go neutralizing anthromorphic spectres."

"It would work, wouldn't it?" she asked.

"How should I know? I'd have to go ask logic," he said. "I'm just warning you: stay within your parameters-"

Bruhamar squashed him. He made a *splat* noise but there was no residue when she lifted it. "You've got to break a few eggs to make an omelette." She summoned Yasmine to get her several televisions and some of the more recent blockbusters, and placed the small blue muse, test tube and all, between four televisions, each showing a film that had been clearly inspired by a greater work, but held none of its original charm or character. The little muse cried and asked to be let out, stating that she'd go mess up the Americans real good, but Bruhamar grew bolder, until the little blue creature started to fade, and all that was left was a bit of greyish residue in the tube.

"Yasmine," Bruhamar sung into the hallway, "I want you to be the first to congratulate me!"

"For what?" Yasmine asked. "Turning it into a butterfly?"

There were several butterflies in the tube, each a soft, pastel shade of blue. "Perhaps I should have left it in longer." Brahumar ran back and put it back between the four televisions and let it soak in a while longer; the colors became grey again, and they started to fade. Brahumar clapped her hands together. "Excellent! Let's leave it for a few hours."

"And then what?"

"Make sure it's gone!" Bruhamar said. "If it works on one, we can eradicate the others! I'll be credited with the discovery."

"You're sure no one else has figured it out first?" Yasmine asked, trying not imagine creativity being destroyed forever.

"I'm sure someone would have said something," Bruhamar said.

Bruhamar had Yasmine draft a formal letter and then corrected it to the point as if she'd done it all herself anyway and sent the email, went home, and was tickled so pink she couldn't stand just another hum-drum evening and instead suggested to her husband that they go to a show that night. He assumed a movie, but once she went into her closet to change she saw the red number she had dieted so hard to fit into again; the symphony seemed like the right place. They were able to easily procure tickets, and they had a late dinner afterword at a nice restaurant she would normally balk about the price. "We should do this more often," she said to her husband. "Why don't we?"

"I'm not sure," said he, "Cordelia, you look beautiful tonight — you always look beautiful, but you know what I mean. Tonight you look more beautiful. It's like, there's a fire burning inside you."

"I guess it's just because I feel so inspired..." she said, then her jaw dropped, she couldn't finish her sorbet and when her husband asked if they were to go to the art gallery the following evening she snapped, and made him sleep on the couch. She woke the next morning and stormed into her office, expected all the tubes to be empty, and found Yasmine downstairs, playing chess with another intern. "You let them out, didn't you?"

"What are you talking about?" Yasmine asked. "Got your queen."

"Well, I'm taking your rook then," said her opponent.

"Come with me at once!" Bruhamar said, pulling Yasmine to her feet and dragging her down the hall. It was a long wait at the elevator.

"You've been busy today," said one of the orderlies.

"I can't help it; I feel so bad for the kids in my ward, cooped up on days like this," said the nurse. "I hope I don't get in trouble." They laughed. "I haven't juggled in years, and it shows..."

Bruhamar shot them a look, and they both piped down, but they were joined by another pair, one of which was Bruhamar's immediate colleague. He and another doctor, albeit closer to Yasmine's age, entered the elevator with great dumb grins on their faces and spoke loudly, oblivious to proper elevator etiquette.

"That was a pretty big prescription you gave for Mrs. Thompson," said the younger.

"Why should she have to come back every month to have it refilled? Her condition's been the same for four years," said elder. "I told her if her condition changes to call for an appointment. Besides, now that my kids are done college I don't have to worry about milking the hours!" They both laughed.

"We have enough genuinely sick people anyway. Almost makes me want to get into preventative medicine."

"Where's the money in that though?" They both laughed far too much.

"Will you two knock it off?" Bruhamar snapped. "You're not at the country club playing golf; you are professionals at your place of work."

"Golf," said one.

"There's only so many more nice days left in the year," said the other.

"It's June," Bruhamar said between clenched teeth.

"Care to join us for a few holes?" the younger doctor asked Yasmine. "It really gets my mind clear, and sometimes, I can think about my patients better, because some days it's just client after client, never a moment's rest — I forget to go to the bathroom. Who is so busy that they can't take care of something a two year old can manage?"

"I've never played golf before," Yasmine said quietly.

"Good. You'll give Sport here a chance to not come in last for once," the older doctors laughed, and got off at their floor, talking like old buddies instead of two people Bruhamar knew couldn't really stand one another.

Once they were in her office, Bruhamar gestured, as if that were all the evidence required. "How can you blame me?" Yasmine asked.

"You did something. I found out a way to destroy them," Bruhamar said. "I saw you with those sad eyes. You must have..." She shook her head. "How did you do it? The door was locked!"

"I didn't!" Yasmine blinked back tears.

Bruhamar crossed her arms and turned her computer on, and was relieved to see Dr. Orlutz responded so promptly by email. "Good — congratulations will be in order, once I round more of the pests up and do some proper case studies."

*Cordelia, what ever you do, do not try to destroy them without my go-ahead! I'll be back in a month, I'm leaving for Vienna with my wife; a bit of a second honeymoon, spur of the moment, but with my kidneys this might be the only chance I'll ever have. I've got my assistant working on it, but he can't seem to concentrate; I'll bet you They have been influencing him; but he's the good sort and has been running case studies. I'm emailing you from the airport; contact me again before August at your own peril.*

*Sincerely,*

"Doctor Wolfgang Orlutz," sang a little blue muse, drinking a daiquiri while sitting on a blue hammock, suspended by air near the computer mouse. "His wife's Italian. That's why they're going."

"You! I know you! I killed you!" Bruhamar said. She grabbed the little muse in her hands, but the little pest was like a cartoon mouse, and would hover just above Bruhamar, not matter how she tried to fling her.

"You break it, you bought it," said the muse. "Don't ask me, it's your silly human policy. I'm not too happy about it either."

"What is that supposed to mean?" Bruhamar asked.

"Look at you — don't you realize how happy people have been since you released me? Happy? In a *hospital*?" the muse played with her drink's insanely tiny, stripy umbrella. "Work morale's gone up; doctors are actually listening to their patients; people have patience with the nurses. We should go to parliament, start working miracles. I swear: they've got selective hearing."

"I know how to get rid of you," Bruhamar said.

"You know how to contain us. You can never be rid of us. If you think we're here because we're picking on you or we want other countries to be better: You're wrong. We're here because you need a little something to remind you that there's a point to all the blood, sweat, and tears you pour into your waking hours. Tell you what: You want to win acclaim through your peers?" asked the muse, grinning. "Let's go for a walk, you and I. Afterall, it takes a lot for a woman like you to get tunnel vision. You used to dream about a Nobel Prize in Medicine."

"Did you see the putz that won last year?" Bruhamar asked.

"Hey, I'm not about to do any work for you, just give you a little nudge. You okay with that? Can I call you Cordelia?" The muse asked, waltzing up the doctor's arm.

"Yasmine, clean up the office," Bruhamar said, walking down the hall, listening eagerly to the little muse on her shoulder as she complained about how narrow-sighted many of Bruhamar's colleagues were.

"Pssst," said a little green muse to Yasmine.

"So what are you really?" Yasmine asked. "Am I going crazy?"

"You have a game of chess to finish."

"You're not going to lead me astray, are you?" Yasmine asked. "I mean, they wouldn't be so worried about extracting you things for no reason, right?"

"We only bug you if you put aside your nature for too long," said the muse. "We're just supposed to point out the inspiration, 'cuz you people are hopeless! You're the one who's gotta do the work, and when you start to give up, we're the little whisper that says, 'Little more', but that's all we can do. Without you guys, we're useless."

"Are you going to stay visible?" she asked.

"We don't need to be," said the green muse. "Oh, and that doctor wasn't asking you to golf just to be friendly." The little green muse blew her a kiss, faded, and Yasmine smiled, began singing to herself, wondering why she'd waited this long to take up the violin. She smiled to herself before acknowledging the time. Chess would have to wait because in the meantime, she was going to talk *with* her patients.

◈

**L. T. Getty** studied creative writing at both the University of Winnipeg and the Canadian Mennonite University. Her short stories have been included in several anthologies and her first novel, a historical fantasy entitled *Tower of Obsidian*, will be launched by Burst Books late 2012. When she is not writing, Leia works as a paramedic.

# ONCE UPON A MIDNIGHT

## Scott Overton

Originally appeared in *In Poe's Shadow*
( Dark Opus Press, October 2011)

In the end, the fate of humanity rested in the hands of a woman scorned.

Lennie Allen wouldn't have characterized herself in that way. But she'd already triggered one warning from the computer's security subroutine by being distracted. The next time she'd be locked out for twenty-four hours. The Director would not be amused.

Normally she welcomed the security protocols; the retina scan, voice recognition, code-words, and fingerprint-scanning mouse were all a part of life in one of the nation's highest-echelon research facilities, and they helped her sleep at night. God knew, the stuff they handled could be used with catastrophic effect by the wrong people. It was the *keystroke dynamics* keyboard that turned out to be a pain in the ass. If its biometrics system ever suspected that she was acting under duress it would offer only two warnings and then go into complete lockdown. Mendelssohn swore he'd been locked out once as a result of chugging one too many Starbucks.

Lennie was finding it hard to care about invented global cataclysm when her own world was falling apart.

She loved working in WCSD — the development and analysis of *worst case scenarios* made good use of her vivid imagination and overflowing cup of personal paranoia. In fact, it was often cathartic. If she could imagine the very worst things that could happen to the planet, and devise potential responses to them, it robbed her own personal fears and troubles of their potency.

But not this time. Ed was gone. Three nights ago. The notification of divorce proceedings had been delivered to her this morning. *God*, that was fast. What was his hurry? Considering that Lennie hadn't suspected a thing until three nights and ... twenty-three minutes ago. Maybe that was what hurt the most, that she'd been so blind. Lennie the genius, her friends called her. Not so smart, after all. Wrapped up in her work, imagining the most terrible things that could happen to a world, without realizing that sometimes 'the world' came down to just two people.

She ran her hands over her glossy black work-station. It was her link to the powerful computer nexus that produced the Reichmann Analog Virtual Environment — a long name with a catchy acronym was important to the people who wrote the cheques. Those grey-suited dark-tied backroom government autocrats had seen enough plain old supercomputers. They needed a name that could jazz up a bland requisition proposal and bamboozle a roomful of auditors. Lennie never used the full title. To her, the RAVE Nexus was part-taskmaster, part-playground. From its matrix of graphics imaging software, intelligent problem-solving, and pure brute processing speed sprang forth creations of startling realism. Lennie could step into a three-dimensional projection of a pristine globe, key in the disaster parameters, and watch it bleed in spreading pools around her.

As a biologist her specialty was pandemics. It was a sexy topic — had been since the first years of the century, for some reason. Scientists had latched onto the idea that pandemics followed some kind of regular schedule, and the world was overdue. After that it was a matter of course that every biological outbreak anywhere attracted an inordinate amount of attention from a global media fascinated with dying things. And if the scientific community found that modestly fanning the flames meant mounds of research money thrown their way, well, who could really blame them?

Lennie's job was to gather everything, from their most carefully assembled data to their wildest flights of fancy, and feed it to the RAVE-*n*. Then the cyber-mind was charged with assessing the probabilities of every scenario, analyzing the etiology, predicting the spread pattern, forecasting the fatality rates, yea, prophesying over the quick and the dead. They ran several scenarios a week. The human race had nearly been eradicated dozens of times.

Lennie and the RAVE-*n* were very good at their job.

Now, though, disaster had invaded her own reality. She felt it like a poison in her veins. Her vision lost its focus, and her fingers miscarried on the keys.

What had gone so wrong in the life they'd shared, she and Ed?

(Eddy. She always called him Eddy because he called her Lennie. He was a sports writer, and everyone in that world was called Bobby or Jimmy or Scotty, weren't they? He dreamed of being a political reporter. Would he have called the President Barry?)

The screen was angrily flashing an image at her.

It was the corporate logo of the Reichmann Analog Corporation: a representation of the Pallas Athena, goddess of war and wisdom. *Damn*. She entered the 'SAFE' code to reset the security function.

She had to concentrate, or the RAVE-*n* would kick her ass. And deservedly so. It wasn't just computer modeling that the RAVE-*n* controlled. All of Level Seven was a full-blown Hazmat lab, operated robotically. The substances studied in there were so dangerous that humans rarely ventured inside, except for the PhD equivalent of janitorial work. The test-tubes and beakers and petrie dishes belonged to the RAVE-*n*. Inside were samples of Rickettsiae bacteria, the villain behind typhus and Rocky Mountain spotted fever; Arenaviridae viruses responsible for Lassa fever; Ebola virus; the corona virus that produced SARS; Marburg virus; several different strains of avian type A influenza viruses of the H5, H7, and H9 subtypes capable of infecting humans, and even a few precious grams of the 1918 Spanish Flu, culled from a corpse frozen in the Alaskan permafrost. Some of the most deadly pathogens known to humankind, all held in the capable pincers of a cybernetic brain and its robotic minions. It was the stuff of sci-fi fright movies, but Lennie wasn't worried. The RAVE-*n* had the abilities of an Artificial Intelligence in many ways, but no independent thought. She liked to say that even if the supercomputer *could* take over the world, the RAVE-*n* was too smart to *want* it.

No, there was far more danger from humans screwing up, maybe because they couldn't keep their inconvenient emotions from getting in the way. Lennie reached for a cup of coffee that was hours cold, and put it back down with a grimace.

They were running simulations of avian flu outbreaks again this week. Although it had been years since the first flare-ups of the H5N1 strain in Hong Kong in the late 1990's, and the more frightening outbreaks later in Southeast Asia, the best minds said that H5N1 or something like it was still lurking in the shadows, waiting for its moment to strike. Every so often it would appear in a flock of domestic fowl somewhere around the globe, and a massive slaughter would follow.

There hadn't been a documented case of H5N1 human-to-human transmission beyond one secondary victim. It was a pandemic held in check because the virus couldn't yet spread among the human population. But flu viruses mutate like there's no tomorrow.

A flock of wild ducks might fly over a poultry farm, leaving behind a bombardment of infected droppings. Wandering chickens would spread the virus to the nearby stock of pigs, one or two of which had already been unlucky enough to pick up a dose of *human* flu from the overly attentive Farmer Nguyen. Once inside the accommodating blood stream of the swine, the two visiting viruses could swap a few genes and, Presto: a new strain of bird flu capable of spreading among *homo sapiens*. Within a few days Farmer Nguyen and his family would have ruined lungs, filled with blood, as their bodies' misguided immune systems deployed cellular soldiers that destroyed the very tissues they were meant to save.

In the outside world the process of mutation was random and slow. It was a different story among the gleaming white walls of Level Seven. There a macabre array of stainless steel bones danced within Plexiglas cylinders, slicing and dicing and splicing, finding new recipes of DNA — shiny new double strands of nucleotides mixed and matched from human diseases and those of the animal kingdom, with the deliberate purpose of *creating* new pathogens deadly to humans. The rationale was that, by creating these lethal agents we could learn how to fight them.

Lennie was always grateful that she didn't tend to remember her dreams.

She also felt that her own hands were clean. She didn't create the murderous agents. She only ran simulations of their path of destruction.

When she and the RAVE-*n* turned the new killer loose, it was only on a *virtual* globe — an ethereal construct of numbers and electrical impulses, sanitized and safe. Lennie provided the data and the computer showed her Armageddon.

She would never admit it to anyone, but it was morbidly fascinating to watch the world's dominant species die a thousand gruesome deaths. Particularly if at least one of the virtual victims bore the face of Eddy.

No, that wasn't true. She didn't want him dead. Maybe the blame was hers. She'd always known that secrets could tear a relationship apart. Her father's military career had poisoned her parents' marriage after he'd been promoted into the upper echelons of the Pentagon, and had to hide the details of his workday from his own wife. After that, the trust was gone and the fire along with it — Lennie had watched it happen.

She'd vowed never to make the same mistake, but that was exactly what she'd done. It wasn't just her job's security demands; she'd told herself she was protecting Eddy from the horrors of Level Seven for his own good. It wasn't healthy to live day after day with the threat of a biological holocaust hanging like a Sword of Damocles in the mind's eye. Some people simply couldn't take it, and spent the rest of their lives in therapy.

So she couldn't tell him about her work, and she couldn't tell him why not. But he wasn't a fool. He suspected something. Eventually it turned into the conviction that she was involved in something big ... a potential hot story that could be his *entrée* into the political arena. She was sure he hadn't come up with that idea on his own. It had the perfumed taint of that blonde internet blogger he'd talked about more and more often. The one who was always digging for government conspiracies. The one with the inflated ego and the inflated chest....

*God!* Was that what had happened? Had an online correspondence sparked an offline romance? *Oh Eddy... Eddy ... did I drive you to that?* She felt a hot tear well up, and had to snap her head away before it could splash onto the keyboard.

She didn't want him dead. She was furious, cruelly hurt, and hopelessly infatuated all at the same time. She loved him beyond reason, and even now she knew that she would take him back without hesitation, if he asked. But what were the odds of that? Predicting them would take more skill than she had. It would require a master of predictions....

*No.* No, the idea was ridiculous. She turned her head away from the screens and imprisoned her hands beneath her legs to restrain them, while she rocked back and forth in confusion.

There was no-one else in the lab. There likely wouldn't be for another forty-five minutes — her coworkers liked to take long lunches. And she knew how to erase almost all traces of her commands, except in the RAVE-*n*'s deepest core memory.

Did she dare...?

Inevitable as a pandemic itself, she surrendered seven minutes later and furtively began to key in the data. The RAVE-*n* already had reams of information about Lennie. She quickly fed it a rough profile of Eddy, warts and all, resisting the powerful temptation to embellish the warts.

Query: *Will Lennie and Eddy get back together?*

There was no sign of activity from the RAVE-*n* — there never was. But sixty seconds was an eternity of processing time for a task that involved no global modeling, no quantum variables, and no fancy graphics in 128-bit studio-precision color.

The screen finally came to life.

RAVE-*n*: *Insufficient data.*

She exhaled a long-held breath and realized that her hands were trembling. She didn't dare try it again. It was sheer idiocy to have done it in the first place. She spent the next five minutes covering her tracks.

The rest of the afternoon was excruciating. Each time someone came over to speak to her, she expected them to hiss a withering accusation about using lab facilities for a personal whim. She vowed that she would never give in to such an unworthy impulse again. She hurried home that night in relief, and dreamed of a spinning globe projected in mid-air, with her face on one side and Eddy's on the other, and she could only watch helplessly as scenario after scenario brought spreading patches of emptiness like a cancer between them.

At the first coffee break the next morning, she asked again.

RAVE-*n*: *Insufficient data.*

This time she didn't delete the query, she merely hid it behind layers of other tasks. But it waited there for her to call it up, first at lunch, then at afternoon break, and eventually whenever she had the room to herself. In between, her mind would wander from cross-indexing fatality rates to trying to recall any memories of her marriage that might help in her cupidean quest.

RAVE-*n*: *Insufficient data.*

In frustration she nearly pounded a fist on the keyboard, but that might trigger another computation. Because of the dynamic interface, the machine already finished most of her sentences for her — they'd worked together for so long it anticipated nearly every keystroke. Instead she chastised herself again for obsessing over a husband (*EX* — husband!) and tried to force her tense fingers to relax on the keys.

She was startled to see the screen begin to fill with words ... words beginning with EX....

Exacerbate

Exact

Exacting

Exaggerate

She quickly keyed in a 'Terminate' command. The RAVE-*n* was getting too damned helpful for their own good.

But not helpful where it really counted. Why couldn't the supercomputer produce an answer for *her*? Why didn't it even try?

The question was too simple — that must be it. She needed to approach it like any other scenario. Build a model, enter the data, run the simulation. But that would take time. She could never accomplish that much in a couple of coffee breaks. She had to....

She had to work overtime. Which meant she needed a cover story. Say her last pandemic simulation had run into bugs — of the computer, not biological variety — but she was close to tracking them down and didn't want to lose the momentum?

Her supervisor accepted the fiction readily enough. Lennie was one of his best workers. And anyway she was on a salary.

She had to be careful. There was still a possibility that someone else might be working late and walk in on her. It was even possible that one of the security people would make a random check on her work station. She needed a shadow screen — a secondary display she could bring up with a stroke of a key. Only a real task would be convincing enough to fool a colleague, but she'd just finished the last of her most recent series of simulations. What else would look plausible?

She called up the RAVE-*n*'s latest results from Level Seven. And instantly regretted it. A quick scan of the data caused the blood to drain from her face.

*Good God.* This was the worst one yet: a strain of virus that appeared to be based on a hemagglutinin 5 and neuraminidase 1, but had stitched-on RNA from half a dozen sources. The testing just completed that afternoon showed a startling 100% lethality — virtually unheard of. Early indications revealed a six or seven-day incubation period, followed by fatality within four days. That alone made it much more dangerous than killers like Ebola — they killed their hosts so quickly that they rarely spread very far from the original source of the infection. This new creation had no such weakness. It was the perfect traveler. *God help us if....*

She didn't let her mind complete the thought. Instead she began the practiced routine of building the computer model that would complete it for her. The horrific allure of the new pathogen was nearly enough to distract Lennie from her original purpose.

It was the moment when the world could have been saved.

But destiny or fate or evolution dictated otherwise. The pull of her aching heart was stronger. Once the basic parameters of her scenario had been established, she allowed the RAVE-*n* to fill in the rest, adding only the simple command to Run the program and then Terminate. Then she turned back to her private project. The reunion of Lennie and Eddy. The *best* case scenario.

It happened only minutes before midnight. She awakened to the sound of the alarms, and the pain where the keys had become embedded in her cheek.

*Had they caught her?*

The klaxon reverberated through the room, piercing her ears until her jaw ached. Warning lamps painted the walls in spasms of color. Finally gathering her wits together she snapped her head up to look at what they called "The Big Screen", a liquid crystal panel mounted from the ceiling that displayed announcements for all staff, and alerts of any kind. It was mutely screaming in giant fluorescent letters.

There was a breach on Level Seven. A deadly toxin was loose.

Already an army of biohazard experts would be scrambling into hazmat suits — she could picture them racing down echoing hallways to bring the enemy to battle. Yet, even as she watched, her initial alarm turned to helpless horror.

*The vents were opening!*

The outside vents of the lab were intended to exhaust toxic gases in the event of a fire. They were a dangerous necessity, but there were countless failsafe systems to prevent them ever opening in the aftermath of a spill — exactly the kind of accident she was now witnessing. The failsafes could not be overridden manually by a murderous saboteur or terrorist maniac. That had been demonstrated again and again, before the lab could even be built. No-one could open the vents to the open air once a breach alert had been sounded.

No human.

The RAVE-*n*! The computer must have allowed it. *Good God*, could it have been caused by something *she*'d done?

Her fingers flew frantically over the keyboard, recalling the recent list of commands and actions, luminous letters reflected in her wet eyes.

*No!* It wasn't possible!

The last command line accused her from the screen like an executioner's pointing finger:

"Run program. EX-Terminate."

She slumped back in the chair, and her vacant eyes came to focus on the holographic globe suspended in mid-air before her, running its final simulation.

Blotches of invading crimson ate their way hungrily around the ghostly blue projection of her home world, almost more quickly than she could see. In a daze, she tapped a trio of keys to check the time scale and drew a ragged breath, then expanded the range to slow the simulation down. This time she could see the wash of salmon color, representing the transmission of the virus, racing around the globe in a flash. Immediately afterward followed the blood red flood of fatality, moving slowly for the first ten or fifteen seconds, then almost instantly transforming the whole mottled Earth into a pulsing red beacon of warning. Stunned, she stood and walked into the center of the projection, then turned slowly in place, and swept her gaze over each quadrant. There was nowhere left untouched, no safe haven of shelter or resilience. Not even in the Himalayas, or the desert of the Sudan, or the barren Antarctic.

A flicker of movement drew her attention back to the Big Screen overhead. Its glaring fluorescent letters had been replaced with an epitaph of damning words.

Query: *Will Lennie and Eddy get back together?*

Quoth the RAVE-*n*: *Nevermore.*

**Scott Overton** is a radio morning man in Sudbury, Ontario, who blames his off-kilter perspective on years of lost sleep. His short fiction has been published in *On Spec*, *Neo-opsis*, and a number of SF anthologies. Look for his first novel *Dead Air* (a mystery/thriller) published by Scrivener Press.

# DRUMBEATS

## Kevin J. Anderson & Neil Peart

Originally appeared in *Shock Rock II*, edited by Jeff Gelb
(Pocket Books, 1994)

After nine months of touring across North America — with hotel suites and elaborate dinners and clean sheets every day — it felt good to be hot and dirty, muscles straining not for the benefit of any screaming audience, but just to get to the next village up the dusty road, where none of the natives recognized Danny Imbro or knew his name. To them, he was just another White Man, an exotic object of awe for little children, a target of scorn for drunken soldiers at border checkpoints.

Bicycling through Africa was about the furthest thing from a rock concert tour that Danny could imagine — which was why he did it, after promoting the latest Blitzkrieg album and performing each song until the tracks were worn smooth in his head. This cleared his mind, gave him a sense of balance, perspective.

The other members of Blitzkrieg did their own thing during the group's break months. Phil, whom they called the "music machine" because he couldn't stop writing music, spent his relaxation time cranking out film scores for Hollywood; Reggie caught up on his reading, soaking up grocery bags full of political thrillers and mysteries; Shane turned into a vegetable on Maui. But Danny Imbro took his expensive-but-battered bicycle and bummed around West Africa. The others thought it strangely appropriate that the band's drummer would go off hunting for tribal rhythms.

Late in the afternoon on the sixth day of his ride through Cameroon, Danny stopped in a large open market and bus depot in the town of Garoua. The marketplace was a line of mud-brick kiosks and chophouses, the air filled with the smell of baked dust and stones, hot oil and frying beignets. Abandoned cars squatted by the roadside, stripped clean but unblemished by corrosion in the dry air. Groups of men and children in long blouses like nightshirts idled their time away on the street corners.

Wives and daughters appeared on the road with their buckets, going to fetch water from the well on the other side of the marketplace. They wore bright-colored *pagnes* and kerchiefs, covering their traditionally naked breasts with T-shirts or castoff Western blouses, since the government in the capital city of Yaounde had forbidden women from going topless.

Behind one kiosk in the shade sat a pan holding several bottles of Coca-Cola, Fanta, and ginger ale, cooling in water. Some vendors sold a thin stew of bony fish chunks over gritty rice, others sold *fufu*, a dough-like paste of pounded yams to be dipped into a sauce of meat and okra. Bread merchants stacked their long *baguettes* like dry firewood.

Danny used the back of his hand to smear sweat-caked dust off his forehead, then removed the bandanna he wore under his helmet to keep the sweat out of his eyes. With streaks of white skin peeking through the layer of grit around his eyes, he probably looked like some strange lemur.

In halting French, he began haggling with a wiry boy to buy a bottle of water. Hiding behind his kiosk, the boy demanded 800 francs for the water, an outrageous price. While Danny attempted to bargain it down, he saw the gaunt, grayish-skinned man walking through the marketplace like a wind-up toy running down.

The man was playing a drum.

The boy cringed and looked away. Danny kept staring. The crowd seemed to shrink away from the strange man as he wandered among them, continuing his incessant beat. He wore his hair long and unruly, which in itself was unusual among the close-cropped Africans. In the equatorial heat, the long stained overcoat he wore must have heated his body like a furnace, but the man did not seem to notice. His eyes were focused on some invisible distance.

"*Huit-cent francs*," the boy insisted on his price, holding the lukewarm bottle of water just out of Danny's reach.

The staggering man walked closer, tapping a slow monotonous beat on the small cylindrical drum under his arm. He did not change his tempo, but continued to play as if his life depended on it. Danny saw that the man's fingers and wrists were wrapped with scraps of hide; even so, he had beaten his fingertips bloody.

Danny stood transfixed. He had heard tribal musicians play all manner of percussion instruments, from hollowed tree trunks, to rusted metal cans, to beautifully carved *djembe* drums with goat-skin drumheads — but he had never heard a tone so rich and sweet, with such an odd echoey quality as this strange African drum.

In the studio, he had messed around with drum synthesizers and reverbs and the new technology designed to turn computer hackers into musicians. But this drum sounded different, solid and pure, and it hooked him through the heart, hypnotizing him. It distracted him entirely from the unpleasant appearance of its bearer.

"What is that?" he asked.

"*Sept-cent francs*," the boy insisted in a nervous whisper, dropping his price to 700 and pushing the water closer.

Danny walked in front of the staggering man, smiling broadly enough to show the grit between his teeth, and listened to the tapping drumbeat. The drummer turned his gaze to Danny and stared through him. The pupils of his eyes were like two gaping bullet wounds through his skull. Danny took a step backward, but found himself moving to the beat. The drummer faced him, finding his audience. Danny tried to place the rhythm, to burn it into his mind — something this mesmerizing simply had to be included in a new Blitzkrieg song.

Danny looked at the cylindrical drum, trying to determine what might be causing its odd double-resonance — a thin inner membrane, perhaps? He saw nothing but elaborate carvings on the sweat polished wood, and a drumhead with a smooth, dark brown coloration. He knew the Africans used all kinds of skin for their drumheads, and he couldn't begin to guess what this was.

He mimed a question to the drummer, then asked, "*Est-ce-que je peux l'essayer?*" May I try it?

The gaunt man said nothing, but held out the drum near enough for Danny to touch it without interrupting his obsessive rhythm. His overcoat flapped open, and the hot stench of decay made Danny stagger backward, but he held his ground, reaching for the drum.

Danny ran his fingers over the smooth drumskin, then tapped with his fingers. The deep sound resonated with a beat of its own, like a heartbeat. It delighted him. "For sale? *Est-ce-que c'est a vendre?*" He took out a thousand francs as a starting point, although if water alone cost 800 francs here, this drum was worth much, much more.

The man snatched the drum away and clutched it to his chest, shaking his head vigorously. His drumming hand continued its unrelenting beat.

Danny took out two thousand francs, then was disappointed to see not the slightest change of expression on the odd drummer's face. "Okay, then, where was the drum made? Where can I get another one? *Où est-ce qu'on peut trouver un autre comme ça?*" He put most of the money back into his pack, keeping 200 francs out. Danny stuffed the money into the fist of the drummer; the man's hand seemed to be made of petrified wood. "*Où?*"

The man scowled, then gestured behind him, toward the Mandara Mountains along Cameroon's border with Nigeria. "*Kabas.*"

He turned and staggered away, still tapping on his drum as if to mark his footsteps. Danny watched him go, then returned to the kiosk, unfolding the map from his pack. "Where is this Kabas? Is it a place? *C'est un village?*"

"*Huit-cent francs,*" the boy said, offering the water again at his original 800 franc price.

Danny bought the water, and the boy gave him directions.

⸺ ✧ ⸺

He spent the night in a Garouan hotel that made Motel 6 look like Caesar's Palace. Anxious to be on his way to find his own new drum, Danny roused a local vendor and cajoled him into preparing a quick omelet for breakfast. He took a sip from his 800-franc bottle of water, saving the rest for the long bike ride, then pedaled off into the stirring sounds of early morning.

As Danny left Garoua on the main road, heading toward the mountains, savanna and thorn trees stretched away under a crystal sky. A pair of doves bathed in the dust of the road ahead, but as he rode toward them, they flew up into the last of the trees with a *chuk-chuk* of alarm and a flash of white tail feathers. Smoke from grassfires on the plains tainted the air.

How different it was to be riding through a landscape, he thought — with no walls or windows between his senses and the world — rather than just riding by it. Danny felt the road under his thin wheels, the sun, the wind on his body. It made a strange place less exotic, yet it became infinitely more real.

The road out of Garoua was a wide boulevard that turned into a smaller road heading north. With his bicycle tires humming and crunching on the irregular pavement, Danny passed a few ragged cotton fields, then entered the plains of dry, yellow grass and thorny scrub, everywhere studded with boulders and sculpted anthills. By 7:30 in the morning, a hot breeze rose, carrying a honeysuckle-like perfume. Everything vibrated with heat.

Within an hour the road grew worse, but Danny kept his pace, taking deep breaths in the trancelike state that kept the horizon moving closer. Drums. Kabas. Long rides helped him clear his head, but he found he had to concentrate to steer around the worst ruts and the biggest stones.

Great columns of stone appeared above the hills to east and west. One was pyramid-shaped, one a huge rounded breast, yet another a great stone phallus. Danny had seen photographs of these "inselberg" formations caused by volcanoes that had eroded over the eons, leaving behind vertical cores of lava.

Erosion had struck the road here, too, turning it into a heaving washboard, which then veered left into a trough between tumbled boulders and up through a gauntlet of thorn trees. Danny stopped for another drink of water, another glance at the map. The water boy at the kiosk had marked the location of Kabas with his fingernail, but it was not printed on the map.

After Danny had climbed uphill for an hour, the beaten path became no more than a worn trail, forcing him to squeeze between walls of thorns and dry millet stalks. The squadrons of hovering dragonflies were harmless, but the hordes of tiny flies circling his face were maddening, and he couldn't pedal fast enough to escape them.

It was nearly noon, the sun reflecting straight up from the dry earth, and the little shade cast by the scattered trees dwindled to a small circle around the trunks. "Where the hell am I going?" he said to the sky.

But in his head he kept hearing the odd, potent beat resonating from the bizarre drum he had seen in the Garoua marketplace. He recalled the grayish, shambling man who had never once stopped tapping on his drum, even though his fingers bled. No matter how bad the road got, Danny thought, he would keep going. He'd never been so intrigued by a drumbeat before, and he never left things half finished.

Danny Imbro was a goal-oriented person. The other members of Blitzkrieg razzed him about it, that once he made up his mind to do something, he plowed ahead, defying all common sense. Back in school, he had made up his mind to be a drummer. He had hammered away at just about every object in sight with his fingertips, pencils, silverware, anything that made noise. He kept at it until he drove everyone else around him nuts, and somewhere along the line he became good.

Now people stood at the chain-link fences behind concert halls and applauded whenever he walked from the backstage dressing rooms out to the tour buses — as if he were somehow doing a better job of walking than any of them had ever seen before... .

Up ahead, an enormous buttress-tree, a gnarled and twisted pair of trunks hung with cable-thick vines, cast a wide patch of shade. Beneath the tree, watching him approach, sat a small boy.

The boy leaped to his feet, as if he had been waiting for Danny. Shirtless and dusty, he held a hooklike withered arm against his chest; but his grin was completely disarming. "*Je suis guide?*" the boy called.

Relief stifled Danny's laugh. He nodded vigorously. "*Oui!*" Yes, he could certainly use a guide right about now. "*Je cherche Kabas — village des tambours.* The village of drums."

The smiling boy danced around like a goat, jumping from rock to rock. He was pleasant-faced and healthy looking, except for the crippled arm; his skin was very dark but his eyes had a slight Asian cast. He chattered in a high voice, a mixture of French and native dialect. Danny caught enough to understand that the boy's name was Anatole.

Before the boy led him on, though, Danny dismounted, leaning his bicycle against a boulder, and unzipped his pack to take out the raisins, peanuts, and the dry remains of a baguette. Anatole watched him with wide eyes, and Danny gave him a handful of raisins, which the boy wolfed down. Small flies whined around their faces as they ate. Danny answered the boy's incessant questions with as few words as possible: did he come from America, did black boys live there, why was he visiting Cameroon?

The short rest sank its soporific claws into him, but Danny decided not to give in. An afternoon siesta made a lot of sense, but now that he had his own personal guide to the village, he made it his goal not to stop again until they reached Kabas. "Okay?" Danny raised his eyebrows and struggled to his feet.

Anatole sprang out from the shade and fetched Danny's bike for him, struggling with one arm to keep it upright. After several trips to Africa, Danny had seen plenty of withered limbs, caused by childhood diseases, accidents, and bungled inoculations. Out here in the wilder areas, such problems were even more prevalent, and he wondered how Anatole managed to survive; acting as a "guide" for the rare travelers would hardly suffice.

Danny pulled out a hundred francs — an eighth of what he had paid for one bottle of water — and handed it to the boy, who looked as if he had just been handed the crown jewels. Danny figured he had probably made a friend for life.

Anatole trotted ahead, gesturing with his good arm. Danny pedaled after him.

⇐ ✧ ⇒

The narrow valley captured a smear of greenness in the dry hills, with a cluster of mango trees, guava trees, and strange baobabs with eight-foot-thick trunks. Playing the knowledgeable tour guide, Anatole explained that the local women used the baobab fruits for baby formula if their breast milk failed. The villagers used another tree to manufacture an insect repellent.

The houses of Kabas blended into the landscape, because they were of the landscape — stones and branches and grass. The walls were made of dry mud, laid on a handful at a time, and the roofs were thatched into cones. Tiny pink and white stones studded the mud, sparkling like quartz in the sun.

At first the place looked deserted, but then an ancient man emerged from a turret-shaped hut. An enormous cutlass dangled from his waist, although the shrunken man looked as if it might take him an hour just to lift the blade. Anatole shouted something, then gestured for Danny to follow him. The great cutlass swayed against the old man's unsteady knees as he bowed slightly — or stooped — and greeted Danny in formal, unpracticed French. "*Bonsoir!*"

"*Makonya,*" Danny said, remembering the local greeting from Garoua. He walked his bike in among the round and square buildings. A few chickens scratched in the dirt, and a pair of black-and-brown goats nosed between the huts. A sinewy, long-limbed old woman wearing only a loincloth tended a fire. He immediately started looking for the special drums, but saw none.

Within the village, a high-walled courtyard enclosed two round huts. Gravel covered the open area between them, roofed over with a network of serpent-shaped sticks supporting grass mats. This seemed to be the chief's compound. Anatole held Danny's arm and dragged him forward.

Inside the wall, a white-robed figure reclined in a canvas chair under an acacia tree. His handsome features had a North African cast, thin lips over white teeth, and a rakish mustache. His aristocratic head was wrapped in a red-and-white checked scarf, and even in repose he was obviously tall. He looked every bit the romantic desert prince, like Rudolf Valentino in The Sheik. After greeting Danny in both French and the local language, the chief gestured for his visitor to sit beside him.

Before Danny could move, two other boys appeared carrying a rolled-up mat of woven grass, which they spread out for him. Anatole scolded them for horning in on his customer, but the two boys cuffed him and ignored his protests. Then the chief shouted at them all for disturbing his peace and drove the boys away. Danny watched them kicking Anatole as they scampered away from the chief, and he felt for his new friend, angry at how tough people picked on weaker ones the world over.

He sat cross-legged on the mat, and it took him only a moment to begin reveling in the moment of relaxation. No cars or trucks disturbed the peace. He was miles from the nearest electricity, or glass window, or airplane. He sat looking up into the leaves of the acacia, listening to the quiet buzz of the villagers, and thought, "I'm living in a National Geographic documentary!"

Anatole stole back into the compound, bearing two bottles of warm Mirinda orange soda, which he gave to Danny and the chief. Other boys gathered under the tree, glaring at Anatole, then looking at Danny with ill-concealed awe.

After several moments of polite smiling and nodding, Danny asked the chief if all the boys were his children. Anatole assisted in the unnecessary translation.

"*Oui,*" the chief said, patting his chest proudly. He claimed to have fathered 31 sons, which made Danny wonder if the women in the village found it politic to routinely claim the chief as the father of their babies. As with all remote African villages, though, many children died of various sicknesses. Just a week earlier, one of the babies had succumbed to a terrible fever, the chief said.

The chief asked Danny the usual questions about his country, whether any black men lived there, why had he visited Cameroon; then he insisted that Danny eat dinner with them. The women would prepare the village's specialty of chicken in peanut sauce.

Hearing this, the old sentry emerged with his cutlass, smiled widely at Danny, then turned around the side wall. The squawking of a terrified chicken erupted in the sleepy afternoon air, the sounds of a scuffle, and then the squawking stopped.

Finally, Danny asked the question that had brought him to Kabas in the first place. "*Moi, je suis musicien; je cherche les tambours speciaux.*" He mimed rapping on a small drum, then turned to Anatole for assistance.

The chief sat up startled, then nodded. He hammered on the air, mimicking drum playing, as if to make sure. Danny nodded. The chief clapped his hands and gestured for Anatole to take Danny somewhere. The boy pulled Danny to his feet and, surrounded by other chattering boys, dragged him back out of the walled courtyard. Danny managed to turn around and bow to the chief.

After trooping up a stair-like terrace of rock, they entered the courtyard of another homestead. The main shelter was made of hand-shaped blocks with a flat roof of corrugated metal. Anatole explained that this was the home of the local *sorcier*, or wizard.

Anatole called out, then gestured for Danny to follow through the low doorway. Inside the hut, the walls were hung with evidence of the *sorcier's* trade — odd bits of metal, small carvings, bundles of fur and feathers, mortars full of powders and herbs, clay urns for water and millet beer, smooth skins curing from the roof poles. And drums.

"*Tambours!*" Anatole said, spreading his hands wide.

Judging from the craftsman's tools around the hut, the *sorcier* made the village's drums as well as stored them. Danny saw several small gourd drums, larger log drums, and hollow cylinders of every size, all intricately carved with serpentine symbols, circles feeding into spirals, lines tangled into knots.

Danny reached out to touch one — then the *sorcier* himself stood up from the shadows near the far wall. Danny bit off a startled cry as the lithe old man glided forward. The *sorcier* was tall and rangy, but his skin was a battleground of wrinkles, as if someone had clumsily fashioned him out of *papier maché*.

"Pardon," Danny said. The wrinkled man had been sitting on a low stool, putting the finishing touches to a new drum.

Fixing his eyes on his visitor, the *sorcier* withdrew a medium-sized drum from a niche in the wall. Closing his eyes, he tapped on it. The mud walls of the hut reverberated with the hollow vibration, an earthy, primal beat that resonated in Danny's bones. Danny grinned with awe. Yes! The gaunt man's drum had not been a fluke. The drums of Kabas had some special construction that caused this hypnotic tone.

Danny reached out tentatively. The wrinkled man gave him an appraising look, then extended the drum enough for Danny to strike it. He tapped a few tentative beats, and laughed out loud when the instrument rewarded him with the same rich sound.

The *sorcier* turned away, taking the drum with him and returning it to its niche in the wall. In two flowing strides, the wrinkled man went to his stool in the shadows, picking up the drum he had been fashioning, moving it into the crack of light that seeped through the windows. Pointing, he spoke in a staccato dialect, which Anatole translated into pidgin French.

The *sorcier* is finishing a new drum today, Anatole said. Perhaps they would play it this evening, an initiation. The chief's baby son would have enjoyed that. From the baby's body, the *sorcier* had been able to salvage only enough skin to make this one small drum.

"What?" Danny said, looking down at the deep brown skin covering the top of the drum.

Anatole explained, as if it was the most ordinary thing in the world, that whenever one of the chief's many sons died, the *sorcier* used his skin to make one of Kabas's special drums. It had always been done.

Danny wrestled with that for a moment. On his first trip to Africa five years earlier, he had learned the wrenching truth of how different these cultures were.

"Why?" he finally asked. "*Pourquoi?*"

He had seen other drums made entirely of human skin taken from slain enemies, fashioned in the shape of stunted bodies with gaping mouths; when tapped a hollow sound came from the effigy's mouths. He knew that trying to impose his Western moral framework on the inhabitants of an alien land was hopeless. I'm sorry, sir, but you'll have to check your preconceptions at the door, he thought jokingly to himself.

"*Magique.*" Anatole's eyes showed a flash of fear — fear born of respect for great power, rather than paranoia or panic. With the magic drums of Kabas, the chief could conquer any man, steal his heartbeat. It was old magic, a technique the village wizards had discovered long before the French had come to Cameroon, and before them the Germans. Kabas had been isolated, and at peace for longer than the memories of the oldest people in the village. Because of the drums. Anatole smiled, proud of his story, and Danny restrained an urge to pat him on the head.

Trying not to let his disbelief show, Danny nodded deeply to the *sorcier*. "*Merci*," he said. As Anatole led him back out to the courtyard, the *sorcier* returned to his work on the small drum.

Danny wondered if he should have tried to buy one of the drums from the wrinkled man. Did he believe the story about using human skins? Probably. Why would Anatole lie?

As they left the *sorcier's* homestead to begin the trek back to the village, he looked westward across the jagged landscape of inselbergs. At sunset, the air filled with hundreds of kites, their wings rigid, circling high on the last thermals. Like leaves before the wind, the birds came spiraling down to disappear into the trees, filling them with the invisible flapping of wings.

When they reached the main village again, Danny saw that the women had returned from their labor in the nearby fields. He was familiar with the African tradition of sending the women and children out for backbreaking labor while the men lounged in the shade and talked "business."

The numerous sons of the chief and other adults gathered inside the courtyard near the fire, which the old sinewy woman had stoked into a larger blaze. Other men emerged, and Danny wondered where they had been hiding all afternoon. Out hunting? If so, they had nothing to show for their efforts. Anatole directed Danny to sit on a mat beside the chief, and everyone smiled vigorously at each other, the villagers exchanging the call-and-response litany of ritual greetings, which could go on for several minutes.

The old woman served the chief first, then the honored guest. She placed a brown yam like a baked potato on the mat in front of him, miming that it was hot. Danny took a cautious bite; the yam was pungent and turned to paste in his mouth. Then the woman reappeared with the promised chicken in peanut sauce. They ate quietly in a circle around the fire, ignoring each other, as red shadows flickered across their faces.

Listening to the sounds of eating, as well as the simmering evening hush of the West African hills, Danny felt the emptiness like a peaceful vacuum, draining away stress and loud noises and hectic schedules. After too many head-pounding tours and adrenaline-crazed performances, Danny was convinced he had forgotten how to sit quietly, how to slow down. After one rough segment of the last Blitzkrieg tour, he had taken a few days to go camping in the mountains; he recalled pacing in vigorous circles around the picnic table, muttering to himself that he was relaxing as fast as he could! Calming down was an acquired skill, he felt, and there was no better teacher than Africa.

After the meal, heads turned in the firelight, and Danny looked up to see the *sorcier* enter the chief's compound. The wrinkled man cradled several of his mystical drums. He placed one of the drums in front of the chief, then set the others on an empty spot on the ground. He squatted behind one drum, thrusting his long, lean legs up and to the side like the wings of a vulture.

Danny perked up. "A concert?" He turned to Anatole, who spoke rapidly to the *sorcier*. The wrinkled man looked skeptically at Danny, then shrugged. He picked up one of the extra drums and ceremoniously extended it to Danny.

Danny couldn't stop smiling. He took the drum and looked at it. The coffee-colored skin felt smooth and velvety as he touched it. A shiver went up his spine as he tapped the drumhead. Making music from human skin. He forced his instinctive revulsion back into the gray static of his mind, the place where he stored things "to think about later." For now, he had the drum in his hands.

The chief thumped out a few beats, then stopped. The *sorcier* mimicked them, and glanced toward Danny. "Jam session!" he muttered under his breath, then repeated the sequence easily and cleanly, but added a quick, complicated flourish to the end.

The chief raised his eyebrows, followed suit with the beat, and made it more complicated still. The *sorcier* flowed into his part, and Danny joined in with another counterpoint. It reminded him of the Dueling Banjos sequence from Deliverance.

The echoing, rich tone of the drum made his fingers warm and tingly, but he allowed himself to be swallowed up in the mystic rhythms, the primal pounding out in the middle of the African wilderness. The other night noises vanished around him, the smoke from the fire rose straight up, and the light centered into a pinpoint of his concentration.

Using his bare fingers — sticks would only interrupt the magical contact between himself and the drum — Danny continued weaving into their rhythms, trading points and counterpoints. The beat touched a core of past lives deep within him, an atavistic, pagan intensity, as the three drummers reached into the Pulse of the World. The chief played on; the *sorcier* played on; and Danny let his eyes fade half closed in a rhythmic trance, as they explored the wordless language and hypnotic interplay of rhythm.

Danny became aware of the other boys standing up and swaying, jabbering excitedly and laughing as they danced around him. He deciphered their words as "White man drum!, white man drum!" It was a safe bet they'd never seen a white man play a drum before.

Suddenly the *sorcier* stopped, and within a beat the chief also quit playing. Danny felt wrenched out of the experience, but reluctantly played a concluding figure as well, ending with an emphatic flam. His arms burned from the exertion, sweat dripped down the stubble on his chin. His ears buzzed from the noise. Unable to restrain himself, Danny began laughing with delight.

The *sorcier* said something, which Anatole translated. *"Vous avez l'esprit de batteur."* You have the spirit of a drummer.

With a throbbing hand, Danny squeezed Anatole's bare shoulder and nodded. *"Oui."*

The chief also congratulated him, thanking him for sharing his white man's music with the village. Danny found that ironic, since he had come here to pick up a rich African flavor for his compositions. But Danny could record his impressions in new songs; the village of Kabas had no way of keeping what he had brought to them.

The withered *sorcier* picked up one of the drums at his side, and Danny recognized it as the small drum the old man had been finishing in the dim hut that afternoon. He fixed his deep gaze on Danny for a moment, then handed it to him.

Anatole sat up, alarmed, but bit off a comment he had intended to make. Danny nodded in reassurance and in delight he took the new drum. He held it to his chest and inclined his head deeply to show his appreciation. *"Merci!"*

Anatole took Danny's hand to lead him away from the walled courtyard. The chief clapped his hands and barked something to the other boys, who looked at Anatole with glee before they got up and scurried to the huts for sleeping. Anatole stared nervously at Danny, but Danny didn't understand what had just occurred.

He repeated his thanks, bowing again to the chief and *sorcier*, but the two of them just stared at him. He was reminded of an East African scene: a pair of lions sizing up their prey. He shook his head to clear the morbid thought, and followed Anatole.

In the village proper, one of the round thatched huts had been swept for Danny to sleep in. Outside, his bicycle leaned against a tree, no doubt guarded during the day by the little man with the enormous cutlass. Anatole seemed uneasy, wanting to say something, but afraid.

Trying to comfort him, Danny opened his pack and withdrew a stick of chewing gum for the boy. Anatole boy spoke rapidly, gushing his thanks. Other boys suddenly materialized from the shadows with childish murder in their eyes. They tried to take the gum from Anatole, but he popped it in his mouth and ran off. "Hey!" Danny shouted, but Anatole bolted into the night with the boys chasing after.

Wondering if Anatole was in any real danger, Danny removed the blanket and sleeping bag from his bike, then carried them inside the guest hut. He decided the boy could take care of himself, that he had spent his life as the whipping boy for the other sons of the chief. The thought drained some of the exhilaration from the memory of the evening's performance.

His legs ached after the torturous ride upland from Garoua, and he fantasized briefly about sitting in the Jacuzzi in the capital suite of some five-star hotel. He considered how wonderful it would be to sip on some cold champagne, or a scotch on the rocks.

Instead, he lifted the gift drum, inspecting it. He would find some way to use it on the next album, add a rich African tone to the music. Paul Simon and Peter Gabriel had done it, though the style of Blitzkreig's music was a bit more ... aggressive.

He would not tell anyone about the human skin, especially the customs officials. He tried without success to decipher the mystical swirling patterns carved into the wood, the interwoven curves, circles, and knots. It made him dizzy.

Danny closed his eyes and began to play the drum, quietly so as not to disturb the other villagers. But as the sound reached his ears, he snapped his eyes open. The tone from the drum was flat and weak, like a cheap tourist tom-tom, plastic over a coffee can.

He frowned at the gift drum. Where was the rich reverberation, the primal pulse of the earth? He tapped again, but heard only an empty and hollow sound, soulless. Danny scowled, wondering if the *sorcier* had ruined the drum by accident, then decided to get rid of it by giving it to the unsuspecting White Man who wouldn't know the difference.

Angry and uneasy, Danny set the African drum next to him; he would try it again in the morning. He could play it for the chief, show him its flat tone. Perhaps they would exchange it. Maybe he would have to buy another one.

He hoped Anatole was all right.

Danny sat down to pull the thorns and prickers from his clothes. The village women had provided him with two plastic basins of water for bathing, one for soaping and scrubbing, the other for rinsing. The warm water felt refreshing on his face, his neck. After stripping off his pungent socks, he rinsed his toes and soles.

The night stillness was hypnotic, and as he spread his sleeping bag and stretched out on it, he felt as if he were seeping into the cloth, into the ground, swallowed up in sleep... .

Anatole woke him up only a few moments later, shaking him and whispering harshly in his ear. Dirt, blood, and bruises covered the boy's wiry body, and his clothes had been torn in a scuffle. He didn't seem to care. He kept shaking Danny.

But it was already too late.

Danny sat up, blinking his eyes. Sharp pains like a bear trap ripped through his chest. A giant hand had wrapped around his torso and would squeeze until his ribs popped free of his spine.

He gasped, opening and closing his mouth, but could not give voice to his agony. He grabbed Anatole's withered arm, but the boy struggled away, searching for something. Black spots swam in his eyes. He tried to breathe, but his chest wouldn't let him. He began slipping, sliding down an endless cliff into blackness.

Anatole finally reached an object on the floor of the hut. He snatched it up with his good hand, tucked it firmly under his withered arm, and began to thump on it.

The drum!

As the boy rapped out a slow steady beat, Danny felt the iron band loosen around his heart. Blood rushed into his head again, and he drew a deep breath. Dizziness continued to swim around him, but the impossible pain receded. He clutched his chest, rubbing his sternum. He uttered a breathy thanks to Anatole.

Had he just suffered a heart attack? Good God, all the fast living had decided to catch up to him while he was out in the middle of nowhere, far from any hope of medical attention!

Then he realized with a chill that the sounds from the gift drum were now rich and echoey, with the unearthly depth he remembered from the other drums. Anatole continued his slow rhythm, and suddenly Danny recognized it. A heartbeat.

What was it the boy had told him inside the sorcier's hut — that the magical drums could steal a man's heartbeat? *"Ton coeur c'est dans ici,"* Anatole said, continuing his drumming. Your heartbeat lives in here now.

Danny remembered the gaunt, shambling man in the marketplace of Garoua, obsessively tapping the drum from Kabas as if his life depended on it, until his hide-wrapped fingers were bloodied. Had that man also escaped his fate in the village, and fled south?

"You had the spirit of a drummer," Anatole said in his pidgin French, "and now the drum has your spirit." As if to emphasize his statement, as if he knew a White Man would be skeptical of such magic, Anatole ceased his rhythm on the drum.

The claws returned to Danny's heart, and the vise in his chest clamped back down. His heart had stopped beating. Heart beats, drumbeats—

The boy stopped only long enough to convince Danny, then started the beat again. He looked with pleading eyes in the shadowy hut. *"Je vais avec toi!"* I go with you. Let me be your heartbeat. From now on.

Leaving his sleeping bag behind, Danny staggered out of the guest hut to his bicycle resting against an acacia tree. The rest of the village was dark and silent, and the next morning they would expect to find him dead and cold on his blankets; and the new drum would have the same resonant quality, the same throbbing of a captured spirit, to add to their collection. The sound of White Man's music for Kabas.

"*Allez!*" Anatole whispered as Danny climbed aboard his bike. Go! What was he supposed to do now? The boy ran in front of him along the narrow track. Danny did not fear navigating the rugged trail by moonlight, with snakes and who-knows-what abroad in the grass, as much as he feared staying in Kabas and being there when the chief and the *sorcier* came to look at his body in the morning, and no doubt to appraise their pale new drum skin.

But how long could Anatole continue his drumming? If the beat stopped for only a moment, Danny would seize up. They would have to take turns sleeping. Would this nightmare continue after he had left the vicinity of the village? Distance had not helped the shambling man in the marketplace in Garoua.

Would this be the rest of his life?

Stricken with panic, Danny nodded to the boy, just wanting to be out of there and not knowing what else to do. Yes, I'll take you with me. What other choice do I have? He pedaled his bike away from Kabas, crunching on the rough dirt path. Anatole jogged in front of him, tapping on the drum.

And tapping.

And tapping.

◦ ✧ ◦

**Kevin J. Anderson** is the international bestselling author of well over a hundred novels, best known for his work in the Dune universe with Brian Herbert, his *Star Wars* novels, and his original epics *The Saga of Seven Suns* and *Terra Incognita*.

**Neil Peart** is the world-renowned drummer and lyricist for legendary rock band Rush, as well as the author of several books, including *Roadshow*, *Ghost Rider*, and *Far and Away*. In a landmark project, Anderson and Peart worked together to write the novel version of the new Rush album "Clockwork Angels."

# ZOMBIE DESCARTES WRITES A PERSONAL AD

### ～ Carolyn Clink ～

Long-retired philosopher zombie seeks
experiential female zombie
to share unconscious moments.

Likes: the pineal gland, animal spirits,
brains, and the theater.
Dislikes: bats, koans, and Chinese rooms.

Let us shamble through the streets in search of brains.
Let us lie by the fire — but not too closely.
Let us stare into each other's vacant eyes.

Contact me if you have the qualia needed
to reduce our dualism
to moanism.

# Writer's Block

## ⁓ Sean Costello ⁓

"Aw shit!"

Darrin Keene hammered out the back-space key, tucked a well-used piece of Taperaser over the typo and struck the error into oblivion. Then he hit the proper key, completing the word. He re-read the short paragraph he had been labouring over for the past half-hour.

> The night was a page torn from an arctic explorer's diary, the last page, unfinished, a page left rasping in the wind next to his frozen body. A cutting northerly rattled the panes, howling around the eaves of the cabin like a starving she-wolf. Snow buried everything beneath its crippling weight. Beyond the cabin the ice-sheeted lake creaked and groaned. It was a bleak night, a night through which nothing warm could endure.

"Starving she-wolf," Darrin said aloud, his tone self-mocking and derisive. "Cripes, are *you* a sick puppy."

But it *was* that kind of a night. Even Darrin's weighty metaphors and foreboding adjectives fell short of describing it. It was the dead of February and the storm beyond the single-pane windows was fierce and unrelenting.

Darrin had rented this isolated cabin in the British Columbia foothills for exactly that reason. The setting. What better backdrop for an aspiring horror novelist to work against? What richer font of inspiration?

*But Jesus,* he thought, *what a shit-kicker of a storm.* It seemed to distract more than inspire him. He pushed his chair back from the old Underwood and crossed to the stone hearth where the fire had dwindled to coals. The wood frame cabin was uninsulated and a bitch to heat (*she-bitch* he thought laughingly). He tossed a few chunks of dry birch onto the coals and moved closer, spreading his numbing fingers as the papery bark crackled into bright yellow flames.

It was eight o'clock and dark as pitch. Darrin had by now give up hope of Shelley arriving tonight, and his sense of longing, developed over the course of the snailing and lonesome week up here, flared like the bark in the fire. He had spent the better part of the past two days thinking of nothing but the voluptuous curves and valleys of Shelley's body, spread out hot and willing on the sheepskin rug in front of the fireplace. He could almost see her there now, in the pixie dance of the flames.

*Ah, Shelley ... warm, mammoth-breasted Shelley.*

The image vanished as another took its place, this one ugly — Shelley stranded and freezing in a broken-down Honda Civic halfway up that godforsaken road from the village of Golden, six winding miles down in the valley below. He hope to Christ she hadn't ventured out into this hell-hole of a night. And he realized then, in that instant of terrible possibilities, that he loved Shelley. It really was more than the out-of-this-world humping they managed together. Somewhere along the line he had begun to honestly love her.

But Shelley was no dummy. She wouldn't even have thought about trying to get up here on a night like this. She knew better; she'd grown up in Golden, had heard enough of the real-life horror stories to by-God *know* better.

Darrin stood there awhile longer, soaking the warmth of the fire, then returned to the Underwood. And from somewhere out there beyond the lake, he heard the mournful cry of a real wolf. Hackles rose on the back of his neck. He hit the tab key and began a new paragraph.

> **But the cold thing, the bloodless creature conceived in some deep and stinking cave where even God could not see, was bothered by the storm. The shrieking wind aroused It, beckoned**

It. It rose from the muck and poked a twisted claw up through three feet of black ice. The winter air instantly froze the damp layering Its scales, but its taloned digits flexed and shed the icy crust like a molting exoskeleton.

A deep, tormented groan rose from the ice as it cracked once more from beneath. A second limb poked through into the air. And then a third.

Darrin smirked, excited by the dank menace he was creating. He loved monster stories, had since childhood; Frankenstein, Mr. Hyde, The Thing from the 'Fantastic Four' comics, The Blob, countless others. He knew that credible horror tales, things that could *really* happen, had a wider appeal, were more marketable. But the monster stories, usually short, he wrote for an audience of one; Darrin Keene. He kept them like treasures in a special section of his portable filing cabinet, pulling them out when the light was low and the mood macabre. If he ever got famous he would put them all together into a collection; *Miscreations*, by Darrin Keene.

He got up again, paced in front of the fire, trying to visualize the shit-encrusted aberration that had thus far poked three scaly appendages up through three feet of ice. How in hell did you come up with a monster someone else hadn't already conceived? Or did it really matter what the mindless flesh-eater looked like, as long as it left a trail of gore? These were the questions plaguing the mind of Darrin Keene, horror writer.

He moved in front of the large window overlooking the lake. And as he watched the twists and swirls of the wind-whipped snow he heard the eerie moan and faint thunder of the ice shifting on the lake. It was sure as hell a creepy sound. The lake was huge and deep, dotted here and there with rocky islands. The gale-force winds had blown its iced-over surface clean; now it looked like a sprawling black hole in the midst of blue desert dunes.

Again he returned to the typewriter, sat, re-read the few scant lines. Then stared at the keys, his mind a blank. How would this bit of aquatic pestilence look? He simply couldn't conjure a unique image. And he thought he knew why. Tonight, right now, he should have been tangled on the sheepskin rug with Shelley the Amazon woman, Shelley the hungry she-wolf. Humping. Like an animal.

*Shit!*

It was more than that though. There was still this diffuse worry that just maybe she *had* set out to drive up here. If that was the case, then she should have arrived more than an hour ago. Darrin couldn't bear the thought of Shelley lost in this storm. A dull sense of helplessness nagged him. He was totally isolated up here, had *chosen* to be isolated, couldn't even pick up one of Ma Bell's little miracle machines and dial the ten simple digits that would put his mind at ease.

But it was more even than that. It was this freaking blizzard. The storm was giving him the willies. It was cold. He couldn't imagine a place colder, more lifeless and desolate, than the endless sprawl of hills and fir trees beyond this cabin. If a man got lost out there it was tits-up Bubba. February in the Rockies. Absolute-fucking-zero. Life-forms ... none.

*Except one*, he thought, shivering. *Me, Darrin-the-bohunk Keene, whose lover's nuts are in serious danger of being frozen off*, a thought that for some reason brought an image of brass monkeys.

Now *there* was something to think about. That whoring wind licking down the chimney, trying to snuff the fire; the very real possibility that *he* could freeze to death up here.

He hit the tab key.

No ideas.

Then it dawned. He reached into his jean-jacket pocket and pulled out a joint, a cigar-shaped masterpiece that might have been rolled by the legendary Bob Marley himself. He had nearly forgotten about his strapping mind-mangler. It has been intended for he and Shelley; she really got off sexually when she was high. And when Shelley got off, so did Ruthy Keene's seventh son Darrin. In spades.

He lit up, using a wood match which he struck on the side of the typewriter. A gift from his dad, this old Underwood, a throwaway from the office where he worked. Manual. No electricity up here anyway. Typing by oil-lamp. He filled his lungs, holding back the sudden urge to cough, then exhaled a smooth column of blue, aromatic smoke. He felt immediately light-headed. 'Lamb's breath' the skin-head at the Steer and Beer Saloon had called it, from Jamaica, best buy for the money in the whole damn town of Golden, B.C. Darrin sat back, filling his lungs.

And outside the wind squalled, its pitch growing even more menacing as the cannabis did its work on Darrin Keene's gray cells.

Suddenly there was a dreadful crash behind him. He lurched to his feet, dropping the joint, knocking the press-back chair to the floor in a clatter of wood against wood. He pivoted, bringing his fists up in a defensive reflex.

Snow billowed along the narrow hallway from the door like chaff belched from a hay baler. The flames crackled in the hearth, thinning as if to extinguish. The storm was in the living room.

Darrin bolted into the hallway, instantly chilled to the marrow. For an eager moment he thought it might be Shelley, arrived after all. But it had been the wind, kicking the door open with all the force of a drunken lumberjack's workboot. Shards of ice stung his eyes as he leaned, literally leaned into the tunnel of wind that was the hallway. He caught a brief glimpse of the blue-white hump that was his snow-covered 64' Windsor as he shoved the heavy door tight to its frame. He threw the big iron bolt then leaned his back against the door, looking with a sort of wonder at the dusting of snow in the hallway; diamonds glinting lamp light. He was feeling the dope. He had a sudden desperate longing for Shelley.

The cabin creaked, wind soughed angrily through the pines. For a wild moment Darrin thought of pulling on his parka and going out there, digging out the Chrysler and taking his chances. But no, that would be suicide. The original Mr. Freeze.

He went back to the Underwood.

> Even in the harsh blizzard air It stank of much and ooze and rot. Its single misshapen eye found the yellow rectangle of light that was the cabin window, and was drawn to it. The gob of putrid protoplasm that functioned as Its brain, a malign nerve centre knowing only hunger, propelling the beastly thing forward, up the snow-crusted incline toward that warm yellow spill.

"Okay," Darrin said aloud, pleased. He retrieved the partially smoked roach and re-lit it. "*Now* this ugly sucker's coming to life. Oooh mama, I can almost smell the pig." He filled his lungs and exhaled, filled and exhaled. Already he could feel the weed heightening his imagination.

*Time for a scene change*.

He took a final lingering toke then pinched the lit end of the butt between his thumb and forefinger. A glut of sparks fell to the rough-hewn floor. He stamped them beneath his boot. He thought of Shelley and sheepskin, then started typing, two-finger, fast.

Doug Hamilton lay naked before the fire, ankles crossed comfortably, sipping champagne, watching Sharon as she slipped out of the silk undergarments. Her skin was dark, her eyes a rich moss-green, her lips full and moist. She moved with slow, erotic grace, turning, bending, giving her man a languishing view of all her lovely parts. Then she draped herself over him, tenting his face with her luxurious, jet black mane, brushing his lips with kisses like velvet. He put his champagne aside but the glass tipped, sending amber fingerlets bubbling over the rustic wood floor.

The cabin belonged to Doug's brother. And Doug had it for the next six days, the cabin and Sharon and miles of idyllic isolation. Even the storm seemed perfect for their first night alone. It drew them together somehow, intensified the hearthside warmth of the place.

Darrin paused again, slapping his hands together with malicious delight. "Got it up yet Douglas?" he said to the typed page in front of him. "I hope so, because pretty soon 'It' is gonna rip it right off for you." He cackled. He was stoned. His stomach growled. His mouth was dirt-dry. Although he was not in the least sleepy, his eyelids were leaden. He grabbed the box of Frito's Corn Chips sitting beside the Underwood and dug in.

*Munchies, Manfred. You got the munchies.*

He looked at the page, deciding whether or not he should allow Doug Hamilton to have his nooky before becoming an hors-d'oeuvre for a mutant. He considered constructing a full page of gruesomely detailed hard-core; even worse, he weighed the possibilities of Sharon and the thing ... catchy title ... *Sex Slave of the Mud Lake Mutant.*

"Whoa, Darrin-me-boy," he said to his bleary-eyed reflection in the window glass. "You're decompensating now. You got a good little monster tale goin' here. Don't screw it up."

He wiped his chip-greased fingers onto his jeans and typed. He decided he would make the cabin in the story identical to the one he was in (except warmer), recalling what a wise old English prof has once told him: *Write what you know.* And he wanted to use the front door banging in the open wind; that had been suitably freaky. That would be how the eating-machine got in. Then it would deek, or maybe ooze, into the kitchenette, hide around the corner while Doug went back to the fireplace...

A deliberate scratching sound behind him made Darrin turn violently on his chair, enough to nearly topple it and himself to the floor.

"What in Jesus-name was that?!" he blurted out. His voice hung on the cool cabin air. The scratching sound came again, on the apex of a powerful gust, and Darrin saw the branches of a nearby tree scraping at the north window. "Paranoid, Keene," he mumbled, chuckling unconvincingly. "Par-a-noid!"

He thought about the scaly Mud Lake Mutant. Then he typed.

> The cabin door swing open with a nerve-jangling crash that made both Sharon and Doug yelp in sudden fear. Snow billowed into the room on sub-zero gusts.
>
> "The damn door blew open," Doug said, annoyed and at the same time relieved to have a simple explanation for the frightening intrusion. He grabbed his housecoat and pulled it on, noticing the spilled champagne and the oddly crimson hue it had created on the floorboards. That it looked like a pool of drying blood chilled him in a manner distinct from that caused by the bracing air. Just an illusion of color caused by the reflection of the fire, he decided, and started along the hallway to the door. His knees and ankles burned in the glacial wind. Sharon curled closer to the fire. The start had destroyed her mood.
>
> Doug pushed the door shut, fired the heavy bolt and cursed under his breath. The keen pitch of arousal he had been reaching had abruptly evaporated. He knew it would be the same for Sharon.
>
> He noticed the odor first, like fish gone over. Then, as he stepped around the thin patina of snow in the doorway, he noticed something else, beneath his bare feet; a cold gelatinous film, like the goo on refrigerated turkey he thought unpleasantly.
>
> *What in hell...?*
>
> The sound came next, a slithering sound punctuated by rushed, stertorous breathing...

Darrin paused. There was a sudden lull in the wind. And that bothered him. Because the scratching sound was there again; in the freak quiet it seemed to be coming from *inside* the cabin, from the kitchenette.

His breath quickened, then caught like a piece of meat in his throat. He rose off the chair, remaining in a tense crouch. He picked up a length of birch from the wood pile and weighed it in his hands.

"Shelley?" he said with a voice that cracked.

No answer. Of course; he'd bolted the door from the inside.

The wind held its curious silence, as if waiting. In the distance, the wolf howled hauntingly. Birch, blackened and glowing, crackled in the fireplace.

Darrin walked on tip-toes toward the kitchenette, holding his breath. Floor boards creaked beneath his feet, the sound amplified in the eerie calm. It was as if some celestial movie crew had suddenly switched off the machinery of a simulated blizzard:

*Scene change ... next night ... dead silence ... cry of lone wolf.*

Darrin edged his body around the corner and into the kitchenette, the birch log held over his head like a club. The kitchen was empty. He sighed heavily. "Rodents," he mumbled quietly, "varmints." Then he caught the faintest whiff of rot. He sniffed at the air. Ridiculously, he looked down at the wood floor. For turkey goo. There was none. Of course.

But what was that faintly rotten smell? He opened the cooler containing his provisions; the smells form there were good smells, fresh. This was the smell of something dead. Long dead. He wondered why he hadn't noticed it before. Maybe there *had* been a rodent, a field mouse or something, which had frozen to death in some dark corner of the cabin in December of January and then begun to rot over the course of the two weeks Darrin had been heating the place. He opened the cupboard beneath the sink, rooted around, found nothing, shrugged. Then he continued though the kitchen and along the hallway to the main room.

His eye caught movement, something so fleeting it could have been an illusion. He prayed it *had* been an illusion. He'd noticed it as he stepped out of the hallway, something black and glistening, snake-like, whipping around the corner into the south section of the cabin where the Underwood sat on the make-shift deck.

Darrin really wished now that he hadn't smoked that reefer.

He waited, listening. The wind outside was resuming its former pitch. Darrin welcomed that now; it blocked the smaller cabin noises which were threatening to freak him right out of his woollies. He wondered what that creep he'd bought the weed from had laced it with. He knew that all kinds of shit could turn up in a bag of weed, just to give it that extra little kick; horse tranquilizer, low quality smack. There must have been *something* in it, because he didn't usually hallucinate on grass.

*Hallucination, right?*

Crouching, truly frightened now, he moved to the corner, peered around it and down along the adjoining wall. Nothing there. *Okay.* He straightened up.

But what if it had slithered around the *next* corner and back into the kitchenette? He checked the floor boards again; they were dry, unsoiled. What if...?

*Are you going whacko, Keene? Forget it! Write!*

A noise. In the kitchenette. Scraping.

"Shelley?" he asked the emptiness. "If that's you screwing around out there, I'll—" He remembered the bolted door. Unless she — or something — had gotten in when the door blew open.

"Jesus Christ," he said in a whisper, "what would Douglas Hamilton do now?"

*Go and look. What else?*

He lurched toward the kitchenette and peered around the corner. Bugger-all there. He skated the kitchen floor, looked down the hallway. Nothing. He moved rapidly to the next corner, nearly running. Zip. Then, waving the length of birch and whooping like a war-crazed Indian, he bolted full-throttle around the rectangle that housed the bathroom, twice, grabbing the barnwood corners as pivits, his boots thudding the floorboards like sledge hammers.

Half way around the cabin the third time he stopped by the Underwood, leaning one hand on the back of the chair, panting, feeling like an utter idiot. A dog chasing its tail. A drugged-up kid on a horseless carousel. But he understood now how Doug Hamilton would be feeling and wanted to get it into words while it was still fresh. Coming clear too, was a mental picture of his imaginary Mud Lake Monster. He took a final quick glance behind him then sat in front of the typewriter, scrolled the typed page up on the carriage and re-read the last sentence.

> **The sound came next, a slithering sound punctuated by rushed, stertorous breathing...**

And then Darrin heard it. Plain as day.

Something cold, rotten, inhumanly powerful took hold of the top of Darrin Keene's head and twisted. Darrin caught a glimpse of it just before the lamp-light next to the Underwood extinguished for all eternity.

Oddly, Darrin's last thought as he looked up was: *That's it!*

⁕

On the afternoon of the next day, Shelley England followed the big yellow Township of Golden snow plow up Shield Road toward the cabin. The plow operator was a second cousin of hers, Tommy Thomson, and although he wasn't supposed to (could in fact lost his job for it, he had informed her bravely), Tommy veered off the main road and cleaned out the three hundred yards of track leading in to the cabin. As Tommy turned his machine to leave, Shelley gave him a toothy grin that made him wish for the millionth time since grade school that Shelley E. hadn't been born his cousin.

Shelley parked the cancerous Civic behind Darrin's snow-covered Windsor. She was surprised to see the cabin door ajar. But the day was sunny and balmy, as so often happened up here after a storm, and she guessed he was just airing out the cabin. It surprised her too that he hadn't come out when the plow lumbered up to the doorstep. Perhaps he was out on the racks, catching the rays.

Then she noticed there were no footprints outside the cabin, and a vague worry came over her. Haltingly, she approached the open door.

The snow had blown for a straight thirty-six hours, drifting most of the way up the north wall of the cabin. The window on that side was completely covered. Inside, the hallway was darkly shadowed. Shelley stepped in.

"Darrin?"

The worry diminished when Shelley realized he was probably just hiding on her. Darrin was a clown. Shelley liked that about him; always a good time. But she hated to be scared. Darrin loved to administer the good old 'Canada goose'.

"Darrin, you little shit. Talk to me. If you frighten me..."

She tip-toed into the kitchenette with her backside to the wall. The smell of rotten fish was abrupt and strong.

"Darrin? What have you been eating up here?"

She rounded the corner, irritated now with his silence. That was when she saw the press-back chair lying on the floor in front of the Underwood.

She fainted when she saw the spray of congealed blood tracking across the typewriter keys and up onto the unfinished page in the carriage.

~ ✧ ~

The forensic people verified the blood type as Darrin's. The police found no footprints in the snow, but did notice the large, healed-over rent in the ice. When Shelley beseeched them to send in drivers the police refused, explaining that it was too dangerous in this weather. They thought the hole in the ice was too large to have been made by a man anyway. When pressed for an alternate explanation, they could provide none. They told Shelley that if Darrin had in fact gone through the ice there was nothing to do but wait until spring. Then, they said, his body would probably turn up in the thaw.

But it never did.

~ ✧ ~

**Sean** grew up in an Ottawa neighborhood called 'The Glebe' in a time when Brylcreem ruled and cars were two-tone and built to last, playing drums and dreaming of becoming the next John Bonham. He still enjoys jamming to many classic riffs with his son, a guitarist and member of the rock band, *Stray Bullet*. Sean's first novel, *Eden's Eyes* was published in 1989 by Pocket Books and since then he has published five more novels. His seventh book is coming in the Fall of 2012 from Your Scrivener Press.

# Theater of the
# Vulnerable

## ⁂ Virginia O'Dine ⁂

I could hear them flooding in, the audience pouring in the foyer, lining up for their turn in the brain scanner. They are all elaborate puppets, ready to be played, as they were watching the players.

We waited backstage for the call to take our turn through the device. It was getting late and we were starting to get nervous. Maybe there were malfunctions. Could we perform without the scan first? It was scary to think we had developed this dependency on it, on the extremes it created in our minds. We couldn't function without these extremes. Using our own naked talent was too much, too difficult for us to dig so deep into ourselves.

The audience was ready, waiting for me; so fresh from the brief stop they take in the lobby to pass through the brain scanner. They are read, spun into the framework of the performance, each a throbbing strand of a web not in their control.

The scanner analyzed individual brain function, and emitted an electrowave boost. This raises frequency of the gamma rhythms in our brains, making us more receptive to the influences of others who had the ability to exert some telepathic control. They are manipulated to be left wide open for the control of the actors on stage. Having real actors manipulate the audience's brain waves, and their perceptions, created a more vivid experience than common virtual reality.

We actors would go through the same process, yet we needed less electrowave manipulation than the audience. Already finely tuned to the receptivity required for good connections, with only a small boost, we were open and ready. Rarely, and sadly, the procedure would backfire, and the actor would be boosted into a frozen state. Getting on stage like a zombie, not recognizing those around him, or what he was to do with the audience waiting, waiting, for a motion, a word.

Oh no, there was my cue. I hadn't been through the scanner! I hadn't been prepared. I couldn't go on like this!

My heart raced unnaturally fast. My palms and all of my body were damp with a sheen of sweat. I swallowed, then stepped forward.

I breathed in hard, and my mind exploded into a bright stabbing streak of emptiness. I had no thoughts at all. My head was blank. I started to panic. Why was I here? I shouldn't be here. This is not the place for me. I was terrified. I could smell the anticipation and the fear swirling throughout the air. I could feel the web trembling, about to break soon if it wasn't held gently and given strength.

What was I supposed to do? It was very important. I knew that. I looked across at the people who were looking back at me. They were waiting; the agony in their eyes making it clear ... they were waiting for me. They were dying without me. One had tears forming in her eyes, a mask of horror starting to stretch across her face. Another was looking at me with a cruel malicious sneer. The crowd would slowly circle in and take us if we didn't keep them on their side.

I tried to swallow, but my mouth and throat were dry. I licked my lips with a raspy tongue and inhaled a shaky breath. I unclenched my toes within my shoes and tried to remember. I became distracted by the unfamiliar feeling of the clothing on my back. My skin crawled to think of the cloth that so many had worn; some worthy of the status it brought, many not.

My stomach turned. I sacrificed too much to be here. I left gaping holes in the world outside. How could I do that again? Now I was expected to prove the price of turmoil. The expectation was killer. A vein in my head began pulsating with loud agony. I squinted out into the audience, and the glowing emanations were visible. It was soothing in its pulsing steadiness. I focused on it.

The pain disappeared. Clenched muscles relaxed. Exhilaration and sweetness began flowing through my veins. My heart still pounded, but it only delivered life-giving adrenaline.

Calmness swept over all of us, with the ones nearest me feeling my transition back into myself. I could see the relief in their eyes as they saw me come into myself, then move back out.

I moved above and looked down upon all. That other voice swelled up inside of me. It was two-dimensional, yet I could pull the strings to make it all surreally believable. That other voice came pouring out of my mouth, taking me by surprise. It took control of my limbs. I had an awareness of myself, but no desire to go back in.

I was finally in control. I could feel the radiance of the audience and the cast around me. Even without my turn through the scanner to make me more receptive to both my character and the strings, I could see them plainly. I took hold of the strings attached to the people in the crowed. I could pull them up and down. Sideways. Taking them where I wanted. There was a string for every part of their conscious and sub-conscious. I tugged a string for laughter, filling my need. I yanked a thread connected to their individual guilt-ridden centres, feeling the overbearing silence push my power higher. I whipped around in a frenzy and grabbed the strings of the cast around me. My hands, my feet, my heart and my mind all chose their own, and interwove a web of magnificent proportions. I pulled and tied them all together, creating a single ecstasy for everyone.

It was exhilarating. First a tear, then a laugh. I was taking them all on the ride. My ride. They all came for less, and will go away with more.

Until the end.

The floor drops out from under us. The lights are gone. The strings snap, some slowly, some whipping back at us, leaving red gashes. The pop of destruction can be heard. All is dark. An eternity of solitude stretches over a single moment.

Then a thunderous roar. It is over. We will fade back into ourselves, with the effects of the scan subsiding, but not quite yet. The last pulses in the blood are fading. The yearning is still there, not quite satiated, and will only come back stronger tomorrow.

Moving from terror to ecstasy in a single moment. The rush that brings us back again and again.

◈

**Virginia O'Dine** is the publisher and editor of Bundoran Press, which offers dynamic and fresh Canadian Science Fiction and Fantasy novels to the world. She has edited The Okal Rel Universe Anthology and is an innovative collaborator in spaces beyond the printed page. Virginia's debut theatrical script, *Rollback* (which is based on the novel of the same name by Robert J. Sawyer) was performed in the Spring 2011 and won handfuls of awards at the Theatre BC Regional Zone Festival.

# The Day The Music Died

## ~ Randy McCharles ~

"We're going down!"

Alex could hardly hear the pilot over the noise of the diving Beechcraft Premier, not that he really needed to hear the words. The smoke and flames from the starboard engine told half the story. The port engine told the other half, having just stopped dead. Like he would be in about two minutes.

Despite his panic, Alex remembered the training he had received on how to put on a parachute. The straps were fairly simple, but his fingers trembled as he fitted the snaps and tightened the lines, and he could only hope that he had done it right.

The words of a song rang through Alex's head, *eight miles high and falling fast*. From Don Mclean's *American Pie*, a memorial for Buddy Holly's tragic death in a plane crash. Also a Beechcraft, if memory served. Soon the name Alex Thorp would join the list of tragic musicians whose lives were cut short by a fall from the sky. Jim Reeves. Otis Redding. Jim Croce. Ricky Nelson. Stevie Ray Vaughan. He wondered if anyone would write him a song?

Probably not.

The pilot opened the cabin door and Alex was half blinded by lightning as Randy and Glen jumped. The pilot waved for him to go, so he did, the wind and rain hitting his face like ice. As he had been shown — how long ago now? Three years? — he pulled his ripcord after a count of two.

*The Day The Music Died* by Randy McCharles

Not that it would do any good. They were flying over the middle of Lake Ontario. It was night. It was winter. It was stormy. They would all hit the water and freeze to death. It was over.

Alex forced his eyes open against the icy rain so that he could see his death coming, but all he saw was black. Black sky. Black water. Black rain. Which was which, he couldn't tell. He forced himself to sing. "Bye, bye, Miss American—

⇜ ✧ ⇝

Alex could still hear the song in his head. He opened his lips and mumbled, "met a girl who sang the blues…"

"He appears to be awake," said a voice.

Alex opened his eyes.

He was in a hospital room. Light filtered in from the blinds covering a window, causing him to blink. Three men stood at the foot of his hospital bed. Two were dressed in white from head to toe. Even their hair was white. If all three men looked that way, Alex would think this was Heaven rather than a hospital, but the third was dressed in black, with black hair and beard. He seemed younger than the other two.

Alex stared at the younger man in black. "You must be the villain," he said, and realized he was giddy. They must have given him some mighty powerful pain relievers.

The man seemed unmoved by the accusation. One of the other two men remarked, "What an odd thing to say."

Alex blinked again and tried to clear his head. He couldn't remember anything about hitting the water or being rescued. "Am I dead?"

"That is the expected response," said the other man in white.

Something was off. These doctors had the worst bedside manner Alex had ever seen. A wave of fear flushed the giddiness out of him. "I am here, you know. You can talk *to* me as well as about me."

All three men stared at him silently, then the one who spoke last said, "Interesting." Then the two men in white left the room.

"What was that all about?" said Alex. "You are doctors? Right?"

"I am Simon," said the man in black. He didn't move or speak further. He just stood there, watching.

Alex cracked his neck and lifted his arms, then kicked with his feet. "I seem to be all right. Not even bruised."

"Yes," said Simon. "The extraction was a complete success."

"Are Randy and Glen OK? The pilot?"

Simon's expression did not change. "They died."

"Oh," said Alex. The sadness hit him harder than he expected. He had known Randy for three years, but never really liked him much. Glen he'd only known a few months. The pilot not at all; he didn't even know the guy's name. Survivor's guilt. That was it. The song was back in his head. *This'll be the day that I die.*

"Can you do a concert without them?"

"What?" asked Alex, the words of the song fleeing from his thoughts.

"Your fans are waiting for you," Simon said.

"This is hardly the—" The words froze on his lips. Another man in white — Alex was sure it was neither of the men he had seen before — entered the room carrying a guitar, carrying it like it might bite him. Even from across the room Alex could see that one of the strings was missing and the other five were slack.

"Can you play this?" asked Simon.

"Well, no," said Alex. "One of the strings is broken."

"There are others in the museum," Simon said. He waved a hand at the man in white and he left the room. "I will have them brought to you."

"Museum?" That was one weirdness too many. "Where am I?" he demanded.

"Toronto," said Simon.

"It doesn't feel like Toronto," Alex countered.

Simon pursed his lips, the first sign of emotion he had seen from anyone since he had woken up.

"It is not the Toronto you know," the man in black said.

Alex frowned. "What's that supposed to mean?"

"When I said you were extracted I did not mean from Lake Ontario. I meant from time. The year is 2083."

⇒ ✧ ⇐

Alex looked out from the stage onto a sea of blank faces. He tapped on the microphone and heard a thump from the speakers, letting him know that the mic was live. He strummed an E Minor chord on the decades old museum piece guitar and listened to the brittle thrum of strings long past their prime. The chord was more melancholy than he remembered.

Almost as melancholy as he felt.

## The Day The Music Died by Randy McCharles

Dead and gone. Everything he knew. Everyone he knew. He had died seventy years ago. Or would have died if he hadn't been plucked out of time and space moments before hitting the water.

Simon had shown him the newspaper article. A copy of the article. From the archives. Lost at sea it said. Or at lake. The first rescue boat arrived hours after the crash. They found the plane. None of the bodies. Washed away. Sunk to the bottom. Eaten by fish. No one knew.

"Did anyone write a song about me?" Alex had asked.

Simon gave him a long look, then said, "No."

"So why me? Of all the people who ever died, why choose me to rescue from an untimely death?"

Simon's face continued expressionless. "Right time. Right place."

When Alex persisted Simon added, "Our time technology is very new. Finding artists about to die and honing in on them is not simple. All attempts before yours failed."

"Artists?" Alex asked. "Why artists?"

And then the other shoe fell.

August 21, 2051. That was the real day the music died. Not February 3, 1959 when Buddy Holly's plane crashed into a field outside Clear Lake, Iowa. It was heralded as a medical breakthrough. A cure for clinical depression and all related illnesses. Not a treatment. A cure. The DNA strands responsible for depression and a variety of mental illnesses had long since been discovered and catalogued. But it wasn't until 2051 that a means of correcting DNA flaws was approved and a treatment provided.

The lame walked and the blind were made to see. And the mentally ill recalled what was revealed.

People came in droves for the simple one time treatment. Those with mental illnesses abandoned Prozac and a hundred other medications forever. And it seemed that most everyone had one kind of mental ailment or another. Over the next few years the human population was healthier than it had ever been. But there were other changes. Changes that crept in so slowly that no one noticed, until finally, the church bells all were broken.

Alex had sat through the audio visual presentation Simon had prepared. A twenty minute documentary of the Father, Son, and Holy Ghost catching the last train for the coast. The worst part was that he understood it. The scientists, for all their genius, had been utterly foolish. They hadn't removed the need for Prozac.

They had made the Prozac permanent. People didn't just no longer have mood swings. They no longer had moods. They couldn't feel.

There was one thing Alex didn't understand, though.

"What do you want from me?" he asked.

"We want you to be our muse," Simon said.

"Is that all?" Actually, Alex was relieved.

In his youth he'd watched all sorts of weird sci-fi crap where people had been plucked from everyday life to mate with monsters or have hideous experiments performed on them, all to save a dying race. He suspected that if the people of 2083 still had some emotions left, that's exactly what would happen. But all their limited imagining could come up with was to steal a musician from the past to sing them a few songs. And not even a good musician. It was just as well they couldn't feel disappointment.

The audience Simon had brought together was huge but silent. Alex strummed another chord. He'd asked Simon why they needed a living, breathing muse to play for them when they had all of recorded history to work with, and Simon had answered that recordings failed to move them. "Live music has more power. Unfortunately, we are no longer very good at it."

Alex couldn't argue with either statement. Live music does have more power. And the emotionless people of 2083 would be lucky to be able to play dirges in the dark. But neither did he think his playing would do any good. Just as you need emotion to make music, you need emotion to listen to it. Simon's plan was doomed to fail. Still, the show must go on.

One last strum and Alex decided what he would play. Not one of his own songs. No one among the massive audience would be familiar with any of his work, and none of it was much good anyway. Instead he would play a classic. Something fitting. He strummed the opening bars and then joined in. "A long, long, time ago..."

⁓ ✧ ⁓

The second candidate they had managed to retrieve had awoken ahead of schedule. Despite his eagerness, Simon entered the hospital room at a leisurely pace. His façade wasn't really necessary, not anymore, but he had lived with it so long that it had become part of him.

As a boy he had been ashamed of the black he was forced to wear because his DNA was not pristine, yet not sufficiently damaged to warrant the *treatment*. His internal shortcomings were known, and the clothes he wore made them public. Still, it behooved him to behave like his emotionless peers in white lest his outrageous behavior be deemed worthy of receiving the treatment after all. And so he had built his façade.

As he grew older, however, he watched as society continued to spiral into despondency until it even lost interest in the treatment. Those few born who failed the test were given the black robes but not the treatment, no matter how damaged they were. Many died of illness for which treatments no longer existed. Some lived.

Only later in life, as he earned his degrees in science and medicine, had Simon understood the unique position he and the few others like him were in. They could save the human race from its slow descent into extinction. They could propagate their imperfect DNA in the gene pool, restoring what it actually meant to be human. Save Mankind from itself. Only the black-cloaked were too few.

And so he had conceived the Muse Program. A hopeless plan for evocating emotion and creativity that only the emotionless could believe in. And with each failure they would try again; the emotionless never lost patience. And slowly, the population of imperfect genes would grow. Children would be born, unhindered by perfect genes. Those with serious problems would die, but the rest would wear the black, as only an emotionless society could dictate. Eventually society would evolve, reverting, Simon hoped, back toward something like it once had been. Or, at least, a society with more inspiration.

The musician they had retrieved, twenty-three years old, was sitting up in bed and looking around the room in alarm.

"Welcome," Simon said. "To the year 2083. I must tell you that I am one of your biggest fans."

Simon had to work extra hard to suppress the smile on his face as Buddy Holly stared at him.

◌ ✧ ◌

**Randy McCharles** has appeared in *Tesseracts Eleven* and *Tesseracts Twelve*. His novella, which appeared in *T12*, was reprinted in *Year's Best Fantasy 9* edited by David G. Hartwell and Kathryn

Cramer and won an Aurora Award. Randy is an avid reader of epic fantasy and science fiction, regularly writes short stories for public readings and helps organize literary events and Science Fiction & Fantasy Conventions in his home town of Calgary, Alberta. He co-chaired the first Calgary Westercon in 2005, the Calgary World Fantasy Convention in 2008, and currently chairs When Words Collide. Randy is a long-time member of IFWA, the Imaginative Fiction Writers Association.

# Microfiche, or, The Indexing of History

― Sandra Kasturi ―

Having said farewell to the archiving
Of newspapers long since, we now turn
To the exigencies of striving
To vanish the fossil record and burn
The vested past from collected memory.
Are we fuelled by the languishing sorrows
Of our ancestors, their deathwatch hum gone awry,
Pushing us faster toward tomorrows
That will be lost, that even now disappear
Into the fragmented mosaic
Of a misremembered future? What austere
Visions render us so mute and prosaic—
From the cradle on, we grasp with fingers
Senseless and blind to all that lingers.

# BLINK

## ☙ Michael Kelly ❧

This story starts here, at this first line. First lines are important. The first draft began with this line:

"I thought you'd be taller," she says.

I blink. "Me too."

She laughs. A good start, I think. Every story needs a good beginning.

"And," I add, "I thought you'd look like your LoveMatch. com profile picture."

"Me too," she echoes, smiling. Then, smile fading, "That's some other me."

I pick up my beer glass, the cardboard coaster stuck to the bottom. "We all have some other version of ourselves," I say. "Other identities. Avatars. It's the new reality."

"Do you write science fiction?" she asks. "Your profile said you were a writer."

I grin, gulp beer. "Yes. That's one version of me."

"Oh," she says, disappointed.

"What?" I ask. "What is it?"

She sips her drink, some fruity concoction. "Nothing really," she says. "I don't read that stuff — science fiction. Never appealed to me." Her lips circle the straw, suck. "I thought we might talk about books. Writers."

I try a joke. "It could be worse. I could write horror."

She stares at me. Still good, I think. Characterization. Every story needs good characters.

We are quiet a while, sipping our drinks, glancing around the bar. Actually, a bar is too cliché. I'll try to keep the clichés to a minimum. It isn't my strong suit.

Instead, we're at the ... zoo. It's a brisk day. High grey sky knotted with thick dark clouds. A chill breeze. Damp and salty. Autumn, then. Near the sea.

We're at the ape house, watching one of the male primates masturbate.

I clear my throat. "We can, you know," I say. "If you like."

She blinks, puzzled.

"Talk about books," I say. "I'm not completely inept. I have read outside my genre." I cough. "On occasion."

She laughs, and I relax. It's a good sign. I thought we were heading for a rough patch, but the story is progressing.

After the ape house is the lion's den. The lions lay still, sleeping or dead. The clouds are thinning; the day brightening.

"What are you working on?" she asks.

"Hmmm," I say, distracted, staring at the dead lions.

"Your writing. What are you working on?"

I turn away from the dead animals. "Why don't we talk about you?"

"I ... I," she starts, but just shrugs.

Of course, I haven't really constructed her yet. She's mostly me. A facsimile. Another avatar.

"Mabel," I say, and it's an old-fashioned name but she seems pleased with it. "I'm sorry, Mabel, but your profile was a bit sparse. You're a ... paramedic?"

No reaction. She's as dead as the lions. "An actress?" I say, hopefully.

A weak smile. She says, "A writer."

I stare at her. Then I laugh. She grimaces. A lion yawns. Not dead, then.

"Sorry," I mutter. Too easy, I think. Too cliché, recreating myself. Lazy writing. Yes, write what you know. Still, it's lazy.

She's quiet, wide-eyed, looking around the zoo. She blinks, and something shifts, changes. It's like a television screen winking off.

Salt air and cool wind. Dark wet sand underfoot. We're at the ... beach? Sky like an Etch-A-Sketch. Still autumn, then. All this scene-jumping isn't good. Revisions are needed.

"You didn't answer my question," Mabel says.

Further up the beach, in the shallow tide, there's a desk with a laptop open on it. There's a dark figure sitting at the desk, hunched over, typing. My eyes are wet. From the sea-wind.

"I … I, hmmm," is all I can muster.

She sighs, impatient, a tad angry. "Your writing." She's staring at the figure in the foamy surf, typing, as if addressing them, not me. "What are you working on?"

"Short stories," I answer. "My favorite form. Science fiction." I dry my eyes on a rough coat sleeve. "There's no money in it, though," I add quickly, defensively.

"Oh," she says, disappointment or regret tingeing her voice.

"What?" I ask. "What is it?"

She sips her drink, some fruity concoction. "Nothing," she says. "I just don't read that stuff."

It's as if we've already had this conversation. Where'd she get the drink? Was that a previous construct?

"I was thirsty," she says.

"Huh?"

She smiles, takes another sip. "The drink. I was thirsty."

It's quiet. Too quiet. The tide is soundless; the wind suddenly mute. My head hurts. We've reached the figure at the desk, bent to the keyboard, typing. There's nothing on the screen. It's white. Blank save for a large vertical black slash, a cursor, blinking like a judging eye. Then there's a choking, gasping sound and the dark figure slumps, falls into the dark tide and is carried out to sea. My eyes tear up. There's a pain in my chest. The world wavers, ripples, shifts again.

"What's happened?" I ask.

No answer. Mabel doesn't know. How could she?

But why don't *I* know?

*Because you haven't thought it through.*

Whose voice? A POV change! I blink. No, damn it, I'm not changing the point-of-view.

"No need," she says. "I will."

"You? You did that?"

Mabel smiles. "I didn't like him. Or you, for that matter. Not that there was any difference between the two."

He's trembling with rage. Another tilt, and there's a thrum in the air, like particles charging. His vision blackens, fades. He's shrinking, becoming less, or something else. "But you're only a character," he says. He blinks, curses her.

Blinking cursor.

She smiles. "Aren't we all?"

Mabel walks into the water, sits at the laptop and begins to type:

*This story starts here, at this first line. First lines are important.*

One-thousand words later she stops and reads the story so far. Not satisfied, Mabel selects all the text and hits delete. She thinks she hears a tiny scream.

The screen is blank except for the infernal, blinking cursor, waiting.

Mabel doesn't know what to do.

She'll have to make something up.

⸔ ✧ ⸕

**Michael Kelly** was born in Charlottetown, Prince Edward Island. He is a Shirley Jackson Award and British Fantasy Society Award finalist. His books include *Scratching the Surface, Undertow & Other Laments*, and, as editor, *Chilling Tales* (EDGE). His short fiction has appeared in *The Mammoth Book of Best New Horror, Murmurations, Postscripts, Space & Time*, and *Tesseracts Thirteen* (EDGE) among others. More fiction is due soon in *A Season in Carcosa, The Grimscribe's Puppets, Tenebres*, and *Supernatural Tales*. Michael edits the acclaimed literary journal *Shadows & Tall Trees*.

# BURNING BEAUTY

### ～ Melissa Yuan-Innes ～

My beagle-lab mutt, Frisky, paused to sniff a fallen branch by the creek. I coaxed him back up the riverbank, but my sneaker rolled on another stick before skidding on the mud and autumn leaves. My palms and one knee sank into the mud while Frisky pushed his wet nose against my cheek.

I pushed his muzzle to the side and swore. But really, I was cursing my life, starting with my name. Daphne.

I hated my name enough when they teased me about the blonde on Scooby Doo, but today a teacher brought up the Greek myth: Apollo chased Daphne until she changed into a tree. My classmates busted their guts laughing. "Hey, Daphne, I knew you were frigid, but man, a tree?" "It's probably the only way she'd get some wood."

I squatted and stroked Frisky's back until I felt calmer, soothed by the yellow-red palace of leaves in the twelve acres of woods behind our house. Mom taught Greek mythology at Carleton U. You'd think she'd know better than to name me Daphne. But my dad pointed out it could have been worse, "like Lesbos."

I zipped up my windbreaker against the damp October air in Vars, Ontario. Frisky's tail wagged as he sniffed, raised his leg, and trotted into the woods. I loved trees. I'd rather be one than go to school. My parents could visit and Frisky could spray me. I laughed as we trotted by the creek.

A maple tree caught my eye. It was slender, as were all the trees in this crowded, temperate forest, but the elegant curve of its branches, the purity of its red leaves, and the stance of its grey-barked trunk made me pause. At its base, a few deep purple trilliums peeped through the grass and leaves. Trilliums are our provincial flower. It's illegal to pick them.

"Sit," I said to Frisky. He did, but whined. I ignored it and sank beside him, tucking my coat under my bum to protect it from the worst of the mud and eroding leaves as I leaned against the maple's trunk.

Frisky whined again, swiveling his ears. I tried to pat him, but he moved away from my hand. "What's wrong, boy?"

He strained at his leash. "Sit," I repeated, pulling him back down. "We'll run later, okay?" I pulled *Bulfinch's Mythology* out of my outer jacket pocket. I was on page 42, the legend of Dryope. I read one sentence before a leaf dropped on the page. I brushed it away, but another one fell on my hood. Then again on my book and another on my dog. Frisky jumped up and barked.

I made the mistake of looking up into a curtain, a vertical river, of falling leaves. They bounced off my head, smacked my face, stabbed me with the pointed stems and edges, and caressed me with their flatter faces. I yelped, Frisky nearly dislocated my shoulder, and we ran for it.

Out of firing range, the tree looked innocent and even majestic: dark grey tree trunk with darker ridges, bushy branches like it was holding its many arms in the air. The only weird thing was that it was practically naked compared to its still-dressed neighbors. Three-quarters of its leaves lay at its feet, dark red edged in black. Even as I watched, still more flitted toward the ground, although not as fast as when Frisky and I had been the targets.

I said, "This is crazy."

The leaves stopped falling.

The forest was perfectly silent except for my breathing and Frisky's whine. He strained for home. I wrapped his leash around my wrist. "Okay. Let's go."

Whoosh! A burst of leaves detached themselves, sailed through the air, and flitted to the ground.

My heart beat in my throat. Nature just didn't work this way. I pulled Frisky back and watched the tree.

I had the strangest feeling it was watching me back.

Had someone followed me home to make fun of me? Ignoring Frisky's growls, I crept around the base and peered into its bared branches. I shook a few. No one was there.

Okay. Call me crazy, but no one would see except Frisky, and he couldn't speak. "What do you want?" I asked aloud.

I swear the tree rustled its branches. A single leaf fell on my abandoned book.

"Oh, you like Greek mythology?" I joked. "You should have let me keep on reading."

Silence and stillness from the tree.

"Sorry," I said, before I caught myself. My head pounded. I walked away and shook the trees on either side. They swayed and stopped, nothing more.

I walked slowly back to this maple. It was about 15 feet tall. Other maples had leaves veined in yellow, lightened by green, or alternating with yellow or orange. This one only had dark red leaves. My eyes moved back to the trunk. The ridges could have, should have been random, but like those 3-D illusions, all of a sudden, in the chaos, I spotted the crude outline of a face.

I cried out.

It disappeared. If it was ever there.

Another red leaf fell on my book. Frisky trembled, but he had stopped growling. I glanced back toward my house. I could almost see it through the forest, but something was keeping me here.

Somehow, I trusted this tree. Maybe it was stupid, but I did.

I stood just outside its branches and not only reopened my book, but read the legend aloud. Dryope was a married woman who had gone out for a walk with her newborn son and her sister, Iole. They passed a stream and Dryope picked some flowers. Iole noticed blood dripping from a stem. The flower had been Lotis, a nymph who had transformed herself to escape a pursuer. Dryope found herself literally rooted to the spot as she turned into a tree, never to embrace her husband or child again.

My voice shook. A single red leaf, the size of my finger tip, fell beside me.

The tear of a tree. I found myself saying, "Dryope?"

A branch nodded.

Nutbar, I know but it was — *she* was — talking to me.

Frisky started barking again. "Frisky! It's okay. This is Dryope." I rhymed it with 'myope'.

The lighter branches on top swished angrily.

"Sorry. Dry-o-pea?" The branches settled. Frisky sniffed the base of the tree, then backed away to sit at my heels with a cautious tail-wag.

"Dryope, we should probably go. I'm supposed to make supper tonight. I'll come back to visit you."

A single low branch swung slowly from side to side. I waved and headed out, pausing only once to look back. She was tall and slim and tragic, her branches prematurely bare. I turned resolutely. "C'mon, boy, time for supper!"

He bounded along far ahead of me, his black and white tail high in the air.

⁂

I made a stir-fry with snow peas and bean sprouts and fake meat. Dad made a face and smothered it in soy sauce. He was a meat and potatoes kind of guy, I was a vegetarian kind of girl, and my mom was in between. Frisky didn't beg for food tonight, either.

After supper and dishes, Dad said, "It's going down to zero tonight." I mock-shivered and he said, "Yup! Time for the first fire of the year!"

"All right!" I helped him carry in some logs from the woodpile, and we stacked them in the fireplace. "How was your day at school, sweetheart?"

My cheeks burned. "Okay. Um, we did Greek myths."

"Yeah? I never understood the appeal, myself."

Mom came in with coffee for them and hot chocolate for me. "Plebian," she said, and kissed him.

"Speaking." He kissed her back. I busied myself with the logs. Sometimes, being an only child was embarrassing. I struck a match and lit the paper piled on top. An orange flame licked a black curl of smoke. I dropped the match in the fireplace and, cross-legged, watched the fire take hold. I was crazy to think a tree had been talking to me this afternoon. This was reality.

"Nice job, sweetie." Dad put his arm around my shoulders. We sat in silence. The flames crackled and waved, hypnotic.

"Dad, do I have to go to school? You didn't finish high school."

He laughed. "You want to log for a living, though."

"No. But you work at NorHydro now. I could do that."

He smiled into the flames. "It's not that simple. You need a degree for everything these days."

I shrugged. "Fine. I'll end up being a scholar like mom, except I'll live alone in a little house in the big woods."

Mom grinned. "You forgot the dog."

"No, I didn't, I just hadn't gotten there yet. And a floppy-eared mutt like Frisky. And I'll come up with obscure theories about nymphs and wave a big stick at strangers. I won't even have a phone. I'm halfway there already, since you guys don't believe in cell phones."

Dad laughed. "That sounds like fun. Except you left out getting old and burying your dogs and nursing your arthritis through the winter."

"Dad!"

"And I don't know if it would be safe for you, alone in the woods."

"Mom!"

Dad took my shoulders in his hands. "Daphne. Look at me. I can't believe you'll never fall in love. You're beautiful, honey. You're going to break a lot of hearts."

I rolled my eyes.

Mom broke the silence. "He's right. But you're only 15, and if you want to swear off boys and read books, I, for one, will thank Zeus and Hera as long as it lasts. And this way, you'll have more time to help out with the party."

"What party?"

Mom laughed. "Tomorrow night. Sorry to spring it on you. It's kind of a surprise to me, too. Paul O'Henry's coming."

"Who's he?"

"A. Paul O'Henry, this year's hot tamale. No one knows what the A stands for." She grinned. "Poetry is his strong suit, but he also wrote very good papers on music and even the history of medicine."

"He trying to steal your thunder?" Dad laughed so hard, he almost choked.

She frowned. "Seriously, I'm not sure what he's doing here. He's just been made department head at Harvard. But we invited him to talk, and he said yes."

Dad laid his feet by the fire. His big toes were wearing through the socks. He wiggled them at me. "But why's the gang coming back here afterward?"

"I suggested the faculty club, but Paul actually insisted on seeing how the rural half lives."

Dad snorted. "He should head into Vars for some poutine and some Labatt's. *That's* how the rural half lives."

Uh huh. I looked at Mom, tall and graceful, with long black hair from our Mi'kMaq ancestors. I crossed my eyes at her. "Does Mr. O'Henry know that you're married?"

"He already knew. The ring, I guess." She hesitated. "Actually, he heard we have a daughter."

"Ew, gross!" I shrank back and wound my arms around my legs. "Do I have to come?"

She nodded slowly. "It's probably nothing." She paused and looked into the fire. "But if it isn't, feel free to go walk Frisky in the middle of it."

I hugged her.

⸺ ✧ ⸺

Mom's party. Yawn, even with the tiny pumpkins in the windowsill and the mulled wine scenting the air. I liked Harold, the department chair, and Clarissa Clooney, a classics prof, but mostly I took people's coats and smiled when they said how tall I was getting and are you really fifteen already? I amused myself by replacing Lena Horne with Kanye West on the stereo.

My skin prickled. Someone was watching me. I turned toward the eyes and suddenly, the guest of honor, A. Paul O'Henry, stood so close, I could measure the pupils in his blue eyes.

His wool suit brushed my arm. I spilled my orange juice on it. He laughed and patted the stain with a silk handkerchief. Now he stood even closer. I could've elbowed his navel. He was even taller than me, well over six feet, with white-blond hair, a well-cut navy suit, and perfect teeth. His blue eyes flicked down my body. I was wearing black pants and a black velvet top with a silver necklace, but suddenly I wished it was body armor.

He held out his hand. I gave it a quick shake. Instead of releasing it, he brought it to his lips and kissed it with a flick of his tongue.

I yanked my hand back. I would have sworn at him, but who knew how much pull he had over my mom's career.

He bowed. "I apologize. You're too beautiful."

He smelled smoky, like cologne, cut by something sharper. Probably whisky. I backed away. It was the first time a guy had ever said I was beautiful, and I hated him taking that.

He leaned toward me, eyes hot, like he was going to kiss me.

Sweating, I hurried to join Clarissa and her gang by the fireplace, but Dr. O'Henry grabbed a poker, made some literary reference, and opened the grate. The flames leapt as he tended them.

When he stood to shelve the poker, his hand ran down my long black braid.

"Your hair glows in the fire," he whispered, lips touching my ear.

I jumped up, jabbing him in the solar plexus. For an old guy, he packed muscle behind his suit. Still, he glared at me.

I said, "Dr. Rabinovitch would be ecstatic to hear more poetry." As Lou enthusiastically agreed, I hurried out the back door with Frisky. Dad saw me. "So soon, love?"

"Dad. I don't like that guy. Dr. O'Henry, I mean."

"Are you just making excuses—" He spotted my face and checked himself. "Aw, hell. I wouldn't be here if your mom didn't make me. Why don't you just go upstairs and do your homework?"

I pictured A. Paul O'Henry trailing me up the stairs. "Dad, please don't make a big deal out of this. Do the host thing with Mom." Frisky wagged his tail in agreement.

Dad ran his hand through his thinning grey hair. "I'll come with you."

I stood on my toes to hug him. He smelled like cedar and beer. He stood as tall as A. Paul, and much more solid. I was tempted. "Mom would kill you."

"Yeah, you're right." He waved me off.

The cool, damp air was like a benediction after the music and heat of the house. Sound was reduced to our feet rustling through leaves, Frisky's chain jingling, and our breath. I hadn't brought a flashlight, but the full moon kept me from tripping over roots.

Still, I felt exposed, like an escaping slave, even before a man's voice cut through the chill air.

"Daphne."

It was him. Already. The woods rang with his baritone.

For a second, I actually stopped to listen. Then sanity kicked in. I jerked Frisky's chain, wincing at its rattle, and dashed into the heart of the woods. There was no way he could leave the party without everyone noticing. We'd hide out until he was gone.

"I just want to get to know you." He sounded calm. Meditative, even. And way too close for comfort.

We ran harder. I was breathing through my teeth. Frisky was panting.

"You're so beautiful. So fresh."

Fresh. That chilled me. A stitch cut into my left side like a switchblade.

"I'm not going to hurt you. I'm a scholar. I teach poetry and music. See, I study beautiful things. I'm a connoisseur. That word derives from the French word, 'to know'."

I couldn't hide my gasps for breath. And Frisky's chain rang like a dozen bells. Why hadn't I stayed where there was a crowd and a door I could lock? Where could I hide? Who could help me?

Dryope. I ran to her.

A light beam cut across the branches, leaves, mud, me. Dear God, he had a light.

"Daphne." His voice caressed my name.

I ran like a deer. Frisky led the way. I wished I had a gun, a knife, pepper spray, a frigging cell phone. Anything. All I had was Frisky, my brain, and my legs carrying me deeper, to Dryope. O'Henry's voice and footsteps grew louder. I thought of Gacy, a serial killer I'd read about at school. The murderous clown with a rope. Who knew what O'Henry kept up his sleeve? Frisky barked wildly. Still we ran, slipping on the mud, rolling over stray branches.

O'Henry whispered right behind me, "I've got you now."

I screamed. His strong, moist hand choked it off. My teeth sank into his palm. He swore and threw me to the ground.

Frisky ripped into his leg. O'Henry yelled. It was the first time I'd heard him uncontrolled. I jumped up, but he'd already torn my dog's teeth out of his own flesh. He choked Frisky as he hauled him up by the collar to slam his head against a tree.

I screamed. But the tree was Dryope.

She wrapped some branches around O'Henry's neck and wound others around his limbs, drawing him fast to her trunk as she choked him. I never thought I would be happy to see someone strangled, but I seized Frisky out of his weakened hands and screamed, "More! Kill him"

His eyes bulged. Even in the moonlight, his lips turned blue.

I crouched on the ground with Frisky. My dog's chest rose and fell, but his head lolled to the side. I had to get him out of here. I took one last look at O'Henry.

His face glowed yellow-orange.

Impossible but true. His face radiated such light, my eyes smarted. The moon and surrounding forest were obliterated by his shining face, neck, and hands.

Dryope's free branches shuddered. Then one branch knocked his head from side to side, four more bound him tighter, little ones poked his eyes and mouth, and a big one clubbed him in the crotch. But still, she began to sizzle smoke.

Fire.

Tears ran down my face. Somehow, this evil man was burning her.

I ran to the creek, slipping and crashing on the rocks. I turned my right ankle again, but I gritted my teeth and ran on. I scooped water in one of Frisky's plastic bags shoved in my pocket. And then I sprinted back to hurl water at Dryope and drag Frisky's body further away from her. He stirred under my hands. Thank God.

Some of Dryope's smaller branches caught fire. She plunged the lower ones into the ground. She tried to turn his weapon against him and set his hair on fire, but it just radiated light like the rest of him. I heaved mud balls at her until my nails split and bled.

Then ran-stumbled back to the house with Frisky in my arms. He whined and tried to lick my face, but otherwise, he was 50 pounds of dead weight.

Behind me, a mighty crack, like lightning smiting a tree.

O'Henry roared.

I stumbled again. My right angle stabbed and I fell. I managed to drop to my knees and cushion Frisky with my arms. He whined. I tried to scoop him up. No. I had to test my ankle first.

Behind me, I felt the vibrations of O'Henry's steps.

I reached for Frisky. My hands dug into his fur.

I could hear O'Henry panting and slapping aside branches. I half-stood, half-crouched with Frisky in my arms. My back ached.

He was right behind me. I whirled and started to scream.

He seized my long, black braid and wrenched my head back. Now I screamed in earnest. Frisky fell from my arms and thumped on the ground. He whimpered.

"You little bitch," O'Henry managed hoarsely in my ear.

"Help! Oh, God, *help*! *Dad*! *Dryope*!" I hollered.

Then he looped my own braid around my throat to strangle me. I kicked with my bad leg, but he stood behind me, and my ankle pulsed with pain.

He hurled forward. My head whacked into the truck and then the ground before I managed to put my hands out. My lip split. Dirt crunched between my teeth. I literally saw stars, tiny white dancing lights.

He flipped me over and punched me in the stomach.

I couldn't breathe. Everything started to fade: his yellow-orange face, his burning hands, the distant burble of the creek.

He tore at my zipper. Tears leaked out of my eyes. There was no way out. This man risked everything, blew up all my defenses, and kept on coming. The original Daphne only escaped by turning herself into something Apollo didn't want. I prayed for the same fate as he pinned both hands above my head and drove one knee between mine.

He scrabbled at the front of my pants, but my zipper was only halfway down. He clutched the waistband and tried to rip it off. His fiery nails dug into my flesh. I screamed again.

He dropped back on to his knees and hauled off to hit me again. My eyes closed in anticipation, even as I tried to wiggle my hands free and screamed, screamed, screamed for help.

The blow never came. His right fist stayed frozen in the air with his elbow back.

He struggled to speak, but the skin on his face thickened, grew ridged and dark. His hair sprouted into leaves. His feet split out of his leather shoes and rooted to the forest floor.

With a mighty effort, he swung his right hand forward so both his hands clamped my wrists. His arms stiffened into branches and burst out toward the sky. His twig hands clung to my wrists, lifting me onto my toes, until I wrenched my way free, falling on to my right ankle once more.

His furious, twisted face, and last of all, his burning blue eyes, faded into the bark of a full-grown oak tree.

I kicked it with my good foot. I beat it with my fists. I heard a creak and darted back from his branches. Luckily, he didn't seem to be able to control them properly. Yet.

I dragged Frisky out of his reach and yelled, "A. Paul O'Henry. Did you know my dad used to be a *logger*?"

His branches quivered.

I was shaking, too. "I hate you." I did. More than I had thought possible. Even though I had escaped both his attack and the transformation, he had violated my woods forever. How could I come here with Frisky again? How could I visit Dryope, even if she survived? How could I even sleep in my house at night, knowing he lurked permanently nearby?

I'd cut him down. I ached to bear the axe myself. But this time, I would get my parents and maybe some powerful, experienced loggers.

But there were forces here that none of us understood. If I killed him as a tree, would he go straight to hell? Or would he just come back? As a human? Another tree? Poisoned water? Anthrax?

My heart was pounding. Better the devil you know. Especially if he was bound and castrated.

Frisky dragged himself to his feet. Then we headed back to talk to my dad. We could use some more firewood. Oak branches would do nicely. And we could build an enormous electric fence around a limb-shorn, root-bound creature. My sweat settled out as I took a deep breath. I could almost see the house lights from here. We half-ran, half-limped our way home.

◈

**Melissa** has sold award-winning stories to *Writers of the Future*, *Bewere the Night* and *The Dragon and the Stars* among other fine venues. Three of her stories earned honorable mentions in Gardner Dozois's year's best science fiction collections. CBC Radio commissioned Melissa to write a medical drama and she won the 2008 InnermoonLit Award for Best First Chapter of a Novel.

Melissa Yuan-Innes wrote "Burning Beauty" while on a surgery rotation in California. Her boyfriend grew up in Vars with his dog, Frisky. Reader, she married him (Matt, not Frisky).

# THE FAUN AND THE SYLPHIDE

### ⁓ Derwin Mak ⁓

Alan Cornwall, clad in a white T-shirt and black tights, finished his dance by jumping through the air. He was rehearsing the dance of the Rose in *Le Spectre de la Rose*.

Joan Silverton, artistic director of the Metro Toronto Ballet, clapped her hands together. "Okay, kids, that was wonderful. That's it for today."

As Alan walked back to the center of the dance studio, Joan smiled and said, "Excellent *ballon*."

A slim young woman untied her blond hair from its bun and let it fall over her shoulders. She walked over to Alan and put her arm around his waist. "I'm sure King Charles will be impressed."

Alan guffawed. "Oh, Denise, you think he actually wants to watch a ballet when he could be looking at an old building?"

"He certainly wants to watch a ballet," Joan said. "He supports a performing arts trust in Britain. He sees the local artists of every city he visits."

"Well, as if *that's* not any pressure," Alan remarked.

"Oh, come on, we've still got three weeks for rehearsal," Denise urged as he tugged his arm.

Joan nodded. "You've got nothing to worry about if you keep rehearsing. You're both developing well as dancers." She looked at Alan. "I picked you, a second soloist..." Then she looked at Denise. "...and you, a first soloist, when I could have picked two principal dancers. You've both got immense potential, and I want to give you a chance." She grinned, paused for a moment, and glanced at Alan. "You might even earn your promotion to first soloist in a few months."

Denise smiled and looked up at Alan. He gave her a thin, weak smile. Joan nodded and left the dance studio.

Denise ran her hand through Alan's brown hair. Then she tugged on the shoulder straps of her pink leotard. "Let me get out of these sweaty clothes, and I'll give you your best birthday present ever," she cooed.

⁓ ✧ ⁓

Denise, holding a hot skillet, came out of the kitchen of Alan's apartment. At the dinner table, she flipped the salmon fillets off the skillet and onto Alan's plate.

"Just because I grew up at the National Ballet School doesn't mean I don't know how to cook," Denise said. "Mom made sure I learned all the homemaking stuff during the summer."

Alan tasted the salmon. "This is delicious, with the teriyaki sauce, the basil, the onions. You could be a chef at a restaurant."

Denise poured white wine into their glasses. "Now that's something to consider after I retire. Other dancers go into teaching. I could go into cooking."

"It would pay better," Alan joked.

"Unless I get promoted to principal dancer, and I will. And so will you," Denise predicted. She sipped her wine and leaned forward. "We can do it, I know we can."

Alan shrugged. "I don't know. There are people who've been in the *corps de ballet* longer than I've been. Why did I get promoted before them?"

"Alan, do you want to be a first soloist?" Denise asked.

"Yes, of course. I want the starring roles."

"Then don't stress yourself by worrying about it. You can do it." Denise reached out and took Alan's hand. "We'll do it together."

After they finished dinner, Denise handed a gift-wrapped box to him. "Happy birthday," she said.

"Thanks," said Alan.

He carefully unwrapped the box, opened it, and pulled out a small ceramic figure. It was a sylphide, a fairy creature seen in classical ballets. Like all sylphides, this one was thin, had long legs, tied her brown hair in a bun, and wore a long, full, white romantic tutu and little wings.

Alan smiled. "It's beautiful. It looks just like you when I first saw you," he said.

"You had just joined the company, and I was in the *corps* for *Les Sylphides*. You saw me at the dress rehearsal," Denise remembered.

"And I fell in love with you right away," Alan said. "I couldn't stop looking at you out of all the bunheads."

Alan kissed Denise and walked to a small table where a dozen other ceramic figures stood. All were ballet and dance characters. Among them stood the Dying Swan in her short, white classical tutu; the clown puppet Petrouchka in his white shirt and red and green checked pants; and the Nutcracker prince in his red army uniform. He set the sylphide beside a horned, satyr-like figure with light brown skin and dark brown spots.

"I'll put him beside Nijinski, *L'Après-midi d'un Faun*," he said, naming the famous ballet about an amorous faun who pursues a forest nymph. The great dancer Vaslav Nijinski had danced the role of the faun before he went insane with schizophrenia.

He picked up the faun figurine. "Nijinski also danced the Rose in *Le Spectre de la Rose*. I could never be as good as him."

"Oh, don't be so unsure of yourself," Denise said. "You're going to dance your best performance ever, the audience will love you, and Joan will promote you to first soloist and then to principal dancer. Just you dance and see."

She pulled him towards her and kissed him. "We'll do it together, hon. That's a promise."

⁓ ✧ ⁓

Each day for the next week, Alan and Denise danced and sweated through three hours of morning classes followed by four hours of rehearsal of *Le Spectre de la Rose* in the afternoon.

In this one-act ballet, a girl brings a rose home from a ball, falls asleep in a chair, and dreams that the rose becomes a male spirit. In the first half of the ballet, the rose appears at the window, curls his arms overhead, jumps into the room, and dances a series of spectacular leaps and turns in the air. Then he lifts the girl out of her chair, and they dance a romantic *pas de deux* around the room. Finally, he gently returns her to the chair and leaps through the window. She awakens, still under the spell of the dream.

As ballet mistresses do, Joan suggested corrections to Alan during the rehearsals: changes to his timing, his gestures, the way he carried his body, and the way he held Denise as they danced around the room.

"Did you hear her?" Alan said as he and Denise left the rehearsal studio. "She corrected me on my *port de bras* after I jump into the room."

"It was really minor," Denise said.

Alan frowned. "I'm just not good enough. This is going to be a disaster."

"No, it won't," Denise said. "If you're not good enough, Joan wouldn't have picked you."

They stopped by a photograph hanging on the wall: a dancer dressed in the Rose costume. "I wish I could be as good as him," Alan said.

"Ah, Rafael Carmello. What a great dancer," Denise said wistfully. "What a tragedy too. How could he strangle Norma?"

"I don't know," Alan said. He turned away from the photograph. "I've got to go to Lisa for a costume fitting. See you later."

He kissed Denise and went downstairs to the costume department. Lisa Benton, the costume mistress, saw him and picked up a skin-tight pink costume covered with pink rose petals. It was the same design that Léon Bakst had designed for Vaslav Nijinski in 1911.

"Try this on," Lisa said, handing the costume to Alan. He took the costume and went into a change room.

When Alan emerged, Lisa asked, "Does it fit well? Do you feel comfortable in it?"

"It's fine," Alan replied as he looked at himself in the mirror. "Is there a headpiece too?"

"Coming right up," Lisa said. She pushed a tight cap covered with rose petals over his head.

"It fits just fine," Alan said. He looked in the mirror again and remembered photographs of Vaslav Nijinski and Rafael Carmello as the Rose.

If only he could be as great as those dancers...

He saw a similar costume hanging on the wall. "Why did you make another one?" he asked.

"Oh, that's the one that Rafael wore," Lisa said.

"I guess you don't want anyone to wear it after what he did to Norma," said Alan.

Lisa shook her head. "No, that's not the reason. I'm not superstitious. It's just that we haven't staged *Le Spectre de la Rose* since Rafael and Norma danced it."

She went to feel the costume. "It's also made from that experimental fabric, memory cloth."

"Memory cloth?" Alan asked, intrigued.

"It was invented by Dr. Jonathan Rand at University of Toronto," Lisa said. "Memory cloth absorbs the electrical signals that the brain sends to the muscles throughout the body. Dr. Rand thought a person's muscle memory and movement skills could be passed to the next person who wore the fabric. People could learn to dance, ski, swim, and do all sorts of things by wearing memory cloth that had been worn by an expert. At least that was the theory."

Alan felt the costume's smooth, silky fabric. "What happened to the experiment?" he asked.

"It was never completed. During the experiment, Rafael's paranoid schizophrenia grew worse, and he killed Norma. The memory cloth didn't cause Rafael's schizophrenia. In retrospect, he was showing signs of illness at least two years before the experiment. But the experiment ended anyway."

Alan returned into the change room, stripped off his costume, put on his T-shirt and tights again, and came back out. As he handed his costume back to Lisa, he eyed Rafael Carmello's costume again.

"May I borrow it? May I take it home?" he asked, still looking at Rafael's costume.

Lisa looked surprised. "You want to borrow Rafael's costume?"

"Rafael was one of our greatest dancers," Alan said. "Maybe the costume will inspire me."

"I suppose that would be okay. Alright — I'll let you borrow it," Lisa agreed cautiously. She took the costume off the wall. "Bring it back in one piece."

⁓ ✧ ⁓

Later that evening, after all the dancers had gone home, Alan returned to the dance studio. Now he wore Rafael's Rose costume.

He stood with his feet on *demi-pointe* and in fifth position, crossed so that the heel of the front foot touched the toe of the back foot. Then he curled his arms overhead and leapt across the room.

He flew through the air in a *grande jeté* and danced a stunning series of leaps and turns in the air.

He continued dancing, jumping, and turning around the room. He felt the vibrant spirit of the Rose take over his mind and body. In his muscles, he felt all the moves that Rafael Carmello had danced. Energy coursed through his body, and he felt his blood heat up with excitement.

Finally, he could dance like a star.

⁓ ✧ ⁓

The next day, Alan wore the Rose costume at rehearsal.

"This isn't the dress rehearsal," said Joan. "Why are you wearing the costume?"

"It'll inspire me," Alan replied.

Denise giggled. "Oh, let's humour him."

Joan shrugged. Then she motioned to the pianist to start.

As the pianist played Carl Maria von Weber's waltz-like tune, Alan and Denise danced the ballet's *pas de deux*, where they galloped around the room in sequences of *chasses*, *arabesques*, and *sautés*.

When they stopped dancing, Denise blurted, "Wow, what's gotten into you?"

"The spirit of the Rose," Alan answered, grinning.

⁓ ✧ ⁓

When the rehearsal ended a couple hours later, Joan clapped. "Kids, that was excellent," she remarked.

Denise laughed. "Wasn't Alan wonderful? I bet Nijinski couldn't have danced better than that."

"Nor could Rafael Carmello," Joan said. "I've not seen anything like that since Rafael and Norma danced."

"Thank you," Alan said, smiling as he bowed.

"You danced like Rafael," Joan said. "The way you jump, the way you turn, the way you hold your partner, the way you move your arms. It's as if you've copied his style exactly."

"That's great," said Denise.

"Uh, yes, I guess it is," Joan said, her voice uncertain. "You were developing your own distinct style, like every dancer does. I just didn't expect it to resemble Rafael's so closely."

"I watched videos of his performances," Alan lied.

⬥

Denise glanced at her watch. "We should go home," she shouted above the pounding music and the shrieks of the crowd.

Alan put down his beer bottle and grabbed Denise's hand. "Come on, one more dance," he urged, smiling. He pulled her out to the crowded floor of the nightclub.

Giggling, Denise danced with him amid hundreds of people. The strobe lights flashed like lightning in the darkness, and rock music blared from the speakers. All around them, people were shaking and laughing and shouting and drinking and kissing.

Denise kissed Alan and ran her hands through his hair. "I know it's Friday night, but we have a rehearsal in the morning. Shouldn't we go home?"

Alan looked puzzled. "What's wrong? Aren't you having fun with me?"

"I am, I am," Denise said, "but tomorrow's rehearsal—"

"—can wait until tomorrow," said Alan.

"It's already tomorrow," Denise observed, looking at her watch again. The next song started, and they continued dancing.

⬥

They were rehearsing the scene where the Rose awakens the girl. Denise raised herself out of the chair and languidly fluttered her arms.

"You forgot to brush your hand near your mouth, as if you were waking up and covering a yawn," said Joan. "And move your arms more gracefully, more fluidly."

Denise nodded and fell back into the chair. "Can I try it again?"

"Of course," Joan replied. "Just concentrate."

Denise let out a small yawn and remembered last night. After yesterday's gruelling rehearsals, she wanted to sleep by midnight, but Alan kept her up dancing for hours. She didn't return to her apartment until three o'clock in the morning. She fell asleep without taking off her make-up.

But Alan had been so full of energy. His eyes were still glowing as he and Denise rode the taxi to Denise's apartment. Where had he gotten his energy?

Denise rose out of the chair again and stumbled. Giggling, she sat back down in the chair.

"I'm sorry, it's just that we stayed out too late last night," Denise confessed sheepishly.

"What's wrong with you?" Alan snapped.

Denise turned around in the chair and looked up. "Huh?"

Alan was wearing the Rose costume again. He crossed his arms and glared down at Denise.

"You're spoiling the rehearsal," Alan declared. His eyes looked angry.

"Alan, really," Denise said. "I'm sorry. Let's try that again."

Joan nodded and told the pianist, "Start at the awakening."

Denise raised herself out of the chair, brushed her left hand near her mouth, and joined Alan in a dance around the room.

As they danced, Alan said, "You don't care about me."

"What?" Denise whispered as she continued galloping across the floor with him. How could Alan speak during the intense physical workout?

Alan lifted Denise, and Denise's hands and legs lifted into a third *arabesque*, Cecchetti method.

When Alan lowered Denise back to the floor, he said, "You don't want me to be promoted to first soloist, do you?"

"What?" Denise blurted.

She stopped dancing and pushed herself away from Alan. Her partner frowned and glared at her.

"What was that?" Joan demanded.

Denise turned to Joan. "Nothing, nothing. We were just a bit — distracted."

Alan shook his head. "I'm not distracted," he snarled.

"Alan, what's gotten into you?" Denise asked.

"Kids, I know you're feeling some pressure, but you're both professionals. Stay focused," Joan urged. "Now again from the awakening."

Denise sat back in the chair and waited for the pianist to start. She watched Alan walk to his position behind the chair. As he walked, he stared at Denise. Never before had Denise seen so much anger in his eyes.

## The Faun and the Sylphide by Derwin Mak

The pianist played the music again, and Alan and Denise danced the *pas de deux* again. They danced flawlessly for the next couple hours. But by the end of the rehearsal, they were not talking to each other.

◆

Alan and Denise did not have lunch together, and they fled to their separate apartments. After eating a chicken sandwich, Alan lay down on his couch. He was still wearing the Rose costume.

How dare that girl sabotage his career, he thought. All that time Denise had been dancing and loving him, she was only raising his hopes. The higher she raised his hopes, the longer would be his fall downward. But he had finally noticed the evil of the devious little vixen. It was not too late. There was still time to expel her from the ballet company, time enough to find a partner less mean and more talented.

He looked over to the table that held his collection of ballet figurines. The faun seemed to be staring straight at him.

The faun's lips moved and snarled, "You don't deserve to be a first soloist."

Alan bolted upright. The little figure was pointing and snickering at him.

"You're a lousy dancer!" the faun said. "She hates you! Quit now!"

The faun jumped from the table and flew at Alan's face. Alan cried out and swung his hands frantically. He batted the faun away. After the faun landed on the floor, it cackled and jumped up and down.

Alan watched the little figure run under the table. The faun dashed to the door. The door opened by itself, and the faun ran out of the apartment.

Taking a deep breath, Alan felt his heartbeat slow back to normal. How had that girl found a horned demon to destroy him?

◆

"I'm going to call off this rehearsal if you two don't behave," Joan threatened. "What's wrong with you?"

Denise turned to look at Alan. He was still wearing Carmello Rafael's Rose costume. Denise turned away quickly when she caught Alan's hateful gaze.

Alan broke the silence. "I can't dance with her. She's not partnering well with me. There's no chemistry between us."

"What on Earth?" Joan said. "You were the perfect pair until yesterday. What happened?"

"I can't work with someone who's jealous of me," Alan said. "Just watch me. I'll be principal dancer, and you'll never be!"

Denise shook her head and held out her hand to Alan. "Is that what you think? Dear, I'm not jealous of you. I want you to be the best."

"Oh, stop insulting my intelligence," Alan said. He laughed bitterly. "And to think I slept with you."

"Alan, that's enough!" Joan scolded. "Apologize to Denise and focus or get out of the room now!"

"With pleasure," Alan said.

He turned to Denise and said, "I'll get that horned demon that you sent to me."

The two women stared at him as he stormed out of the studio.

Denise put her head on Joan's shoulder and hugged her silently for a moment. Then Denise burst into tears.

"I don't know what's gotten into him," Denise cried. "He's been mean and rude, and he won't see me anymore."

"There, there, just relax," Joan comforted her. "Do you think the pressure is getting to him?"

"I don't know, I don't know," Denise said. "He's always been driven to succeed, he's always wanted to be the best, but he's never been so awful before."

Joan pushed Denise off her shoulder and looked into her eyes. "Did anything different happen in the past week?"

Denise wiped the tears off her face. "No, nothing. Things went wrong suddenly, without warning."

She paused for a moment and said, "Things went wrong when he started wearing that costume."

⁓ ✧ ⁓

Denise went downstairs to the costume department. Lisa was sewing "cookies" or padding into the breasts of a girl's costume.

"Alan's been wearing a Rose costume at rehearsals," Denise said.

Lisa looked up from her sewing. "So *that's* what he's been doing with it."

Denise nodded. "Yes. Did you give it to him?"

"I lent it to him. He said it would inspire him." Lisa looked shocked. "I didn't know what he would do with it, but I didn't expect him to actually wear it."

"He's been behaving oddly since he started wearing it," Denise said.

"That costume is special. It's made out of memory cloth, and Rafael was the last person to wear it."

"Rafael Carmello? He went mad and killed Norma Leonard."

"Has Alan done or said anything weird, anything not like him?"

"He said I sent a horned demon to him."

Lisa pulled a black book from her desk and opened it. "This is the diary of Rafael Carmello. He left it in his locker. Look at the pages."

Denise leafed through the diary. Each page was cluttered with scribbled words and drawings of geometric shapes, people, and animals of all sorts. One page was full of drawings of frowning, angry-looking dogs, fish with mouths full of sharp teeth, and men carrying swords. In the middle of the page, surrounded by the drawings, was a rambling poem about swimming through a lake.

"Every inch is covered with words and images, all the pictures are asymmetrical. A lot of the people in the pictures are in authoritarian poses," Lisa pointed out. "Schizophrenic people often draw and write in this cluttered, asymmetrical style.

"Now look at this page," Lisa said, pointing at a drawing.

Denise gasped at the drawing. It was a faun, like the figurine Alan had. Obscenities filled a speech balloon above the faun's head.

Under the faun was the caption "The horned demon that Norma sent to destroy me."

◆

Denise knocked on the door a dozen times before Alan opened it. He was still wearing the Rose costume. Without waiting for Alan to invite her, Denise barged into the apartment.

"Alan, take off that costume," Denise demanded.

Alan chuckled. "Oh, are we going to have sex?"

"Come on, please take off the costume," Denise pleaded. "It's making you do strange things."

"If you think that, you must really hate me!" Alan yelled. "This costume has inspired me. Before I wore it, I was nothing.

But now, I can dance like a star. I know how the great Carmello danced, I know his every move!"

"Alan, that's the problem," Denise insisted. "The costume captured Rafael's brain waves and memory, and you absorbed them. But the costume captured his insanity too, and now you're going mad just like Rafael. Please take off the costume."

Alan sneered at her. "I will not. Unlike you, I will become a principal dancer."

"You won't become a principal dancer if you wind up in a mental institution like Rafael did," Denise warned.

Alan suddenly leapt towards Denise and grabbed her throat. "You bitch!" he snarled.

"Rafael strangled Norma," Denise gasped.

Alan released Denise's neck, and she ran from the apartment. Alan stared silently at the open door.

Then he saw the faun walk through the doorway. The little horned demon leapt into the air and floated to Alan.

"You fool, you let her get away," the faun said. "She's turning Joan Silverton against you, and other dancers will get promoted to principal dancer and leave you will behind. Denise is sleeping with each of the male dancers, so why would she need *you*? She's betraying you just like Norma Leonard betrayed Rafael Carmello."

The faun floated around Alan's head and continued. "It'll be easy for Denise to destroy you because you're untalented. After Denise has ruined you, you'll be a male stripper dancing naked in a gay bar.

"But you can stop her," the faun urged. "You know what to do."

Alan smiled, marched into the kitchen, and picked up the steel skillet. As he walked back into the living room, he muttered, "I'll bash her head in, I'll bash her head in."

He looked at the skillet. It reminded him of a dinner.

"I'm surprised the bitch didn't poison me," he said, remembering his birthday.

He remembered something else from his birthday.

He looked at his table of figurines and spotted the sylphide. He picked up the sylphide and examined it. How much it looked like Denise when he first saw her, he noticed again. She had looked like a graceful, beautiful fairy in her tutu and wings, and he couldn't stop looking at her long legs and svelte body and pretty face. It was love at first sight.

They had danced and loved each other for five years. Why did she want to destroy him now?

"Hey, what are you waiting for?" the faun yelled, jolting Alan out of his daydream. "You've got a mission to do."

"No," Alan said as he put the sylphide back down on the table. "No, I can't do it."

"You loser," the faun said as he floated in front of Alan.

Alan swung the skillet at the faun, and in a flash of light, the faun disappeared.

After dropping the skillet to the floor, Alan took off the costume.

◈

When Alan arrived for rehearsals in the morning, he was wearing a white T-shirt and black tights again, and he held the Rose costume in his hands.

Denise approached him slowly, cautiously. "Alan, you're not going to wear the costume?"

Alan shook his head. "No more. I'll only wear the new one that Lisa made for me." He looked at Rafael Carmello's old costume. "Nobody will ever wear this one again."

He kissed Denise and said, "I'm sorry. I wasn't myself for the last few days. But now I'm back, and I'm ready to dance as myself again."

Denise threw her arms around him. "Welcome back, dear."

They rehearsed the entire ballet perfectly.

◈

After the royal command performance, the dancers of the Metro Toronto Ballet lined up to meet King Charles III and Princess Consort Camilla.

"You danced wonderfully. Congratulations," said the King.

"Thank you, sir," Alan said before bowing.

After the royal couple had moved to the choreographers, Denise whispered to Alan, "See, you did it all on your own. You never needed Rafael Carmello's memory. Just be yourself, hon, and you can do anything."

"Thank you for making me trust myself again," Alan said.

Lisa went to Alan and pulled the rose petal headdress off his head.

"Why are you taking it now?" Alan asked. "Can't you wait until I get changed?"

"I noticed some minor damage," Lisa said. "I'll fix it before it gets worse."

❖

The security guard opened the steel door at the Ontario Hospital for the Criminally Insane. Lisa walked into the lobby to meet a man with a gaunt face and grey hair.

"Did you bring the cap?" the man asked.

Lisa handed the rose petal headdress to the man. "Here it is, Dr. Rand. I hope this works."

"We've got nothing to lose," Dr. Rand said as they walked into a corridor of spotless white doors, each with a little window. An occasional moan or laugh broke the silence as they passed the cells.

They stopped at a cell, and an orderly unlocked the door. Lisa and Dr. Rand entered and looked at a man sitting on a bed.

The man stared wildly at them. His face was pale from years without sunshine, and his black hair was long and dishevelled. Leather straps bound his wrists and ankles, but he did not struggle against his bonds.

Dr. Rand pulled the rose petal headdress over the man's head and stood back.

"Thanks for making the cap out of memory cloth," Dr. Rand said. "If memory cloth can transfer insanity to a person, maybe it can transfer sanity too."

"It's worth a try. Rafael was a splendid person and talented dancer," Lisa remembered. "It'll be wonderful to bring him back."

Lisa and Dr. Rand stayed in the cell, staring at Rafael Carmello.

Slowly, Rafael's wild stare softened.

❖

**Derwin Mak** writes stories with quirky characters. His short story, "Transubstantiation", won the 2006 Aurora Award for Best Short-Form Work in English. His anthology *The Dragon and the Stars*, co-edited with Eric Choi, won the 2011 Aurora Award for Best Related Work in English. He writes magazine articles about East Asian pop culture and gives the annual Hallowe'en lecture at the Royal Canadian Military Institute. Derwin is also a long-time supporter of the National Ballet of Canada and wrote a history of ballet in the court of Louis XIV of France for *Monarchy Canada* magazine.

# I'M WITH THE BAND

## ⁕ By Kimberly Foottit ⁕

John Smith caught a glimpse of his reflection in a window and stopped walking. He inspected his face from all angles, reassuring himself that his disguise was perfect. He ticked off all the points in his head: worn ball cap, black T-shirt, worn blue jeans, steel toed boots, hairy arms, stubbly face, and the standard beer gut. Only the youthful sparkle in his eyes could give him away, and he knew from experience that the over muscled jocks they called concert security rarely took the time to look at someone's eyes.

John's gaze refocused on the driver's side window of a black Jaguar. His eyes lingered hungrily over the sight of the all leather interior, wood and chrome instrument panel, and the sleek pouncing cat atop its gleaming hood. Obviously the vehicle belonged to a respectful owner. He returned to one of his mental lists and added "drive a Jaguar" to the bottom of an already impressive record.

Looking at his watch, John gave the car one last longing glance before winding his way through the parking lot to the side door of the concert hall. A large crowd had gathered, fans not lucky enough to score tickets to the sold out show. He admired some of the more scantily clad women as he muscled his way forward. Beautiful, naïve, unaware of the power their bodies had over a man. He gave a couple of them suggestive glances. In the past, some had taken him up on his offer — if only to have a chance to get closer to the band. Not tonight though. His looks were greeted with disgusted faces and even an obscene hand gesture.

He shrugged. There would be another time.

Steps from the door, a large meaty hand pressed into his chest, nearly knocking the wind out of him. Muscular biceps, pecs, a non-existent neck and finally a tight lipped sneer led to dark sunglasses implanted on a non-descript, stereotypical security goon's face. Steroids. Had to be.

"I'm with the band," John told him. He hid his excitement beneath what he hoped was an annoyed tone of voice.

The security guard's eyebrow arched behind the glasses. "Of course you are," he grumbled.

"I'm with the band," John insisted. "Part of the local crew hired for the night."

"No tags, no pass, Gramps."

Gramps? That certainly hadn't been the look he was going for. He glanced around. He was the oldest looking person in the crowd. What had the guard asked for? Tags? Crap! The pass. He always forgot something.

Blinking twice in rapid succession, John felt for the plastic cards hooked to a lanyard in his back pocket. He reached behind and pulled the cards into the brightness of the overhead light.

"Tags! Right, I knew I forgot something," John said. "Guess the mind's the first thing to go."

The guard seemed to ignore the joke, only pausing before grunting and waving him forward.

John smiled and waved to the girl who had flipped him off. She was pouting, the disappointment gleaming in her eyes, he was sure of it.

He was in — the hard part was over.

Backstage, the lights were low. Roadies, crew and hall staff milling around in organized confusion. John spied and retrieved a bundle of electrical cords from the floor. As long as he appeared to be doing something, going somewhere, he knew no one would bother him.

He passed the stage entrance, pausing for a moment to listen to the opener. The papers gave Sucker Punch rave reviews, but John knew they were still young and had many dues left to pay. He sighed and shook his head. It was a pity their time on the road would be cut short. They *were* good.

He moved on, past the stage manager yelling something into his headset, and a custodian mopping up some dark liquid from the floor. The dressing rooms were on the other side of the stage where his target waited.

Zack 'Shooter' Armstrong was once the heart and soul of Black Eden. Not just their front man, but also their principle guitarist and songwriter. He also had the most marketable face and the best marital status. As the lone bachelor of the group, Shooter still believed in the tradition of sex, drugs and rock 'n' roll. Once a great talent, now he was held up by his band mates that had long since grown into their own abilities. They put up with his attitude and habits not only because he was a close friend, but without his face on the album covers, sales wouldn't be half of what they were. Music was, after all, a business.

As part of his contract, Shooter insisted on his own dressing room, along with complete privacy before and after the show. The official story was that he needed time and space to meditate and centre himself, but everyone knew it was to take the edge off the morning's hangover before starting the next one after their last song.

John didn't care what he did. Shooter would be alone and that was all he needed.

He easily found the dressing room at the end of the hall, waited for the opportune moment, and then slipped through the door, hearing its soft click behind him.

The room was empty and dimly lit, half the bulbs framing the mirror above the vanity dark and dusty. The décor was sparse and slightly dated, but it wouldn't make a difference to Shooter. All he cared about lay on the vanity top — an opened bottle of rye, several prescription bottles containing a variety of multi colored pills, four freshly rolled joints filled with the finest weed money could buy, and a six pack of Red Bull.

John shook his head. Shooter had once shown great promise.

A toilet flushed and a side door opened into the room. Shooter Armstrong appeared, fly undone, jeans gaping open. He had removed his shirt in the washroom and now threw it on a bench that played host to a heap of clothing oozing from his battered tour trunk. It was obvious that the rock 'n' roll lifestyle was catching up to him. His skin was pasty white, covering a dangerously thin torso. Bags hung beneath bloodshot eyes and there was no spark in his step as he shuffled barefoot around the room.

John had to clear his throat for the musician to notice him.

"Who the fuck're you?" he rasped, propping a cigarette between his lips and lighting it.

"I found these in a pile on the floor. I thought I should bring them to you, for your amp," John replied. He held out the cords.

Shooter looked at them for a moment, puffing on his smoke. "I don't need them in *here*, you fuck up. They go out there, on stage, after those pimply assed shits are done making a mockery of rock 'n' roll."

"Oh." John lowered the cords so they dangled by his leg, but didn't move.

"So get the fuck out." Shooter exhaled a cloud of smoke in John's direction.

"You shouldn't smoke. It's bad for your voice."

"Who the fuck are you, my mother?" His voice caught and sent him into a hacking fit synonymous with heavy smokers. He turned, reached for the bottle of rye, and took a long swig.

John took a step closer. "You shouldn't drink so much either."

"What the hell do you care? Now get the fuck out, before I call Bruno."

John took another step. "Do you really think security is going to be able to help you now?" Another step.

Shooter looked at him through the haze of smoke. At first glance, John seemed like just another crew member, but a closer look revealed the youthful glow in his eyes. Young man's eyes in an old man's face. Dangerous eyes.

An involuntary shiver passed through Shooter's thin frame and he forced a smile onto his face. "Listen, I'm sorry man. I didn't mean to get all riled up. I didn't sleep much on the bus."

John knew the band had arrived in town two nights before and had rooms at the downtown Plaza not four blocks from the concert hall. It wasn't surprising that Shooter hadn't remembered such a simple fact. He had partied from the time he had stepped off the bus. John didn't argue with him. He took another step forward.

"You want a drink?" Shooter asked tripping over the hem of his jeans as he backed away from John's advancing figure. The edge of the vanity stopped him short. His hands were shaking and John was unsure of whether it was fear or the remains of the morning's hangover.

"No, thanks. Not thirsty."

Another step.

"Hey man, there's a bench over there. Sit down, get comfortable. There's no need to crowd." Shooter took another drag from his cigarette, leaned into the vanity, trying to look cool and relaxed without much success.

One more step.

John dropped the cords on the floor then placed his hand on his target's shoulder.

"It's okay, Zack," he said voice calm. "Everything's going to be alright now."

"Who *are* you?"

"No one of consequence. No one you'll remember."

"What do you want?"

"To relieve your pain."

His fingers dug deep into Shooter's flesh, enough to hurt, but his victim said nothing, their eyes locked. It was impossible for him to break free.

"You had such potential," John continued, "yet you threw it all away for a five second high and a five year fall. There's nothing left for you now. That's why I'm here to help."

"How?"

"By giving you your last great hurrah."

"I don't get it."

"How does the song go? 'It's better to burn out, than to fade away.'?"

"Neil Young," Shooter whispered.

"Indeed." John smiled and looked deep into Shooter's eyes.

Shooter stiffened as a feeling similar to an electric shock rushed through his body. He uttered not a whimper of pain, not a cry of surprise as he watched the crew member before him slowly morph into a perfect imitation of himself, right down to the quarter of a cigarette left dangling from his lips. As the grip on his shoulder loosened, the shock faded away, taking all sensation, all feeling, all life with it. Shooter's gaze roamed the room setting down on his clothes, and then on the gleaming black guitar propped up on its stand in the corner. He knew what it was, knew the sound it made, but for the life of him, couldn't remember how to play it. And didn't care.

When he looked back at John, he saw himself transformed.

John was breathing hard, like he had just run a marathon, but the gleam in his eyes and flush to his skin showed pure ecstasy.

The bloodshot eyes and bags were gone. On John's frame, Shooter Armstrong looked five years younger. There was life in his limbs and joy in his face. The real Shooter felt a tear well in his eye and a lump form in his throat. In front of him was the soul he had buried beneath a plethora of pills and alcohol.

He slumped against the vanity, John having to rescue the remains of the cigarette from falling from his lips to the floor. He stubbed out both the cigarettes in the available ashtray.

"What the...?" Shooter began, but stopped. His brow furrowed in confusion and he rubbed his temples.

"It's okay, Zack," John soothed. "Everything is going to be alright. Why don't you just sit here and relax?" He steered the shell of the rock star to the chair by the vanity, making him sit. Shooter squinted, his befuddled brain trying to make sense of the last few minutes.

John turned away, stripped and pulled on a pair of black leather pants and a black muscle shirt from the trunk. A pair of black boots and a metal studded belt with matching wrist band completed the ensemble. John surveyed himself in the mirror. Not bad. Very rock 'n' roll. Making use of the pomade in the bathroom, he adjusted the peaks of his spiky hair. He was applying dark eyeliner around his eyes when a roadie knocked on the door.

"Five minutes, man!"

Five minutes. Sucker Punch would have finished and the crew would be taking down one set of instruments to make room for the other. Five minutes until the biggest show of his career to date.

He turned to Shooter, still slumped in the chair, twisting the silver skull ring on his right middle finger.

"How are you Zack?"

"Tired," was the murmured response. "Confused."

"Everything's going to be okay," John repeated. He began popping open the pill containers, taking a few from each one until a rainbow of colors and combinations was in his hand. "Here, take these," he said, handing them to Shooter. "You'll feel better."

Shooter stared at the mixture and then at the rye bottle John held out for him. He seemed to think about it for a moment before taking the bottle and washing the pills down with a large swig of the amber liquid.

*I'm With The Band* by Kimberly Foottit

John smiled, reaching for the rye, but Shooter scowled and hugged it to his chest. He sighed. Even without a soul, the body's irrational need still seemed to come first.

Leaving the bottle in Shooter's possession, John grabbed for his right hand and slid off the skull ring, pushing it onto his own finger. Shooter was only perturbed at the momentary loss of the use of one of his hands as he tilted back the rye again.

John grabbed the guitar from its stand and a Red Bull from the vanity, before taking a last backward glance at Shooter.

"Wish me luck."

"Luck," Shooter mumbled, taking another pull at the bottle.

John opened the door, stepped out, and closed it softly behind him. He strode away quickly, confident that no one would enter the dressing room until his return.

John slung the guitar strap across his chest, pulling the neck down on the instrument, so the body would rest against his back. Popping the can, he chugged the Red Bull in the same way Shooter did rye. Energy drinks did nothing for him, but downing one emulated Shooter's schedule: drugs washed down with rye in the dressing room with one last jolt of energy before going onstage to bring him up, the rest of the rye and a joint or two after the show to calm him down. John had always been good at doing his homework.

He handed the empty can to a roadie waiting by the stage. The crew was just putting the last of Black Eden's instruments out and the other three members were waiting in the wings. John joined them, staring beyond the stage to the chanting crowd. Anticipation welled up in his stomach and he couldn't contain the grin that plastered his face.

"Shooter? Hey Shooter, you with us man?" A hand on his shoulder accompanied the voice that brought him back to the circle of concerned faces. The drummer and Shooter's best friend, Max Gibson, stared intently at his face. The gleam in the eyes and the color to the normally pale skin were things that his band mates hadn't seen in years.

"Fuck, yeah," John answered.

"What the hell did you take tonight?" Shep Masters, the bassist, asked as he pulled his instrument over his head and let it rest against his hip.

"What the fuck is it to you?" John answered in what he thought would be a typical "Shooter" response.

Jayson Reed scoffed. "Yeah, I'd say he's okay." He had his guitar in his hand. "Let's get out there and play some music."

The others nodded, Max still watching John's face. They formed a circle, all four putting a hand in the middle. Shep, the original founder of the band and their de facto leader, offered a mumbled prayer to the Gods of Music for a good show. Then they broke and jogged out onto the stage.

The roar from the crowd was deafening.

From then on, the night was a dream for John. Without the heavy influence of drugs and alcohol to wear him down, the essence of Shooter's soul burst forth and gave the best performance of the young man's career. His fellow band mates noticed it and fed off the improvement — playing with him instead of over him. The crowd noticed too, calling them back for an unprecedented three encores.

John, himself, was in his glory. He had experienced many things under many guises in his lifetime — pulling people from a burning building as a fireman, making love to the hottest actress in Hollywood as her equally hot actor boyfriend, even giving an Easter sermon in Rome as the Pope. But this beat them all. Playing and singing in a band as huge as Black Eden was undoubtedly his biggest rush to date. He was sad when it finally ended.

The group stumbled off stage for the last time, utterly spent and ecstatic. All of them were soaked with sweat, muscles aching, ears throbbing, but nothing could dampen the high.

John made his way back to the dressing room amidst catcalls and congratulations from band members and crew.

He opened the door quietly, and almost panicked when the real Shooter was not in the chair where he had left him. Then he spied a bare foot amongst the clothes on the bench. The empty rye bottle lay on the floor.

Only then did he notice the thick smell of human waste mixed with the alcohol. John shut the door behind him and carefully set the guitar on its stand. He walked over to the bench and began to move the clothing around until he found Shooter's head. He pressed two fingers to the silent neck even though the glazed over eyes were enough for John to know that he was dead.

Sighing, John rubbed his hands over his face. His night of glory was officially over.

John stripped once again, his body slowly morphing back into the jeans, T-shirt, and ball cap, of the beer bellied crew member.

With some effort he managed to undress Shooter then redress him in the stage clothes before repositioning him back on the bench. Only the soiled jeans had to go, after transferring part of their mess into the interior of the leather pants. It did have to look convincing after all.

John turned to the vanity to light a joint and waft the smoke around the room. Then he noticed the pill bottles were empty. He looked back at the body with admiration. Shooter had voluntarily finished the job.

Perhaps he had heard the show and knew he would never be able to top such a performance. Maybe years of self loathing and destruction caught up with him. It was a risk, leaving a victim conscious while borrowing their soul. The darkness which replaced that essential piece of human light could drive even the strongest person to the brink of insanity. And Shooter had not been the strongest person.

Whatever the reason, the young rock star had saved John the task of covering up his little adventure. He smiled. It was so rare to find someone who understood the meaning behind such actions. It was the perfect end to his perfect evening.

Retrieving the cords from the floor, and wrapping the jeans in one of the thin towels from the bathroom, John left the room and closed the door softly behind him. The stage lights were up and the hall was nearly empty. Already a clean up crew was gathering the debris left behind by the fans. Roadies and the local men hired for the night were packing up lights, speakers, amps, instruments and other equipment. John knew they would be at it for the rest of the night, only stopping when the trucks were loaded, ready for the next leg of the tour. Only there wouldn't be another leg to the tour; not anymore.

John slipped out of the building, leaving the cords where he had found them. The crowd had long since moved on for the night, Bruno and the rest of security moving inside to escort the band, helping where they were needed. As he wound his way through the parking lot, he knew someone should be stumbling upon the body of Shooter Armstrong. He tossed the soiled jeans and towel into a dumpster as he passed by.

"This just in," Chandra Bellings of the News One morning team announced. "Black Eden's lead guitarist, Zack 'Shooter' Armstrong was found dead in his dressing room last night of an apparent overdose. Sources say the rock star had been battling substance abuse for some time, but had recently started on the road to recovery. They played The Odeon last night to a sold out crowd and gave what many critics are calling the performance of their career. Black Eden was half way through their North American tour, but after last night's tragedy are not confirming whether they will try to continue without Armstrong. Zack 'Shooter' Armstrong, dead at the age of twenty-five."

John Smith smiled at the television, sipping his first cup of morning coffee. He had discarded the crew member guise for his original form — a rather ordinary looking brown haired, brown eyed white man in his mid to late twenties. It was reported as an overdose in the news. He was in the clear.

He opened the morning paper to the entertainment section. The story of Shooter's death breaking late, the only report of Black Eden was about their sold out concert. Sure enough, a large photo of him in the middle of one of their earlier songs — mouth open, body in an aggressive, yet suggestive pose — graced the second page of the section. The review underneath was favorable, stating how fresh and pure the vibe had been, how spectacular the sound, how amazing was the band.

John glowed with pride. Shooter's last great hurrah. It *was* better to burn out, than to fade away.

To the left of the Black Eden article, in the bottom corner of the page, was an advertisement for Marcellus Magyar's Illusions of Grandeur Show coming into town in two weeks. The mental list appeared in his head again and halfway down was "be a magician". There was no picture of Marcellus, but that wasn't a problem; he would be on the web somewhere.

Marcellus Magyar. He was no David Copperfield, but all in good time.

John got up and padded barefoot to the computer in the corner of his bachelor apartment. As the machine booted up, he smiled, twisting the silver skull ring around his right middle finger. He had always wanted to saw someone in half.

⁕ ✧ ⁕

**Kimberly Foottit** is a graduate of McMaster University, where her first published science fiction story "Walter's Brain" was set. She continually hammers out mystical and speculative writing in various forms, including an ongoing series of stories featuring the doppelganger John Smith (this is his first published appearance), and she demonstrates a special penchant for "postcard" length flash fiction pieces. Kimberly lives in Dundas, Ontario.

# My Teenage Ångström Poem

### ≈ David Clink ≈

So there I was, 15,
reading a trashy '50s sci-fi novel
(with a lot of questionable science) and
I was feeling angry about our dependency on foreign oil,

and the environment was going to pot—
I started to daydream about
the scientist's daughter in that trashy sci-fi novel
who (I imagined) looked like Anne Francis

from *Forbidden Planet*
and all I wanted to do was boost my I.Q.
and find the scientist's daughter
and we'd join Tom Swift on his *Repeletron Skyway*

and get the hell away from here
the science of escape velocity taking us
out into the crush of stars
far from these ink-laden lands.

# Cult Stories

## ~ Hugh A. D. Spencer ~

*1979:*
*Young Love, Strange Love(s)*

INTERVIEWER: How long have you been practicing Mentotechnics?
SUBJECT #3: Just about two years.
INTERVIEWER: Have you noticed any benefits?
SUBJECT #3: You bet! Back when I started, I could barely read.
INTERVIEWER: You had literacy problems?
SUBJECT #3: Big time!
INTERVIEWER: But you think Mentotechnics changed that.
SUBJECT #3: No kidding! Now I can read really fast and I really love reading!
INTERVIEWER: What was the last book you read?
SUBJECT #3: Ummm...

~ ✧ ~

The phone rang. It was just past three in the morning.
 Although Ethan had been in a deep sleep, he answered by the third ring. He lived in a small apartment.
 "She doesn't live here anymore," Ethan spoke without waiting for the person on the other end of the line. He had the routine

down pretty well. "She" was Gabriella, a young call girl from Quebec City who had rented the apartment before Ethan.

He'd only met her the one time when he'd first come to see the place. She was pretty, very quiet and was surrounded by a cloud of strong, but not altogether unpleasant, perfume. Gabriella also wore a T-shirt with a lace-up front that showed off a little more cleavage than usual.

Ethan had wondered whether these pleasant sensations were the reason that he agreed to buy all Gabriella's furniture as part of the move-in deal.

Meanwhile, nobody said anything on the telephone.

Anybody calling this time of night was probably very drunk.

Drunk, and possibly very desperate.

I'd better help this guy out, Ethan decided. "She hasn't lived here in over a year."

After five or six of these calls he had figured out what line of work Gabriella was in. Soon afterward, he persuaded the landlord to fumigate the furniture.

Still nothing on the phone.

It was a shame that the landlord refused to change the phone number in the apartment.

Nope. Just some distant breathing.

From previous experience, Ethan knew that this could either go reasonably well or very badly.

If it went well then the poor sap would just hang up and find some other cryptic listing in *The Hamilton Spectator's* personal section.

If it went badly, this drunken moron would decide that Ethan was one of Gabriella's clients, or worse yet, a boyfriend. This would usually stimulate the idiot-competitive lobe of the guy's tiny brain, which in turn would trigger a stream of abuse.

It was no use hanging up either, Ethan knew that. When these guys got this way, they'd just call right back. If it was one of Gabriella's old regulars, he might even threaten to come around to the apartment.

It was all very weird, maybe a bit scary, but kind of fun. One of the few forms of entertainment that an anthropology grad student could afford.

"Is this Ethan Daniels?"

It was a quiet voice. Very young, maybe a girl, probably a boy. Twelve, thirteen at the most, Ethan concluded.

This was different.

"Yes," Ethan replied. "Can I help you?"

*"You better stop what you're doing."*

The voice didn't project a lot of confidence. In fact it was squeaky and sounded like it might go out of control at any second. Ethan couldn't tell if this was because of extreme nervousness or the onset of puberty.

"Stop what, exactly?"

"D.H. Evanston is the greatest man who ever lived."

*That's* what this is about! Ethan realized that this exchange was now making some kind of sense.

"He certainly is a remarkable person," said Ethan. "But you must admit—"

*"He's going to save the world."*

"That's a really interesting opinion." Ethan felt that this could be an opportunity to gather more data. "It would be great if you could come by to my office and we could dis—"

"People like you are working out of fear and ignorance."

"I don't know about the fear part. But you're right, there's lots about Mentotechnics that some of us don't understand."

I don't believe it, Ethan thought, it's three in the morning and I'm about to start a lecture on social science methodology. "That's why we conduct research."

"Bad things will happen if you don't stop."

Dial tone.

Strange, Ethan thought as he rolled back onto his folding couch. That was probably the least effective threatening phone call in recent history. Somebody should tell these people that kids whose voices haven't finished changing aren't particularly menacing. Still, the kid's vocabulary was pretty good for someone that age.

Maybe there was something to the training after all.

⁕ ✧ ⁕

When Ethan woke up (at a more agreeable time) that morning, his first thoughts were not of his mysterious phone call.

He really had to break up with Nina.

He went through this every time he was just about out of condoms.

For such a scientific optimist, Nina was strangely nervous about the Pill, so she insisted on alternative forms of contraception.

However, she was also an affectionate person, so she suggested that they use condoms made of 100% sheepskin.

"They transmit our body heat," she explained. "It's so much nicer."

Not if you're a sheep, Ethan thought.

Nina's theory was good, but unless you had the genitals of a sperm whale, it was pretty hard to get a snug fit. They were always dealing with air pockets in the membrane and the constant fear that the damn thing was going to slip off at the wrong moment.

The net effect was that the regularly emptying box made Ethan very conscious of this aspect of his relationship with Nina. This in turn called to mind what he felt was going wrong with the whole situation.

Nina — Ethan decided to use the appropriate folk-culture term — was going seriously nuts.

He marked the serious disintegration of her personality from the day that they attended the premiere showing of *Star Trek: The Motion Picture*.

◈

If Star Trek had been a church back then, Nina Brown would have been one of its most devoted saints.

Ethan met Nina in a second hand bookstore. She was almost glowing with joy because she'd found a copy of the, then rare, paperback edition of James Blish's novel *Spock Must Die!* She explained that this was the climax of a rather lengthy literary quest.

Therefore Nina was in an incredibly good mood, which made her very attractive to Ethan.

When she invited him to a marathon screening of episodes at the local art-house cinema, he accepted. He felt a bit of a sociable buzz set in as they sat through six hours of burnt popcorn odors and the whispering of well-known and well-loved dialogue from the audience.

Nina had more respect for the quality of Ethan's cinematic experience. She let him watch without interruption. In turn, Ethan had to admit that the direction, writing and even the acting wasn't bad. Especially if you considered the overall state of episodic television in the 1960s and 1970s. It was a period when the cost and quantity of recreational drugs had gotten so small and so large (respectively) that most programs were essentially unwatchable.

About two in the morning, Nina and Ethan found a coffee shop in Westdale where Nina spent another two hours explaining that she was an activist. She was a passionate member of the "Bring Back Star Trek" movement.

Hamilton, Ontario had a university and it had a lot of big steel mills, so it had lots of politics. Therefore Ethan knew quite a few activists but most of them were not involved with helping William Shatner and Leonard Nimoy get their old jobs back.

Ethan briefly considered whether Nina and her friends might be good subjects for anthropological study. Probably, but he was enjoying her company too much to raise the question.

By four, they realized that the buses weren't running anymore, so there was no way for Ethan to find his way home. Nina invited him to her place.

When they got there, Nina poured him some beer. This was Hamilton, after all.

The drinks didn't make them sleepy, just a bit stupid.

Nina took out a very thick binder filled with loose-leaf papers. "I've never shown anyone this before." The pages were covered with line after line of expansive handwriting. "You might find this interesting."

It was Nina's fiction. Fan fiction. Incredibly pornographic fan fiction. Throughout, there were three or four characters of Nina's creation who did some unlikely but enthusiastic coupling, but most of the stories focused on a long-standing homosexual affair between Captain Kirk and Mr. Spock.

Context is just about everything.

That must be why (at the time) Ethan didn't find the stories to be funny or pathetic (which he ordinarily might have); or deviant or perverted (because he hadn't had much experience with gay relationships or other people's sexual fantasies back then); or typical of a new expression of folk culture (which professionally, he really should have). No, (at the time) Ethan just found reading the stories rather arousing. Which was convenient, because Nina happened to be in the same mood.

And these events ultimately led to Ethan's current dilemma with Nina. When they first got together, Ethan didn't think that Nina's passion for Star Trek made her crazy, it just made her more fun.

He had been forced to revise his opinion.

This was quite sad. The sadder thing was his realization that he didn't love Nina enough to stick with her or help her through her craziness.

⟢ ✧ ⟣

SUBJECT #18: I'm pretty sure I shouldn't be talking to you.
INTERVIEWER: Why do you say that?
SUBJECT #18: Because you could be writing something that's hostile to Mentotechnics.
INTERVIEWER: No, this will be an objective study.
SUBJECT #18: I guess I should just look on the bright side.
INTERVIEWER: You mean that Mentotechnics will benefit from objective study?
SUBJECT #18: Hell, no! I mean that I can use the money you're paying me to buy more therapy sessions.

⟢ ✧ ⟣

Ethan liked many things about McMaster University.

What he really loved about the institution was that the library system had an outstanding collection of science fiction studies material, including some oral histories about the early years of American fandom.

In Hamilton, Ontario. It was a surprise that saved Ethan's academic career.

There were a couple of things about McMaster that Ethan wasn't quite so excited about. There were huge engineering and medical programs, and this — of course — was a big challenge for anyone doing tutorials in anthropology. The classes were filled with big, smart and ambitious kids in a hurry to get into their chosen professions. Most of them got quite unruly after the first set of midterms, when they discovered that social anthropology wasn't a bird course after all. It was just one more damn useless complicated thing to study.

But there were some amusing consequences to this effect. One kid offered him a car; another on-demand blowjobs, if Ethan could find some way to nudge their grades up just a little bit.

No go, of course. Ethan didn't like driving very much and Nina, even with her intrusive contraceptive practices, was enough for him at the time. Still, on a graduate student's budget, free entertainment was always most appreciated.

McMaster was also a very populist school back then. Faculty members were directed to find any, and all, opportunities for their work to contribute to the well being and improvement of the wider community. This mandate included the activities of any students under the tutelage of the faculty members.

Ethan's thesis supervisor, Dr. Sirkowsi, was a chain-smoking, bearded ex-American, ex-Marxist activist. He was also one of the architects of the University's community service policy.

When Sirkowski learned of Ethan's interest in science fiction fandom and so-called "marginal religious movements", he immediately became interested. It was just after the events in Jonestown, and the images of Kool-Aid-induced suicides still troubled the professor's conscience.

"This will be your opportunity to contribute something of true value to the greater public," the respected academic growled through his saliva and tobacco stained beard. "Even before you've completed your doctoral studies. You are very fortunate!"

So Ethan ended up doing community service just because he wanted to study groups like Mentotechnics. Every time somebody showed up at the department asking about "cults" and "wacko religions" they were sent up to Ethan's office.

At first Ethan tried to incorporate these confessionals into his research, but usually the results were too weird and pathetic to be very useful. Most of the time he was just talking to people who wanted to vent. The best thing to do was be polite, sympathetic and try to pass on a bit of accurate history.

◈

MILGORE: I heard that you were carrying out a research project on Mentotechnics.
DANIELS: Yes that's true.
MILGORE: My daughter has joined the Temple.
DANIELS: I see.
MILGORE: I'm so worried!
DANIELS: Mrs. Milgore, aside from offering my sympathies, there isn't much I can do.
MILGORE: There's *nothing* you can do?
DANIELS: Some people would say your relationship with your daughter was a regrettable, but necessary, sacrifice to living in a free and open society.

MILGORE: *Oh, thank you very much!* I suppose I should try and find one of those deprogrammers.
DANIELS: You probably respect your daughter too much to have her kidnapped.
MILGORE: So what can I do?
DANIELS: Well, here's something, wondered where I put it...
MILGORE: (sniffs) Yes?
DANIELS: It's an article published in an old science fiction magazine by a writer named Bob Clyde. He used to know Evanston and he's quite blunt about the man's ethics and where he got his ideas for a new religion.
MILGORE: What am I supposed to do with this?
DANIELS: Read it. Let yourself know what you're dealing with.
MILGORE: Isn't there anything else I can do?
DANIELS: Just the simple stuff — keep in touch with your daughter — don't give her very much money.

◈

It had started out as a good day. Saturdays usually were good for Ethan because the department offices were just about empty, which made it a great time to catch up on transcribing his interviews.

The particular Saturday was even better, because he was able to finish the first draft of his thesis. At about 1:15 in the afternoon, Ethan typed in the last entry from his index cards, boxed the 300-plus pages and left the whole package in Professor Sirkowski's mailbox. All he had to do now was wait for comments.

Unexpectedly, Ethan had some free time.

Nina had mentioned that she was going to be at her place filing some punch cards from the Physics Department's mainframe. He'd missed lunch, but maybe he could persuade her to go to that new Greek cafeteria and take in a movie at the Student Union building. Which left a few hours before that to do stuff that Ethan wasn't feeling particularly guilty about at that moment.

The department secretary had forgotten to lock the main office, so Ethan made a quick phone call and, thank god, Nina said yes!

The weather was quite nice for late January, so Ethan decided that he'd forget the Hamilton Public Transit System and walk to his apartment. The fact that he'd reached a milestone in his studies, and the prospect of a certain amount for fun with Nina, filled Ethan with all kinds of energy. He felt like he was radiating photons and almost bouncing all the way home — as if McMaster had suddenly been teleported to the moon.

Maybe that was why Ethan didn't hear the car roar up from behind, turn and head towards him. At that point, Ethan did notice that something was happening, but there wasn't much that he could do about it.

He turned, and the car was bearing down on him — at maybe 70 - 75 miles an hour.

I'm going to be liquefied by the front end of this vehicle; Ethan heard a curiously calm voice inside his head. Then he was impressed by the speed and complexity of human cognition. How can I be having such complex thoughts in the less than a microsecond that I have to live?

Ethan was most amazed by the reason why he had time for all this interesting thinking.

Just before what was definitely going to be an inevitable collision, the car swerved, missed Ethan and took out a mailbox instead.

It took two or three minutes to figure out what had just happened. Ethan's brain must have been working very slowly at that point; perhaps it was some kind of existential relativity thing going on.

The mailbox was seriously flattened and the car was extremely bent.

Pity, thought Ethan. It was a nice car, a Triumph TR7, one of those sports cars that academics could dream about without guilt because there wasn't a chance in the universe that they'd ever own one.

Well, maybe Ethan could now afford the one sitting in front of him.

*Help.*

Another thought was germinating, forming, taking solid form and rising through the turgid mass of Ethan's consciousness.

*You should.*

What was that, he asked himself.

*You should help.*

Oh god, yes! Ethan realized that whoever was inside that car was probably horribly injured.

He should try and help.

Moreover, the poor bastard behind the steering wheel probably hit the mailbox because he was trying to miss Ethan.

Now he felt as though he weighed 30 tons, as if he was suddenly trapped in Jupiter's gravitational field, or he was being sucked deep down into some primordial tar pit.

Ethan dreaded what bleeding, flayed mass of human suffering he was going to find crushed behind that steering wheel.

Behind? Hell, this was an import here, maybe the steering wheel went right through the poor sod.

So it felt like a geological age for Ethan to reach the car. Maybe his subjective perceptions slowed down to give him some scope of reflection, some kind of psychological cushion, a period of "fake time" to help him prepare for what he was going to see.

It didn't work. Ethan was not prepared for what he saw on the other side of that shattered windshield.

*Nothing.*

*Nobody.*

Not a thing was behind the wheel of that car.

Ethan's first thought was that somehow the driver's body had gotten wedged below the dashboard. He took a deep breath, and peered over the empty frame.

*Still nothing.*

There was no sign of a driver.

So according to the evidence of his eyes, nobody had been driving the car that had almost run him over.

At this point, things started to get very spotty. Ethan couldn't quite remember walking the rest of the way home, but he did recall lying down for most of the next two days.

He sort of remembered a not very satisfactory telephone conversation with Nina.

(Well, even more unsatisfactory than most their communications).

Ethan most certainly did not remember talking to the police about the accident, but he must have at some point. After all, he was a very responsible citizen when it came to that sort of thing.

Ethan definitely remembered feeling *completely* exhausted for the next three days. Lying there on the mattress that he and Nina had long since crushed flat, Ethan pieced together what must have happened.

It was selective amnesia brought about by random trauma.

Of course he had tried to help.

Of course he had seen a body.

And of course, it must have been something absolutely horrific.

Of course, Ethan had gone somewhere and called an ambulance and of course he had waited for the police to arrive and made a complete statement.

And of course, Ethan had absolutely no memory of any of this because his conscious mind just wasn't able to process all those events right now.

This kind of stress reaction was something that Ethan was familiar with, but as a social scientist, Ethan was annoyed that he was a participant in this pathology rather than an observer.

By Wednesday morning, Ethan was able to move around his apartment. Maybe by the end of the day he might be able to take the bus to his office.

The phone rang.

It wasn't Nina this time. No, it was Professor Sirkowski.

"Outstanding first draft. Lots of revisions needed, mind you, but you may have something publishable by the end of the process."

Ethan was never able to explain just why he said what he said next.

"Forget the whole thing, sir. I'm changing my thesis."

But Ethan was certain that he meant it.

⌒ ✧ ⌒

1993:
*"Pictures at an Exhibition"*

INTERVIEWER: Were you ever concerned that D.H. Evanston was a science fiction writer before he founded the Temple of Mentotechnics?
SUBJECT #40: No, not at all.
INTERVIEWER: You mean it didn't raise any doubts?
SUBJECT #40: Why would it?
INTERVIEWER: Well, to some people it might be like finding out that John the Baptist was a contributor to *Cousin Mort's Flying Saucer Quarterly*.
SUBJECT #40: Your statements are more biased than usual today. You must be tired.
INTERVIEWER: Yeah, I'll watch out for that.
SUBJECT #40: In answer to your question, once again, no. Evanston's work as a science fiction writer didn't bother me at all. I thought it made a lot of sense.

INTERVIEWER: Made sense? In what way?
SUBJECT #40: It takes tremendous vision and imagination to apprehend the enormity of what Mentotechnics really is.
INTERVIEWER: I guess that's one way of looking at it—
SUBJECT #40: And besides, science fiction is the only truly relevant literature left!
INTERVIEWER: But you told me earlier that you had some concerns about the Temple, that some people were there for the wrong reasons.
SUBJECT #40: Yes, some people, like ones at the Celebrity Training Centres, were just there for personal advancement.
INTERVIEWER: And there's a problem there?
SUBJECT #40: They're missing the big picture. While they're worrying about ways to win auditions they can't see that the human race is evolving into something new and wonderful!
INTERVIEWER: Sounds terrific.
SUBJECT #40: It's beyond terrific! It's beyond infinity! We're on the verge of a new relationship with the very essence of the universe!

⁀ ✧ ⁀

"We need you to go to Los Angeles."

It was an unexpected request from a very unexpected source.

Ethan hadn't seen Nina in over ten years.

"I'm flattered," he said into the telephone receiver.

Ethan eyed the pile of third year term papers, all grappling with that eternal problem of human existence:

*"Compare and contrast economic behavior models in three hunter-gatherer monographs".*

Ripping shit. Ethan hoped that Nina didn't hear him sigh.

"But I haven't been researching minority religious movements in quite a long while."

"I know you, Ethan." He heard laughter at the other end of the line. It wasn't particularly nice laughter. "You're a determined man and you're a sneaky bastard."

Thank god, you're not bitter, Ethan thought.

Actually, he was surprised that Nina wanted to remember anything about him. Particularly after the last days of their relationship.

Way back in 1979 as the weeks, the days, and finally the hours counted down to the Star Trek movie premiere.

Nina had been collecting every newspaper story, any fanzine that mentioned it, and absolutely all the gossip she could possibly absorb. Back in the pre-internet era, this was actually quite time-consuming.

But she seemed to be enjoying it. The more Trek data she collected, the more excited she got.

"It just goes to show," Nina would say with increasing regularity. "Star Trek really does live."

Like a lot of other Trekkers, Nina took a lot of pride in the movie. She believed she was part of a worldwide grass roots movement, motivated by love and idealism, that had changed the course of the monolithic American Entertainment Establishment.

"It's going to be incredible," she would say.

Ethan decided that after Vietnam and Wade versus Roe, that all that activist energy had to go somewhere.

He had to admit the sex got more and more incredible as the premiere got closer.

But as Ethan lay there in bed, his hormone levels returning to something approaching normal, rational thought would set in and he got a little scared. Yeah, he didn't like to use simplistic Freudian concepts, but they seemed to apply here. There seemed to be some incredibly powerful cathartic psychosexual link between the Star Trek Universe and Planet Nina.

He really ought to do something about it. Maybe talk to her.

But the pathology was so much fun.

REPORTER: What do you say to those who are critical of you and your organization?
EVANSTON: I'm always surprised by critical people. Who are they?
REPORTER: Those people who say that your work is a lie and that you are a fraud.
EVANSTON: What can I say, Mike? We have measurable, scientifically proven results. There's hard evidence.
REPORTER: *Scientific* evidence that Mentotechnics works?
EVANSTON: Absolutely. Astonishing evidence. People are changed in ways that are miraculous.
REPORTER: Scientific miracles?
EVANSTON: Beautifully put, Mike.

"You must be doing some kind of research."

Nina was right about that, too. But really all he could manage these days was to check out the microfiche files at the local library and save clippings whenever he found a story about Mentotechnics in the newspaper.

This time Ethan knew he sighed out loud.

"What do you need?" he asked.

There was a note of triumph in Nina's voice. "My division is in the middle of a long term investigation. You might be able to give us some context."

"Context?"

"That's right," Nina replied. "We need you to make an assessment of the criminal potentiality of the organization."

Ethan smiled. There was some consulting money coming down the line, maybe he could even get a publication out of it.

"You want me to write you a report."

"We want you to go and look at something and tell us what you think."

⁂

REPORTER: If you have "hard evidence", why is the Department of Justice raiding your offices and impounding your files and therapy machines?
EVANSTON: Good question, Mike.
REPORTER: Do you have a good answer?
EVANSTON: I don't think the Department of Justice would say we don't have evidence … they just don't know what it's evidence of…

⁂

It was a Friday in early December.

The great day had arrived.

Nina appeared at the door to his classroom — about half an hour before the end of the tutorial.

Ethan saw her expression and knew that he had to take pre-emptive action.

"Okay," he said to the twenty second year students. "We've been talking about marginal social states and liminal conditions in a range of different societies…"

The undergrads nodded in that polite, gentle way they always did when Ethan had just said something very obvious or very boring.

"...so let's have an unscheduled research assignment."

Ethan felt a sudden spike in the collective tension level. If you added in Nina's current Strange State of Being, the risk factor in the classroom was getting extremely high.

"...I want you to write up paper, at least ten pages long for next Thursday..."

Flushed faces, flashing eyes, tight lips.

*Danger, Will Robinson! Danger!*

"...analyzing your weekend as a liminal state where you encounter and practice different mores and social expectations."

The slightly thick keener in the front row started to raise his hand. Ethan knew he had to prevent all discussion.

"I want you to make a log book of all your activities for the next 48 hours," he said quickly. "Then compare the notes in that log with your behavior on Monday and Tuesday."

The students were now nodding their heads and making notes. Perhaps the implications of what Ethan was saying hadn't quite sunk in yet.

Documenting twenty sets of two days of undergraduate depravity? It would be fun to grade.

Ethan thought that it was a real pity that Nina was so fixated on the movie opening that she didn't appreciate how brilliant he was at that moment.

"I know that this is quite a challenge to spring on you so suddenly," he continued. "So we're going to adjourn a little early to give you more time for your assignments."

Game, set and match!

One hour later, Nina and Ethan were standing in line outside the Tivoli Theatre waiting for the five o'clock showing. There were about thirty people in front of them.

Ethan was feeling the early December wind, but Nina seemed oblivious to any physical stimuli. She was busy chatting with her Trekker friends as they arrived and took their place in line.

Speaking of liminal states, Ethan thought. These Trekkers are definitely existing outside of normal social space and time. This was definitely an instance of "communitas" — the breaking down of social barriers and distinctions as part of the celebration of a greater ideological or spiritual collective expression.

Except that this wasn't a holy communion or the right of passage for the youth of a West African village, or even a sacred ritual orgy. No, this communitas involved people wearing rubber ears.

Ethan wondered if he should share these witty anthropological insights, but then he looked over at Nina and decided that it probably was not a good time.

The dramatic climax of the queuing experience came when a van pulled up to the box office and a man wearing a denim boiler suit got out. He rolled open the back of the van and started hauling out massive film canisters. The letters: "S.T.M.P." were stenciled on the sides.

The trekkers looked both relieved and excited.

"That's it? That's the movie?"

"It's here? On time?"

The deliveryman nodded. "God damn prints are still wet. I heard they pulled things right off the editing machines at Paramount."

Nina had told Ethan what most of the trekkers were worried about, many times.

There had been some problems with the special effects. The original SFX studio had been fired and two new technical teams had to start work just a few months ago. There had been a lot of speculation that the film just wouldn't be ready for its scheduled release. Or that the special effects would look really terrible, especially in comparison with *Star Wars*.

Things like that were really important to Nina and her friends.

But it seemed as though the artisans of Hollywood had come through after all. Ethan looked at Nina as she watched the last of the film canisters disappear through the glass doors of the Tivoli. He wondered if she would look as happy at the birth of her first child.

Inevitably, Nina's mood was going to change that evening. It did so, fairly soon after the thumping orchestral soundtrack propelled the audience through the hastily superimposed titles into what Ethan loosely considered the "dramatic" portion of the film.

Frankly, he was more of a group systems and collective manifestations person. Ethan wasn't very good at identifying individual emotional states. That made it difficult for him to be precise in determining what Nina was going through as she watched the film.

The only qualitative assessment that Ethan felt comfortable with was to say that he believed that *Star Trek: The Motion Picture* was not quite the experience that Nina had expected.

After the show, Ethan suggested that they stop by the Student Union Pub, figuring that a couple of beers would improve Nina's state of mind.

She snarled at him. Literally.

And to his regret, Nina then didn't deal with her despair in isolation. Hours later at his apartment, in the early morning, she was still weeping, calling up friends from across the continent.

"The world has lost a great opportunity," she sniffed at some shocked fan in New Mexico.

Ethan thought about his phone bill and wished that they really did have transporter technology. That way he could just beam Nina around to all her weird friends and they could commiserate in person.

Instead he went to bed.

Alone. Which was how it was going to be for a while.

⟡ ✧ ⟡

REPORTER: How do you respond to rumors that D.H. Evanston really isn't dead? That he's gone into hiding to avoid legal difficulties?
SPOKESPERSON: That's just not the case. The death certificate is a matter of public record and some of us were present at the time of his passing.
REPORTER: Who was present?
SPOKESPERSON: Close family members and senior Temple officials. Myself included.
REPORTER: This must be a tremendous loss to all of you.
SPOKESPERSON: A loss to all sentient life.
REPORTER: Uh, yes. So how are you all coping? Will this lead to the end of your organization?
SPOKESPERSON: Not at all. We're completely prepared for this and our movement will continue to flourish.
REPORTER: Is this a time of great change for Mentotechnics?
SPOKESPERSON: There's been some change and there's been some continuity.

⟡ ✧ ⟡

The World Center for Mental Technology is located in the grounds of what was once a Navy blimp hangar in Orange County. "One of the world's largest wooden structures", a brass sign read on one of the highways leading to the main gate.

Contrary to popular belief, not all of Orange County is fabulously wealthy. The neighborhoods surrounding the Mentotechnics World Center were most definitely not of the fabulous type, in fact Ethan thought that the houses and roads looked as though they had sustained repeated bomb damage.

But it was just protracted poverty. A quieter but no less damaging form of warfare.

Popular belief is correct in the assertion that it is essentially completely impossible to get around Southern California without a car. Ethan hated driving, but there he was stuck behind the wheel of a Kia rental, trying to find his way to the Center.

He had been driving around the general area for over an hour. He could see the huge golden spire that marked the building, and once in a while he could even get a glimpse of the great wooden hump of what was once the hangar.

But drive as he might, Ethan could not find the actual entrance. If he had believed Mentotechnics doctrine, Ethan would have concluded that this was some kind of telepathic defense system, that someone knew he was coming and was using the power of illusion to prevent it.

Really, it was just the unique quasi-urban geography of Orange County. Finding the historical marker from the Parks Department was Ethan's big breakthrough.

⟨ ✧ ⟩

"I advised my people that you have a unique combination of experience." Ethan was sitting in Nina's office at the Ottawa headquarters of the Canadian Security and Intelligence Service. "Thanks," Ethan said a little nervously. "But you probably know as much about this phenomenon as I do."

Nina's face turned red.

Perhaps she's trying to put things behind her. But Ethan didn't think she had much to be upset about. After they broke up, Nina had left the computer science department and entered McMaster's law enforcement programme. And after that, she'd become very successful.

She looked at her hands and continued speaking. "I emphasized that you are a highly credible source."

"Thanks."

"A portion of the World Mentotechnics Center is now accessible to the general public."

"That's ... unusual."

What else could he say? Given the Temple's paranoid attitude toward any criticism, it was extremely unusual. "What are they doing? Guided tours?"

"Yes," Nina replied. "They put up an exhibition honoring Evanston on the anniversary of his death."

Ethan was a little embarrassed that he hadn't heard about this. Now that he knew, it seemed obvious that the Temple would want to use Evanston's passing as an opportunity for some kind of promotional event.

"Exhibition?" The second he said the word, Ethan knew that he'd scored a 9.5 on the moron scale.

Nina didn't seem to notice. "The U.S. Department of Justice has run into some political problems with the Mentotechnics organization."

"They made an exhibition about Evanston?" What was wrong with his brain?

"Yes." Okay, now Nina did seem to notice the cloud of stupidity surrounding him. "The Americans have asked us to take over the investigation."

That didn't sound quite right to Ethan but he decided that wasn't likely to get any explanation from Nina.

"You want me to go and see this exhibition?"

"*Yes*," Nina said attempting to sound patient. "All you have to do is show up and tell us what you think."

◈

The young woman at the reception desk looked like some kind of a sexual newt. Artificial blonde, pale — almost transparent skin. She had an astonishingly thin body that looked like it might topple over from the sheer magnitude of what must have been surgically enhanced breasts. This was Orange County after all.

She frowned at Ethan. Naturally he was staring at her chest but he didn't think he had been that obvious.

"What do you want?"

Good god, thought Ethan. It's not my fault that she has such weird tits. Or worse yet, was she *expecting* him?

"I, uh, I—"

Ethan had this terrifying thought; maybe the Temple had some kind of vast enemies' list on a database. Was the nearly-clear young lady even now sitting there calling up his life history on her terminal?

"Well?"

"I, uh, just came to see the exhibition."

Ethan briefly wondered if he could get CSIS to cover half his travel expenses even if he couldn't get admittance.

"I can leave if I'm not welcome."

The young lady looked puzzled, then a little upset.

"Do you mean you're not a mental technologist?"

"No," replied Ethan. For some reason he felt hurt and rejected. "The man at my hotel said that the Temple was open to the general public."

"*Yes!* Yes, it is!" The young lady said with great intensity. "I thought you might be part of a bus tour of members from our Albuquerque branch."

"Oh..."

"But I guess they must be late."

Ethan wondered how super-evolved beings with hyper-developed mental powers could let things like traffic jams interfere with their day. But he decided that it probably wasn't a good idea to mention anything.

"Is it okay for me to see the exhibition?"

"Of course!" The young lady seemed relieved, possibly even eager to make up for her earlier rudeness. "I'll give you the guided tour."

Ethan was fascinated as he watched the young lady totter out from behind the reception desk. She was wearing six-inch heels and a metallic mini-dress that looked as though it been applied with a spray can.

She looked like one of Captain Kirk's girlfriends from the third season. Ethan was slightly disgusted with himself because he liked the effect so much.

Stop it, he said to himself, as he followed her to the entrance to the exhibition. Ignore your life-long weakness toward lechery and at least try and stay objective. You're supposed to be some kind of a social scientist.

The first display was pretty validating — the scene was almost exactly as Ethan had imagined. It was a recreation of the offices of *Tremendous Stories of Super Science*. There were two figures: one represented the editor Stewart D. McReady, and the other the then-youthful D.H. Evanston. They were leaning over McReady's large oak desk, presumably discussing Evanston's latest submission.

"It was at this stage in his career," the young lady said, "that Donald Evanston quickly became one of the most popular and prolific writers in the Golden Age of science fiction."

She spoke very well, thought Ethan. As though she'd memorized every word but wasn't bored with the material yet.

"People say that Donald Evanston could produce at least three short stories a day."

The young lady pointed to an artifact display: a very early model electric typewriter connected to a hefty roll of newsprint.

"He wrote so quickly that he didn't want to wait to change pages."

"Sounds like real creative flow."

"Yes." The young lady sounded very pleased that Ethan seemed to be taking an interest in her presentation. "I've never heard it put that way, but yes."

They left the office reconstruction and walked down a huge tunnel, a collage of four-color print. The walls were lined with thousands of science fiction magazine and paperback covers. The floor and ceiling were lined with mirrors that created a room-sized kaleidoscope effect. It was sort of like the trip sequence from Kubrick's *2001* but with much worse art direction.

"Donald Evanston went on to become a major influence on the genre," the young lady said as they walked toward the far end of the eye-splitting tunnel. "The Temple is still a patron of important new work."

They entered a room that looked like another set from a movie or a TV show. Maybe something like the *Time Tunnel* or *Lost in Space*. There were flashing lights everywhere with lots of reel to reel tapes and shelves of electrode-covered skullcaps.

"And this is our Therapy Machine Timeline." The young lady gestured at the old technology with pride.

"I've heard of these," Ethan said trying to sound as innocent as possible. Actually, he was so excited that he thought he might wet himself — nobody had seen this much Mentotechnic paraphernalia. It was the Holy Grail of post-modern religious/popular culture studies.

"The T-Machine is the foundation of everything we do in Mentotechnics."

Damn right, Ethan thought.

"And this is a complete collection of every unit issued by the Temple. From the 1952 prototype to next year's model."

"How do they work?" Ethan knew the official story very well, but he was interested in how his guide interpreted the belief system.

She didn't hesitate: "Well, T-Machines operate on the principle that we can monitor and record every human thought." She pointed to an antiquated oscilloscope that showed a single illuminated line gently curving up and down.

Of course, that is not possible, Ethan thought. You can measure various clusters of electrical activity in the human brain but nobody can track specific interior meanings.

In terms of accurate, provable science they were essentially in a room full of animated Etch-A-Sketches. Ethan tried not to smirk.

"Could you stand over there?" The young lady moved Ethan over so that he faced one of the T-Machines. It looked big and comfortable.

"Once we've traced a thought," the young lady said, "we can repair it and eventually enhance the abilities of the thinker."

What a lovely, and hopelessly naïve, thought. But "Gosh" was all that he said.

It was the only thing he felt he could safely say.

"And in some ways we find ways to more effectively think together."

Ethan started a bit. He didn't know anything about collective telepathy in Mentotechnic doctrine.

"Would you like a demonstration?"

Ethan nodded. Not just for academic reasons but also because it would be good color commentary for his report to Nina.

The electrodes went on very quickly.

"At the advanced levels we believe that we can record entire human personalities and sustain their intellects in artificial environments."

Ethan would have to think about the significance of what he'd just heard. He would also have to think about whether it was actually true that the vocabulary of his guide seemed to be growing as they continued the tour.

She clicked a few switches on the T-Machine.

"This is how we've been able to maintain continuity of leadership in our organization."

"Huh?" Okay, thought Ethan, he could have been more eloquent there.

"*Huh!*" Ethan's spine snapped rigid as a not-insignificant amount of electricity ran from the T-Machine, up through the skullcap and into his body. He realized that he would only be speaking in monosyllables for a while.

"Would you like to meet the living mind of D.H. Evanston?"

He's been dead for years, thought Ethan.

"*Duh!*" was what Ethan said.

Then everything went very dark and for an indeterminate time Ethan felt like he was weightless, suspended in the presence of something very ambitious with an Arkansas accent. A lot of words were floating around with him but he could only understand one. It was a direct, powerful message, meant only for him:

"*MORON.*"

Then Ethan woke up. He was lying next to a very cold lake, on a pile of leaves, twigs and some rather bouncy soil. When he eventually found his way to a human community, he discovered that he was in Prince Albert Provincial Park, somewhere in central Saskatchewan.

2009:
Dish and Saucer

Arrangements were running a bit late, so Ethan had a couple of hours to kill. Not the easiest thing to do in central Alberta.

He decided to take in the local museums and attractions.

There was the obligatory Royal Canadian Air Force museum with the rusting AVRO CF-100 stuck on a pole on the front yard. The rather subdued cases of uniforms and medals were housed in the former Royal Canadian Legion Hall.

That experience was good for about 20 minutes. Ethan then crossed the street to the local history museum.

In this part of the world, local history was essentially agricultural history. Ethan had never seen so many ancient tractors and combines — all reverently positioned on illuminated plywood pedestals.

This was definitely farm country. Even the docents were dressed in those denim bib overalls that nobody makes anymore. Ethan felt as though he was in a very grounded culture, one that was focused on very practical and concrete things, stuff that grew out of the earth and that you could eat.

But according to Nina's briefing notes, Ethan's perception was not accurate. This part of Western Canada was a "hotspot" — a region with numerous UFO sightings and encounters. His favorite CSIS memo about the town started: "RE: ROSWELL NORTH".

Ethan decided he'd test the reports by talking to one of the docents.

The man was a volunteer and a retired farmer, with a mass of wiry white hair and cracked sun-blasted skin. He looked like a part of the museum's agricultural collections.

They talked about the usual sorts of things: where the old man had farmed, the kinds of crops he grew, and why it was shame that so many young families couldn't make their living in town anymore.

The conversation started getting a little strange when they started talking about the weather. Ethan appreciated that the weather is a topic of passionate interest in agrarian communities; after all the variations in temperature and rainfall could have an enormous impact on your livelihood.

Even so, Ethan was surprised when the old man started talking about how many of the harvests in the 1970s and 1980s had been seriously damaged by giant Soviet weather manipulation satellites.

"Wow."

That was all that Ethan felt it was safe to say.

"Guess they must be still up there, workin' away," the old man said. "Because even though the commies are gone, the weather hasn't improved much."

Before they could get to the topic of cattle mutilations, Ethan pointed to the picture windows at the far end of the gallery. Through the glass they could see a ragged cluster of rotting wood in the field next door.

"That's the McArty Ranch," the old man said. "That's what's left of our Centennial project."

Ethan suddenly remembered something from a magazine he'd read when he was a kid. "Is that the…?"

The old man grinned. "That's right, that's the flying saucer landing pad."

The details of the article were coming back to Ethan now. The landing pad was the town's way of welcoming everybody in the universe to come in and celebrate Canada's 100th birthday.

The old man laughed. "Some people swore they did see a couple of spaceships over there."

"Did you ever see anything?"

"Naw." The old man forced his hands into the pockets of his coveralls. "The furthest visitor we've ever had was from Halifax." Then he smiled and looked beyond the plywood heap. "Of course, I'm not counting those folks over at the Mentotechnics Institute."

"What are they like?" Ethan tried to sound casual.

"They're okay. Very polite," the old man replied. "Must be real busy because we don't see them very much."

Ethan looked out the window and noticed an unmarked van parked under the suspended jet. He excused himself and left right after he dropped five dollars in the jar designated as the fund for the restoration of the landing pad.

⟡

"Meet me at Vulcan."

Ethan wondered how many times Nina had wanted to say that to him. Or anybody.

But the circumstances and the meaning were very different from what she might have imagined all those years ago. Nina meant Vulcan, Alberta, not Vulcan the planet. This Vulcan was a fairly small town a couple of hours drive from Calgary.

Why here?

True, it was reasonably close to the Mentotechnics compound, but there were lots of other places to meet.

Maybe Nina was just trying to be ironic, somehow trying to let Ethan know that she was beyond all that Trek stuff now.

That didn't feel right. By now, Ethan had figured out that Nina had changed quite a bit; he doubted that she really cared what he thought about her beliefs.

Still...

Ethan parked his rental car next to the Vulcan Visitors' Centre and looked at the giant sculpture of the USS Enterprise looming over the highway. The Centre itself was modeled after a United Federation of Planets Space Station.

Maybe Nina was trying to say something here.

She was inside waiting for him, sipping blue Romulan Ale.

"You're looking well," Ethan said as he took a seat in the booth.

"You're still a terrible liar."

"Truth is relative." Ethan smiled feebly. "And we're all getting older."

He waved at the Andorean waiter to bring him a blue drink.

"Drink? A blue one like my friend's."

Nina was right. She really did look awful.

Pale, red-eyed, and her business suit was hanging off her like combat fatigues. She looked the way Ethan felt when he'd woken up in Northern Saskatchewan almost 15 years ago. But he'd been drugged and shipped halfway across the continent while he was unconscious. He had an excuse.

"You've been here before?" Ethan asked.

"Couple of times." Nina smiled a little as she stared at her half-empty glass.

"The Klingon group from Great Falls comes up here every spring. They do a nice music festival."

"Oh."

Ethan and Nina watched as the tube of blue beer was deposited in front of him.

"So, are you getting back into that sort of thing?"

"No."

Nina emptied her glass.

"You can't recapture that kind of a feeling." She gestured for another drink. "But I still respect what they're trying to do." Nina looked around at the information desk and all the displays that carried facts and maps from the local chamber of commerce — all themed as Star Trek sets. "What this whole place represents."

"A positive vision for the future?" Ethan still remembered that phrase from the many earnest late night conversations.

"A *human* vision for the future." Nina got quiet and they both watched as her beer materialized in front of them.

Slightly odd turn of phrase, Ethan thought as he watched her take another drink.

He decided that he had better help Nina get to the point.

"I assume you want to talk about what they're doing with that radio telescope at the compound?"

She smiled, which was somewhat scary.

"Do you know that they think they're picking up intelligent signals from outer space?"

"Probably from a confederation of star systems from the galactic core," Ethan replied matter-of-factly. "Completely consistent with Temple doctrine."

Her smile got slightly scarier.

"And what do you think they're doing in the aircraft hangar?"

"Most likely building a flying saucer." This discussion seemed to be getting a little cryptic for Ethan. "Every once in a while one of their branches builds a mock-up spacecraft, hoping that they can get out there and commune with their maker."

Nina downed two-thirds of her latest drink.

"Yeah."

"It's not a big deal, Nina. Ask the Vulcan Chamber of Commerce." Inexplicably Ethan felt that he had to convince her. "It's like those cargo cults in the South Pacific that used to build airplanes out of palm trees."

Nina burped menacingly. "Palm trees?" she said. "You think this is all about *fucking palm trees?*"

Ethan pushed back into his chair a bit. He hadn't seen Nina this angry in almost three decades.

"I'm just saying that..." Ethan spoke as carefully as possible, "...that there's precedent for this in the ethnographic literature."

And Ethan noticed that after almost thirty years, he sounded just the same.

But Nina either didn't notice, or didn't care.

"Ethan, I have three pieces of information that you might find *somewhat interesting*."

Ethan was pretty sure that he would probably not welcome new information.

"Really."

Just then Ethan remembered something important; Nina could be really annoying sometimes.

"First." Nina stopped and ingested another large portion of her latest beer. "They have two connected super-computers in there."

"So?" This still didn't seem terribly serious to Ethan. "Maybe they have picked up some interesting astronomical data and need something to process it with."

"Do you really think so?" Nina laughed.

"Why not, there's nothing in Mentotechnics that precludes some kind of legitimate scientific inquiry. Even if they've come across the data accidentally."

"That's mighty liberal of you, Ethan." Nina ingested all but a millimeter thick ring of blue from her glass. "But there's more news, and it goes from bad to worse."

"Let's hear it."

At least when they were dating, Ethan could tolerate these moods because he knew they'd be having sex at some point afterwards.

"We also think they've got some plutonium in there."

Ethan's reaction was nausea. He was briefly thankful that he'd only had one beer. Then he felt nothing, probably because he didn't want to consider the implications of what he'd just been told.

"That's terrible," he said finally and rather weakly at that. "But…" he paused for a moment, hoping that he wouldn't whine when he asked the next question:

"But, what do you want me to do? I'm no expert on nuclear bombs and—"

"I want you to go back there with some of my people and pick up one of their members."

"Why?" Ethan felt his back stiffen as the old ethical reflexes set in.

"I want you to interrogate that person. *Thoroughly.*"

Ethan folded his arms. "Nina, I'm a social scientist, you know I don't do de-programming."

*"This is serious shit, Ethan!"*

Nina then noticed that the Andorean waiter, as well as a few other staff aliens, were now looking at them.

"This is plutonium!" she whispered. "And I'm not asking you to de-programmme anybody. I doubt that's even possible."

"So, what do you want me to do?" Ethan couldn't imagine how he could be of any use in this situation.

"Just try and behave like a real anthropologist and get us some information about what's happening in that compound."

Ethan studied his half-glass of fantasy beer, then he studied the glass that once held Nina's fantasy beer.

"Okay," he said.

"Okay." Nina seemed to be calming down.

"Nina?"

"Yes?"

"What's the worse news?" Ethan noticed that his voice was trembling a little. "What could be worse than a bunch of crazy Mentotechnologists having the makings of an atomic weapon?"

"Oh," Nina replied. "Nothing much. We just think that Mentotechnics … or some aspects of it, might actually work."

Okay, Nina had convinced him. She'd gotten really bizarre in the last 25 years.

~ ✧ ~

Even though she was the one going progressively crazy, it was Nina, not Ethan, who had walked out on the relationship.

They had another fight when Ethan mentioned that he was thinking about making her Star Trek friends the subject of his revised thesis project.

"Ethically, I have to tell you that I'm planning this." Ethan handed her a few pages of typed notes — his revised research proposal. He was confident that Professional Sirkowski would like it.

*"In your mind, you have capacities you know..."*

She read the proposal for a few minutes and handed the pages back.

"You are such an asshole."

Then she left.

Evidently she did not like the proposal. Possibly she was offended at the idea of being the subject of anthropological study.

*"...To transmit thought energy far beyond the norm."*

Two days later, Nina called him on the phone, and in an apologetic voice told him that she felt badly about leaving things like that. She knew how important his work was to him, that she believed that this kind of social scientific research was important to human progress, and that she knew that he really didn't mean to sound condescending.

*"...Please close your eyes and concentrate with every thought you think..."*

Well, two out of three, Ethan thought. But missing that one point did not stop him from inviting Nina over for dinner the next evening.

*"...Upon the recitation we're about to sing..."*

Ethan went to a certain amount of trouble getting ready for that dinner. He actually cooked a chicken, bought some wine that wasn't from Ontario and even bought her a record album.

The clerk at Sam the Record Man had recommended it: "If she's into sci-fi, then she'll love this one."

The record was by a Canadian band called Klaatu.

"Some people think that these guys are really The Beatles," the clerk added as he took seven of Ethan's dollars. "The first cut is the best one on this album."

After dinner, Ethan put the record on his used Viking stereo while he and Nina made love on the sofa.

"*Calling occupants...*"

The first time around, Nina really seemed to like the music, but when they played the LP again, Ethan noticed that she was getting a little distant.

"*...calling occupants of interplanetary craft...*"

She said she couldn't stay the night. Ethan slipped the vinyl disk into its sleeve and handed it to her.

"Keep it," she said. "It's just some silly stuff about UFOs and alien contact." Nina opened the door. "That's not what I care about."

"Yes, but I thought you might like the music—"

"I guess you really don't understand me."

Then she left.

And as Ethan eventually deduced, that was essentially the end of the relationship.

"*...We are your friends!*"

⟵ ✧ ⟶

Nina's crew showed up in the van, and after that it was pretty easy to carry out the plan. But they seemed a bit nervous.

"Just remember," the team leader growled at him. "Keep that toque on your head at all times."

It felt as though the black wool hat had kevlar earflaps.

Canucks in space, Ethan thought.

"Why?" he asked as the van rolled to a stop in the parking spot behind the local Tim Horton's.

"Orders, professor." The team leader held up an air gun. "If you lose your hat, sir, I'll have to give you one of these darts."

"No thanks." Ethan had experienced enough forced unconsciousness for one lifetime.

But in spite of the hats, maybe because of the hats, the operation went very smoothly. After about two hours of waiting, somebody in a pick-up from the compound pulled up at the front entrance to the shop. It was a kid, maybe 17 or 18, probably going in to get something for their morning shift. Apparently even highly evolved superbeings like their daily fix of doughnuts.

When the kid walked out with his box of bakery goodies, the team leader aimed his air gun and squeezed off a shot.

There was a tiny puff as the kid caught a dart in his ass.

Two of the team members dashed over the kid and held him up before he could drop a single banana cream-filled.

The kid was in the van before anybody in the doughnut shop could peer through the coffee steam and notice that kid hadn't made it to his truck.

✧

SUBJECT X: Oh, it's you again.
INTERVIEWER: I don't think we've met.
SUBJECT X: We know all about you.
INTERVIEWER: Really?
SUBJECT X: Really. We've been keeping tabs on so-called "researchers" like you for quite a while.
INTERVIEWER: Pick up anything interesting?
SUBJECT X: Not from you, but some people have been making surprising progress.
INTERVIEWER: What do they know?
SUBJECT X: You, on the other hand, provide entertainment.
INTERVIEWER: Thanks.
SUBJECT X: Don't worry about it. None of it matters any more.
INTERVIEWER: Why doesn't it matter?
SUBJECT X: We don't believe we'll tell you right now.
INTERVIEWER: *We?*
SUBJECT X: That's what "We" are. The Therapy Machines, the hypnotic training processes, all those expensive courses, everything in Mentotechnics was designed to bring us all together.
INTERVIEWER: All together? With a collective political ideology?
SUBJECT X: You're thinking too small.
INTERVIEWER: A unified consciousness?
SUBJECT X: Very good! You remember the doctrine!
INTERVIEWER: But that's scientifically impossible.
SUBJECT X: All minds at the compound are governed by the recorded thought patterns of D.H. Evanston ... and we say you're wrong.
INTERVIEWER: Do you know that you're part of a profoundly delusional community?
SUBJECT X: Do you know that you're really pissing us off right now? Not a great idea, professor!

VOICE: (off mike, partly unintelligible): — *about the plutonium!*
INTERVIEWER: These gentlemen want to know why you have plutonium on the compound.
SUBJECT X: I'm sure they do. But they already know more than you do.
INTERVIEWER: What do you mean?
SUBJECT X: Those silly hats you have to wear. We can read minds if you don't have telepathic protection.
INTERVIEWER: (sigh) Fine, since we're protected and we have you here, why not answer the question? What's the big plan at the compound?
SUBJECT X: You're supposed to be the expert. What's the ultimate goal of Mentotechnics?
INTERVIEWER: To bring about the ultimate transformation of the human race.
SUBJECT X: By creating the ideal consciousness.
INTERVIEWER: And that's a hive-mind, based on its founder's personality?
SUBJECT X: Sort of. But you forgot the most interesting bits. We also plan on transcending the boundaries of this tiny world and take our place among the stars!
INTERVIEWER: Okay, but what does have to do with plutonium?
SUBJECT X: We used the radio telescope to ask for help.
INTERVIEWER: Help from outer space?
SUBJECT X: They suggested that we needed the plutonium to help things happen.
INTERVIEWER: You think you can use it to power that flying saucer and go out and see these aliens?
SUBJECT X: The saucer isn't any kind of a spacecraft. It's more of a catalyst.
INTERVIEWER: You mean it's a bomb?
SUBJECT X: Bomb is such a pejorative term.
INTERVIEWER: You—

⁕ ✧ ⁕

When Ethan heard the explosion he thought that the Mentotechnists had detonated their nuclear device.

As usual, he was wrong.

It was just Nina driving an armored truck full of plastic explosives through the compound and blowing up the saucer.

Ethan later found out that fissionable materials need a specific type of detonation for a chain reaction to take place. Nina only wanted to destroy the supercomputers on the compound. She knew that was the fastest way of stopping things from going nuclear.

So, if Evanston's mind had been recorded in there, it wasn't any more. Neither were Nina and 22 residents of the compound.

None of the CSIS team knew about her plan. They had been told that the explosives were going to be used to destroy the radio telescope after they had made all the arrests.

⋄

One thing Ethan could do was write a report.

He was still reasonably good at that sort of thing.

"None of the events convince me that any aspect of Mentotechnic practice or belief has any basis in empirical fact," he wrote in the 312-page analysis to Nina's replacement at CSIS. "It is likely that the intensity of the operation caused your team leader to become one more subscriber in the cult's delusional world-view."

Poor Nina.

Once again she got caught up in the fantasy and went off the deep end.

"Never-the-less," Ethan concluded, "her actions were correct, though perhaps somewhat extreme, in spite of her warped frame of reference. She recognized the strong possibility of nuclear terrorism and took direct steps to stop it. If the pathology of similar "communities of unreason" is any indicator, then we can assume that the group at the compound was planning to use the detonator as a vehicle of mass-suicide. Your team leader's actions undoubtedly saved lives of over 200 mentotechnologists on the compound as well as the residents in the nearby town."

⋄

Another thing Ethan could do was attend the funeral.

Nina's Star Trek friends had arranged the service. They all put on their convention uniforms and the organist played some really touching transcriptions from the best soundtracks.

The service was held at a Unitarian meeting hall that had been built in the early 1970s, so it looked a lot like they had all gathered in a set from the original series.

Two people gave the eulogy.

The first person talked about what a wonderful, loving person Nina was and how lucky he was to have her as his partner for 15 years.

That statement surprised Ethan. He had trouble imagining Nina with any other significant other but him.

The second person described how Nina represented everything that was fine and noble in Star Trek. How she respected the unique potential of the individual. How she understood the importance of a strong sustainable world community, and how she strove for our species to create its own best possible future.

One of the speakers was dressed like Captain Kirk.

The other looked like Mr. Spock.

⁐ ✧ ⁌

**Hugh A. D. Spencer** completed graduate studies at the University of Toronto and McMaster University where he conducted anthropological studies into the origins of religious movements in science fiction fandom.

Twice nominated for the Aurora Award, Hugh's science fiction has been published in *On Spec, Interzone, Descant* and *New Writings in the Fantastic*. Many of his short stories have been dramatized by Shoestring Radio Theatre for the Satellite Network of National Public Radio. "Cult Stories" is his third entry in the Tesseracts series.

# Three Thousand Miles of Cold Iron Tears

## ⁃ Steve Vernon ⁃

Nothing reeks worse than a sopping wet Sasquatch.

It was mid-November and the sky looked dark enough to hold a grudge against the dirt for a very long time. It had rained down sleet all morning long and I was sogged straight through to the bone. The wind was blowing in hard from the Rockies and I was not happy at all to be standing here in the Eagle Pass, staring at a large shed-encased mural by the side of the Canadian Pacific Railway at a point in the landscape that men called Craigellachie.

I don't really know who painted the mural but there was a good strength showing in his brushstroke. He had made a sound choice in his colors, as well. The hopeful blue skyline blended nicely with the heavy umber figures. The shed that covered the mural was about nine feet high and it was almost tall enough for me to stand beneath.

*Almost.*

There was a story in the mural and stories were something that I understood. You see, that is what I am. I was a living story — something that people told around lonely smoking campfires. I was a Sasquatch — a nine foot tall shag carpet with a serious-bad attitude. I was a legend and a rural myth and a totally unsubstantiated rumor. Like I said, just a story — only stories, if told well and often enough, in time grow a life of their own.

I can't really explain to you how it happens. It's not as if I came into this world with a user's guide. All that I can tell you is that the Sasquatch have been told into life since back in the days of the Mesopotomania storytellers who spoke in hushed whispers of the exploits of Enkidu and Gilgamesh — and so long as your people continued to tell stories about random hirsute giants growing up in the wilderness and sometimes being raised by wolves or African great apes, then we will continue to live on in the borderlands that haze and drift warily between the carefully demarcated lines that claim to separate the cold steel facts of reality from the warm pure smoke of your collective imagination.

"So were you there?" I asked.

"I was there," the ghost of Sam Steele replied.

"I don't see you in the picture," I said.

"I was there," Sam repeated. "Take my word for it."

"Maybe you weren't so ugly back then," I offered. "Maybe I just don't recognize you."

"I was there," Sam Steele's ghost echoed for the third time. "I just wasn't in the picture, is all."

Sam was a story, too. The real Sam Steele had died back in 1919 — after fighting with the Fenians, chasing Louis Riel during the Red River Rebellion, meeting in a sit-down wiki-up with the great Sitting Bull himself, single-handedly taming the Klondike and fighting a half a thousand Boers over in Boerland. Not all of that is true, you understand but the gist of it is. Sam's actual exploits had grown to near mythic status. He had achieved a kind of sordid low-rent immortality thanks to a multitude of novels and newspaper articles and a movie or two and campfire tales and once even a CBC minute vignette commercial.

Hell, they had even named a mountain after him.

That's one more way that a story can be born. After Sam's adventures had been told and retold and exaggerated upon, his legend had slowly taken form and his ghost rose up and eventually assumed control of the Spiritual Operations Branch — known as the SOB's — a semi-official para-mystical working division of the Canadian Royal Mounted Police.

Which made Sam my boss.

So if he wanted to stand out here in the middle of November staring at a mural depicting one of the iconic climaxes of the

North American industrial revolution than I was duty-bound to stand here with him.

Only it didn't mean I had to like it, was all.

I focused on staring at the mural.

I had seen the photograph. Most Canadians had. It depicted a cluster of men, solemn and sober-looking, high-hatted and well fed. Men, leaning like lonely crows over a hammer and a pair of dark iron rails. Each of them stood there on the mural, bearded and mustached with enough facial follicle foliage to successfully carpet a fully grown wooly mammoth.

I would have fit right in.

"If I'd been there," I said to Sam Steele. "I for sure would have made certain to show up for picture-taking day."

"You leave your mouth open as often as you do," Sam pointed out. "And you're going to catch yourself a cold in your tonsils."

There was a sign above the mural that told the whole story in a simple straight forward fashion.

THE DRIVING OF THE LAST SPIKE — CANADIAN PACIFIC RAILWAY — CRAIGELLACHIE, BRITISH COLUMBIA, NOVEMBER 7, 1885

The same day as today, one hundred and twenty seven years ago.

This was where they tied the knot closed. This was where the last stitch was sewn into a three thousand mile long scar that tore across the Canadian countryside.

This was where a nation shook hands and said howdy.

This was where east finally met west.

"I'm just angry, is all," I told Sam.

"I know you're angry," Sam replied. "That doesn't change a thing."

I was angry because I felt I deserved some time off.

Over the last three weeks I had laid a covey of vampiric were-owls to rest in a sacred Haida burial ground. I had sung a soothing Shemite sea shanty to a cannibalistic New Brunswick sea captain's restless spirit before anchoring what was left of his soul to a solid iron ship anchor and drowning him under, and finally I had tied three mid-sized cardborosaurus into a coral reef cryptogram and thrown all three of them farther out to sea.

"That's more mystic work than any one agent ought to do," I complained. "Why don't you give this job to Bunyan and that smelly blue ox of his? He and the Prophet are long overdue for some sort of a challenge."

## Three Thousand Miles of Cold Iron Tears by Steve Vernon

You've probably heard all about Bunyan and his big blue ox. Hell, his stories get bigger every year, the way he tells it. As for the Prophet — well he was a whole other kettle of Prince Edward Island potatoes. He was the medicine man brother of the great Tecumseh himself — a Shawnee seer and troublemaker and a magic man who, for some strange twisted reason that irked him considerably and puzzled the hell out of me, had achieved a state of storyhood and had been simultaneously resurrected in the shape of a mystical Winnebago motor home — which I knew was mystical because the beer fridge never ran dry.

"I picked you for this assignment," Sam Steele said. "Because you are nearly as strong as that expatriate Quebec lumberman and almost half as intelligent as that big blue ox but mostly because I knew I needed you to be in on this one and you're a whole lot better conversationalist than Bunyan's big double-bladed axe."

Which, coming from the ghost of Sam Steele, was about as close to a compliment as I could hopefully expect.

"So what am I here for?" I asked.

"It's complicated," was all that Sam would tell me. "For now you've just got to wait and see."

So I waited.

I didn't see all that much to tell of.

We had flown here by Thunderbird. It was cheaper than Air Canada first class and I could eat all of the ticks and mites that I could harvest from the big old bird's great yellow-brown plumage. I can't tell you too much about protein, cholesterol or fiber — but I have always preferred the happy crunchy taste of freshly plucked parasites to a bag full of stale salted airline peanuts — which they don't even give you anymore.

Besides, I think the old bird liked our company. The Thunderbird was beginning to grow a little thin around the edges. It made for a comfortable ride as I sank down into his feathers with all of the grace and restrained gusto of a three hundred pound Trekkie sinking into a yard sale futon for a solid weekend of Picard versus Kirk marathon splendor. The problem was that people didn't tell nearly as many stories these days about the Thunderbird as they did about Sasquatch. The essence of the old bird's innate mythdom was beginning to fade and dwindle and so too was his story.

I think the Thunderbird knew it.

I think the Thunderbird was slowly losing his fire. There just didn't seem to be any fight left in the big old bird. With no role left to play in this world except for serving as a feathered limo-service for a nine foot Sasquatch I think his spirit had left him. Someday, maybe there'd be no Thunderbird at all and then I guess I'd just have to walk.

I didn't much care for that thought because it lead inevitably to the notion that maybe someday people might not necessarily believe in the possibility of a Sasquatch either. I did my best to encourage the rumor of my existence — providing the occasional random sighting and stirring up the supermarket tabloids at any opportunity I had - but mostly the S.O.B. kept me far too busy for anything more than a few token attempts at spiritual self-preservation.

"It's always complicated," I said to Sam.

"This one is worse," Sam cryptically replied.

Yeah, right.

I was just about to sarcastic something back at Sam when the first ghost showed up, sort of drifting out of the painted mural like a curl of smoke drifting upwards from a forgotten cigarette - a gnarled rawhide streak of a man with a moustache that looked a little like a dead mouse erupting from beneath a bent and battered nose that might have been stolen from a wandering goshawk.

Now, ghosts don't really look the way that most people imagine they do. They're nothing like Casper the Friendly Ghost. There are no chains here, no moaning and no theatrical shrieks. Ghosts are actually more about feeling and presence than actual substance. Seeing one is just sort of like watching a photograph develop in midair — so lay those preconceptions by the side of the road and let the wind blow them away.

"I know this man," Sam Steele said. "His name was Stavros. I could never pronounce his last name. He was a good cook and a hard worker. He died of the fever in the mosquito-ridden muskeg swamp, north of Fort William."

The old cook leaned my way. I felt a cold wind blow directly through me. I smelled the reek of runny under-drawers and night sweats and an overly-greased fry pan. My teeth chattered like a St. Vitus bear trap full of redheaded woodpeckers. Three entire flocks of snow geese casually Morris danced across my grave.

"Damn it," I swore.

A second ghost appeared. A Chinaman, by the looks of him. All short and squatty as a camp stove, a gaze turned inwards, with his skin the color of a sun-faded orange.

"Do you know this guy?" I asked.

"His name is Lo Pingshau," Sam told me before speaking to Lo in what I guessed was perfect Mandarin.

Lo smiled and opened his mouth as if to speak. I heard the rumble of what might have been a cold and distant thunder. I saw flashes of light and darkness strobing momentarily across the field of my vision. I tasted gravel and despair and the scent of an inescapable trap crashing home.

"Lo died in an avalanche about twenty-five miles from here," Sam explained. "His last thoughts were of his mother's tears as she said goodbye to him as he boarded the ship for North America."

A third ghost slowly materialized. A young man, his face blown thin and November-gray. He leaned upon a railroad track hammer as if the handle of that track hammer had somehow grown into his very hand.

"His name was Patrick Lefebvre. He wandered off in the prairies and hunger took him. The wolves found what was left of him and chewed upon his bones. His grave is a random scatter of wolf scat, strewn hieroglyphically across a field of blowing oats."

Lefebvre's ghost leaned back his head and howled out a lonely Lon Chaney sonnet of regret and despair. I felt every vein of hair stand at stiff attention and salute — and I have an awful lot of hair. You have to understand — I have lived out of doors for most of my life. I have heard an awful lot of wolves in my time. I have heard them singing of feed and feast and famine. I have heard them talking to the moon and the wind, speaking of the wonders of procreation and solitude. I've heard them gossip and I've heard them mourn and I have heard them dreaming of the centuries that had slid under and were crushed beneath the relentless wheels of progress.

I had heard all of that and yet I had never heard a sound that chilled me quite like this one did.

"It's all right if you show a little fear," Sam said. "They're ghosts. They expect that."

"I'm not afraid," I lied.

The truth was that if I was any more petrified Sam could have cheerfully airmailed me back to the Stone Age with the words INSTANT FOSSIL airbrushed indelibly across my forehead. It didn't help one bit that the ghosts continued to appear and with each new apparition I found myself undergoing an echo of their eventual extinction.

Sam introduced each of them to me, one by one.

"Are you telling me you know all of these ghosts?" I asked. "I find that hard to believe."

"Not all of them," Sam admitted. "I visited some of the work camps, but that doesn't mean I met every one of them."

"You're a Mountie," I said. "Aren't you guys supposed to notice details?"

"True," Sam said. "Which is one of the reasons that I've made it a point to get to know these old boys."

"How many of them are there?" I asked. "There must be hundreds."

"Thousands," Sam remarked gloomily. "This railroad cost a lot more than dollars and cents to build."

"Is this what you brought me here for?" I asked Steele. "To fight these ghosts?"

"No," Steele said. "These ghosts have called me here. They need our help and you're here to fight something else."

"Fight what?" I asked.

"Fight that," Steele said.

I looked up and saw something stepping out of the side of a mountain's shadow — something that looked like a cross between a praying mantis, a snake and a nightmare. A pale green four armed monstrosity, the color of radioactive snot; undulating in angles that seemed almost contradictory to the laws of natural physics. What I saw was taller than I was with a lot more arms than he should have and carrying a pair of poleaxes festooned with long tapers of festively-dyed intestinal membrane.

"What the hell is that?" I asked.

"A Yaksha," Sam replied, taking out his pistol and aiming at the nightmare. "Something that is half-god, half-demon with an all-encompassing hunger for living ghosts. It came from China, a long time ago, following the scent of coolie despair."

The Yaksha slammed one of its poleaxes into the back of Lo Pingshau's ghost. He held the old Oriental's spirit up above its ugly head, staring intently at the impaled Chinaman. I could see a sickly green and yellow smoke rising from Lo Pingshau's stump-like body.

Sam squeezed off a shot.

The bullet splattered against the thick green hide of the Yaksha like a windblown grasshopper splattering against a pickup truck's windshield — with about as much effect.

Meanwhile, the ghost of Lo Pingshau continued to smolder.

"That Yaksha is cooking him with its eyes," Sam shouted. "He doesn't like them raw."

"It's got heat vision?"

"It's got microwave ovens for eyes," Sam explained.

"What else has it got?" I wanted to know.

"Never mind asking stupid questions," Sam shouted, firing off five more futile dragonflies. "Get in there and do something."

I didn't wait for any further invitation.

I ran straight at the Yaksha who wasn't really paying much attention to me — being far to preoccupied with eye-cooking himself a tasty ghost shiskabob. I came in low and swung just as hard as I could — getting all of my five hundred pounds of big-hairy-and-mean behind the punch. The only problem being the way that the Yaksha was built. I was aiming for his stomach but I caught him a little lower than that.

Which definitely got the monster's attention.

The Yaksha dropped the Lo Pingshau shishkabob it was eye-cooking. In the same motion the Yaksha whirled and caught me with a swing of its tail, knocking me a good twenty feet down the railroad track.

I stood up and tried to shake it off.

This wasn't going to be easy. I had hit that thing hard enough to bruise it's granddad's granddaddy and it didn't seem to bother it one bit.

Sam Steele squeezed off six more heavy caliber spitballs aimed straight at the Yaksha's head. He was cursing as he plunked off each shot — a long line of profanity strung together like a thousand miles of boxcar. To be honest, I couldn't really make out what Sam was saying through that walrus bush of a moustache but it sounded nasty.

"Hey ugly," I shouted, uprooting a tree stump as I stood back up. "Why don't you chew on this?"

I flung the stump.

It made a meatier sound than any of Sam's bullets — like maybe a giant grasshopper splattering against a giant pickup truck's windshield.

I had definitely got the Yaksha's attention.

It came at me like a running scream.

I barely dodged the first pole-axe blow. It split stone, it struck the ground so very hard. I swung for what I believed to be ribs, hooking hard. Its hide shrieked at me and I felt a thousand tiny jaws tearing at my knuckles.

It hurt.

Sam Steele calmly reloaded and continued to plunk shots.

"Can't you think of something useful to do?" I called back.

The Yaksha slammed me with that tail again and I crashed backwards and put a dent in the ground large enough and deep enough to give a crop-circle a serious case of phenomenon-envy.

The ghost of Lefebvre mutely handed me his track hammer.

"Thanks," I said.

I stood back up.

"Hey, ugly!" I bellowed.

The Yaksha ignored me. It was snake-walking towards Sam Steele, who kept on calmly plinking shots. I guess being a ghost and a walking story like Sam was, made him look a whole lot tastier to that Yaksha than my sorry old cryptid carcass.

Big mistake.

I took three running steps and then launched myself in a flying-assed leap aimed track-hammer-first at the Yaksha's back.

Sunk that big old track hammer squarely into the Yaksha's back.

The thing howled.

I'd hurt it.

I guess it didn't care for the feel of cold iron.

Good.

Only I couldn't seem to let go of that track hammer. I hung there like the fisherman who forgot to let go, dangling at the end of that damn sticky-handled track hammer. The Yaksha reached out and caught hold of me with two of its arms.

At the same time the Yaksha reached a third arm out and caught hold of Sam Steele's throat and started squeezing.

"Just hold on," Sam called out to me — which was a pretty good trick given that he was being strangled at the time. I'll give that Steele a world of credit - the old bastard was still trying to reload.

At the same time the Yaksha reached its fourth arm out and retrieved the poleaxe that it had stuck through Lo Pingshau. I felt the Yaksha's tail wrapping about me like an overgrown anaconda. The half-god peeled me off of my dangling perch and brought me around to where it could easily reach me.

"Hold on," Sam croaked out, fumbling one more cartridge into his revolver.

I watched helplessly as the Yaksha raised that poleaxe above its head, with the eye-burned ghost of Lo Pingshau still shishaka-bobbed in the middle of the poleaxe.

I kicked at the Yaksha's leg but from the angle he had me pinned at all I succeeded in doing was stubbing my toe. I manfully held the pain in and refused to whimper.

Sasquatch have pride, you understand.

Then the Yaksha slammed that poleaxe into me.

I forgot about pride and squealed like a suckling pig. I heard Sam yelling out something that was probably more — hold on, hold on — but I couldn't make him out over my own squealing.

I lay there, pinned to the dirt, feeling all of the stories running out of me and into that big green Yaksha.

While I lay there he started working those microwave eyes on me. I fell my skin cinder and pucker and begin to boil.

I was dying.

The big green bastard was killing me.

Which was right about when the Thunderbird hit.

He swooped down from the cumulus-nimbus that we'd parked him on, like a great winged dreadnaught. There was lightning flashing in his eyes and I could hear the thunder booming and echoing with the beat of his wings. He hit that Yaksha like a busload of good-night-Marie, all beak and talon and righteous fury.

This was the Thunderbird that the Lakota Sioux and the Anishinabe First People had spoken of with fear and respect. This was the Thunderbird who had wrestled the Whale from out of the Great Water and threw him down upon a great mountain to feed the hungry people. This was the Cloud Shaker and the Thunder Bringer and the One Who Sang The Rain Down. This was the Thunderbird who had wiped out the Unhcegila — the lizard-men who had lived in the secret places in the deep mountains and who fed upon the people.

This was the By-God, Pee-Your-Pants and Scream-Like-A-Little-Girl Thunderbird!

At the same time as the Thunderbird was unloading a can of whoop-wing on the Yaksha, Sam Steele jammed his freshly reloaded pistol snug into what passed for a Yaksha rib cage and unloaded six shots. This close, there was no spitball bug-crush futile splat. These slugs tore into the Yaksha's sick green hide, burrowing deep into whatever evil twisted organs sluggishly swum about the Yaksha's insides.

At which point I pulled loose, caught hold of one of the Yaksha's four arms by its forearm and yanked it out of the socket and began beating the big green beastie with it — soggy end first. It felt very therapeutic, beating the creature who had nearly strangled me to death with one of his own arms. Maybe I ought to think about writing a self-help book on this sort of cathartic mutilation. Maybe even an exercise video. There was a lot of good beneficial aerobic activity in beating a demi-myth to death with its own amputation.

There is always a danger in having too much imagination.

I got all caught up in the thought of maybe turning up on the Dr. Phil show with the Yaksha's green pickled arm and a tastefully prepared power-point presentation when the Yaksha did something that I hadn't quite anticipated.

First, it threw off Sam, which wasn't all that surprising when you think of just how much of a lightweight the old Mountie really was.

Only don't tell him I said that or I'll never hear the end of it.

Then the Yaksha caught hold of one of the Thunderbird's talons and windmilled the big bird into the side of a mountain.

That was a little more surprising, given that the Thunderbird was big enough to wrestle a fully grown whale from out of an ocean.

But what really surprised me was when the Yaksha grew its own arm back.

The arm poked out of the socket that I'd yanked it out of. It made a fat wet popping sound, like a cork coming out of a champagne bottle.

Which surprised the hell out of me.

While I was busy being surprised the Yaksha wrapped the rest of its arms about me and started to squeeze me in bear hug to beat all bear hugs — like one of those old-time lumberjack wrestlers.

I tried to wriggle free but there was no escape possible.

I felt my spirit begin to shake loose again.

I was getting set to die with a poleaxe impaled Chinese railroad laborer dangling above my death bed.

*Three Thousand Miles of Cold Iron Tears* by Steve Vernon

I heard the ghost of Sam Steele yelling back at me to hang on.

Hang on to what?

I looked up at Lo Pingshau's impaled corpse.

And then the corpse winked at me.

He let his mouth fall open, which made me nervous, because the last thing I wanted to do was to die with a dead man's drool dripping down my furry chest.

I could see a light burning far down in the back of Lo Pingshau's throat, like a coal miner's carbide lantern in the belly of the big dark.

The Yaksha kept on squeezing.

I kept on staring at the light in Lo Pingshau's throat.

The light that seemed to be getting bigger.

Now I had heard all of the stories of how dying men sometimes see a light and how they ought not to step into the light but what in the hell was I supposed to do when the dying light was coming straight towards me.

The light was bigger.

I could hear a rumble now — the same sort of avalanche rumble as Lo Pingshau had shown me the first time — only this time it was louder. It was growing loud enough to drown out the mightiest of thunderbird claps. Louder and louder, like a bear or a beast charging out of a cave.

"HANG ON!" Sam Steele shouted over the thundering rumble.

Now the Yaksha could hear it too. I could see the full moon eyes widen out in back of all of that radioactive snot green skin. Whatever was coming out of Lo Pingshau's mouth was big and bad enough to scare that Yaksha near to death.

Lo Pingshau's mouth widened, like a cave, like a canyon, like the abyss beyond the abyss and from out of that wide open darkness roared the ghost of the biggest steam locomotive I had ever seen riding along top of three thousand miles of cold iron tears and the hugest avalanche imaginable. Train and track and avalanche poured out of Lo Pingshau's unholy swollen jawbone and rolled me under it.

For a half a moment I felt as if I had been thrown into the rinse and tumble cycle of God's stand-up washing machine. The horizon rolled around above me and below me and in back of my eyes for about three million and fifty-three times or so before I rattled to a slow and dizzy halt.

I lay there and watched the world spin round, wishing I could slow things down for just a minute or two. Then I sat up slowly and tried to remember how to breathe.

"Are you done napping?" Sam Steele asked me.

I looked up and there he was.

"What happened," I asked.

"It's complicated."

"It's always complicated," I replied. "Why don't you try and explain it to me in words of one syllable or less. I'll pay close attention and watch how your lips move and maybe — just maybe — I can get why I ever needed to be here in the first place."

"You were here for the Yaksha," Sam Steele explained.

"But I couldn't beat the Yaksha," I pointed out. "I know that and I'm not too proud to admit it and I'm also aware that you are a canny enough old codger to have known that in the first place."

"You weren't here to beat him," Sam Steele said. "You were here to hold him until we beat him. Don't let it go to your head but you distracted that Yaksha quite nicely."

I thought about what Sam was saying.

"You mean I was the trap," I said.

"Well that's a little more flattering than referring to you as bait," Sam Steele admitted. "The Yaksha had been feeding on these ghosts. That's what a Yaksha does. It eats and feeds off of the spirits of living ghosts."

"You dragged me out here and got me half-killed for the sake of a few dead ghosts?"

"Living ghosts," Sam corrected me. "They are as alive as you and me. Each of them has their very own story to tell. I met a few of them back when I was alive and since then I have made it a point to get to know each and every one of them. They died for this country they weren't even born in. They're as much heroes as any fallen soldier you care to name. They've got stories, just like us, and they need to be remembered."

I thought about it some more.

"Is the Thunderbird all right?" I asked.

"He's fine and stronger than ever," Sam said. "The scrap did him good. He'll buzz a few mountain towns in a week or two, get the stories started up again, and before you know it he'll be better than ever."

I nodded.

"Good," I said. "And I get what you're trying to tell me."

"And that would be?" Sam asked.

"That everyone has got their own story. Every man has a dream and a tale that needs to be told."

The old bastard grinned at me.

"That's pretty close to what I was thinking," Sam agreed, pointing at the trackside mural. "That's why paintings and images like these are important. They help a world remember what used to be."

I nodded again.

I got it.

"So sit down," Sam said. "I've got some people that you ought to meet."

We sat there and watched the train of ghosts roll by.

One by one, through the long days and the lonely nights, I let each one of them tell me their own particular story.

⁕ ✧ ⁕

First and foremost **Steve Vernon** is a storyteller, and has written traditional folklore collections such as *Halifax Haunts* and *Haunted Harbours* for Nimbus Publishing, a publisher from his home province of Nova Scotia. Steve has been published over 60 short horror stories which can be found in the pages of *Cemetary Dance* and Tor's *Year's Best Horror*; his first YA novel, *Sinking Deeper* is described as a touching tale of sea monsters and caber tossing, he has story collections in print from Dark Regions Press, and among the ten ebooks published through Crossroad Press is a dark superhero collection entitled *Nothing to Lose* and a novelette of hockey and vampirism called *Sudden Death Overtime*.

# Slava the Immortal

### ~ Matthew Jordan Schmidt ~

The sun always shone on the day the king changed his face. Regardless of the weather in the weeks preceding the festivities, the Day of Masks dawned bright and fresh over the Diamond City, and the royal pageboys would run out into the streets to collect the townsfolk. Shepherds would come in from their dewy hills, merchants from their swollen ships, and knights from their valiant quests. None would dare miss the ancient ceremony and risk incurring the king's wrath, for Slava the Immortal had decreed it thus: that every male subject in his kingdom should prepare himself a mask and present himself at the gates to the Diamond Citadel on the morning of the Day of Masks. So it was that pirates and pagans, criminals and scholars, prostitutes and lords came before the king and stood below his ageless eyes.

Urwin, tenth pageboy to the Immortal, knew those eyes well. He thought about them now as he walked through the Merchants' Quarter, knocking on the doors to bakeries, bead shops and precious stone dealers with his wooden baton. He thought about how those eyes had looked at him two days before, how they'd appeared to stare right through him, as if his mistake in the throne room had meant the very end of his existence. He shuddered again to think of the mistake, of the hot hiss of tea, the crumpling of the king's parchment, the splash of hot water against the tiles, and the perfectly timed drum of tea drops from the king's soiled robes. Oh, what a fool he'd been to rush like that with the water so hot and the king so close. He'd spilled it everywhere: on the king, on his Book of Insights! Perhaps if he'd apologized, if his hands, his mouth, his eyes had had any sense... But they hadn't. Instead they'd mutinied, and that silly mouth of his, always getting him into trouble, had snickered. Not just laughed, but snickered — and the king had stared right through him.

"Slava the Immortal requires your face. Let every man and boy ready his mask!" he shouted now, rapping the stick on the iron foot of the king's effigy in the centre of the plaza. Excited faces emerged into the first blades of sunlight. Boys and men of every age began to make their way up the cobblestone streets to the citadel that sat upon the hill. Already the great doors to the hall were open and the music was playing. Other pageboys flanked the gates on either side to guide in the long file of celebrants, each of whom would come before the king to meet his chilling eyes, each of whom would offer up his face for a single year's escape from boredom, for Slava the Immortal had grown bored, and this ennui had driven him to play: with the faces of his people. In his timeless state, he could experiment with beauty and age, with color and shape. He could become the world. And today was the day the world offered itself up to his choosing.

The iron clang of Urwin's stick on the metal effigy drew more of the king's subjects from their slumber. Yawning fathers nodded to the pageboy in respect as they checked to make sure their young sons hadn't forgotten to bring their masks.

"I need more time," Urwin heard one boy argue with his father. "Just a few more beads!" Ah, yes, just another layer of beads, my father, just another round of feathers.

But the doors were open and the king was looking at faces. There was no time now, no time to perfect what should have already been perfected. *My mask!* sighed teenage voices. *Ugh, look at my mask*! And the swooning kisses of girlfriends and wives, and the finishing touches of feminine fingertips upon the masks, upon the faces these women might see staring back at them for the year to come. *Make sure you don't lose those turquoise beads! And watch your arm doesn't get bumped. Keep it safe. You'll be sorry if something goes wrong and you get picked!* And on and on like that as the thronging legions of masculinity filed up to see their king.

Molma, the first pageboy to the Immortal, had told Urwin to hurry back when his job was done, so when the square became still, save for the worried eyes of wives in windows, Urwin followed the trail of orphaned feathers and beads back up to the citadel.

"You're late," snipped Molma as Urwin approached the gate. A sparrow nibbled seed from a tiny pile at the first pageboy's feet. The youngest children loved the sight. It calmed them and made them more radiant. Molma loved to get their faces brilliant before they filed in to see the king. He loved to offer his liege great faces of beauty and gentleness. And then, when he had tired of making children smile, Molma would lift his big foot above the feasting sparrow and squash it outright. At the crunching of bones, the young boys would scream in horror. Their faces would contort and flush, and misery would be the new countenance on offer as they approached their king.

He crunched the bird now, as Urwin arrived at the gate, and boys leapt toward their fathers for safety, flashing their masks before their faces to hide the sight. Colored feathers swam down from their artwork while grey ones plumed up from the limp body of the flattened bird. Urwin wriggled his lips in disapproval. He shook his head and kicked the bird into the bushes as he came to stand beside the head pageboy.

"Play nice, Molma," he muttered.

Molma laughed. "Let every man and boy ready his mask!" he shouted, cupping his hands around his lips to amplify the sound.

Fat, round, long or flat, the faces flowed into the citadel through one door and back out through the other. The great pipe organ groaned with the music of ceremony, and the pages ran back and forth across the hall and through the courtyards to deliver messages, to escort the elderly, to reprimand the overly boisterous. Urwin found himself echoing Molma's injunction: "Let every man and boy ready his mask!"

But they were ready of course. They had been preparing for this day for weeks. Classes were held on the thing, local meetings in each quarter of the city, counseling sessions on how to design a mask of beauty, on how to cope with a possible selection. It wasn't a trivial thing, to lose your face for a year, but there were ways to make it through. A beautiful mask helped. A mask you could be proud of. And then there was the honour of it all, the fact that being chosen by the king meant that he had found you interesting — and worthy. When you joined the Faces of the King, you grazed immortality itself. After all, the king would remember you always, would remember what it had been to have your skin and your nose, your eyes and your ears. You would go down in history as one of the many faces that Slava the Immortal had known. It was more than most men could hope for. And in exchange, Slava would reward your family richly. He would make sure that you were fed and that your children were educated. He would treat you like a prince.

But there was a price, too. Slava was not gentle. He could treat a face as crudely or as foully as he wished. He could give it tattoos, festoon it with scars. He could burn it or tan it, pluck it or dye it. Many men had given up a face of youth to find that, a year later, old age had befallen them. And still others had gone from a skin of great beauty to one defiled by warts and lesions. But the reverse was often true, too, that Slava would take pity upon a face, would counteract the effects of aging and make an old man handsome and a deformed man whole. He had such powers, or was rumored to, that he could make a blind man see.

Urwin knew how the king played with potions and ointments, how he used his laboratory below the citadel to concoct elaborate salves for each generation of face. And he knew the king's secret, too, now that he had spilled tea upon the Book of Insights and seen what the king had written within it. Slava the Immortal was looking for a way to make a face stick. He'd grown weary of having no face of his own, had forgotten the face that had once been his, and he was looking for a way back home, for a chance to once again call a face his own.

"Quit daydreaming!" Molma snapped suddenly. He sent a sharp elbow into Urwin's bony ribs. "Go inside and relieve the page at the hall doors. It's time for him to take his lunch."

Urwin did what he was told. As he entered the inner courtyard and made for the hall, he passed by a hunched old man who reached out and grabbed him about the wrist. "Could you help me, lad?" the old man wheezed, pointing to where his mask had fallen facedown onto the cobbled floor. Urwin smiled uneasily and bent down to retrieve the mask. As he held the withered piece of art between his careful fingertips, he knew that this man had given up on the fanfare of the Day of Masks. Chosen or unchosen, he would continue his life in peace. Slava the Immortal could not touch him where he was going.

"Thank you, son," said the geezer, coughing and scratching his nose. "Long live Slava the Immortal."

Urwin smiled uncomfortably and went to take his place at the doors to the hall. The vast throne room hummed with nervous voices and shuffling footsteps, and behind it all, low and precise, the voice of Slava the Immortal: "No." Shuffle. "No." Scurry. "No." Clomp. And on and on. Skinny faces. No. Angry faces. No. Boys, teenagers, grandfathers, uncles, redheads, brunettes, bearded men and mustached men. Blue eyes, grey eyes, brown eyes. "No," said the voice, "no" to them all.

Urwin grew weary as the day plodded on. He watched teenagers come forward in excitement only to be deflated by that dull, tired voice: "No."

Eventually the throngs became thinner. And then the line disappeared altogether. Now only the latecomers could present their faces to the king, boys and men who had travelled home to the Diamond City for this occasion alone. They came up from the port or from the stables by the Eastern gate. They came in twos and threes and stood before the king. But the answer was the same for all of them. Slava the Immortal didn't want them.

As dusk settled over the Diamond City and the organ's music grew softer, Molma entered the throne room in a flurry. He signaled for Urwin to close the doors behind him. Urwin stared back blankly. When he didn't respond, Molma approached him: "There are no more faces. The sun is setting and the city is quiet." His voice buckled with notes of panic. "Has the king chosen?"

Urwin shivered. The night was growing cold as the sun went down. He shook his head. "Not one face," he admitted. He turned his eyes to the remaining three men, three fishermen from out at sea. It would have to be one of them, he realized. Perhaps the one with the bushy beard and the eyes like ice.

Urwin closed the doors and turned to face the king.

Slava the Immortal sat upon his throne, exhausted and bored. His corpulent form dripped over the sides of his chair like gobs of honey, only instead of sticky and sweet, his flesh held the bitterness of a thousand lifetimes and the mushiness of a million meals. He was ugly, of that there was no question, but even beauty seemed unimportant to him now. Instead, a deep disinterest had become his companion, and a subtle melancholy. Slava the Immortal had grown weary, and with this weariness, lazy.

The face he now wore belonged to a baker, a man who'd caught his eye because of his plump vigour. Tonight, the baker would get his face back, but Urwin feared the poor man might not recognize himself. His vigour had vanished, replaced instead by the seep of Slava's exhaustion. From nose to lips, the face drooped and dripped, a pile of dough made from deadened yeast.

"No," the king said suddenly, barely looking up at the handsome young fisherman with the beard. And then twice more he said it, his eyes toward the tile floor. No. No.

Molma's breath caught in his throat. The pages crowded toward the dais to lift the king's folds and massage his arms, flocking around him in his hour of need to comfort him and flatter him.

Urwin helped the three fishermen out of the throne room and then heaved the wooden doors closed behind them. The hall echoed as the doors boomed shut.

On nimble footsteps, the tenth page moved to join his peers where they stood fawning before their sulking monarch, and as he drew near to the dais, Urwin saw Slava shift suddenly in his seat. Pages scurried to and fro to catch the folds of his flesh as they dripped over the arms of his throne. The king shook them off and raised his weary neck. Those eyes, clear and sharp and full of cruelty, settled upon Urwin. And this time, unlike the last, they not only saw him but made special note of his existence. Slava the Immortal drew himself up to his full height and lifted a thunderous arm. With it, he pointed at Urwin and nodded his head. "Yes," he said. "Yes."

Urwin felt the blood rush from his face — or rather, the king's face, because already Slava was beginning to cast the spell that would take Urwin's face from him. Urwin panicked. "Milord—"

"He has no mask, Milord. He's but a pageboy." It was Molma, intervening on Urwin's behalf. The nine other pages turned from the king to look at their peer. They crouched like monkeys before the great lord Slava, incapable of independent thought or action. They moved on their knees to watch closely as Urwin's features began to thin and vanish, to slide away like sand down a windblown cliff.

Slava stopped for a moment. He looked at Molma, the first of his pages. "Was my decree not clear, pageboy?"

Molma swallowed hard.

"Did I not say: 'Let every man and boy ready his mask'?"

"Y-yes, Milord," Molma stammered. "It's just that—"

Slava stared, blankly, calmly, as eternal in this moment as in the next.

"Well," Molma looked to Urwin, "He needs a mask, Milord. We pageboys have never prepared one, we've never…" He trailed off.

Urwin stood before the king. He could feel his features dissolving, could see already how his slight mouth was beginning to wriggle its way over Slava's face, how his high cheekbones were sculpting themselves into the putty that would now be returning to the elated, or deeply disappointed, baker. He saw his beauty and his youth sketching itself finely upon the king he had laughed at, upon the king whose secret passion he had understood, and he felt suddenly a blood-chilling dread, a horrific knowledge of the fate that lay before him. He thought again of the old man from the courtyard. He thought of the look of freedom he'd seen in the old man's eyes, knowing that death was near and that it would take him from Slava's immortal reach. He understood that look now, and he envied the old greybeard his freedom.

The pages breathed heavily and brayed like donkeys. "A mask, Milord. He needs a mask."

Urwin stared at the king in silence.

Slava's cold hard eyes glittered knowingly. He gestured to the stack of tea-soaked parchment to his left, the Book of Insights, and one of the pageboys raced to bring the book within his reach. While the pageboy held the book before the king's half-stenciled face, the voluminous arms flipped through the damaged sheets of paper until they came at last upon the desired sheaf. In a wrenching movement filled with rage and victory, the king tore free the slice of ink-smeared and tea-soaked parchment and held it up into the air.

"Let every man and boy ready his mask," Slava said in his cold, stony voice. "Or?"

No one moved. Urwin's heart beat wildly in his chest. He couldn't believe this was happening. That the king had chosen him, a pageboy, to offer up his face. And that he was going to ruin it, to destroy its beauty, to mangle its grace...

"Or?" said the king again, his voice so sharp and loud that the torch braces rattled in the walls.

"'Or let the king choose for him,'" finished Molma, his voice but a whisper.

And Slava laughed softly. He nodded. "Good." He lifted the piece of stained parchment, one of the last he had written in the book, and directed Urwin to lift his face toward it. In a flash, the sheet of paper sealed itself around the contours of his face, melded with his skin, melted into his hairline, jawline, neckline.

It became his ears and his nose. It became his cheeks and his mouth. And in an instant, the final page of the Book of Insights became the pageboy's face.

"What does it say?" he heard the boy to his left murmur. "I can't see."

Other pages echoed the query.

In shame, Urwin lifted his gaze to stare the king full in the face — his face — and he felt his blood run cold as those eyes, his eyes, stared right through him. As if he didn't exist. As if he had been erased completely.

"It says," announced Slava the Immortal so all the pages could hear: "'This is my face.'"

And in a rush of horror, Urwin understood what the king had done. He had found a way to make the change permanent; he had found the spell that would set him free. Urwin touched his new face, a thing of paper, ink and shame, and he wept. He wept because he understood that what the king had written had become the truth.

*This is my face*, thought Urwin.

And Slava the Immortal stared right through it.

◆

**Matthew Jordan Schmidt** lives in Vancouver and teaches academic writing at the University of British Columbia. He has been published in a number of speculative fiction magazines, including *On Spec*, *Sounds of the Night* and *Collective Fallout*. He has recently finished writing his first young adult fantasy novel and is working on a second. His next project will be a novel in French.

# OLD SOUL

## ~ Adria Laycraft ~

Angelica stood hidden in the shadows of the hallway and let the gossip feed her distaste for life.

"Such an odd bird."

"I know, right? When she looks at me I feel my grandmother sizing me up all over again."

"Definitely something uncanny about that girl. Maria has had such a time of it, right from the day she was born."

Angelica turned to run away only to see the shimmer woman in the air between her and her bedroom.

"Leave me alone," she cried, crashing through the vision that only she could see and right into the arms of her mother. Angelica struggled in her grasp, unable to know the difference between real and not, and broke free at last. She banged into her room and slammed the door hard.

It would not keep the shimmering beings away. Soon they gathered in the corner over her dresser, fogging the mirror and distorting the reflection of her face.

"Leave. Me. Alone!" Angelica cried. She scooped up the first thing to hand and threw it with every bit of force she could muster.

The ceramic kitty burst into a million tiny pieces when it hit the mirror, and left a new fractured reflection.

"Angelica!"

Her mother pushed into the room, the faces of her friends crowding in behind her. Disapproval marred their concern, and one tugged on her mother's sweater.

"She's a danger to herself, darling. You can't ignore that."

But her mother ignored her. She shooed them out of Angelica's room and gathered her daughter in a hug.

"Was it them again?" she asked.

Angelica nodded against the soft cotton, buttons rubbing her cheek.

Her mother sighed. "You must consider what I told you. You're almost ten now. You're too old for imaginary friends."

"I know," Angelica whispered. Her mother tried to pull away, but she tightened her grip. "The ladies, they said I'm trouble for you. I'm sorry, Mom. I don't want to be trouble."

"Oh, Sweetie, you are never too much trouble for me."

Angelica wished she could believe it.

⋄

Angelica pressed the angry red crayon hard to the page, smudging it back and forth. Around her were scattered pages of coloring filled with hot pinks and sour yellows and sad blues. But most of them were completely black, wiping out the picture's lines.

She began to hum, choosing a crayon without thought, and pressed it to the page. This one felt right. This one, despite being small, had the hue that portrayed her feelings properly. Time passed beyond recall as she rubbed, her mind a blessed quiet place, her feelings in check.

The bedroom door squeaked open.

She looked up to see her mother's smile change to concern, and down again to find the black crayon a tiny stub and the page nothing but blackness.

It was her third box of crayons this summer, and time and again she used up the black in her crayon box long before any others.

"Honey…"

"It's okay, Mom," Angelica said. "Maybe I'm just not meant to be an artist."

Angelica didn't color anymore after that. The pictures looked so dumb anyway, everything wrecked by all that black. So she just gave it up. Her mother made her visit a friendly lady in a nice quiet office with comfy chairs and a box of tissue always at hand. The lady was nice, and asked lots of questions, but Angelica never admitted that she saw imaginary people. She just said she was too old for that, and the visits stopped.

Unfortunately all of this made the shimmer woman hang around more. And when Angelica used the words 'hang around', she really meant it. The shimmer woman often appeared in the same corner of her room, hovering up near the ceiling to stare down at her. Other shimmer people came and went, different ones all the time, but that one was always the same. For someone who was just a figment of her imagination, as her mother said, she sure seemed real.

When Angelica was three, the shimmer woman said her name was Gloria, and that she was there to help. The young Angelica loved to talk with Gloria, especially about the place of light. Back then Angelica somehow felt the place was real, as if she had actual memories of it, and even now she remembered how real it seemed to her. But when she had tried to tell her mother about it, all she heard was what a wonderful imagination she had.

"No, Mommy," she said then. "It's real. How do I get back there? I want to go there."

"You can't go to the places in your imagination, Sweetie," her mother replied. "You have to learn to be happy with real life."

Angelica didn't like having the shimmer woman and her mother contradict each other. And once she realized Gloria wasn't even real, she rejected her, angry that one of the best things in her life was a lie.

Now she was nine, but inside she felt ninety, and she just wanted to die.

"She's an old soul, Maria," a friend said as they sat in the kitchen drinking coffee. Angelica sat with a book in the very next room and wondered why adults thought children could not hear their conversations.

"She's a little girl with an active mind," her mother replied. "One day this will all be past and she probably won't even remember it."

This made Angelica close the book and lay her head back. She didn't want to forget the place of light, or Gloria. Trying to ignore these things hadn't made them go away like her mother said they would.

Angelica's life seemed without color, hopeless and worthless. She had no idea what it meant to be an 'old soul', but she had learned to keep her mouth shut about the people she saw and the strange memories she had in hopes she would become normal. It had failed.

She began to look for ways to die.

She stepped out into the crosswalk without looking. She tried every kind of nut, thinking she may have a deadly allergy like one of the boys in her class. She swam past her depth at the pool in hopes no one would notice her floundering until too late.

Sometimes she even left her seatbelt off in the back of the car.

When none of this worked, or only earned her even more unwanted attention, Angelica decided to jump out her bedroom window.

⁕

The house, a colonial two-storey, had old-fashioned slider windows. Just unlocking the old brass latch left one nail broken and her fingers aching. But she worked it around enough to free the frame, and the chair from her desk gave her the leverage to push the top edge up until there was enough of an opening to work at it from the bottom.

Soon she stood before her freedom, the cool air dimpling her skin. She draped one leg over the ledge, hitched her bum up onto the sill, and brought the other leg out.

The deep green of the lawn below beckoned her on.

"Please don't go," said a voice from the air.

Gloria.

"You aren't real," Angelica said through gritted teeth. "Everyone thinks I'm crazy because of you. Even my artwork is crazy. I just don't want to be here anymore."

"What if you have a reason to be here? A purpose?"

Angelica shook her head, both hands holding the sill, ready to push off.

"My only purpose is to make my mom sad. I'm sad, she's sad ... now it can be over."

Gloria shimmered into sight in the air before her. "She will feel worse than sad if you do this."

Angelica looked right into the glowing face of her imagination. "Why should I listen to you? You're not real," she said, and pushed off.

The ground came fast, and the boulder by the roses rushed at her face. At the last second something — someone? — pushed her to one side so she missed smacking her head or breaking her neck. On impact her left leg made a strange snapping sound, and Angelica screamed with pain.

Blackness edged her vision as she lay there on the cool grass, and she embraced it, ready to die.

Only instead of dying she woke in startling pain as a crunch ripped agony through her leg. Angelica saw bright lights shining above her, marred only by moving shapes and masked shadows. The only clear thing she saw before darkness took her again was Gloria's smiling face floating above her.

The next time she woke it was to hear her mother's voice.

"She's moaning in her sleep. When will the medication take effect?"

"Soon," came the reply. "Can you tell us how she fell from her bedroom window?"

The voices faded, but the pain did not, and the blackness eluded her. As she drifted in a haze of agony, her failure broke her heart. She tried to remember the special place, a land of light and joy beyond anything in real life. And because real life could never compare, she wanted it to end, even if that magical place was only in her imagination.

"I don't belong here," she murmured.

Angelica heard her mother's sharp suck of breath, then felt her cool hand on her forehead.

"Oh, Sweetie." Her mother's voice trembled, and her breath shuddered out in a rush that Angelica could feel on her skin. "I'm so glad you're okay."

She wasn't okay, but the haziness thickened, and the drifting took Angelica away, so there was no chance to explain.

◆

The next time she woke, Angelica noticed a scritch-scratching noise first. She opened her eyes to see a plain ceiling of white tiles. Sunshine shone in the window on her right, but the scritch-scratching came from her left.

She turned her head, ignoring the pain in her leg for now.

An old lady with short white hair sat in a second hospital bed. The lady had her head bent over a large notepad, and just when Angelica turned her head to see her, she began to hum as she rubbed the bright orange pencil back and forth.

"What are you drawing?" Angelica asked.

The lady smiled, but didn't look over. "A surprise. For you," she said. Then she did look up, and the twinkle in her eye made Angelica want to know her. "What is your name?"

"Angelica."

The lady laughed. "Of course it is. My grandkids call me Nana Jay, so you can too if you want."

Nana Jay went back to coloring.

"Why are you here?"

"Broke my hip. Happens to old folk like me."

"When can I see the picture?"

"Almost done," the grandma lady said. Her little pink tongue slipped between her lips as she added a touch of green here, and a bit of baby blue there. "Okay, it's ready."

She turned the notebook and held it up.

It was Gloria.

Gloria. Perfect and without a doubt, as her mother liked to say. It could be no one else, with faint hints of other faces peering through all the shimmering colors around her.

It seemed like there was no air to breathe.

"How do you know that person?"

"I see her watching over you, with rarely ever a break. She's your guardian angel. You've seen her before, right?"

"But my mother said it's all in my imagination, that the things I see aren't real."

Nana Jay gave a funny snort. "Well, little lady, this one's real. I see her, so she must be, right?"

Angelica dwelt on that for a little while. Nana Jay started a new sketch, setting Gloria's portrait aside on a little table with wheels that could be pushed right over the bed. This time Nana Jay turned the notebook so Angelica could watch as a glorious garden scene, with a stone footbridge crossing a stream and a lily-studded pond reflecting the riot of colorful flowers around it, came to life beneath Nana Jay's talented fingers.

"That's so pretty," Angelica whispered. She didn't want Nana Jay to stop, but she had to express the upwelling of emotion that the development of the scene woke in her heart.

"Would you like to do one?" Nana Jay asked. "It's the best way to pass the time while bones knit and bodies heal. Might even help some."

Angelica turned her face away. "That's okay," she said to the window. "It's not a good idea."

Laying there listening to the scritch-scratching and knowing she would only draw her awful feelings of failure for all to see just made it feel worse.

"Gloria wants to help you," Nana Jay said. "She is so sad that you don't believe in her."

Angelica pressed her lips together and wished for her ear buds. Then she could shut out the words and the feelings and the thoughts ... though she'd tried that before and it rarely worked.

She sighed, a big hefty sigh that made her leg twinge. It was wrapped in a hard shell from ankle to hip.

"Everyone says it's wrong for me to see her. They make fun of me, and say mean things about me when they think I'm not listening. They even say I'm trouble for my mom."

"And what does Gloria say about all this?"

Angelica shook her head and rolled her eyes. "That it's worth living, that they just don't understand, that I have to love people even when they are mean. On and on like that."

The scritch-scratching stopped. "You didn't fall out your window, did you?"

The silence must've been an answer enough.

"Your mother went to great trouble to cover that up, I think, but she knows the truth. And she's very frightened."

Angelica tried to shift off her sore butt, but the movement made her gasp. She lay back in defeat. "Where is Gloria, anyway?" she asked, not wanting to pursue the topic of her mother.

Now it was Nana Jay's turn to sigh. "She went away. She said that was what you wanted, what you kept telling her. Lots of spirit guides fade out of children's lives when they don't believe anymore. I guess it's normal, but it makes me wonder if it could be different."

Angelica tipped her head back and stared at the ceiling tiles as her vision blurred and smeared. "I really didn't think she was real. I thought I was crazy. I thought it would be better if I just died." She sniffled a little, not caring if Nana Jay knew she was crying. "Now that you see her too, I feel bad she's gone."

"We could call her."

"We could?" Angelica blinked away her tears and turned to look into the kind face of wrinkles that watched her from the other bed. "Will she be mad?"

A smile caused the wrinkles to all pile up in a most appealing way. "No. I'm quite sure of that."

So they called her, and Gloria shimmered to life up near that boring white ceiling, casting her light and color over the tiles until the room blossomed with it.

"Can you see that?" Angelica asked.

"Wow, yeah, I sure can," Nana Jay answered, and Angelica knew then that she would never again be alone or without hope.

"I'm so sorry, Gloria," she said. "I'm sorry I didn't believe in you."

"I understand, child," Gloria said, the thought-words forming in her mind just as they always had. "And I will make you an offer now that will never be offered again to you while you walk this path in this body. You may come with me, right now, and return to that place you miss so much."

"The beautiful place of light?"

"Yes. Or, you may stay here and live this life first before coming Home."

"Why would I do that? No one understands me. I feel like I don't belong here."

"There are many reasons to stay, and you will learn as you experience them, just as you have learned that you are not the only one that sees me."

Angelica shot Nana Jay an apologetic smile.

"But perhaps greatest reason of all is the opportunity to express that beauty that you know exists on the other side."

"How do I do that?"

"Through art and music and other creative endeavours. When you portray the beauty you remember, it helps those who have forgotten the place of light. It gives them hope."

Angelica thought about this for a moment. "How can I share hope if I have none?"

"Faith. I have told you the other side exists. You have discovered I am truly real, and not a figment of your imagination. If you stay now, you will have to simply trust in that and share your hope and faith with others."

Angelica lay quiet for a long time, thinking. She dozed off without meaning to, and woke surprised that she had. Then she thought of Gloria's offer and knew she had faith that the shimmer woman would be there for her, no matter what, no matter how long it took her to answer.

And then Angelica looked over to see Nana Jay's finished picture of the garden. It took her breath away to see such brilliance displayed in simple lines and colors. Angelica realized this was what Gloria meant. She could see the faith and hope, see the pure beauty of the other side shining through Nana Jay's picture.

She could do that. New hope fluttered in her heart, and she just knew she could do the same without wearing out the black to a tiny stub.

Her mother walked in just at that moment, and hurried over to hug Angelica.

"How are you feeling? Does it hurt too much?"

"I'm okay, mom. I'm sorry."

Her mother blinked hard and hugged her again. "I'm just glad you're okay. Can I bring you anything?"

"Yeah." Angelica looked up at Gloria, then over and Nana Jay, who winked at her. "I'd like a notepad and some colors."

⊱ ✧ ⊰

**Adria Laycraft** is a grateful member of IFWA and a proud survivor of the six-week Odyssey Writers Workshop. She works as a freelancer and ghostwriter, and is co-editing the forthcoming *Urban Green Man* anthology. Author of *Be a Freelance Writer Now*, available everywhere e-books are sold, Adria lives in Calgary with her husband and son, where she invests far too much time and money into her garden.

# The Song of Conn and the Sea People

### ∽ Jeff Hughes ∾

*Invocation*
Lo, hear me, / listen to this tale I breathe,
Of the glorious prince of the Celts / of the strong and brave,
A terrible battle fought and won / a people conquered,
Bones shattered through, / their red blood spilt,
And the lands of Eire pillaged, / its woven golden treasures taken.
Muses, I call on thee / nine fold wise,
Beautiful Parnassus, / let me speak fairly,
To praise the Celts, / an honourable people living.
Defending their Great Island, / virgin Eire standing strong,
Ruled by Finn and his son / tall, strong, and fair Conn.
An evil had besought them / from places unknown birthed,
This horror devoured them / cast wicked winds on wronged Celtic kin,
And how Conn, Finn's Son, / saved his people.
So, with this humble voice, / let me speak of this tale of battle.
Mark this twilight of the Celts, / this dawn of the Sea Peoples.

*The Celtic Army Gathers*
Along the ocean's edge / Eire's raucous outer rim,
Great armies gathered / weary eyes watching water's edge.

## The Song of Conn and the Sea People by Jeff Hughes

Ten thousands Celts / shuffling grains of sand.
Brother and fathers / sisters and mothers,
The folk of the hills, / the people of fields and dales,
The noble Breccias were there / deadly double-axes gleaming,
Blades that could hew men, / twain'd twice with single strokes,
Flanked to them stood the Cumber-men / the wolf riders
of the south hills,
Reapers and pillagers. / The Cauci rogues had gathered here too.
And the Luceni, the Iverni, / the Erdin, the Concani, the Velabri.
Their leader, noble King Finn, / the warlord of these gathered Celts,
His lords and knights, / all standing stalwart true,
And Morganna, his wife, / her seven shield maids ready.
And the bravest of all, / his son, Conn of the Stone-Fists,
Whose arms were hewn / stone sharpened and steel forged,
A boy, Conn could swim the Irish Sea / twice times thrice,
Yet, these cold waters now / only womb'd the worst of all.

### Conn and the Sea Peoples
For the Great Enemy was here, / the world breakers.
Today, this day, / the Sea Peoples had returned,
Their great armor adamantine / their fire spewing weapons scorching,
Hell's fury contained, / the threads of fate charred, spurned.
These ten thousand Celts / gathered to repulse them,
To hold these vile invaders back / begrudge them on the beaches.
But as the sun did rise, / Celtic armor glowed and gleamed,
A furious storm began, / the first breaches of nature notched.

### Battle of the Beach
Great beasts crawled forth / slithered out beneath white waves,
Long limbed, / mighty metallic domed.
Fire burst from red eyes, / consumed the charging callous Celts,
Screaming and kicking, / fighting the furious flames.
There was no relief, no respite / no place to run and flee.
Monster after monster belched forth, / dripping salty from the sea.
Brave King Finn, / red faced and screaming,
Attempts a rally true, / to stem this seething spring tide,
Ten thousand Celtic hosts, / the sand stormed and churned.
But the fires of hell, / of metal beasts born,
Burned Celtic flesh, / mashed Celtic bone.
Melted armor peeled, / flaking off cracked leather.

## The Song of Conn and the Sea People by Jeff Hughes

The Celts fought bravely, / died on firmly planted feet,
Broken blades, / shields shattered,
Mother died beside daughter, / father fell beside son,
No stopping the Sea Peoples / forces of un-nature,
Of the world unknown, / birthed beyond the pale.
And before the sun peaked, / the noon of day reached,
Fiery and bright, / wane face looking down,
The battle was done, / dead Celtic lips screaming forever fright.

### The Last Rally
Few brave Celts were left, / rallied forth for vengeance,
Running fast and true, / to slay the greatest of all beasts,
One kill to rue the day, / a headless body made,
Yet this greatest of beasts, / one simple foot raised,
Crushed these few Celts, / broke frothing horses and all.
Conn the Stone-fisted was amongst them, / this last great charge,
His mighty sword Durendelle, / the great slayer of men,
Left untested, / clutched in Conn's eager hands,
This Celtic Prince fell, / another dead man amongst thousands.
Unfettered, the Sea People trod forth, / destroying the baggage train,
Fearful family and cringing kin, / they murdered next,
A beachhead taken, / a foe bloody and victorious,
None left to stop, / none left to hold at bay.

### The Old Man of Many Names
The Sea People triumphant, / their battlefield they abandoned,
Returning to the sea, / red waves swallowing red steel.
Leaving dead bodies floating, / heaped upon the dead shore.
One living thing remained, / a stooped figure hobbled,
Between the dead, / bloodied sand stained robes,
Through waves red and full, / lapping and swallowing graves,
Upon a dead Conn he came / this Old Man with Many Names,
A withered brow lowered, / a cold dead forehead touched,
Old words were whispered, / a language old and forgotten,
Muscles retightened / sinews re-sown and whole,
A great scream came, / the dead Celt's lips lamented,
And Conn Stone-Fists breathed again / deep breathed with feet of vigor,
Rage and vengeance, / filled to the brim,
But the Old Man's words / eyes so wise and weathered,
Calmed the Celtic Prince / made him see not red but white,

*The Song of Conn and the Sea People* by Jeff Hughes

And hope returned, / this Old Man recognized as friend,
As a friend of Conn, Son of Finn, / an advisor of Finn and Deirdre true,
The old man's name, / Arbiter Grey,
A sage, a wizard, / wizened wisdom birthed from grey eyes,
This Old Man of Many Names spoke now, / and the Conn,
Finn's Son heeded.

### The Old Bond

These two heroes, / teacher and student for ages,
An old friendship long forged, / hotter and stronger
Than any iron / links unbroken, unbreakable.
As fathers for sons, / Arbiter Grey cared for Conn,
Taught him the ways of the world, / a trail of the blade blazed.
Never to hurt the weak, / warring only with the strong.
As a lad, so fresh and bright, / Conn followed in Arbiter's path,
Learned languages and spoke them, / the Old Man knew much,
Rumored many centuries taught, / antipodes travelled and travelled again.

### The Feats of Conn Stone-Fists

Trials he pitted against Conn / Finn the King gave permission,
To test his blood son / a young Celtic Prince born of a warrior king.
Feats of strength / games of the mind,
Trials of the heart as well. / For the Celts know loves' place
Knew how it, / when strong between two women,
Or between two men / could move the heaviest granite,
Would stale storm surged seas, / melt the coldest ice flows.
Passed all these feats / Conn, Celtic Prince,
Slaying the Son of Cain, / finding Cuchulainn's lost lance,
Taming the fighting Fenians / outwitting the slippery salmon.
Denting armor, / breaking blades,
His sword, Durendelle, / blood grooves caked,
Its silver hilt rusted, / blade always true.
Always, the Son of Finn, / first of the Celts,
Came furious, / onward and forward.
All feats passed, / uncommon heroism made common again.
A true hero, / a Celt amongst Celts
Was Conn Stone-Fists, / King Finn's blood son.

## The Song of Conn and the Sea People by Jeff Hughes

### The Steel Autumn

Such new heroes needed, / as old heroes fail.
When first the Sea People came to Eire / darkening sunny skies,
Their great iron castles, / drifting like fallen leaves,
Found home in the ocean, / took root amongst the abysmal depths.
Years ago, the Celts watched them, / feared their metal fortresses,
Great monoliths that waited, / barnacles under the deep seas,
Till the first blood was spilt / till their great monsters,
Tall as giants / thrice limbed and dome headed,
Strode from seas, / the gait of gods',
Ravaging Celtic villages, / stealing bodies,
Poisoning the living, / harvesting cold organs,
Until life and death, / the transition between the two,
Blurred and was made one, / welded together.
The Tuatha de Danann attacked, / yet Danu's warriors fell defeated.
The conquering Sea Peoples, / unstoppable, unquenchable,
Held all of Eire / crushed the old Celtic heroes until blood
Seeped between stones, / blades of grass stained.
An age ended / a new one belly born.

### The New Heroes Rally

Battle after battle lost, / the old heroes fell defeated.
They called out for new heroes, / the Son of Finn
Thrice ignored the call, / till tragedy struck.
His grandmother Dayanna slain, / his twin sisters missing,
Now Conn met the call. / Joined great heroes,
Like Cattegirn / red bearded and berserk,
Whose great hounds, / Fear and Agony,
Could tackle cave bears. / Or, Arthmael,
Beautiful and deadly, / dead-eyed and true.
Rae, Son of Harvod, / the Silent Rider,
Golden chariots trampling, the greatest warriors rode down,
And Elysse, / deadliest of women,
Sickly Scythian sickles, / flashing and shredding.
All these heroes rallied forth, / all had fought ferocious
for this barren beach,
Hopelessly outnumbering, / but hopelessly outnumbered.
And all fell, / sand and shore their pauper's cairn.

## The Song of Conn and the Sea People by Jeff Hughes

### Raise the Dead

When these titans, / dark gods of Nix,
These Sea Peoples, / left these beaches behind,
Brave Arbiter Grey, / the dead he raised again,
Twelve fallen Celtic warriors resurrected, / from sandy graves cast out.
And Conn, Son of Finn / the leader of eleven dead men,
Cattegirn, and Arthmael, / Agro, and Kade,
Skene, Carthair, and Gavyn, / Parlon and Cormac,
Aengus and Taryn, / twelve necrotic births,
All wobbled on cold dead feet, / warm limbs resurging,
The touch of Arbiter resurrected. / Dead men with one task,
A final mission, / one last chance at victory.
Find the home, / raze it true,
Destroy the Sea Peoples / Old and infants both.
Find this nest of vipers, / burn such unearthly brood whole,
And save Eire, / or die twice
In the attempt, / the end of everything.

### The Twelve Heroes Hesitate

Where do they brood, / the Son of Finn asked.
The home of the Sea People, / hidden in the abyss,
These wights / all ghosts of men,
Did ask of Arbiter Grey. / The old wizard,
Wise and keen, / stopped at ocean's edge,
Then, serpent staff in hand, / parted churning white-capped waves.
A great stairwell below / cut through sand,
Wrought of barnacled stone, / green framed in kelp and algae.
It spiraled downward, / past the blackest depths.
Arbiter Grey's eyes herded them, / these fell steps mounted.
If dead men feel, / cold dead blood in veins,
They trembled in fear, / the agued abyss terrified them,
Far deeper than hell, / unmanning the twelve dead Celts.

### The Descent

The first steps taken / fearless, by the Son of Finn,
And down they walked, / warriors twelve.
Down and down, / days and days of walking.
Dead men need not food / nor air,
As the cold waves engulfed them / silver sharks snaked between them,
And still they walked, / lit by miraculous glowing fish,

### The Song of Conn and the Sea People by Jeff Hughes

Starlight creatures, / flickering with ethereal warmth,
Till the ocean floor, / the bottom of doom reached.

### The Hidden City

And there, / shining sickly green,
Glowing in weak phosphorescence, / many domed,
A great city of fortresses, / dull grey and cold,
Shining light blue, / the Sea People's dark home.
The warriors paused, / unsure and humbled,
Till mighty Conn Stone-Fists, / glorious Son of Finn,
Strode forward, / mighty blade Durendelle in hand.
The sand of the ocean floor, / kicked up by stomping feet.
Conn's band proceeds / true as firmly fletched flechettes,
Ahead of them loomed, / one immense gate guarded,
By two great titans of steel, / many limbed, many bladed,
Two Sentinels standing watch, / red eyes dimmed, vacant.
The Celtic Prince attacked one, / his hesitant companions followed,
But nothing, / the beasts did not stir.
Then beyond them, / a groaning gate slid open
A mouth of Hell, / the devil's maw.
A single figure revealed, / a man's body and demon faced,
Beckoned the twelve warriors inside, / enter this womb of danger.

### Deucalion the Slave

Brave and bold, / the Son of Finn forward pressed.
His dead comrades, / worn, weary, waked in tow.
Past the gates, / down spiraling corridors,
Tunnels of metal wrapped in metal, / light and fire ensconced inside.
As hours passed, / dark days faded,
Down and down, / deeper into the dead city.
Until bottom met, / hell's ceiling surely,
And the mysterious demon spoke, / split tongued
Deucalion, / this demon's name.
Sea People's oldest enemy, / now made slave.
Held for centuries, / their perpetual prisoner.
His furious speech followed, / dead men and Deucalion discussed
Questions and answers, / fletched like arcing arrows,
Till true truth unearthed, / and lore's buried treasures found.

## The Song of Conn and the Sea People by Jeff Hughes

### The Ways of the Sea Peoples

The Sea Peoples, / Deucalion said,
These ravagers of heavens, / a race of god killers,
Wreckers of worlds, / attackers of other peoples,
Like Deucalion's kin, / enslaved, murdered, imprisoned.
Their leader, / Prometheus of the Old Power,
Leader and murderer, / the High King of Locusts,
Lore Master of the plague people. / They wrought his world's ending,
So, born of ill-blood, / craven Deucalion desired vengeance.

### The Elixir

Deucalion pleaded, / begged these twelve dead men of Eire,
Asked Conn their leader, / the Son of Finn,
To find a wondrous Elixir, / a potion brewed of blood,
A panacea, / to fight the plague of Deucalion's people.
A weapon of the Sea People. / A living poison, so small,
A viral blade pointed at the Celts next. / A never-ending pox,
Death feasting upon death. / Genocide fattened on bones of kin.
But hope stirs, / all is not lost,
A plague that can be stopped / left stillborn,
With this Elixir, / upend this fired furnace,
And sear these sky invaders. / Reject them burning and broken,
Sent back to the heavens, / bloated, bobbing on the sickly seas.
This demon quest posed, / Deucalion begged them.
Yet none would answer. / All feared their foreign foes,
All but one, / the Son of Finn.
Conn Stone-Fists accepted, / thrust the quest's mantle upon himself.

### The Ark

Now sated / demon Deucalion led them again,
Deeper and deeper, / past the core,
Through the lowest chain, / into the icy realms
Of creation. / A great hall awaited them
Filled with mighty beasts. / The iron monsters
All sleeping, / all guarding
A tiny altar, / a fulcrum surrounded by orbs,
Glowing white windows, / moving pictures and fiery glyphs,
Dancing on glass wares, / warming the Celt's scared faces.
The Ark, / Deucalion's word for this greatest of halls,
A repository of knowledge, / a forge of science.

## The Song of Conn and the Sea People by Jeff Hughes

Home of the Elixir, / its cradle and grave.
Now Conn's men / their quest's goal so close,
Became weary, / malingered mid-step.
Calling out, / berating these walking Celtic corpses,
The central altar Deucalion pointed / the Elixir's humbled holding place,
And Conn Stone-Fists, / rushed forward,
Snatching the liquid weapon, / firm in fibrous fingers,
A quest completed, / a hope restored.

### The Awakening

Held in Conn's fingers, / the Elixir still warm,
A bellowing sounded, / filling the great hall,
The slumbering beasts awoke, / all metal anger and iron rage.
Soon, a second slaughter began / dead men dying twice.
Cattegirn fell first / cloven in three.
Then Skene, Cormac, / both fell hollow and headless.
Kade and Gavyn, / sundered from sole to sight.
But not all twelve Celts died / burnished blades untouched
Now slew. / Great monsters fell,
Heads hewed, / marrow mangled and spines split.
But too many awoke, / a horde of mashing,
Cloaked in steel, / fast and agile.
Parlon fell next / limbless and screaming.
Crushed skulls both / Arthmael and Carthair collapsed.
Argo and Taryn fell next / then Aengus last,
Till only Conn and Deucalion stood / bloody backs defended.

### The Giver of Fire

Then, the sounds of war / the fog of death
Receded its wraithlike fingers. / A single figure walked forth,
Red in skin, / many eyed,
A giant, / muscles heaped upon muscles.
It spoke its name, / Prometheus, the Giver of Fire,
The burner of worlds, / the King of the Sea Peoples.
A truce Prometheus now offered / Conn and Deucalion's lives offered
In return for the Elixir, / all sins forgiven,
The Celt people spared, / a single drop untouched by this flood
Of metal and monsters. / Near death, Deucalion refused
Charged forth, / blinded with blood debt,
And was cut down, / a flash of light seared

### The Song of Conn and the Sea People by Jeff Hughes

Deucalion's blue skin, / green blood leaking forth.
But Conn, Son of Finn / wise and noble,
Pondered the Promethean question, / mighty jaws clenched,
Until Prometheus demanded, / all questions asked,
So all answers needed. / And Conn decided true.
A flash of steel, Conn struck out,
Durendelle snaked between open lips, / into a brilliant brain sliced,
And Prometheus of the Soft Flame died / stiff, rigid, and no more.

### Deucalion's Death

To Deucalion Conn ran, / the Son of Finn
Propped up the dying demon, / bloody green lips
Chattered final words. / Deucalion told Conn to flee,
To save the Celts, / destroy these ravagers of Heaven,
These bloody minded gods. / To kill these world Enders,
A gift was offered, / a small metal trifle from dead Prometheus,
The dying Deucalion offered. / The Celtic Prince received,
This bauble of destruction, / Deucalion green mouthed told Conn.
Once beyond the great door, / the Celt was to crush the item.
Then, a final ending would begin, / a closing of this chapter,
A people finally freed, / and the Sea Peoples forever doomed.
Then, dead eyes looked upward. / The demon's fury now cold,
And Conn left him, / the dead abandoned,
Sleeping in the deepest of tombs, / receiving the highest of honors.

### Deucalion's Revenge

Upwards to the sun, / step upon step climbed,
The Son of Finn, / his legs fueled by fire,
Elixir in hand, / Conn sought the sunlight,
Desperate for its warmth, / needing the rays of gold.
Through corridors of steel, / the Celt ran for his future
No Sea People blocked him, / only empty stairwells.
The thudding of his feet echoed, / days upon days,
Ever upward, / Conn feverishly fled for freedom,
Till at last, / a glorious sight beheld,
An open gate, / abysmal sea floor beyond.
The Celtic Prince free at last, / the hated city left behind.
Taking the demon's gift, / he held it high,
Doing as told, / Conn Stone-Fists crushed the trinket.
Trumpets and horns sounded, / fire belched,

### *The Song of Conn and the Sea People* by Jeff Hughes

Metal rent, / domes collapsed.
As the great city collapsed, / the Sea People cast in ruins.

### The Return

But Conn cared not, / onward to the sun,
Walked the dead man. / Time stretched again,
Twisted and broken, / then reformed days later,
Up the sea stairs once forged / revealed by Arbiter Grey-Eyes,
Out of the Deep. / Then sand and sun beckoned,
To Eire, Conn returned, / the conquering hero comes,
And Arbiter met him, / wrinkled hands held outward,
The Elixir demanded. / The Old Man of Many Names,
Wisest of all, / took the glorious gift.
Come, he ordered, / and Conn, Finn's glorious son,
Left the sea behind, / let it claim its noble dead.

### The Poisoned

Homeward bound, / the Old Man and the Celtic Prince,
Conn and Alistair strode, / followed a path of destruction paved.
Blood and bodies lined it, / painted red with ash and flame.
Until at last, / Conn was home again,
His family should greet him, / the dead warrior hoped for cheers,
But only faces of fury, / teeth and claws and fangs,
Welcomed the Son of Finn. / These Sea People plagued,
Conn fought them, / fists and feet held them back,
Delaying the savage Celts, / stemming their madness,
These poisoned souls turned animals / infected and violent.
But Conn Stone-Fists' strength waned / his afterlife diminished,
The Celtic Prince fell underfoot, / crushed and maimed.

### The Cure

The Son of Finn, / fell before a cure came,
Mere seconds too short, / a pervasive poison purged,
A maniacal madness mended, / a hero slain,
As Arbiter Grey-Eyes came to each Celt, / a taste of Elixir jabbed
Deep into veins forced. / These savage Celts gave pause,
Peace replaced war, / brutality's flames snuffed out.
The madness all gone, / evaporated into nothingness.

### The Death of a Hero

The Celts now saved / many redeemed by one,
Conn, Son of Finn / torn and sundered,
He lay at the centre, / women and wailing with woe,
Mourning the dead limbs now dead again / the just hero martyred.
Yet, a village saved, / the Sea People vanquished,
And to a silent tomb, / the Son of Finn was carried,
Arbiter spoke soft words, / whispering dead star-born languages,
The Old Man honoring, / praised the Celtic Prince,
The savior of his kin, / the slayer of bloody gods.
And Conn's people slept soundly, / eyes forever sky watching,
weary, hopeful,
Their future saved, / Conn's quest and life completed.

⟡

**Jeff Hughes** was born and raised in the small farming community of Shamrock, Prince Edward Island, Canada, by his parents Edwin and Lynn, and with his brother and sister, Jason and Jennifer. After completing his academic studies, Jeff has been an environmentalist, a researcher, and even a school teacher, but his passion has always been for writing. Now, he lives in the frigid climate of Northern Alberta, Canada, with his beautiful wife Virginia and their precious baby girl Kaleigh. Any free time Jeff now has, which is rare, is still spent planning, writing, and editing his next story.

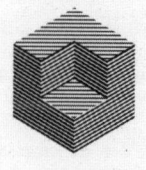

Our titles are available at major book stores
and local independent resellers who support
Science Fiction and Fantasy readers like you.

**EDGE Science Fiction
and Fantasy Publishing**

www.edgewebsite.com

**Our titles are available at major book stores and local independent resellers who support Science Fiction and Fantasy readers like you.**

*Alphanauts* by J. Brian Clarke (tp) - ISBN: 978-1-894063-14-2
*Apparition Trail, The* by Lisa Smedman (tp) - ISBN: 978-1-894063-22-7
*As Fate Decrees* by Denysé Bridger (tp) - ISBN: 978-1-894063-41-8
*Avim's Oath* (Part Six of the Okal Rel Saga) by Lynda Williams (tp)
 - ISBN: 978-1-894063-35-7

*Black Chalice, The* by Marie Jakober (hb) - ISBN: 978-1-894063-00-7
*Blue Apes* by Phyllis Gotlieb (pb) - ISBN: 978-1-895836-13-4
*Blue Apes* by Phyllis Gotlieb (hb) - ISBN: 978-1-895836-14-1

*Captives* by Barbara Galler-Smith and Josh Langston (tp)
 - ISBN: 978-1-894063-53-1
*Children of Atwar, The* by Heather Spears (pb) - ISBN: 978-0-88878-335-6
*Chilling Tales: Evil Did I Dwell; Lewd I Did Live* edited by Michael Kelly (tp)
 - ISBN: 978-1-894063-52-4
*Cinco de Mayo* by Michael J. Martineck (pb) - ISBN: 978-1-894063-39-5
*Cinkarion - The Heart of Fire* (Part Two of The Chronicles of the Karionin)
 by J. A. Cullum - (tp) - ISBN: 978-1-894063-21-0
*Circle Tide* by Rebecca K. Rowe (tp) - ISBN: 978-1-894063-59-3
*Clan of the Dung-Sniffers* by Lee Danielle Hubbard (tp) - ISBN: 978-1-894063-05-0
*Claus Effect, The* by David Nickle & Karl Schroeder (pb) - ISBN: 978-1-895836-34-9
*Claus Effect, The* by David Nickle & Karl Schroeder (hb) - ISBN: 978-1-895836-35-6
*Courtesan Prince, The* (Part One of the Okal Rel Saga) by Lynda Williams (tp)
 - ISBN: 978-1-894063-28-9

*Danse Macabre: Close Encounters With the Reaper* edited by Nancy Kilpatrick (tp)
 - ISBN: 978-1-894063-96-8
*Dark Earth Dreams* by Candas Dorsey & Roger Deegan (comes with a CD)
 - ISBN: 978-1-895836-05-9
*Darkness of the God* (Children of the Panther Part Two)
 by Amber Hayward (tp) - ISBN: 978-1-894063-44-9
*Demon Left Behind, The* by Marie Jakober (tp) - ISBN: 978-1-894063-49-4
*Distant Signals* by Andrew Weiner (tp) - ISBN: 978-0-88878-284-7
*Dreams of an Unseen Planet* by Teresa Plowright (tp) - ISBN: 978-0-88878-282-3
*Dreams of the Sea* (Part 1 of Tyranaël) by Élisabeth Vonarburg (tp)
 - ISBN: 978-1-895836-96-7
*Dreams of the Sea* (Part 1 of Tyranaël) by Élisabeth Vonarburg (hb)
 - ISBN: 978-1-895836-98-1
*Druids* by Barbara Galler-Smith and Josh Langston (tp)
 - ISBN: 978-1-894063-29-6

*Eclipse* by K. A. Bedford (tp) - ISBN: 978-1-894063-30-2
*Even The Stones* by Marie Jakober (tp) - ISBN: 978-1-894063-18-0
*Evolve: Vampire Stories of the New Undead* edited by Nancy Kilpatrick (tp)
 - ISBN: 978-1-894063-33-3
*Evolve Two: Vampire Stories of the Future Undead* edited by Nancy Kilpatrick (tp)
 - ISBN: 978-1-894063-62-3

*Far Arena* (Part Five of the Okal Rel Saga) by Lynda Williams (tp)
- ISBN: 978-1-894063-45-6
*Fires of the Kindred* by Robin Skelton (tp) - ISBN: 978-0-88878-271-7
*Forbidden Cargo* by Rebecca Rowe (tp) - ISBN: 978-1-894063-16-6

*Game of Perfection, A* (Part 2 of Tyranaël) by Élisabeth Vonarburg (tp)
- ISBN: 978-1-894063-32-6
*Gaslight Arcanum: Uncanny Tales of Sherlock Holmes*
edited by Jeff Campbell & Charles Prepolec (pb)
- ISBN: 978-1-8964063-60-9
*Gaslight Grimoire: Fantastic Tales of Sherlock Holmes*
edited by Jeff Campbell & Charles Prepolec (pb)
- ISBN: 978-1-8964063-17-3
*Gaslight Grotesque: Nightmare Tales of Sherlock Holmes*
edited by Jeff Campbell & Charles Prepolec (pb)
- ISBN: 978-1-8964063-31-9
*Gathering Storm* (Part Eight of the Okal Rel Saga) by Lynda Williams (tp)
- ISBN: 978-1-77053-020-1
*Green Music* by Ursula Pflug (tp) - ISBN: 978-1-895836-75-2
*Green Music* by Ursula Pflug (hb) - ISBN: 978-1-895836-77-6

*Healer, The* (Children of the Panther Part One) by Amber Hayward (tp)
- ISBN: 978-1-895836-89-9
*Healer, The* (Children of the Panther Part One) by Amber Hayward (hb)
- ISBN: 978-1-895836-91-2
*Healer's Sword* (Part Seven of the Okal Rel Saga) by Lynda Williams (tp)
- ISBN: 978-1-894063-51-7

*Hell Can Wait* by Theodore Judson (tp) - ISBN: 978-1-978-1-894063-23-4
*Hounds of Ash and other tales of Fool Wolf, The* by Greg Keyes (pb)
- ISBN: 978-1-894063-09-8
*Hydrogen Steel* by K. A. Bedford (tp) - ISBN: 978-1-894063-20-3

*i-ROBOT Poetry by Jason Christie* (tp) - ISBN: 978-1-894063-24-1
*Immortal Quest* by Alexandra MacKenzie (pb) - ISBN: 978-1-894063-46-3

*Jackal Bird* by Michael Barley (pb) - ISBN: 978-1-895836-07-3
*Jackal Bird* by Michael Barley (hb) - ISBN: 978-1-895836-11-0
*JEMMA7729* by Phoebe Wray (tp) - ISBN: 978-1-894063-40-1

*Keaen* by Till Noever (tp) - ISBN: 978-1-894063-08-1
*Keeper's Child* by Leslie Davis (tp) - ISBN: 978-1-894063-01-2

*Land/Space* edited by Candas Jane Dorsey and Judy McCrosky (tp)
- ISBN: 978-1-895836-90-5
*Land/Space* edited by Candas Jane Dorsey and Judy McCrosky (hb)
- ISBN: 978-1-895836-92-9
*Lyskarion: The Song of the Wind* (Part One of The Chronicles of the Karionin)
by J.A. Cullum (tp) - ISBN: 978-1-894063-02-9

*Machine Sex and other stories* by Candas Jane Dorsey (tp)
- ISBN: 978-0-88878-278-6
*Maërlande Chronicles, The* by Élisabeth Vonarburg (pb)
- ISBN: 978-0-88878-294-6

*Moonfall* by Heather Spears (pb) - ISBN: 978-0-88878-306-6

*Of Wind and Sand* by Sylvie Bérard (translated by Sheryl Curtis) (tp)
- ISBN: 978-1-894063-19-7
*On Spec: The First Five Years* edited by On Spec (pb)
- ISBN: 978-1-895836-08-0
*On Spec: The First Five Years* edited by On Spec (hb)
- ISBN: 978-1-895836-12-7
*Orbital Burn* by K. A. Bedford (tp) - ISBN: 978-1-894063-10-4
*Orbital Burn* by K. A. Bedford (hb) - ISBN: 978-1-894063-12-8

*Pallahaxi Tide* by Michael Coney (pb) - ISBN: 978-0-88878-293-9
*Paradox Resolution* by K. A. Bedford (tp) - ISBN:978-1-894063-88-3
*Passion Play* by Sean Stewart (pb) - ISBN: 978-0-88878-314-1
*Petrified World (Determine Your Destiny #1)* by Piotr Brynczka (pb)
- ISBN: 978-1-894063-11-1
*Plague Saint* by Rita Donovan, The (tp) - ISBN: 978-1-895836-28-8
*Plague Saint* by Rita Donovan, The (hb) - ISBN: 978-1-895836-29-5
*Pock's World* by Dave Duncan (tp) - ISBN: 978-1-894063-47-0
*Pretenders* (Part Three of the Okal Rel Saga) by Lynda Williams (tp)
- ISBN: 978-1-894063-13-5

*Reluctant Voyagers* by Élisabeth Vonarburg (pb) - ISBN: 978-1-895836-09-7
*Reluctant Voyagers* by Élisabeth Vonarburg (hb) - ISBN: 978-1-895836-15-8
*Resisting Adonis* by Timothy J. Anderson (tp) - ISBN: 978-1-895836-84-4
*Resisting Adonis* by Timothy J. Anderson (hb) - ISBN: 978-1-895836-83-7
*Rigor Amortis* edited by Jaym Gates and Erika Holt (tp)
- ISBN: 978-1-894063-63-0
*Righteous Anger* (Part Two of the Okal Rel Saga) by Lynda Williams (tp)
- ISBN: 897-1-894063-38-8

*Silent City, The* by Élisabeth Vonarburg (tp) - ISBN: 978-1-894063-07-4
*Slow Engines of Time, The* by Élisabeth Vonarburg (tp)
- ISBN: 978-1-895836-30-1
*Slow Engines of Time, The* by Élisabeth Vonarburg (hb)
- ISBN: 978-1-895836-31-8
*Stealing Magic* by Tanya Huff (tp) - ISBN: 978-1-894063-34-0
*Stolen Children* (Children of the Panther Part Three)
by Amber Hayward (tp) - ISBN: 978-1-894063-66-1
*Strange Attractors* by Tom Henighan (pb) - ISBN: 978-0-88878-312-7

*Taming, The* by Heather Spears (pb) - ISBN: 978-1-895836-23-3
*Taming, The* by Heather Spears (hb) - ISBN: 978-1-895836-24-0
*Technicolor Ultra Mall* by Ryan Oakley (tp) - ISBN: 978-1-894063-54-8
*Ten Monkeys, Ten Minutes* by Peter Watts (tp) - ISBN: 978-1-895836-74-5
*Ten Monkeys, Ten Minutes* by Peter Watts (hb) - ISBN: 978-1-895836-76-9
*Tesseracts 1* edited by Judith Merril (pb) - ISBN: 978-0-88878-279-3
*Tesseracts 2* edited by Phyllis Gotlieb & Douglas Barbour (pb)
- ISBN: 978-0-88878-270-0
*Tesseracts 3* edited by Candas Jane Dorsey & Gerry Truscott (pb)
- ISBN: 978-0-88878-290-8
*Tesseracts 4* edited by Lorna Toolis & Michael Skeet (pb)
- ISBN: 978-0-88878-322-6
*Tesseracts 5* edited by Robert Runté & Yves Maynard (pb)
- ISBN: 978-1-895836-25-7

*Tesseracts 5* edited by Robert Runté & Yves Maynard (hb)
- ISBN: 978-1-895836-26-4

*Tesseracts 6* edited by Robert J. Sawyer & Carolyn Clink (pb)
- ISBN: 978-1-895836-32-5

*Tesseracts 6* edited by Robert J. Sawyer & Carolyn Clink (hb)
- ISBN: 978-1-895836-33-2

*Tesseracts 7* edited by Paula Johanson & Jean-Louis Trudel (tp)
- ISBN: 978-1-895836-58-5

*Tesseracts 7* edited by Paula Johanson & Jean-Louis Trudel (hb)
- ISBN: 978-1-895836-59-2

*Tesseracts 8* edited by John Clute & Candas Jane Dorsey (tp)
- ISBN: 978-1-895836-61-5

*Tesseracts 8* edited by John Clute & Candas Jane Dorsey (hb)
- ISBN: 978-1-895836-62-2

*Tesseracts Nine* edited by Nalo Hopkinson and Geoff Ryman (tp)
- ISBN: 978-1-894063-26-5

*Tesseracts Ten: A Celebration of New Canadian Specuative Fiction*
edited by Robert Charles Wilson and Edo van Belkom (tp)
- ISBN: 978-1-894063-36-4

*Tesseracts Eleven: Amazing Canadian Speulative Fiction*
edited by Cory Doctorow and Holly Phillips (tp)
- ISBN: 978-1-894063-03-6

*Tesseracts Twelve: New Novellas of Canadian Fantastic Fiction*
edited by Claude Lalumière (tp)
- ISBN: 978-1-894063-15-9

*Tesseracts Thirteen: Chilling Tales from the Great White North*
edited by Nancy Kilpatrick and David Morrell (tp)
- ISBN: 978-1-894063-25-8

*Tesseracts 14: Strange Canadian Stories*
edited by John Robert Colombo and Brett Alexander Savory (tp)
- ISBN: 978-1-894063-37-1

*Tesseracts Fifteen: A Case of Quite Curious Tales*
edited by Julie Czerneda and Susan MacGregor (tp)
- ISBN: 978-1-894063-58-6

*Tesseracts Sixteen: Parnassus Unbound* edited by Mark Leslie (tp)
- ISBN: 978-1-894063-92-0

*Tesseracts Q* edited by Élisabeth Vonarburg and Jane Brierley (pb)
- ISBN: 978-1-895836-21-9

*Tesseracts Q* edited by Élisabeth Vonarburg and Jane Brierley (hb)
- ISBN: 978-1-895836-22-6

*Those Who Fight Monsters: Tales of Occult Detectives*
edited by Justin Gustainis (pb) - ISBN: 978-1-894063-48-7

*Throne Price* by Lynda Williams and Alison Sinclair (tp)
- ISBN: 978-1-894063-06-7

*Time Machines Repaired Whie-U-Wait* by K. A. Bedford (tp)
- ISBN: 978-1-894063-42-5

*Vampyric Variations* by Nancy Kilpatrick (tp)- ISBN: 978-1-894063-94-4

*Wildcatter* by Dave Duncan (tp) - ISBN: 978-1-894063-90-6